Readers love *In the Middle of Somewhe* by ROAN PARRISH

"*In the Middle of Somewhere* is a deeply ————————— h I found at turns to be charming, delightfu—————————— ne prose is beautiful and so very apt."
—Dear Author

"So you know when you read a book and it just makes you happy? That is exactly what happened after reading *In the Middle of Somewhere*. I loved every minute of it and finished the book just so content."
—Joyfully Jay

"*In the Middle of Somewhere* is tender and domestic and funny and often steaming hot."
—Heroes and Heartbreakers

"This is a very enjoyable book, beautifully written, with well-drawn characters and just the right mix of angst, emotion and sensuality to make it a beautiful romance."
—Prism Book Alliance

"I really enjoyed this novel. It was so well written, with great dialogue, I can't believe it's the author's first book!"
—Sinfully

OUT OF
NOWHERE

Roan Parrish

Published by

DREAMSPINNER PRESS

5032 Capital Circle SW, Suite 2, PMB# 279, Tallahassee, FL 32305-7886 USA
www.dreamspinnerpress.com

Out of Nowhere

Cover Art

ISBN: 978-1-63476-902-0
Digital ISBN: 978-1-63476-903-7
Library of Congress Control Number: 2015921022
Published February 2016
v. 1.0

For the ones trying to envision new worlds
and the ones working to bring them into being.

Acknowledgments

THANKS TO Anni, who was the first to get excited about this book with me and whose enthusiasm never flagged. And to Judith, whose work may sometimes be invisible, but never goes unnoticed.

Thanks to my comrades in Philly, for years of talk about all of the things, and for both the worlds you envision and the work you do to make them a reality.

It's impossible to write a book about siblings without thinking a lot about mine. Thanks to my sister, who, in addition to being a major badass, was thrilled about this book the second I said, "I want to write about an asshole older sibling," and didn't make too many jokes about it being autobiographical.

Over the past few months, I've had the unexpected pleasure of meeting amazing writers and the immeasurable privilege of learning from them. This book has benefitted greatly from both. Thank you.

Chapter 1

THE FIST comes toward me in slow motion like some fucked-up cartoon, slamming into my jaw and knocking me sideways. My head hits the metal garbage can, and a few seconds later the blond guy's load hits my neck and drips onto the cobblestones of the alley. Blond guy's boots scuff cigarette butts, condoms, and wads of mucky leaves as he stalks toward the back door of the bar, cursing me out.

I didn't peg him as being able to hit quite that hard when I chose him. He'd looked smaller in the bar, though once we got outside I realized he was about my height—six feet or so. Must've been the paisley shirt. Fucking paisley made him look like a wuss. I definitely ripped off a button or two when I shoved him to his knees in front of me, but he didn't seem to mind. Didn't mind when I shoved myself down his throat, either, staring past his light hair to the dark brick behind him and trying to pretend I was somewhere else… someone else. He minded being pushed away when he asked me to return the favor, though, and he sure as hell minded when I said I wasn't a faggot.

My jaw gives a throb and my breath finally comes effortlessly. But it won't last. It never does.

My vision's blurry, but that's probably mostly the whiskey. I drag myself up and stumble the few blocks to the subway, trying desperately to hold on to the calm and think of anything but the feel of another man. When my mind starts to wander to his firm chest and the rasp of stubble on my dick, I run through tomorrow's transmission rebuild on Mr. Coop's '87 Volkswagen Fox until I can relax a little.

The calm's gone by the time my dingy green-and-white awning is in sight, though, and the catch in my breathing is back, like I can't quite inhale fully. Because I know what's waiting for me inside. Nothing. An empty house filled with it. My quickening heartbeat throbs in the bruise emerging on my jaw.

Worse, I've sobered up on the walk from the subway and it's still hours until I can go to work in the morning. The more aware I am of my breathing, the more labored it seems, and I bend slightly at the waist, taking a deep breath with my hands on my thighs. Desperate for something, anything, to distract from the quiet of the walls pressing in on me, I strip off and hit the weight bench. The familiar heft and clank of metal scraping metal and thudding on cheap carpet helps a bit. I lift until my muscles shake and my sweat smells whiskey sweet. If I'm lucky, it'll be enough to let me fall asleep. But I'm usually not.

The second I flop onto the bed, still damp from the shower, the images start playing behind my closed eyes. Blond guy from earlier, but it could've been any of them, really—nameless, interchangeable, seen through a fog of whiskey and revulsion. Their mouths, their sweat, their dirty hands…. But I keep going back even though the thoughts make me squirm.

I GET to Big Jenny's Dive around nine to meet Xavier. X has been my best friend since we played high school football. The guys on the team teased him for being a black kid from North Philly who loved hair metal instead of rap, and since I loved it too, we spent most of our time arguing about Poison, Mötley Crüe, Def Leppard (which Xavier contended was only pop metal but I worshipped), Twisted Sister, Van Halen, and, of course, since they were from Philly, Cinderella. We'd replace Nas and Goodie Mob with Quiet Riot in the locker room stereo and push Play just as our teammates got in the showers, posing and roughhousing; then we'd crack up as they were stuck doing so naked to the soundtrack of "Cum On Feel the Noize."

X left for a few years to get his MBA and we lost touch. While he was in North Carolina, he got married and cleaned up a bit. Not that he had ever been into much. Just selling a little pot when he'd needed the money and pills when he could get them. He seemed different when he got back, though. More focused. He put it down to his wife, Angela. I never got the whole story, but I think she basically told him he was acting like a dumb kid and needed to grow the fuck up. Angela doesn't like me. Xavier denies it, but I know it's true.

We meet at Big Jenny's most Thursday evenings to watch two cover bands battle it out, playing hits from the seventies, eighties, and nineties. How loud the audience sings along acts as an applause-o-meter, and the winning band gets free drinks for the week. Cover band night reminds me of singing along to the radio in our garage when Pop still worked at the other shop, my younger brother, Daniel, sitting on the steps into the kitchen watching me and trying to sing but getting all the words wrong.

X is late so I'm stuck at the bar by myself. A couple of ladies in their forties chat me up. They're clearly slumming it, their clothes a little too fancy, their heels too high to fit in here. They ask the usual questions: What do you do? Do you come here often? Are you married?—this last with exchanged looks and laughs like they're reveling in breaking some rule they've set for themselves. It's embarrassing and exhausting, so I do what I always do.

"You ladies want to see me pass a coin through solid glass?"

They make the usual expressions of disbelief and jokes about me being a magic man. Then I do the trick I've done a thousand times at a hundred bars, the motions as natural as changing a tire or unlocking my front door. The women's delight brings others over and I do it again and again. An older guy buys me a whiskey and everyone's laughing, and now talking is easy. I'm nodding and bumping him with my elbow at the appropriate times, delivering one-liners like it's my fucking job, and he's laughing and leaning in like I'm the second coming, and signaling for another round, and all I can think is that he likes me. They like me. This person I'm pretending to be. I do the trick again and again as more people wander over.

It's just misdirection and practice.

"MY MOM and Angela had a total throwdown at Nika's birthday party," X tells me once he finally shows up, harried. X's mom, Sheila, is a maternal beast. She's totally protective of X and his sister. And now, of X's niece Nika, the first and only grandchild, who just turned three. Sheila and Angela have been locked in a fiery battle of wills from the moment they met, which amuses me to hear about but stresses X out.

"What was it this time?" I ask. "Did Sheila accidentally buy nonorganic juice?" Angela is one of those super healthy people who drinks smoothies and eats nuts as a snack.

"Bro, when Sheila buys nonorganic juice, that shit is *not* by accident. It's waving the red flag in front of the bull." He shakes his head.

"Dude, did you just call your wife a bull?"

"What? No! I… oh." He chuckles. Angela is kind of… forceful.

"No, Angela bought Nika some kind of... I dunno, car toy? A plastic car that Nika can sit in and pedal and it has wheels. Anyway, it's cool. Like a mini VW Bug. And Nika *loves* it. But my mom has decided that it's too dangerous because Nika could pedal out into traffic. And Angela has decided that my mom just wants her to take it away from Nika so that Nika resents her." He shakes his head and downs his drink.

"Jesus Christ," I say. "Hang on." I grab us another round and X has perked up considerably by the time the music starts. He never stays mad long. It's one of the things I've always liked about him.

X elbows me discreetly in the side to point out that Katie has come in. I wink at her and she smiles broadly but doesn't come over. Katie's the kind of girl my mother always said she wanted me to marry: sweet and smart and not mixed up in anything shady. A nice girl. We've slept together a handful of times over the last year, and I know she likes me. But every time I scramble home afterward, or accidentally fall asleep and wake up to feel her in the bed next to me, her pillows smelling of strawberry shampoo, my guts clench and my chest tightens, and the next time she offers, I say no. She never forces the issue, but I can tell how disappointed she is when I don't go home with her. I don't know if she's too proud, too scared, or too embarrassed to demand more from me. Whatever her motivation, it's a relief.

When I was a kid, my mom used to tell me that I had to be a good man or I wouldn't attract a good wife and have a family. Her words. Being a good man meant treating nice girls nicely. My mom worked as the receptionist for a doctor's office, and she would bring home out-of-date waiting room magazines that she quoted as gospel. *You have to listen to her. Don't go to bed angry. Buy her unexpected gifts. Tell her she looks beautiful no matter what. Marry a woman who will make a good mother.* She would sling them at me like boomerangs as she cooked and I did my homework at the kitchen table, neatly pocketing each one after it had hit me so she could deploy it again.

She would've liked Katie. *I* like Katie. But the idea of Katie as my wife... of us with children... a family.... Yeah, I'm panicked just thinking about it.

X hands me another drink. "Katie's looking for you, bro," he says, gesturing behind me.

"Uh, yeah, thanks."

"Don't sound too excited that a beautiful woman wants you, man. Wouldn't want anyone to think you're *that* into her." He rolls his eyes at me.

"No, yeah, it's cool; I'll just—"

Xavier nods exaggeratedly, like I'm an idiot.

Which I pretty much am. Katie's beautiful, smart, and sweet, and she wants me. And I....

"Hey, Col," Katie drawls from behind me, running a hand over my shoulder. I stand in case she sits down, trapping me at the table. "Great set, huh? I liked the U2." She looks up at me. Her eyes are almost the same blue as mine, but where mine always seem cold when I catch a glimpse of myself in the mirror, hers are as warm and uncomplicated as a summer sky.

"Yeah, I like that song."

"Me too," she says excitedly, like it means we're similar. Katie truly believes the best of people. Thinks they're inherently good. Of course, in my case, she couldn't be more wrong. All I want is for her to disappear forever and never look at me again with those hopeful eyes. But Xavier's grinning at me over Katie's head, so I do what they both want. I kiss her.

When I pull back, she grabs my biceps and leans into me, part shy and part turned on. It should be sweet, endearing, hot—something—but it just makes me wish I were somewhere else. I turn to Rawlins, an annoying regular who always finds his way over to X and me, and take the whiskey out of his hand. He deserves it for always being such a dork. He doesn't complain and I slam the whiskey, Katie still clinging to me.

"Sooo," she says, running a provocative hand up my arm to my chest, "you wanna...?" She nods toward the door. I can tell she's pretty sure I'll say yes tonight. I'm already drunk; I could go with her and pretend to pass out, but then I'd be stuck at her place. I could say I have to work early tomorrow and beg off, but the thought of going home to my empty house sets my heart beating even faster.

"Colin?" Katie sounds concerned and I realize I've been staring at the wall behind her. Fuck, I don't want her to touch me, but I don't want to be alone. I pinch the bridge of my nose and squeeze my eyes shut, trying to buy a minute to think of an excuse that the guys won't laugh out of the bar.

"Not tonight, sugar." I immediately hate myself as her eyes dim and she sets her jaw, taking it like a champ.

"Sure," she says. "Sure, some other time."

I give her a weak smile and run my hand over my buzzed hair, feeling sick. Then I pat her on the shoulder and split.

I MEANT to take the long way home, change my clothes, and go for a run so I could sleep.

At first. But then, yeah, all right, even with my jaw still throbbing from last night's encounter, I kind of knew I'd end up here again. The Cellar.

It started when my youngest brother, Daniel, moved away last month. I don't remember where I heard about it. Okay, maybe I looked it up online. While Daniel lived in Philly, there was no way I could go to… that kind of place. There was always the chance, no matter how slim, that he might be there. But once he was gone, I couldn't stay away. It was like there was a light blinking in my periphery that I had to go turn off. Of course, when I flipped the switch, the light just burned brighter, hotter. Impossible to ignore.

Inside, it's so dark that all I can see is the curve of a chin, the bulk of a rounded shoulder, a gesturing hand as it catches the light. For a second, my eyes land on an uncommonly tall guy at the end of the bar who's staring at me. In the whirlwind of seeking bodies, he's noticeably still. I lose track of him fast as I scan the crowd for a likely target. When a built blond guy settles on the stool next to me and orders a beer, I lean toward him and grin. I nod toward the tip I've put on the bar and slide his bottle on top.

"Betcha I can get that dollar out without touching the bottle."

He just raises an eyebrow, clearly unimpressed, eyes icy and face hard. His remoteness suits me fine. He doesn't snatch his beer back, so I do the trick, rolling the bill with my fingers on either side so it nudges the beer onto the bar top. It's usually enough for at least a smile, but he just picks up the beer and drains it. Then he nods at me and tips his chin toward the alley, and the tightness in my chest loosens a little even as my stomach clenches. The room tilts when I slide off the stool, but I steady myself and follow him.

It happens so fast that it takes me a moment to understand that what's going on isn't what I planned for. I was distracted, one hand at my fly. The second man must've been behind me and I didn't notice. He's squat and heavily muscled, but I could definitely take him one-on-one. Could probably take either of them one-on-one, but the hits are coming too fast, and when a hard shove sends my face into the greasy brick and then me to the ground, I can't quite get my feet under me again. And maybe I don't try that hard. When they start kicking me, I close my eyes because the alley is spinning and focus on each distinct point of impact, each throbbing, stinging locus of hurt.

Like a sick meditation, I can lose myself inside the pain, make it bigger than I am, pull it around me like a blanket.

Then someone rips the blanket away and my eyes jerk open. There's a third guy, and for a moment I panic. But he's pulled the other two off me and is—Jesus, he's systematically taking them apart. He fights dirty, but every motion is perfectly controlled, as if he were making a science of hitting exactly as hard as is necessary to take these guys down and not one bit harder. I've been in a lot of fights and seen even more, but I've rarely seen anything like this level of control. His face is expressionless and he's totally silent. He shoves the men down the alley and they scamper off like rats. I close my eyes and try to sink back down into my body, hoping that when I open my eyes, the alley will be empty just like all the other times.

The guy grabs me by the shoulders and pulls me up. His grip is unbreakable, but I try anyway because sitting up doesn't agree with my spinning head.

"Get the fuck off." I try to push against him, but he may as well be the brick wall behind me for all that he gives. Irritation is quickly overshadowed by the humiliating impulse to puke, and I shove at him again.

"Get *off*." He doesn't let go, just keeps holding me steady with that maddening pressure: not tight enough to hurt me, not loose enough to let me go.

"Oh fuck," I groan after I've puked my guts out against the wall. I twisted at the last minute and avoided vomiting on the guy. Mostly. His fault, though, since he wouldn't let me go. Now that I've thrown up, the shame hits. I'm in a filthy alley where I followed a complete stranger in the hopes of getting my dick sucked. I got the ever-loving crap kicked out of me and was too wasted to fight back. I got rescued by some hulking giant who—shit—may actually be mute. And to say thanks? I puked on him. Heat rises in my cheeks and throat, and I need to get the hell away.

Suddenly, I become aware of my breathing and that thing happens where I can't quite take a deep breath. I scramble to my knees and hunch my shoulders, willing my lungs to expand that last little bit, but the more I pay attention to it, the worse it gets.

"Is there blood in it?" The man's voice is low and detached.

"Huh?"

"The vomit. Is there blood in it?" He leans down to look at the puke on the ground, nodding once at whatever he sees. He slides a hand under my shirt and pulls it up.

"The fuck?" I say, pushing him away again. He's looking at where they kicked me, leaning me forward to examine my back and sides.

"You a doctor or something?"

He shakes his head, then slowly pulls me up to a standing position.

"I'll call you a cab," he says, propping me against the wall like a bike or a piece of furniture, one arm loosely across my chest.

"Uh, no, man, I'm fine."

He snorts. And finally looks at me. Well, looks down at me. Dude's even taller than I thought when I saw him in the bar. And bulky with muscle. He has shoulder-length brown hair, and his left eyebrow is broken by scars, the kind you usually see when someone's taken a bottle to the face. His mouth is grim and his brown eyes are sharp, and he's looking at me with a combination of amusement and scorn that immediately pisses me off. Like he knows me or some shit.

"You're wasted," he says. "Those guys would've killed you." My brain shies away from this piece of information and focuses back on my breathing. As I try to get a deep breath, the edge of panic is back. I know I can get enough air in, but the sensation freaks me out every time. Like at any moment I could drown where I stand.

"Come on," he says, patting my shoulder lightly, like my old Little League coach—*You've got it, tiger; back in the game!*—like I did to Katie.

Suddenly, I'm so humiliated that I think I might puke again. Pathetic. I squeeze my eyes shut.

"I'm fucking fine, dude," I say coldly. "I could've handled it."

I jerk away from him and stagger down the alley. When I glance back, he's still standing there, completely still, watching me.

Chapter 2

THE ORANGE BMW 320i rolls in just as I swallow the last bite of a mediocre hoagie. Next to me, my younger brother Brian lets out a low whistle. That is one ugly color. It was probably originally a bright orange, but it's faded and patched and has been painted over a few times. The driver's side door is maroon and the diving boards are spotted with rust.

I've been out of it all day. I took a bunch of Tylenol this morning, but my head is still killing me and my whole body aches. I don't remember it happening, but there's a deep scrape on my shoulder so I guess that's where I hit either the brick wall or the ground in the alley last night. I keep leaning against it to remind myself of what an idiot I am.

"Eighty-one?" Brian asks me. Pop shakes his head in disgust.

"Naw, man," I tell him, pointing at the elongated aluminum bumpers, "That's the E30. In '81 it would've been the E21." I turn to Pop. "I'd go '85." He nods.

I actually love the early to mideighties BMWs. Underneath that shitty paint job and mismatched door, the lines of the car are pure, the boxy form sharp and perfectly balanced.

When that maroon door opens, though, it drives away any thoughts about the car. Because the long legs and broad shoulders that emerge belong to the guy from last night. My ears start to buzz and my heart beats unnaturally fast. He scans the garage, and when his eyes land on me, it's like a physical force catches my breath and pulls it from my chest.

"What?" Brian pokes me in the shoulder. "You know him or something?"

I shake my head and walk toward him before Brian or Pop can.

"Um, hi."

"Hi," he says, his voice low.

"Uh, can I help you?" I'm trying to keep my voice steady and professional, but with my eyes I'm begging him not to say anything. To be just another customer.

He jabs his thumb behind him at his car and says, "I wonder if you could take a look. I think I'm leaking oil."

I grab my clipboard and his key and take down his driver's license information. Rafael Guerrera. He's thirty-eight, two years older than me.

"Pop the hood," I tell him, and I definitely *don't* stare when he bends over to pull the lever, his hips twisting and his shirt rucking up just enough to show a sliver of light brown skin. I look at the engine blankly, taking in no information whatsoever. I close the hood and nod at Rafael.

"I'll take a look, but you'll need to leave it. That okay?"

"How long will it take?" he asks, and there's something about the way he says it that makes me think he knows exactly what I'm doing. That I don't want him to wait here while I look at the car now. That I want him gone, stat.

I shrug, trying to look casual, but it's more of a twitch. "Tomorrow most likely."

Rafael nods. He picks up my clipboard and writes something on it. Then he hands it back to me with a completely neutral look and walks out of the garage.

I look at the clipboard. He's written a phone number and, below it, a note: *Your sweatshirt is in the trunk.*

Shit. I do vaguely remember dropping it on the barstool last night. For a second, it occurs to me that it was nice of him to bring it back. But then my stomach tightens and my skin starts to crawl with unease.

I CATCH up to him at the corner.

"Hey!" I reach for his shoulder, but before I come close to touching him, he whips around, looming over me, feet set shoulder width apart. "How the hell did you know where I work?"

"How's your stomach?" he asks as if I haven't spoken. His stance has relaxed slightly.

"Look, man. I don't know what the fuck you think is going on here, okay. But how did you know where I work?"

Rafael runs a hand through his hair and looks away.

I take a good look at him, trying to focus on not punching him. His thick, wavy brown hair is shoulder length, but neat, not like he forgot to cut it. There are freckles across his nose, barely darker than his skin. Judging by his skin and his name, I'm guessing he's Latino. Is that the right term? I'm not sure. Hispanic? Shit, I don't know. His lips are full, and his teeth are sharp and crowded, the left front one chipped. His long stubble looks soft, but his mouth turns down in a snarl. I shake my head to clear it.

"Look," he says, "I wasn't going to say anything about how we met if that's what you're worried about."

I nod my thanks. "Dude, seriously, how'd you—"

"Colin." He says it like I'm a skittish animal he doesn't want to freak out. Damn name tags. "I was concerned last night. It wasn't safe for you to be wandering around that drunk in the middle of the night. I followed you to make sure you got home okay. That's all." He puts his hands up.

"Wait, you followed me. All the way home? I didn't… I didn't see you."

"I know."

"But wait, how'd you… did you…?" Did I talk to him and not remember it?

"There was a car parked outside your house. It had a bumper sticker for the garage on the back. I figured I'd take a chance it was yours."

"Um." Who the fuck would go to that much trouble for someone they don't even know—especially someone who blew them off—unless they wanted something? Unless—oh, jeez, unless he's one of those wannabe vigilante freaks with a superhero complex who think they have some mandate to beat up evildoers in alleys and protect the downtrodden…. I saw a movie like that once. Of course, that's better than the alternative, which is that he's an entirely different kind of freak.

"Listen," he says, "can we—"

"Okay," I say, cutting him off. "So, I'll be in touch about your car."

Then I hurry back to the shop before he can say anything else.

THE AXE comes down before the man has time to scream, blood splattering the barn, the hay, and the rakes that lean ominously against the wall, and I look away from the TV. I put the movie on in the background for some noise. Usually, I love horror movies and gory war movies. Tonight, though, the sounds are getting to me. Every time someone screams, I find myself looking up. I'm trying to finish the model of the DeLorean DMC-12 that I started months ago and abandoned for a while because the plasticard I got from the hardware store wasn't setting properly and it was pissing me off. I got new sheet plastic at a hobby shop that's malleable enough that I can dunk it in hot water and mold it around a can, secure it with rubber bands, and it'll hold a curve without cracking.

A knock on the door startles me. It's got to be Brian. He's the only one who stops by unannounced.

Still, I yell, "Who is it?" at the door as the deranged killer mows down an attractive young couple with a thresher.

"Uh, me."

I'm lucky Brian didn't just use his key. Thank god I pretty much broke him of that habit last month when he walked in on me jerking off.

A chorus of screams and revving motors is the soundtrack to my brother grinning in the doorway, holding up a six-pack of Yuengling bombers. A few years ago we saved a bunch of those twenty-four ounce cans to be the base of a beer-can Christmas tree, moving to twelve-ouncers toward the top. It was pretty epic.

"Game's on," Brian says, tromping in and plopping down on my couch. He cracks open a Yuengling and tosses one to me. It's warm. "Dude, what the fuck is this gonna be?" he asks, waving around one wing of the DeLorean's chassis.

"Dude," I mock, "aren't you supposed to be a fucking mechanic? What does it look like?"

Brian, impervious and immediately bored as ever, drops it on the coffee table and changes the channel to the Penn State–Michigan game. We watch in silence for a while as Michigan pulls ahead by a touchdown. After a commercial, during which Brian explains how he could tell that the woman who brought her Accord in for an oil change wanted to sleep with him, the broadcast shows an aerial shot of Michigan stadium, teeming with maize and blue, that pulls out to include the fall leaves and artificially green grass of what must be a golf course nearby.

"Hey, Col? Do you think Daniel's okay?"

Daniel. Our youngest brother moved to Michigan last month for an English professor job. He didn't even tell us he was leaving until the night before he split. Which was par for the course, considering he didn't really give a shit about any of us anyway.

"Okay, how?"

"Well, just. *Michigan*. Like, what do they even do there? Is it near Ann Arbor, where he is?"

"Nah, it's north."

"So he's not teaching, like, *at* Michigan." Brian points to the TV, and I shake my head. Brian's never looked at a map in his life. Hell, I don't think he's ever been anywhere outside the Philly area except a few trips to the Jersey shore and one ill-conceived trip to New York to see a Rangers game at Madison Square Garden. He ended up getting trashed and puking into my empty popcorn bucket—well, mostly empty.

"You heard from him?" I ask, trying to sound casual. I'm definitely last on Daniel's to-call list.

"Nope." Brian fiddles with the remote. "Do you think—I mean, did you know he was going to move?"

"He certainly didn't fucking discuss it with me, no."

No, Daniel hasn't discussed anything with me since he was about twelve—hell, he's barely spoken to me since the day he told me he was gay. It's like there are two different Daniels. There's gay Daniel who couldn't be bothered to hang around with us, who thought he was too good to let anyone know he was related to mechanics, who thought we were stupid because we didn't walk around with our noses shoved in books the way he did. Then there's normal Daniel, which is how I remember him from when he was a kid. Normal Daniel used to follow me around and dress like me. Hang out with us, watching Pop fix cars and running around the garage playing our brutal version of Marco Polo that usually ended in one of us walking, eyes closed, into some sharp car part or piece of machinery and Pop cursing us out as he poured alcohol on our cuts and slapped Band-Aids over them.

"It's just weird," Brian's saying. "Like, I know he was busy with school and stuff, but I never thought he'd just… not be here anymore." Brian starts biting at his cuticles, which is truly disgusting because he always has grease on his hands. "I guess he wouldn't've been happy working with us anyway, though, huh? But remember how good he used to be with the cars?"

I remember. He was a natural, quickly sorting out what information was relevant to diagnosing a problem and what was secondary or unrelated.

"Remember the time that old buddy of Pop's brought his truck in and was trying to explain some complicated problem about a fuel line?

Daniel wandered in from school and looked at it and was like, 'Hey, Mr. McShea, you got a loose gas cap, huh?'"

I snort. Daniel had been about ten, a skinny pale kid with jet-black hair that was always in his face. He wore our old hand-me-down clothes, so they hung on him, making him look even smaller. Mr. McShea had turned bright red and Pop had pulled Daniel close to his side and rubbed his head. Daniel kept a straight face until Mr. McShea turned around. Then he grinned up at Pop and over at me and ran inside to do his homework.

That memory is immediately followed by one from six years later when I came home from getting high at Xavier's house to find Daniel on his knees in the alley outside the garage with that fuckwad Buddy McKenzie holding him down and—

My expression must be hostile because Brian changes the subject and starts talking about the Michigan marching band and how hot he thinks the girls in uniform are. I swear to god, my brother really needs to get laid.

As usual, Brian leaves a mess of beer cans, shredded napkins, and crumbs on the coffee table and between the couch cushions. They stand out, white against the dark blue fabric, and make my head buzz with the need to make them disappear. I slide the nozzle attachment onto the vacuum cleaner and go to work on the crumbs, then take the cushions off and vacuum underneath them for good measure.

When I shut the vacuum off, an unholy noise comes from outside. At first I ignore it, assuming it's a neighbor's TV. But it sounds like someone screaming, and unless they're watching the horror movie I had on earlier....

If I had an ounce of sense, that'd be reason enough to keep my door shut and locked. But the noise is horrific. It sounds like a baby or something. I look out the small window in my front door and don't see anyone outside, so I turn the doorknob slowly. As I push the door open, something streaks inside.

"What the—"

From the porch comes a scuffle and the high-pitched sound of a cat in heat. Jesus, I thought that was over for the year. Then, from just inside the door, comes an answering whimper. I shut the door and look around. Shaking under the recliner is a tiny, filthy cat—kitten, whatever. It mews and backs away from me, but its claws get stuck in the worn blue-and-white-striped fabric of the chair.

Oh man. Animals do *not* like me—not even the ones people say like everyone. And this is just a baby; I'll probably squish it. I reach under the chair slowly and, in what I hope is a nonthreatening gesture, try to unstick it from the chair.

Not good. The kitten chomps down on my hand with teeth that are much sharper than I expected and starts scrabbling at my wrist with its back paws.

"Fuck, cat!"

It's left bloody scratches down my arm. Jesus, I hope it's not rabid. Probably there are animal control people or something that I could call…. I find a can of tuna in the back of the cupboard and dump it onto a plate a few feet away from the chair, trying to draw the kitten out, then go to clean the scratches it left on my arm. Within a minute, there's a tug at my ankle, the kitten trying to crawl up my leg.

It's filthy. I cuff my jeans and hoist the kitten into the cuff, where it grabs at the fabric, pricking my calf with its needle claws. In the time it takes to squeeze soap into a big pot and fill it with warm water, the kitten has fallen asleep, but the second it hits the water, it hisses and scrambles to get out. I hold it still with a towel and rub it clean, making sure to keep the soap out of its eyes and mouth the way my mom always did when I was little. *Tilt your head back, close your eyes, and hold your nose, love.*

It tires itself out pretty quickly, and I wrap it in a towel and put it on my bed. I'm flipping through an old issue of *Rolling Stone* when the cat wakes up and pushes up out of its towel. It stretches obscenely and pads over to me, suspicious at first, then pushes into my stomach with its paws. I lie back, and as I stop paying attention to it, the kitten jumps onto my stomach and curls into a tiny ball, tucking its head beneath its tail.

After a few minutes of rumbling, it flips over onto its stomach with all four paws spread out and its tail tickling my belly button. It's pretty fucking cute. White with a black tail and a grayish stripe running from the top of its head all the way down its back, it reminds me of the original 1965 Shelby Mustangs, which were white with a dark blue stripe, so I name it Shelby in my head.

Not that I'm keeping it or anything.

When I run a finger over its head, though, it wakes up and takes a swipe at me. Which is good. The cat may be tiny, but it sure as shit isn't going to let me hurt it.

SATURDAY MORNING, as soon as the first hood's open, I lose myself in the guts of the car. Here, at least, are problems I can solve. If it's bouncing excessively going over bumps, check for a worn shock or strut. If heat's coming from the floor, then the catalytic converter is probably clogged. It's a system, predictable and logical, and anything I break, anything I mess up, I can fix or replace.

Hell, given enough time and materials, I can take a car that seems beyond help and rebuild it, piece by piece. Give it a new life.

Not only does Rafael not have an oil leak, but nothing seems to be wrong with the car. It's old, sure, but the 3 Series have great engines, some power, and good acceleration for an E-class. I drive it around the block just to be sure, and the only issues I can see are that I don't know how such a big guy fits in such a small car and that all he has is a tape deck but no tapes. In fact, there's nothing personal in the car at all: no change of clothes, no junk mail, no toolbox, no soccer cleats or gym bag. It's clean inside, but not pristine. There are some cigarette burns on the passenger-side interior door and the backseats are a bit shabby. The lighter is missing from the console and there's a ding in the windshield that hasn't spiderwebbed. But nothing whatsoever that gives me a clue about who this guy is.

As I dial the number on my clipboard, my heart starts to race and my palms sweat.

"Yeah?" he answers, and there are voices in the background, like he's in a park or something.

"Um, is this Rafael Guerrera?"

"Hello, Colin."

"Hey, uh, just wanted to let you know your car's all set. No leak. Just needed an oil change. We're open till two if you want to come get it."

The sound on Rafael's side of the phone gets a little muted, like he covered it, and I hear sharp words in Spanish.

"Two, huh? I don't think I'll be able to get there before you close. Are you open tomorrow?"

"Nope. Monday, eight thirty to six."

"Monday, then. Thank you, Colin." The noise on his end crescendos to a crash that cuts off the call, and I'm surprised to find that I'm a little… disappointed?

Sam, my older brother, spends Saturdays in the office getting us caught up on paperwork, but Pop and Brian come out of the house around ten, when the usual Saturday stream of quick fixes begins. Oil changes, tire rotations, flats, busted windshields. Saturdays are dull but they always move fast. Hell, even Brian can hold his own with most Saturday issues.

"Maybe we should paint," Pop muses over a beer after we close.

"The garage?" I ask. It's been the same yellowish-tan since I can remember.

"The outside of the shop," Pop says. "Maybe brighten the place up a little."

Every few years Pop undertakes some scheme to try and make the shop more successful, and every few years he leaves it uncompleted. We have some clients that Pop brought over from his last job when he opened this place. They're loyal and they don't give a crap what color the outside of the shop is. There are the neighborhood clients who come to us because we're the closest garage. Some come back, some don't, but it's a steady stream. It's clear who Pop is hoping to entice with a scheme to "brighten the place up," then: the twenty- and thirtysomething hipsters who've swarmed to the neighborhood in the last ten years. Daniel always called them gentrifiers, whatever that means. They look just like him.

"Sure. What're you thinking?"

"Shit, I dunno. What's popular these days?"

"Um." I'm not really the right one to ask. "There's a new place— opened at, uh, 22nd and Washington. Kermit's. It's cakes and pizza." Xavier dragged me there once. Said he wanted to check out their cupcakes for Angela's birthday. They had a bunch of fancy flavors that he thought she'd love.

"The outside of it's cool—it's like an old-school tattoo of pink roses and black vines. Kinda like—"

"Pink roses?" Pop grunts. "Sounds faggy. I don't want flowers on the outside of my shop."

Shame curls up from my stomach like a snake. "Right. I didn't mean—I just meant, the style—"

"Psh," he snorts. "Never mind. Maybe a new sign."

"Yeah, sure. Sounds good. You want me to look into it?"

He pats me on the back and pulls himself up to get another beer.

"Yeah. Thanks, kid." He runs his rough hand over my buzzed hair. "You do a good job, Colin. A real good job."

I can't remember the last time Pop has touched me that wasn't to slap me on the back or push me out of his way. Usually he acts like it's his due to have us working in the shop, carrying out his plans, playing by his rules. His compliments come irregularly, and always just at the moment I'm almost fed up with him.

The joy of his approval burns away the shame, and I feel lighter than I have in months. I remember this feeling from when I was a kid. Pop would muck around with friends' cars in what was then our garage, pointing and asking us what was wrong with them, how to fix them. As the oldest, Sam was quickest, for a while. He had a good memory and could always repeat back ways of fixing things that Pop had explained. Brian didn't really try, just wanted to play the game because the rest of us were. Daniel was better, even as the youngest, and he could make leaps of logic that Sam couldn't. That was before Daniel lost all interest in cars, and in us.

I was the best, though. I could remember things like Sam and come up with creative solutions like Daniel. I cared the most, too. I wanted to be just like Pop and bring cars back to life. A few years later, when Pop opened his own shop, expanding our garage into the empty lot next door, I spent almost all my free time there, watching Pop and the men who worked with him, learning everything I could. And every time he nodded at me, clapped me on the back, or grunted at me to go ahead with the repair I'd laid out, I felt it. That warm, fizzy feeling.

MONDAY MORNING it's as if the sky opened up and dumped every single asshole with a license to operate a motor vehicle into the shop. When I come back from getting a cup of coffee, I find Sam contending with some dick who seems to think that because he googled "why does my car make that noise," he's qualified to argue with Sam about the work that needs to be done. Sam, always diplomatic, is being stupidly polite because—I'm sure—this guy has a nice SUV and the repairs would be expensive.

Next is a woman who must've listened to an NPR segment called "How Your Mechanic Is Ripping You Off," because she wants a fully written-out description of all the work we're going to do so she can get a second opinion. Like I'm diagnosing her car with a damn brain tumor or something, fucking second opinion.

I don't get lunch because Brian trips the master breaker in the office and I spend forty-five minutes resetting it so everything is getting the right power.

On top of all that, I'm furious at myself because every time the bell over the door tinkles, I look up, my stomach clenching, to see if it's Rafael coming to pick up his car.

Right before closing, I'm arguing with a kid who can't be more than seventeen, feeling like an old man. He wants me to install hydraulics in the beige 2007 Volkswagen Jetta that his parents gave him for his birthday. I've told him all the reasons it's a stupid idea and he's still standing there with this "but, really, why not?" look on his weaselly little face.

"You really want to know why?" I finally ask him. "I mean, besides the fact that it's not a lowrider, it's a fucking Jetta, and besides the fact that it's 2014? Because you'll look like a class-A douchebag. That's why."

This is not how I'm supposed to talk to customers, but this kid is seventeen and I'm sure he's called worse in this neighborhood every day. Besides, there's no one around to hear me.

Except that as I finish the thought, someone snorts in amusement, and when I look up, there's Rafael.

The kid turns and seems excited when he sees Rafael. "You get it, right, yo?" he says, his speech sliding into a new cadence.

"Listen to him, man," Rafael says, not unkindly. "Rich white kid gets hydraulics in a clean-looking car? Your shit'll be gone from the parking lot by lunchtime the first day you drive it."

The kid just grins, sticks his hand out, and tries to high-five Rafael.

"Okay, cool, man, cool," he says, mostly to himself, as he drifts out the door.

"He's probably going to go get it done somewhere else," Rafael says. I nod.

"You got kids or something?"

"Nope."

"Um, okay. So, like I said, there was no leak. Engine's in good condition. I changed the oil, topped off your fluids, and put some air in your tires, but other than that, she's good."

"Great. What do I owe you?"

"Thirty-five." I know I shouldn't charge him—the guy stepped into a fight for me when we'd never even met—but Brian and Pop both saw him bring the car in and if either of them notice there's no receipt, they'll want to know why. Rafael steps close enough to hand me the cash, and doesn't step away. I find myself looking up at him because it's less awkward than staring at the skin of his throat.

"Listen," he says, his voice pitched low even though there's no one else on the floor, "there's something I'd like to talk to you about. Are you free sometime this week to grab a coffee or some dinner?"

He's not asking me on a date, is he? He doesn't seem flirtatious; pretty serious, in fact.

"Uh...."

"I'd like to ask for your help with something. If it turns out you're interested."

I do owe him a pretty massive favor. But I don't want to go out for coffee or dinner with the guy. Someone might see us.

"Yeah. Okay. Um, why don't you come to my place. Since you already know where it is," I can't help but add under my breath.

"Okay. Are you free tomorrow night?"

I nod. "Come over around 7:30?" I hand him his key and a receipt.

"See you tomorrow, Colin," he says slowly, looking right at me, and folds himself into his car. And that? That was flirtatious.

THE NEXT day when I get home from work, I get right in the shower and blast the water as hot as it will go, my skin pinking in seconds. Sometimes it feels like, no matter how hard I scrub, I never get the grime off. Then the next day I'm filthy all over again. My mom used to say she even smelled like oil because Pop could never completely get rid of the smell. It clung to his hair, their linens, and eventually, to her.

Today is her birthday. She would've been sixty. When I left the shop, Pop was already drunk, and Sam gave me a look that meant he knew what today is and we should let him be.

Even though I just got out of the shower, I'm already feeling sweaty and anxious, so I grab a beer to calm my nerves and cool me off.

In the second after the doorbell rings but before I pull the door open, this absurd image flashes through my head: Rafael standing there in a tuxedo, with a corsage in a plastic clamshell and a limo waiting in the background. Something is seriously wrong with me. *Get it together, asshole.*

Rafael is not wearing a tux. He's wearing jeans that fit him perfectly, navy-and-gray New Balance classics, and a tight black T-shirt. With his hair pulled back, his prominent cheekbones make him look even more severe.

He sticks out a hand and at first I fumble, thinking he wants to shake, but he's passing me a carton of Turkey Hill Cookies 'n Cream and I can't help but smile at how much better than a corsage that is.

"Oh, awesome, thanks. C'mon in."

As I close the door, though, there's the disconcerting sound of a thump from behind me. I hit the bedroom door with Rafael right on my heel. Then from the closet comes a quiet mewling, and I relax. Beneath a newly fallen pile of towels, old shoes, and baseball caps is Shelby, scrabbling while wrapped up in a flannel shirt. Cradling the ice cream like a football in the crook of my arm, I pluck the kitten out of the mess and give it a pat on the head. When it launches itself off my chest to land on Rafael's crossed arms, he looks startled, but quickly recovers, petting the cat until it purrs like a real Mustang.

"What's your name?" he asks the cat. Why do people do that?

"I named it Shelby. You know, because of the stripe."

Rafael's raised eyebrows and blank look suggest he's not familiar with the Shelby Mustang.

"It? Is it a boy or a girl?" he asks.

I shrug. Rafael clicks his tongue at the cat and flips it on its back in his hand.

"Girl," he announces. Shelby rolls over and kneads Rafael's chest with a deep purr. "She do that to you?"

"Huh?"

Rafael runs a warm finger down my forearm.

"Oh yeah. It—uh, she—just showed up the other night. Can't let her go back out there yet. Too little."

Rafael trails after me, Shelby still in his arms, as I stick the ice cream in the freezer, order pizza, and grab another beer.

"Want one?"

"No thanks."

"Or I have whiskey if you want."

"No, I don't drink. Water would be good, though."

Wow, I don't think I know anyone who doesn't drink.

We sit on the couch with our drinks, Shelby now permanently attached to Rafael. He runs a finger over the kitten's back, making her wriggle closer to him.

"She likes you more than me," I joke.

"Maybe she doesn't want to get attached if you're not planning to let her stay."

I laugh. "Yeah, she's reading my mind. I wish. Then maybe she'd stop unrolling all the toilet paper."

But Rafael isn't smiling. "Animals can sense peace or anxiety, dedication or disinterest. They're incredibly attuned to people's moods. They pick up things we're not even aware we're transmitting."

"Transmitting? Man, you make it sound like a radio or something."

"I think it kind of is like a radio. The way our feelings and thoughts are expressed without words. It's not mind reading. If you pay attention, you get better at it. Animals do it automatically because they don't have the option of verbal communication." He looks strangely comfortable on my couch, talking about animal radios and shit. I'm never that relaxed on my own damn couch.

"You, for example," he says, and I tense. "Not hard to read. You're anxious about what I want to talk to you about but you think you owe me something because I saved your ass the other day." His version of a smile is just small enough to move his mouth to neutral.

"I would've been fine," I say automatically. "Um, so what *do* you want to talk to me about?"

He sits up a bit straighter, slowly, so he doesn't dislodge Shelby.

"I work with an organization in North Philly that does programming for youth in the neighborhood. Giving them activities and a safe space so they stay off the streets. We have after-school programs, sports, art and music programs, mentorship and counseling. And on Saturdays we have drop-in hours all day, but we try to also schedule some special programs. Workshops on things the kids might be interested in, performances, demonstrations, that kind of thing."

"That's cool, man." Jesus, I hope he doesn't want me to be some kind of Big Brother volunteer. Because I kind of already fucked that up with my real little brothers.

"So, I think some of the kids would really like to learn about cars. Knowing how to do basic maintenance would help their families save a little money. And if any of them get into it, it'd give them a skill so they could potentially get a job—that's a big part of what we do, too, trying to connect these kids up with long-term strategies for success, like jobs or internships. And I think some of them probably just think cars are cool. So, would you be interested in teaching a workshop about cars or what it's like working as a mechanic?"

"Wait, seriously? That's what you wanted to talk to me about? If I would teach auto mechanics to some kids?"

"Yeah."

I'm not sure what I was expecting, but not that. Maybe some kind of blackmail for the other night, or—fuck, I don't know. This guy's tripping me out, though. He's handsome, looks like he could be an MMA fighter or a gang leader or something—wait, is that racist?—and he works to keep youth off the streets. I guess that's why he was so good with that kid at the shop last night. Telling him a hard truth in a kind way.

It sounds like a pain in the ass, honestly. I don't know anything about kids and I've never taught anyone anything—unless you count teaching Brian and Daniel how to fight. But I don't really feel like I can say no after he helped me the other night.

"Uh, yeah, I could do that?"

"Yeah?" He smiles, the first one I've seen from him that's bigger than an amused quirk of the lip. "That's great, Colin. I think you'll be good at it."

"Well, you don't really know me. For all you know, I'll fuck it up. Hell, shouldn't you make sure I'm not a child molester or something?"

"Are you?" he asks evenly.

"Uh, no."

"Good. I'll be there. You'll never be left with the kids unsupervised."

"I was just kidding," I clarify. "Obviously. I wouldn't hurt a kid."

Rafael nods and an incredibly awkward silence engulfs the room. Yeah, that's kind of what happens when you try to lighten the mood by bringing up child abuse, asshole.

Once the pizza arrives, Rafael explains the particulars of the workshop, then falls silent. He seems comfortable, but I hate the quiet. I'm hyperaware of the sound of my refrigerator running and the fact that I need to blow my nose because when I inhale there's a slight whistling sound. So I start breathing through my mouth. That makes me hyperconscious of my breathing. Every third or fourth breath, I'm straining to breathe in fully.

"I want to be clear," he says. "I'm gay. I was at that bar the other night to pick someone up. My sexuality isn't an issue for me, and all the kids I work with know about it. I'm assuming that isn't the case for you, and that's fine. It's not my business. I'm not going to bring up how we met in front of anyone. Okay? Does that help?"

"Help what?" I croak.

"Help whatever you freak out about every time you talk to me."

I go into the kitchen and scoop some ice cream for us, trying to pinpoint what it is about Rafael that I keep reacting to so strongly. My mental picture keeps focusing on his eyes and his mouth and his thick arms, but that's not it. That's what I'd notice at the bar.

It's more that Rafael is the first person who knows about… me. The first person who knows I'm—that I would let a dude suck me off—and who I've had an actual conversation with. I've been sitting with him, eating pizza with him, hanging out, and he's gay. And knows about me.

A wave of heat flushes through my stomach and chest, and when I turn around to find him standing next to my hand-me-down red Formica table, looking at me curiously, I can't quite meet his gaze.

"Having second thoughts?"

"No, no, I'm cool." I hand him a bowl of ice cream and stand there awkwardly. "So, uh, how'd you get involved with the—what'd you call it? Organization?"

"My mentor, Javier, started it about thirteen years ago. At first it was an after-school program and some sports. Help with homework, football, safer sex pamphlets, stuff like that. As he got the word out and more people started using the resources, they got more funding. I started volunteering there a few years after it opened. Helping Javier out."

He kind of smiles and frowns every time he says Javier's name. It's more of a reaction than he's had to most things, so this guy must be someone important.

"I've been working there full-time about eight years now."

I nod, but I'm not sure how this is supposed to go. I'm not good at actually talking to people. Small talk at the bar, shooting the shit, sure. But it's easier to just joke around or talk about nothing. And honestly, that's what I mostly do. Talk about nothing.

"So, was that your brother and your father at the shop the other day?"

The bowl Rafael washed is dripping water onto the counter below and my fingers itch to dry it. After resisting for as long as I can (about ten seconds), I reach past him, grab the dish, and dry it, irritated at myself for probably seeming prissy.

"I get those, uh, water bugs," I say lamely. "Yeah, my brother Brian and my dad. Sam, my older brother, works there too."

"Two brothers, huh. I always wanted a brother. I'm crazy about my sisters, but it seems nice to have brothers."

"Three, actually."

"What?"

"I have three brothers. My youngest brother, Daniel, doesn't work with us. Actually, he just moved." Why am I talking about Daniel? "To Michigan."

"Oh, where in Michigan?"

"I don't know exactly. Somewhere in the north. He's an English professor."

"That's interesting. Where does he teach?"

"Um, I'm not sure the name of it," I say, and it hits me for the first time, really, that Daniel lives somewhere in Michigan, but I don't know where. I don't have his address. I have his phone number, I guess. Unless he changed it. But if something happened to him, I don't know where he is. Even though we're not close anymore—hell, he drives me nuts—I used to be the one who looked out for him. And realizing that he's out there, in god-knows-where Michigan, is… unsettling.

"Colin?" Rafael is looking at me, but I can't tell if his expression is concerned or if he just realized that I'm a total asshole who doesn't even know where his own brother lives.

"Huh?"

"I said I've never been to the Midwest."

"Yeah, me neither."

Rafael nods slowly and checks his watch. "I should go. How about I text you the address and the info for Saturday?"

"Sure." I follow him into the living room. "Let me give you my cell number. I called you from the shop phone before."

"What's your last name?" he asks as he adds me to his phone.

"Already have another Colin in there, huh?" I tease, but he just shakes his head. Jeez, this guy has no sense of humor at all. "It's Mulligan."

"Okay," he says. "I'll be in touch. I think this is going to be great." He pats Shelby good-bye.

When he opens the door, I almost don't want him to go. This is the first actual conversation I've had—one that wasn't about beer, sports, or music—in… well, in I don't know how long, and I want to give him… something.

"Listen, Rafael," I say. "Thanks." He looks down at me and his open expression encourages me. "For asking me to do this and—and for the other night. You were right. I was getting my ass handed to me."

A real smile this time, lips and crooked teeth and warm eyes.

"You're welcome. Call me Rafe. Only my mother calls me Rafael."

Chapter 3

WE'RE ON for Sat. 10-1. 11th & Mt. Vernon. Park on Mt. Vernon if you drive. The kids are really excited, Colin. Rafe's text comes in just as I'm starting my last job of the day.

"What're you smiling at?" Brian asks, trying to look over my shoulder at my phone. I quickly shove it back in my pocket and swat him away.

"Can you do some work for once, dipshit? Clean that crap up." I point to the corner of the shop where Luther knocked over a bucket filled with burnt transmission fluid and threw sawdust over it to deal with later. But now it's later and he already left and I'll be damned if I get stuck with it again.

"Hey," I ask Pop as we jack up an Audi, "how did you start explaining cars to us?"

"When you were kids? Christ, I don't remember. I talked out loud about whatever I was doing and you boys were always there, so you listened, I guess. Why do you want to know all of a sudden?"

I shrug, distracted by how he looks a little unsteady as he works.

"Hey, you feeling okay?" I ask him.

"Yep, just felt a little dizzy."

"I thought Sam said you had a headache earlier."

"Eh." He waves a hand, dismissing the subject.

"Uh, hey, listen, Pop, I need to take this Saturday off."

"Oh?" He wanders around the garage and fiddles with some odds and ends lying around, then wanders back to me.

"Colin," he says seriously, looking me right in the eye, "you got some girl knocked up again?"

My face heats up instantly and my palms start to sweat just thinking about Maya. "No! Why would you think that?"

"Well, what am I supposed to think? You're asking shit like how to teach a kid to fix cars and taking a Saturday off. I figure you've got some girl."

"No, no. I just need the day, Pop, that's all."

"Yeah, okay." He pauses and studies me. "You're sure it ain't about some girl?"

I shake my head.

"Huh. Too bad," he says and leaves me to finish the Audi, heart pounding.

SOME GIRL. Jesus. Maya.

I was seventeen and every little thing that anyone did—the way they tapped their pencils or flicked their hair or cleared their throats; the way they said "hey" or fist-bumped or smiled kindly—stirred a rage inside me that was just looking for a target. And god help anyone who gave me one.

Brandon Starkfield caught me looking at him near the auditorium one day, so I kicked the crap out of him and he never made eye contact again. Mrs. Goldzer, the German teacher, offered to let me retake a test I failed and I called her a fat cow. In German. Girls would smile at me and I'd fix my expression into an uncaring neutrality so cold that I would watch them startle and look away. I hurt everyone around me. Everyone. But Maya was the worst.

I had sixth period free that semester so sometimes I'd cut seventh period study hall, leaving after fifth to wander around until football. In the previous few months, though, my grades had been shitty enough that I was worried I'd become ineligible to play, so I started doing homework in the library during sixth period. Maya always came in after choir. She lived in my neighborhood, so I'd known her awhile, though we weren't really friends. We'd chat a little, or sometimes just sit at the same table doing homework. She was a pretty girl—dark skin, big hazel eyes, curvy, great smile. And somehow she didn't trigger the furious reactions that I had so little control over with most everyone else. Because she was an exception in that way, I thought maybe she would be an exception in the other.

I spent a lot of time staring at her, not listening to what she was saying, just trying desperately to catalogue her physical attributes and figure out my reactions to them. I'd stare at her tits and appreciate how round they were, how soft they looked; sometimes I'd even pop wood because tits reminded me of sex and sex was... well, sex, and I was seventeen. I'd look at her mouth and recognize that her lips were full and she looked devious when she grinned, which was cool, but… it didn't make me feel anything.

One afternoon after a few weeks of this, Maya caught me by the wrist and pulled me into the choir room music closet. She was the instrument monitor for the orchestra—she played violin and always had this mark on her neck from it that boys would tease her about, like it was a hickey—so she had keys. She pushed me up against the inside of the door and told me that she'd seen the way I was always staring at her and she was into it. Then she kissed me and grabbed my dick through my jeans.

A few hours before, I'd gotten hard sitting behind Jake, the new kid in my English class who transferred from somewhere in California. He had longish dark blond hair and blue eyes so light they were almost silver. He'd turned around to ask if he could share my book, and those eyes had made my stomach tremble. When I nodded my assent and he leaned closer, the smell of him—something blue and fresh, oceanic—got me hard in five seconds flat, and I'd been on edge ever since.

When Maya grabbed me, I think she felt the effects of Jake, because she grinned that devious grin and started stripping off both of our clothes. She was pretty tall and I hadn't grown my last few inches yet, so we managed to do it standing up, against the door. At one point I knocked into some triangles that were on a hook against the wall and the sound of tinny percussion nearly gave me a heart attack. The whole thing was incredibly awkward. It felt good the way getting enough sleep feels good, or eating a burger when you're really, really hungry—the fulfillment of a physical need that doesn't touch anything deeper—but the second it was over, I felt a rush of hot shame so intense I squatted down on the floor of the music closet, the smell of all those dusty instrument cases and resin making me feel sick. When Maya asked if I was okay, I said I dropped my lighter and pulled my pants up quickly.

That night I dreamt of a smothering blackness that wrapped around me like a midnight ocean, seeping into every pore and plugging up my nostrils, my mouth, my eyes, until it consumed me.

I never went back to the library during sixth period. I ignored Maya when she tried to talk to me, cutting her as hard as I'd cut all those other girls. I wandered the halls like a poltergeist, invisible in my misery until someone set me off, then the very picture of fury.

About two months later, I got home to find Maya and a man who must've been her father at the kitchen table with Pop. Maya was crying and wouldn't meet my eyes, and her father looked at me like I was a turd he'd just stepped in. She was pregnant, and like a scene from one of those awful books we read in English class where the girl is going to be cast out of society unless she can find someone to make an honest woman of her, Maya's father was there to demand that I do the right thing: marry Maya and help her raise the baby.

Pop agreed. And in that moment, I looked at the life ahead of me and saw only the smothering blackness from my dream rushing to drown me.

I don't remember a lot of what happened in the month that followed. Pop tried to talk to me, and I think I nodded but never heard anything he said. At school, the voices blended together into a kind of aural static that set my nerves on buzzing edge and gave me a near-constant stomachache. I felt the way I imagined people feel in a war zone: aware that every step could trigger the explosion or signal the shot that would end them but too exhausted by that reality to watch where they walked.

At football practice I ran until I puked and set blocks I knew would get me steamrolled. At home, I put so much hot sauce on my food that my lips burned for hours after dinner. I turned the shower painfully hot and cut myself when shaving.

Maya lost the baby. I felt such a wash of relief when she called to tell me that I had to sit down, my legs unsteady and my feet numb. For a few days, I felt alive again, like the sword that had been hanging over my head had finally disappeared. But the relief quickly faded back to neutrality again, and I found that my panic over Maya and the baby had only temporarily overshadowed the other thing. The bigger, scarier, more permanent thing. The thing that had made me go along with Maya's seduction in the first place. Now that I wasn't going to be married with a baby to take care of, the problem that was *me* returned with a vengeance.

THE WORKSHOP is in a church, across the street from a basketball court, and there's a colorful sign in the window that says "Use side entrance for North Philly Youth Alliance" with an arrow pointing me in the right direction. I'm a little early, so I wander in, hoping I'll stumble across Rafe.

"Oh, good," a gray-haired black woman says when she sees me. "I thought you weren't coming until tomorrow."

"Uh, excuse me?" I say, looking behind me.

"To fix the sink."

"Oh, no, ma'am—"

"He's with me, Ms. Lilly." Rafe comes from somewhere to my right and puts his hand on my shoulder. "This is Colin. He's doing a workshop with the kids."

"Oh, hello, dear," the woman says, but she looks disappointed that I'm not the plumber.

Rafe takes my arm and leads me to a large multipurpose room where I put down my stuff.

"How are you?" Rafe asks. He's more animated than he was the other night.

"Kinda nervous. Just, I mean, I've never taught anyone anything." I was thinking about Daniel on the drive over and how weird it is that this is what he does every day. But at least he went to school; I'm totally winging it.

"Don't worry. The kids are going to be really into it. Just talk. Just explain. You'll be fine." Then his tone changes. "I'm excited about it too."

"Yeah?"

"Yeah. The only thing I know about cars is how to hot-wire one. And I haven't done that since about 1994." He winks at me. "But don't tell the kids."

"Oi, Conan!" someone yells as the doors open and kids start coming in.

"Hey," another kid says to Rafe, but he calls him something I can't make out.

"What are they calling you?"

He snorts and rolls his eyes in the kids' direction.

"Conan, like Conan the Barbarian, and Khal Drogo. They think I look like this actor who played those characters. I don't know who he is, but they think it's hilarious. I keep meaning to look it up online."

"Uh, like Arnold Schwarzenegger?" Rafe looks confused. "Wait, who's Khal Drogo?"

"Someone in that show *Game of Thrones*. I've never seen it."

"Huh. I don't know."

After a few minutes, about a dozen kids have arrived, chatting, teasing, and hanging all over each other. A few of them look in their early teens and one or two look seventeen or eighteen, but the majority are fourteen or fifteen. At about five after eleven, Rafe addresses the group.

"Hi, folks. Welcome. Today we have a special guest who's going to do a workshop on auto maintenance and cars. Maybe he'll talk a little bit about what it's like to work as a mechanic." He looks to me and I nod. Hell, at least that's something I *know* how to talk about. "So, this is Colin. Why don't you introduce yourselves and then we'll head out to the lot."

The kids all look at each other in an attempt to avoid going first. Finally, the kid who called Rafe "Conan" speaks up. He's one of the oldest ones there. He's wearing a white wifebeater and has the arm muscles of someone who only lifts weights to look tough.

"I'm Carlos," he says. He tips me a little head nod, like he's giving me permission to hang out with him or something. Jesus, I feel like I'm back in high school again. I nod back.

"Ricky," a skinny white girl says, pointing to herself. She doesn't look older than fourteen, but she has a nose ring and a crude tattoo on her thin wrist. Her bleached-white bangs almost cover eyes ringed with black makeup. I smile at her and she looks away.

"Hey, sweetie. I'm Mikal, but you can call me anything you like," says a pretty-boy black kid wearing denim overalls and a shiny purple shirt. Is this kid flirting with me? I expect the rest of the group to turn on him—Carlos looks like the type to react poorly to a gay kid—but most of them just smile.

"Uh, Mikal works for me," I say, trying not to be a total asshole.

Most of the others say their names too quickly for me to retain. Among them are a tall blond guy wearing a plain white T-shirt and jeans like a Gap model who mutters his name like he wants me to forget it; a pair of brightly dressed girls who introduce each other, but do it so quickly I don't catch either name; a beautiful girl who looks Latina—or, shit, is it Hispanic? I really need to ask Rafe about that—and says her name like she's daring me to use it. One guy just waves at me, smiling sweetly. He looks about fourteen or fifteen and has bright blond hair, blue eyes, and pale skin that look otherworldly against his all-black clothes. The smallest one says his name is Stuart, but he says it so softly I can hardly hear him, and one of the older girls, who introduced herself as "Dorothy, but way smarter than that dumb-ass white girl in that Oz movie," repeats it for me.

Last is the oldest and biggest of them: a tall muscular guy I would've put in his early twenties, except that Rafe told me only kids up to age eighteen are allowed here. He's black, with a shaved head and white glasses, and his expression is serious and a bit suspicious. Like he's waiting to decide if he's happy to have me here or not. He's taller than me—maybe six foot two—but not as tall as Rafe, and his worn white chinos, white tank top, and white Converse are all spotless.

"DeShawn," he says in a voice softer than I expected.

"Okay," Rafe says, "let's go talk about cars." And he does seem excited, rubbing his palms together like he's one of the kids.

"So," I say once we're standing in a ring around Rafe's BMW, "this is a 1985 BMW 320i. I know that sounds like just a bunch of numbers and letters, but it's actually kind of like a... a... a secret language that gives you clues about the car. And when you know how to decode the secret language, it saves lots of time because you can shorthand stuff. Okay, so it always goes in that order. The first thing you say is the year. So, Rafe's car was born in 1985."

"Dude," Carlos says, "your car's ancient. It's older than me!"

"Not older than me," Rafe says, raising his scarred eyebrow in warning.

"Me either," I say. "So, okay, next: BMW. That's the name of the manufacturer. Anyone know where BMWs are from?"

"Germany," says Ricky. She's moved her bangs aside enough so that she can see the car with one eye.

"Yeah, that's right." I smile at her, but she keeps staring at the car. "Know what it stands for?" No way will any of them know this. Hell, most people who *own* BMWs don't know what it stands for. I look at Rafe, who shrugs, proving my point.

"Bayerische Motoren Werke."

Ricky again. Holy shit.

"Uh, yeah, that's right." She's staring blankly at the car. "Do you know a lot about cars?" She shakes her head. "Do you know anything else about BMWs?"

"BMW. Established 1916. Produced aircraft engines but forced to stop based on the terms of the Treaty of Versailles prohibiting the manufacture and stockpile of arms or armored vehicles. Began producing motorcycles in 1923 and cars in 1928. In the 1930s, BMW engine designs were used for Luftwaffe aircraft, including the first four-jet aircraft to be flown—"

"Holy crap, so Conan has a Nazi car?" Carlos says.

I can't take my eyes off Ricky. She's staring straight ahead like she's reading this information out of the air.

"Hey, Ricky?" I say. She jerks her gaze toward me. "That's really impressive. How do you know all that?"

"Yo, Ricky Recordo right here! She's got a straight-up photographic memory," Mikal says, stepping closer to me and winking.

"Oh. Cool," I say. "Great. So, we've got the year, the manufacturer. Then the model of the car. In this case, 320. Well, 320i, but the *i* just means it has fuel injection—anyway, the 320 refers to *which* BMW it is."

The kids are looking a little blank.

"But, okay, so a 2014 Honda Civic is simpler: it was made in 2014, by Honda, and the model is a Civic. Got it?"

"Got it," a few of them echo.

"Pop the hood?" I ask Rafe. He has to contort to do it from outside the car and he's surprisingly flexible. He has on worn black jeans that sit low on his hips and hug his ass perfectly and a gray henley with the sleeves pushed up his muscular forearms. Damn, I am *not* paying attention to that right now because I'm supposed to be talking about cars. Uh, no, I'm not paying attention to that *period*.

I force my eyes to the car and resolve not to look at Rafe again. Under the hood is familiar territory, and I lose myself for a moment in the satisfaction of seeing everything exactly where it should be. When Daniel was little, he had these books he would beg me to read to him that he got from the school library where a wacky science teacher miniaturized the kids in her class so that they could see things at the micro level. Daniel would sit on my lap and we'd trace the students' path through the human body, through a hurricane, through the solar system. That's how I feel when I look at a car. Like I'm tiny and can imagine a path through all its different systems. It's dumb, I guess, but it helps me picture everything.

I figured that I'd start by explaining how each of the systems work—engine, exhaust, brakes, cooling, electrical, fuel, suspension, etc. It will give them a good sense of the basics and how all the systems interrelate.

"So, does anyone know what makes a car starts when you turn the key?"

Blank looks and narrowed eyes.

Ignition is so cool—like an action movie. I can see it in my head: the combustion chamber and the crankcase, the pistons floating on a layer of oil in the cylinder, moving up and down, rotating the crankshaft and starting rotary motion; the valve train; the camshaft opening the intake valve as the piston moves down, forming a vacuum that sucks air and fuel into the combustion chamber where they're compressed; the spark plug firing, igniting fuel and air, the explosion pushing the piston back down the cylinder and driving the crankshaft; the exhaust valve opening and the excess gasses being pushed out to the exhaust system. Each tiny piece has one job, and when they work together perfectly, they power this one-and-a-half-ton machine. It amazes me every time I think about it.

I realize I haven't said anything out loud and the kids are still staring at me, and I immediately rethink my plan to explain all the systems. I don't know how to express to them the… magic that I see.

"Um," I say. "Well, really, it's an explosion. Fuel—the gas you put in the car—and air get compressed, squeezed into a really small space, and then a spark ignites them and the explosion starts the car. Like a bullet."

"Whoa, cool," the kids chorus.

"So why doesn't the whole car explode?" asks one of the girls who introduced each other earlier.

"Yeah," says the other. "And sometimes *don't* they just explode?"

"Totally," Carlos says. "Hey, do real cars explode like in the movies? Like… what do you call it…?"

"Spontaneous combustion," supplies Gap Model quietly.

"Yeah," says Carlos, pounding on Gap Model's shoulder in thanks, "spontaneous combustion! That's so sweet."

"Ooh, honey, I saw a car on *fire* once, at 12th and Girard. I bet it totes blew up," Mikal says.

"Oh my god, would you stop it with 'totes,' Mikey. You sound like a twelve-year-old white girl."

"Shut up with that Mikey shit, *Dot*."

"Boy, don't call me that or I'll make you wish—"

"Stop." Rafe's voice cuts through the squabbling. "We have a guest. Can we please save the discussion of nicknames for later?"

Dorothy rolls her eyes but nods. Mikal turns to me and gives me a look that is clearly meant to be charming or seductive, but is mostly just amusing.

"Sorry, sweetie," he says, pouting and opening his eyes wide.

"Uh, no problem," I say. I turn back to Carlos and the twins. "Well, most cars aren't going to randomly catch on fire or explode." A few people exhale with relief and I debate whether I should go on. Eh, shit, everyone likes explosions, right? "But it can happen. Sometimes a battery will be defective and it'll explode, and that looks like the car itself is exploding. When you're charging your car battery, it releases hydrogen, and if a spark were to ignite the hydrogen, it would definitely explode.

"Or, you know, if you had a gas or oil leak in your car and the fuel dripped onto something really hot, that could cause an explosion too. Oh, and sometimes electrical systems go all weird. They can overheat or short out, which can cause a fire, and that can cause an explosion if the fire hits fuel."

Everyone is staring at me. Rafe has his right hand protectively on the roof of his car as if it's going to explode at any moment.

"But, um, those are all really rare occurrences. Really, really rare," I reassure them. "I've never seen it happen and I've been a mechanic for almost twenty years." This seems to put them at ease a little.

"So, what kind of car do *you* have," Mikal asks, his tone flirtatious. People always expect that if you're a mechanic, then you're going to have some tricked-out showy car, but I've never known any mechanic who did.

"A '93 VW Rabbit," I say. "Right now."

They look supremely unimpressed.

"Like, but why?" asks Carlos. "That's almost as old as Conan's car. Couldn't you, like, put together any car you want?"

"Hey, let's not insult our guest's car," Rafe says.

"No, it's cool," I say. "Well, most mechanics I know drive junkers. For one thing, people are always offering to sell us crappy cars for really cheap. And when you know what you're doing, you can fix it up so it runs just fine. So why spend a ton of money when you know you have an endless supply of four-hundred-dollar cars that you can cycle through? Plus, I hate to shatter your illusions, but we don't make that much money. It's not like people are giving away their fancy sports cars when they have something wrong with them. So, yeah, mostly, it's just really easy to have a car I don't have to worry about.

"That's how I got my first car, actually. A customer brought in a falling-apart piece of crap and my dad told him it was worth a few bucks as scrap but would cost a fortune to fix, and the guy sold it to him for two hundred dollars. I bought it off my dad and fixed it up." I painstakingly replaced each busted, rusted-out part in that car, one by one, until it ran as well as anything—hell, better than anything I could've afforded. It took almost a year, but had the bonus of familiarizing me with every scrapyard and junk shop in a thirty-block radius.

This seems to have gotten a few of them interested.

"Could we learn to do that?" Gap Model asks.

"Oh yeah," I say. "It would take a lot of practice, but now there are some really good videos on YouTube of people fixing different parts of cars and stuff."

"Why don't we take ten and then meet back here, okay?" Rafe says. The kids wander back into the church. Rafe is so close I can smell him, can feel his warmth at my side.

"Listen," he says, his voice low. "You're doing great. Just be careful you don't promise them anything you won't follow through with, okay?"

"What do you mean?"

"Most of these kids don't have people who will spend time teaching them things. So, when they do—look, you just don't want to make it sound like you'll be around to help them learn all this stuff if you won't be. It's hard for them if they start counting on you to come back and you don't. They already have a lot of that in their lives. People disappearing. Breaking promises. You know?"

Rafe looks sad, gazing toward the door the kids left through.

"Yeah, I get it."

He squeezes my biceps and nods.

Mikal is the first one back, and it looks like he's applied some kind of glittery lip gloss.

"So," he says, standing about a foot too close to me, "what's wrong with you?"

"Um, excuse me?"

"Well, there must be something wrong with you; you're here." Mikal gestures around him.

I look at Rafe, unsure of what to say.

"Besides, Khal Drogo here is a sucker for a lost cause. Just look around." Mikal's trying to tease, I know, but his voice has changed, his flirty tone gone flat.

"Hey," says Rafe, holding Mikal's gaze. "There's nothing wrong with you. Any of you. You aren't... lost causes." He practically spits the words out. Mikal nods but drops his eyes. I can tell Rafe wants to say more but he bites it back as the other kids join us.

The rest of the workshop goes better now that I'm not so nervous. I demonstrate a few things on Rafe's car, things that I think would be most useful to the kids in case their family cars have problems—how to change a flat tire, how to add oil and top off other fluids. And I look like a complete ass when I try and imitate common noises that cars make when certain things are wrong with them, which quickly devolves into us all making weird shrieking and groaning noises like a pack of wild dogs.

I also answer some of the weirdest questions about cars I've ever heard, including, "Could you put together a car that had two front ends or two back ends?" from Gap Model, to which someone replies, "Course you want something with two back ends," whatever that means; "Is it possible to have a second set of wheels so cars could move side to side?" from one of the twins; and "You know that flying car in *Harry Potter*? Could you make that?" from the kid in all black who hasn't spoken since he walked in. I don't know the flying car in *Harry Potter*, but the rest of the kids greet this idea with enthusiasm.

Then it's over, and the time has gone so fast that I feel like I didn't get to talk about even 10 percent of what I'd wanted to. The twins, Gap Model, and Dorothy wave good-bye to me and call out their thanks as they leave. Carlos thanks me and turns to Rafe.

"Good one, Conan. Way better than that modern dance bullshit."

"You think I didn't see you enjoying the hell out of modern dance, Carlito?"

Carlos mutters something and jogs away. The kid in all black waves good-bye just as he waved hello and wanders off in the other direction.

"Thank you," says DeShawn, holding out his hand. "That was interesting." Again, I'm struck by the softness of his voice, though his handshake is firm. Something about the way he's trying not to seem threatening reminds me of Rafe. I mostly do the opposite.

"You're welcome," I say. He nods solemnly and starts to walk off, but Rafe catches up to him and they start talking about something I can't hear.

Only Ricky is left, staring at Rafe's car as if she's still seeing its guts even though the hood is down now.

"You know," I say quietly to Ricky, taking a page out of DeShawn's book so as not to startle her, "with a photographic memory, you could learn cars really easily. So much of it is just remembering how the pieces interact; what goes where; which are the things that are different in one model versus another. You'd probably be real good at it."

She sighs but doesn't look at me.

"Probably," she says. And she walks away, thin arms wrapped around her chest, hugging herself.

I'm packing up my tools when Rafe comes back over.

"That went well, huh?"

"You think? I—there was so much I could've told them. I don't know if I picked the right stuff. Or if it'll be useful to them."

"They seemed to really enjoy it," he says, and he sounds completely sure. "It interested them, caught their attention. That was my goal for it, and by that measure it was a definite success."

"Oh, okay. Well, that's good, then."

"It is. So, thank you. Let me buy you lunch? There's a great burger place a couple blocks from here."

As I load my tools into the trunk, Rafe stands close enough that I can smell him—warm and spicy and clean—and I fight the urge to lean in and sniff him by slamming the trunk shut hard and digging my car keys into my palm.

The burger place is a little hole-in-the-wall with stools under a bar built into the wall. Rafe's posture is casual and he seems totally concentrated on enjoying his burger, so I try to do the same. I force myself to relax, muscle by muscle, like I do when I can't sleep.

I have the strangest feeling that I've been transported to some other world, like in a science fiction movie. Like I woke up this morning, got in my car, and at some point, drove through a—what do they call them in those movies: wormholes? Yeah, I drove through a wormhole and now I'm here in some alternate North Philly with this person who doesn't exist in my real life, doing things I'd never do in my real life, like the workshop, feeling like I never feel in my real life. Almost… what's the opposite of miserable? It's like a warm charge in my chest. Energy, maybe, but not the kind of fidgety energy I usually have that compels me to run or lift until I can sit still without ripping myself apart. This is—fuck, I don't know.

"Are you going to eat?"

"Huh?"

Rafe points to my burger, which only has one bite taken out of it.

"Oh," I say. "Yeah."

I haven't figured out how to talk to Rafe yet. Fortunately, shoving food in my face gives me a great excuse not to. We don't know each other, so there's nothing to catch up on like there is with Xavier. No "How's your mom?" or "Is your officemate still a jerkoff?" Usually, that would mean small talk, but Rafe has shown himself to be uninterested in that so it seems silly to bother.

"So, um," I say, "I didn't catch some of the kids' names. Can you go through them again?"

Rafe's eyes light up and I know I picked the right topic.

"Carlos," he begins, and I nod. That one I got. "He's a nice kid. I think he'll calm down some. He's been coming to the YA for about three years."

"YA?"

"Youth Alliance."

I nod and keep eating. The burger is really good, despite the fact that the floor is dirty and I can't even tell what color the walls are supposed to be.

"Then there's Dorothy. She talks tough, but she looks out for everyone. She's a poet. Really amazing."

"Who were the twins?"

"Oh, that's Sammi and Tynesha. They're not twins, they're cousins, but they do everything together. They just started coming a few months ago, so I don't know them that well. Edward is quiet—"

"Is that the Gap model? White T-shirt?"

"Shit, he does look like a Gap model." Rafe smiles. "From the nineties." He shakes his head. "Yeah, he's quiet, but if you get him talking about music, he's all right."

"What kind of music?"

"Not sure, exactly. I don't usually know most of what they listen to. But I've heard him talk a lot with Mikal about experimental music from, I don't know, Sweden or Iceland or something. Not really stuff I know anything about, though it sounds interesting."

He gets a look in his eye that I take to mean he's going to look into it. Rafe seems interested in everything. I respect it, that curiosity. Like he genuinely cares enough about some teenager to look into the music he likes so he can talk to him about it. I can't even imagine Pop doing something like that. Or my brothers, for that matter. Well. No, Daniel would do that. Hell, Daniel did do that. He'd ask me who did a song and then ask me things about the band. Then the next time that song came on the radio, he always remembered it.

"So what kind of music do you like?" I ask.

"Honestly?" Rafe runs a hand through his hair. "I mostly end up listening to whatever radio station the kids put on: Top 40 or hip-hop or alternative, usually. I think I know the words to every Taylor Swift song, but I wouldn't know her if I fell over her."

"Taylor Swift—I—wow." I can't help but laugh at the picture of Rafe singing along to Taylor Swift, but he smiles at me, not seeming embarrassed by it, really.

"What would you listen to at home, then?" I try to predict what he's going to say; I'm usually pretty good at that, but he's jammed every signal I have for this sort of thing and I really have no idea.

"I don't listen to music that much," he says. "Mostly in the car, and I don't drive that often. I like country some. I used to listen to mostly rap and hip-hop when I was younger, but that was when I was with friends. Yeah, country. Bluesy country I like a lot. Mostly when I'm home, though, I listen to podcasts."

"Like the news?" Just the sound of those people talking puts me to sleep.

"No. I like ones about history or politics, sometimes science. Do you listen to podcasts?"

I shake my head, my mouth full.

"They're usually about specific topics, like… the Boxer Rebellion or black holes or how icebergs work. And then, depending on the show, they go into different levels of detail on the topic, tell stories about it, that kind of thing."

"So, they're like little documentaries?"

"Basically, yeah."

Hmm. Sounds like school. But, again, he seems so interested in everything. "Black holes… I guess that's pretty cool."

"Actually, DeShawn's the one who first turned me on to the podcast about astrophysics—black holes. DeShawn's the—"

"Big black dude?"

Rafe nods. "He's incredibly smart. Obsessed with science. He wants to be a geneticist." A shadow crosses Rafe's expression, as if that makes him sad or something.

"Hey, what's the deal with Ricky? Does she really have a photographic memory? I didn't know that was a real thing."

"I heard a podcast about that too. Most people don't believe in photographic memory, per se. Not as we think of it, anyway, with someone looking at a book and being able to see each page in their head later on. But people, especially kids, have an incredible ability to recall huge amounts of information, especially if they actively work at it. Like you saw, Ricky does have amazing recall, but I don't think her memory's actually photographic. She doesn't like to talk about it, so I only know what I've seen."

"Is she like—sorry, I don't know the right term or whatever, but does she have that, uh, *Rain Man* thing going on?"

"Autism," Rafe supplies. He runs a hand through his hair, which seems to be an indicator that he's uncertain. "Colin, I'm sorry, but I can't really tell you anything personal like that about the kids. Confidentiality, you know?"

"Oh yeah, of course."

I feel like an idiot for asking. Of *course* he's not going to just tell shit about the kids to some random mechanic who met them once.

"But I can tell you that I've never seen her that intent on something at a workshop before. She was really into it. Mostly, she's interested in military history, like you probably noticed from the stuff she was saying about the world wars. That kid can tell you every battle that was fought during World War II, in order. It's pretty amazing."

"Wow. Isn't it a little strange for a kid to be obsessed with military history? She's, what, like thirteen, fourteen?"

"She's sixteen. I don't think so. Not any weirder than being obsessed with cars when you're sixteen, is it?"

"Yeah, I guess not." But I was only interested in cars because they were around all the time, because Pop was always talking about them and I wanted to be just like him. But hey, maybe Ricky feels the same way about history.

"You were good with them, Colin." Every time he says my name, a little shiver runs down my spine. It makes me realize that people almost never say my name at all. Pop calls us all "kid," Xavier usually calls me "man" or "bro" or something. "You gave them a lot of information but still made it fun. And they responded well to you."

"Heh, yeah, well, I really like explosions, what can I say." Rafe nods. "Um," I start, but then I shove the rest of my burger in my mouth, hoping Rafe'll just keep talking about the kids. But he doesn't. He looks at me, waiting for me to go on.

I choke a little under his regard. It feels like everywhere he looks, I can feel his eyes on me. No one else in the burger place is paying any attention to us, but I suddenly feel like everyone is staring at me, able to read every thought in my head. Rafe pats me on the back as I cough and I flinch. He takes his hand away.

"What were you going to say?"

"Oh well, I remember you said that maybe I could do more workshops—I mean, if the kids'd want me to come back...."

Rafe smiles at me. "You'd want to come back?"

I nod.

"Why?" he asks, and though his tone is matter-of-fact, I can tell my answer is important. He's obviously really protective of the kids.

"It was cool," I say automatically, "getting to shoot the shit about cars."

When he says nothing, just keeps looking at me like he's waiting for my real answer, I try to pinpoint it for myself so I can have some hope of explaining it to him. It's not the cars. Not really. Hell, I talk about cars all day long most days. And it's not the kids, exactly. I mean, I liked them a lot, but... it's me.

"I don't know how to explain it, but... it feels different from the other stuff I do. Like, I go to work and I run and I... I just. It's nice to do something that's not about... me, I guess." Shit, that's it. I don't do anything for anyone else. I mean, I fix cars because I get paid to do it. I listen to music and watch movies for entertainment. I run and lift weights because if I don't, I'll go crazy. But none of that feels good; it's... necessary. Even building my models is just a distraction. Something to do with my hands, a problem to solve, like fixing cars, so I don't have to think.

Rafe is looking at me intently, nodding.

"Javier was the first one who got me to understand that. That doing something for someone else, for a cause, was the best way to get outside of myself, of my own shit. That being a part of something—at least *trying* to make things better—was a way to feel like I had something to offer." His voice is fierce.

Something to offer. Yeah, that's how I feel. In the shop I have something to offer, sure, but it's always been more about getting to a place where I could offer the same thing as Pop or Luther or the other guys who I learned from. But this—I get what he's saying. It's not just information about cars that I'm offering these kids; it's, like, the possibility that they can be good at something.

"I thought, um, Javier might be there today. Since you've talked so much about him," I say, and I cringe a little because I sound… jealous.

Rafe's eyes widen and he swallows hard. He shakes his head and looks at his hands, fisted on his knees. Not so relaxed now.

"Javi's dead," he says, his voice breaking. "He died three months ago."

"What? Fuck, man, I'm—shit! I just thought… shit, sorry."

Rafe's arms are crossed over his chest, the fabric of his shirt pulling taut. His posture reminds me of Ricky's as she walked away, her skinny arms holding herself tight against the world. He shakes his head like he wants very much for me not to make him talk about it.

"I run it now. The YA. I've run it since Javi died." Rafe clears his throat, and I can tell he's making a conscious effort to keep his voice steady. He fists his hands but uncrosses his arms. "So, if you want to make these workshops a regular thing, I think that'd be great. Maybe we could figure out a way to get a car you could actually work on."

"Yeah," I agree. Rafe obviously wants to change the subject and it seems like the least I can do after stumbling into it. "Um, we get piece-of-shit cars at the shop all the time, like I was saying. I could bring one over and leave it in the parking lot? I guess I could tow it over; that way I could get one that didn't run and it'd be more stuff for me to show the kids how to fix? Oh yeah, well, I have one that came in the other day—the engine basically seized completely and it would've cost about five grand to fix so the guy just left it there. That'd be awesome to show them because the whole engine kind of melted…."

Rafe's staring at me. He seems to realize he's doing it and clears his throat.

"Let me check with Marcus. He's in charge of the actual church and the parking lot. He'll know if it's okay to leave the car there. I think it sounds great, though, if he's all right with it."

Then he gets a wicked gleam in his eye.

"I know someone who will be very excited to see you again," he says. "Mikal took quite a shine to you."

"Yeah, what was the deal with that, man? I'm surprised some of the other kids don't want to kick his ass, being so obvious like that. Like, uh, Carlos? He seems like the type… well, at least when I was in school, he would've been the type to kick someone's ass for acting, um—"

"Gay," Rafe supplies easily.

I nod and Rafe's smile turns wry.

"Colin," he says, shaking his head, "YA is a queer youth group."

"Uh, what?"

"Did I not mention that? Huh. I guess I forgot."

"Queer? Like… *all* of them?"

Rafe nods.

"Wait, seriously?"

"Seriously," Rafe says calmly.

My heart starts to pound. "Wait, wait, so do they think *I'm*—" My breath starts coming faster than it should, and I note, absently, that I haven't had any problems with my breathing all day.

Rafe puts his hand on my forearm. I jerk my arm away and look around to make sure no one saw. He sighs and leans back.

"No," Rafe says. "We have straight volunteers. They don't know anything. I promised you I wouldn't expose you like that and I meant it. I wouldn't expose you by implication either. I swear." He's careful not to touch me, but he's looking at me intently, like he can will me to trust him.

"So, then, why didn't you tell me it was a… queer"—the word sounds wrong in my mouth, like it should be an insult but it isn't— "group? And drop that bullshit about forgetting. You seem like you never forget anything."

"Fine. I didn't mention it because I wanted you to go into it with an open mind. Not only for yourself, but for the kids. A lot of people bring a shitload of stereotypes to working with queer youth. I'll bet you know exactly the stereotypes I'm talking about, because I think you might have them for yourself."

What the fuck is that supposed to mean?

"If you want to change your mind now that you know, I suppose that's your prerogative."

Wow, way to totally put me in a tight spot, dude. Now I'll look like a complete asshole if I don't come back. But if someone found out about it, they'd ask all kinds of questions—questions about me. Then I think about how DeShawn shook my hand, so polite and grateful; how Ricky seemed mesmerized by the insides of the car just like I am; how kid-in-black seems to love *Harry Potter*.... He kind of reminded me of Daniel, relating real shit to books.

"No, I—I'm not changing my mind. Next Saturday?"

Relaxed Rafe is back.

"Yes, absolutely," he says, smiling at me. "If it's going to be a regular thing, I'll look at our schedule and see if we want to keep it at this time or if another time is better. Do you have a preference?"

"Well, ordinarily I work Saturday mornings until two. If it was in the afternoon, I guess I could still go to work and—" I break off. It was nice this morning to wake up and know that I had something to do but have it *not* be going to work. "You know what, actually, the morning is great."

"Hey," Rafe says suddenly, "did you say you run?"

"Yeah."

"Me too. We should go running some time."

"Sure, man, that sounds good."

Rafe nods. "Thanks, Colin. For today." His voice is warm and when we shake, his hand swallows mine up, embraces it. He holds on a second longer than most guys would, and looks right in my eyes. "I'll see you soon," he says. And it sounds like a promise.

Chapter 4

ON A good day, running is when I feel most... normal. The tension slowly drains out of me and after a few miles I'm relaxed, floating, like the buzz off a few beers. I'm weightless, suspended between each step as if I might never land, muscles, joints, blood, breath all working together like the parts of a perfectly functioning vehicle.

"How far do you like to go?" Rafe asks.

"I don't really keep track. You?"

"About five miles, usually. But I'll follow your lead, okay?"

I set a steady pace to get warmed up and Rafe follows me, speeding up when I do. After about ten blocks, we settle in, him on my left. His strides are longer than mine since he's so freaking tall, but I'm faster. He's steady, each footfall in perfect rhythm, almost like he's running in place, whereas I know I speed up and slow down a little as the rhythm of my music changes. Since I never ran track, I never bothered with things like keeping a consistent pace or paying attention to how far or how fast I ran. Mostly I just run until I'm tired. Or, depending on the day, until I'm so exhausted that I can't run anymore.

Today I'm taking it easy, though, because when Rafe texted to invite me to go running, I'd already gone.

It's kind of nice to have him by my side. Every now and then, I'll drop the slightest bit back and get a glimpse of lean calves and thickly muscled thighs, of his broad back, sweat turning his white T-shirt translucent along his spine and in the small of his back.

When my thighs start to burn and my knees begin to complain about two runs in one day with a bunch of kneeling on cement in between, I slow to a jog, looking to Rafe, who gives me a thumbs-up.

I jog us back to my house, and Rafe sinks onto the porch steps, breathing heavily.

"You're fast," he says, quirking that broken eyebrow at me. His thick hair is bunched into a kind of knot or something, like a ponytail that he folded in half. It should look girly—like a bun or something—but it's just the opposite. He looks like a warrior, hair tied back for battle. When he reclines on the porch, his arms and neck shiny with sweat, his legs splayed, and closes his eyes, it takes every ounce of concentration I have left not to mold myself to him and taste the salt in the dip of his neck.

He opens his eyes suddenly and I tear mine away so he won't see me staring, but when I look back, his gaze is steady and he's smiling a little.

"What are you up to now?" he asks.

"Nothing. Gotta feed the cat."

"Can I say hi?"

"To the cat?"

"Mmhmm," he drawls.

"Sure." The second I unlock the door, Shelby's right there, attacking Rafe's shoelaces and making little yipping sounds as the loops flop back and forth. When Rafe squats down to pet her, I can't look away from the straight groove of his spine and the way his shorts ride up high on his powerful thighs, dark hair dusting golden skin and tight muscle.

"You want to watch a movie or something?" he asks as he entices Shelby to jump for his wiggling fingers.

I clear my throat. "Um, sure. Let me just shower. You can too, if you want," I say, trying to remember to be polite, which I'm not used to. Sam and Brian just make themselves at home, and Xavier and I have known each other too long to bother with that shit.

"With you?"

"What?"

"You offering to let me shower with you?"

"Holy shit," I say, "did you finally make a joke?" But Rafe just raises an eyebrow.

After my shower I tidy my already tidy house to keep myself from picturing Rafe naked in my bathroom. But I can't stop thinking about what he said. About showering with me. Because Rafe doesn't actually seem to ever be joking. Sometimes he says things lightly, but…. So, then, what would he have done if I said yes? Does that mean he wants to…?

I'm standing in the middle of my floor, so paralyzed by the implications of this that I guess I didn't even hear the shower turn off. Rafe's suddenly right next to me and the sight of him makes my stomach tighten. Wet, his hair is nearly black, waving wildly around his face, cheekbones flushed from the run and the hot water. His gray T-shirt is threadbare and molded to his muscular chest and stomach in damp spots. His jeans are the ones he was wearing on Saturday at the workshop, and his feet are bare. He's so intensely, unavoidably *here*.

"You don't have any shampoo," he says, cocking his head confusedly. It makes him look kind of sweet.

"I don't have any hair."

He reaches up, ghosts a palm over my nearly dry hair.

"It's growing out a little," he says.

"Yeah, I need to cut it."

We get hoagies from down the street and settle on the couch. Rafe's so big that any way I sit, I'm closer to him than I'm used to with Brian or Sam or X.

"What do you want to watch?" I ask, flipping through the On Demand channels.

"Oh, *Runaway Jury*," he says. "I liked that movie." I shrug. "There's a big trial about this tobacco company that's hiding really shady business practices and John Cusack and Rachel… something—that pretty British lady—are trying to trick them into admitting it."

"Um…." That sounds like the most boring movie ever.

"Or *The Bourne Ultimatum*. Did you see the other ones?"

"Is that the dude who's really good at reading maps or something?" So. Boring. Rafe must hear it in my voice because he leans back and says, "Why don't you pick."

"Ooh, *Cube*. It's awesome. All these people wake up locked inside a cube that tries to kill them in different ways…." I trail off, realizing how stupid it sounds when I describe it. Rafe looks uncertain. "Or, how about *Cabin in the Woods*? Did you see it? It's like a horror movie about horror movies—well, I don't want to give anything away."

Rafe's mouth is open, like he's not sure what to say.

"Horror movies…," he says slowly. "Not really my thing. Do you like fantasy? Or… action?"

"Sometimes?"

"Here, *Gladiator*. Have you seen that?"

"No. But, uh, I kind of wanted to."

This is not true, but I'd rather watch almost anything than have an endless negotiation about it.

The movie's… long. I kind of dig it, I guess. I really like the music, and the scenes of them actually gladiating—is that a word?—

are pretty awesome. Russell Crowe is badass. But all the, like, royal intrigue and plotting is dull. Rafe seems to like that stuff, though. The scheming, talky parts. In all the slow parts, I'm mostly aware of Rafe. Leaning forward at things that catch his attention. Leaning back and relaxing into the couch. Sometimes he'll look over at me, almost like he's checking to make sure I'm still there. I don't know if it's because it's loose or because of the no-shampoo thing, but his hair has dried wavier than usual and I have the strangest urge to touch it, to push it back from his forehead and neck.

I've been so relaxed all evening, but then Russell Crowe's character, Maximus, is stabbed by a coward. And even though he keeps fighting, there's nothing he can do. I know he's going to die, and for some reason, I hate it. Yeah, okay, Maximus was a warrior, but war is different—people *know* they might die and they do it anyway, and these warriors seem to welcome a death in battle. But Maximus didn't want to hurt anyone in the arena. He just wanted to be left alone on his farm with his wife and kid, but they made him hurt people and then killed him because he was a threat that they created. I hate it and my stupid fucking breathing thing starts. I hadn't even noticed it was gone until this second. I sit up very straight, trying to breathe deeply and evenly, but once I'm aware of it, it's too late. It's all I can think about.

The movie ends and even though they make it look happy—like Maximus is getting what he wants and being reunited with his family—everyone knows that's bullshit. The dead are just dead and you never see them again. Hell, at least people remember Maximus. I've never done anything more memorable than fixing someone's damn transmission. If I died tomorrow, no one would remember me and no one would care except Pop, Brian, and Sam.

Rafe's not like that. I bet if he died tomorrow, tons of people would remember him. I mean, all those kids at the Youth Alliance would definitely care. They all seemed crazy about him.

The music in the closing credits is incredibly fucking depressing.

"Hey." A tentative hand on the back of my neck startles me and I pull away. "What brought that on?"

"Brought what on?" I breathe as quietly as I can, taking shallow sips of air.

"That change in your breathing?"

"Dude," I say, trying to play it off, "are you listening to me breathe? Sounds like you're the one with the problem."

"Mmhmm," he says, like he's humoring me.

No one's ever noticed it before. Okay, so usually it happens when I'm alone, when I have time to think. But it's definitely happened while I was watching TV with Sam, Brian, and Pop, and none of them ever noticed a thing.

"Um, it's getting a little late," I say. As if I'll be able to sleep anyway. "And I have to work in the morning, so."

I go to open the door, but before I can, he steps right up next to me, and then that warm hand is back on my neck and he's so close I can smell my soap, and *damn*, why does it smell so much better on him?

He leans toward me, and for one panicky second I think... I don't know what I think. I can feel his breath on my face and see the thick spread of his eyelashes.

"You don't have to talk to me," he says, voice low and calm. "But don't think for one second that I buy your bullshit." One side of his mouth tenses in what I'm learning is his version of a knowing smile. "And don't think I don't know exactly what's going on here."

He leans a fraction of an inch closer and strokes my throat with his thumb. I hear my gasp before I'm aware it's happening.

"Good night, Colin. I'll see you on Saturday." He opens the door, then turns back to me. "Sweet dreams."

"GOD FUCKING—MMMF." I cradle my right hand, looking around for a cloth and finding none. I dart into the office for some paper towel before I bleed all over the concrete.

"Colin!" Sam's followed me into the office. "Are you okay?"

It's not so deep that I need stitches, I don't think, but it's bleeding pretty good. It's the third time in two days that I've hurt myself because I wasn't paying attention. The third time since Rafe left my house the other night after his mysterious pronouncement and goddamned perfect face.

"Jesus, what's got you so distracted, bro?" Sam asks, his brow furrowed. "You've been wandering around like a fucking space cadet all day."

"Nothing, man. Just an accident."

"Are you sure? Is it okay? Do you need me to get Pop?" He looks down at my hand. God knows Pop's bandaged up enough of us over the years to know when it's bad.

"Nah, I'm fine. I'm almost done anyway."

I tape the paper towel over my hand and go back to Mrs. Wilson's truck. She's only got a broken drive belt, so it shouldn't take too long to finish. That is, if I can get my head out of my ass long enough to avoid chopping a finger off.

"You're bleeding all over Mrs. Wilson's belt, you knucklehead. Get out of there!"

Pop jerks me up by the shoulder and grabs my hand.

"You idiot—did you even clean that?"

"It's fine, Pop."

"It's not *fine*. Get out of here and take care of it."

He looks disgusted with my stupidity, but with Pop that disgust is always mixed with a little bit of pride that I'm dedicated enough to my work—well, to *his* garage—that I'd stay.

I've been putting off this moment because I know Pop'll be mad, but now I'm right down to the wire so I figure I may as well do it while he can see I'm dedicated.

"Uh, hey, Pop, listen. I need to take Saturdays off for a while."

He gapes at me.

"You're telling me this on a Thursday afternoon? What's wrong with you?" The disgust is back, and this time it's not mixed with anything. "That's not how we do things, Colin."

His nostrils are flared the way they usually are when he's talking to Brian about his incompetence or when Daniel says things that make him sound like a sissy.

"Well," I try and explain, "I talked to Luther and he says he could use the extra—"

"Do you run this garage, Colin?"

His voice is ice-cold. This is don't-cross-me territory that I don't usually stumble into.

"No, sir." I drop my gaze to the floor. Pop and I have the same boots. The toes are pocked down to the steel and stained with oil from years of repairs. He's come so close to me that they're almost touching.

"Do you make the schedule here?"

I shake my head. "No, sir."

"You want Saturdays off?"

I don't say anything, swallowing against a lump in my throat that threatens to cut off my oxygen.

"Sure, son. Take Saturdays off."

His voice is deceptively silky and would sound friendly to someone who didn't know him. I jerk my head up to look at him.

"In fact, why don't you take tomorrow off, too?"

My stomach clenches. "No, I—"

"Do you make the schedule?" There are razor blades beneath the silk.

"No, sir." It comes out as a whisper.

He nods once. "I don't want to see you tomorrow."

I EASE the Beretta into the Youth Alliance parking lot, wincing as it practically bottoms out on the half curb, just as it has on every dip and bump on the drive over. Frankly, I'm lucky it started at all.

I feel fucking rough.

Yesterday was a misery. When my alarm went off, I started getting ready for work as usual, until my brain woke up and I remembered that Pop kicked my ass out. I hadn't had a weekday off in... I can't even remember, and I had no idea what to do with myself.

I did laundry, scrubbed the kitchen floor and behind the refrigerator, scoured the grout in the shower, and cleaned the toilet tank. I rerolled my socks tighter so they took up less space in the drawer, rearranged my shirts by color, and lined up my shoes with military precision.

Shelby started rocketing around my bedroom like a furry missile trying to get at my shoelaces, so I took one out of my boot and let her chase it all over the apartment. I wiggled my fingers for her the way I saw Rafe do and she worked herself up into a frenzy, finally launching herself off the ground and grabbing my left hand in her mouth, front paws anchoring it there and back paws raking my forearm as she scrabbled frantically to dig in and bite down. When I ripped my hand away, there were bright red lines standing out on my arm and scrape marks from her teeth on my hand. Once I got over being startled, I enjoyed the pain—sharp, stinging evidence of what happens when you give something the chance to get a good hit in. By the time she got bored and scampered away to lick herself in the middle of the couch, my forearm and hand were a mess of bright red scratches and welts.

I ran until I was exhausted and then lifted weights until my cut hand throbbed and my muscles gave out and the dumbbell dropped to the floor with a reverberating thud I could feel in my knees.

By the time Brian called after work, I'd done a thousand sit-ups and taken two showers.

"Dude, what the hell?"

I knew the second I heard his voice that I shouldn't have answered because the fire of fury had slid over me, and there was no way to combat it except with ice.

"What the hell, what?"

"Um. Well, you're… you weren't here."

Yeah, no fucking shit, idiot. "Yeah, Pop told me to fuck off."

"Why?"

"I don't fucking know, Brian. Ask Pop."

"Oh. Um, are you coming in tomorrow?"

"Nope."

All I wanted was for Brian to hang up and leave me alone before I said something to really hurt him. When I feel like that, there's nothing I can do. I can't be nice; I can't chat; I can't even end the conversation. There is only one way out: to clench my jaw and my fists until it ends on its own, a wall of ice between me and anything that might delay that end.

"Um. Monday?"

"Yep."

"So, uh, do you want to hang out? The game's on."

"Nope."

I was physically incapable of getting more than one word out—like my whole body's energy worked and worked and worked and all that cranked out was one syllable.

"Oh. Okay, no problem," he stammered. "It's just Florida State anyway, so it probably won't be that good." He paused awkwardly. "I mean, not like you can't watch the game without me. You probably will. So. Okay." He floundered on the end of the line and it was my fault because I'm a shitty brother and basically an asshole. But I couldn't muster another word. "So, then, I guess I'll see you tomorr—or, I mean, Monday."

"Mmhmm."

"Okay, well, bye, bro."

I hung up, relieved to have him off the line, and immediately wished he were there so I wasn't alone.

By ten, I was three whiskeys down, and for some stupid reason, I put that fucking gladiator movie on again. I just really liked the soundtrack—score—whatever you call it. I was feeling the whiskey more than I usually would have because I hadn't eaten anything but cereal when I woke up. But something about my exhausting workout and how hungry I was combined to make my breathing not so bad, so I was afraid to eat. Except then I went to take a piss and saw blackness at the edges of my vision, so I ate a sandwich, cursing each bite that seemed to soak up the warm, tipsy feeling.

I woke up twisted in the covers with a wicked headache and a very disgruntled cat half buried under the blanket, her fur mussed.

Now, my stomach is tight and my breathing is jerky. I think maybe I really should've listened to Pop and gotten stitches, too, because the cut on my hand is throbbing with every heartbeat. I made it worse holding the weights yesterday—tore it open and slapped a bandage on it so I didn't have to look. I press on Shelby's scratches through the rough flannel of my shirt to remind me they're there. To remind me that anything can turn on you in a second. Mostly, I'm just glad for the distraction of the workshop. Another day alone in my house and I don't know what the fuck I would've done.

Before I even get inside, Rafe is striding toward me across the parking lot.

"Hey," he says, and he seems genuinely glad to see me.

"Morning." My voice comes out as a croak, and Rafe leans closer.

"What's going on?"

"Not much."

"You look like shit."

"Wow, thanks, dude. You really know how to brighten a guy's day."

Rafe steps closer, crowding me against the Beretta. "Are you sick?"

"Nah, I'm fine. Just didn't sleep too well."

"What happened to your hand?" He takes my right wrist in his hand like he has every fucking right in the world to touch me, and what is that about?

"Oh, you know. Occupational hazard." I clear my throat. "So, I brought this guy." I thump the roof of the Beretta.

Rafe grabs my left hand where it rests on the roof of the car. "Another occupational hazard?"

He's looking at Shelby's scratches. Then he starts to trace them up from my hand to my arm and I pull away.

"Colin. Are you okay to do this right now?" He puts his hands on my shoulders and it feels strangely good to have all that warm attention focused on me. Different than Brian grilling me.

"Yeah, course."

"The kids are really excited, so if you're not up to giving it your full attention, I don't want to bring them out here."

And damn, that stings. Of course he's not concerned about me. He's worried that I'm going to hurt his kids like I hurt everyone else I fucking come in contact with.

"No, man, I'm fine, really. I'll be good. Scout's honor." I hold up a salute. Rafe frowns, looking me over. I slug him in the shoulder. "Dude, no worries. It'll be great. Get the kids."

His eyes are fixed on the smile I've plastered on my face, and he raises an eyebrow like he's going to call me on it but then just claps me on the back and goes inside, leaving me to set up my tools and search out his lingering smell.

"Yo, yo, yo, Colin," Carlos says, the first one out the door. "How's it hanging, my man?" He tries to execute a complicated handshake, but since I don't have any idea what I'm supposed to do, we just kind of end up flopping our hands against each other's.

"How's it going?" I ask, and Carlos grins at me, like he thought I might ignore him or something.

"Oh, you know, you know, not bad."

It's still a few minutes before eleven, so the kids are chatting and goofing off. DeShawn is back, polite and quiet, wearing all white again, and so are the twins—Sammi and Tynesha, I correct myself. Pretty girl isn't back—guess she wasn't impressed with me—but the rest are, and there are a few new kids who Rafe introduces. I forget their names immediately, as usual.

"Hey, Ricky," I say, waving to her even though she barely seems to notice I'm there.

"Hi," she says, flicking her eyes to me for a second, then looking away.

Last out of the gate is the kid in all black who was into *Harry Potter*. Rafe called him Anders. He's clutching his violin case in hand. When he gets closer, the first thing I notice is that his expression looks different than it did last week. Then he looked... I dunno... sweet and happy, even if he was shy. Now, his expression is shuttered, distant, like he's thinking hard about something. And if he reminded me of Daniel before, with his dreaminess and his little-kid enthusiasm for some weird book, now I can see it quite clearly.

Today, he looks like Daniel did after kids at school started picking on him—after we started teasing him more, moving from the typical brother ribbing to giving him shit because we thought it was girly that he wanted us to read to him and would sometimes absently pull on our mother's too-large robe if he got cold. But most of all, after he realized that he didn't have anything in common with us anymore.

He'd come into the garage sometimes when he was twelve or thirteen—around the time it became clear he was just… different than us—and he'd look around like he was spooked. Like he wanted to hang out but was afraid we wouldn't let him.

"Let's welcome Colin back," Rafe says to the kids. "And let's wish Anders a belated happy birthday."

"A be-what now?" says Carlos.

"Belated. Late. It was Anders' seventeenth birthday yesterday." Jesus, I thought the kid was fourteen or fifteen, he's so small.

"Well, why didn't you just say that, Conan?" says Carlos, his joy at fucking with Rafe clear in his expression.

"You got a problem with my vocabulary, Carlito?" Rafe says, his consonants crisp and mock fierceness in his voice.

"Nope." Carlos grins, and I get the feeling they do this often.

Various versions of *Happy birthday* issue from the group, including a lingering kiss on his cheek from Mikal—who's wearing a sweatshirt with a glittery unicorn on it that says "I even *shit* rainbows"—which makes Anders blush.

I start by taking them on a tour of the Beretta's ruination, explaining why the owner decided to scrap it. The kids are pretty into it, especially when I assure them that they're going to get to actually work on the car, but none of them approach when I ask them where they want to start.

I thought Ricky might step up, but she's like a ghost today, hovering at the edge of the group, her white-blonde hair in her face so I can barely even tell if she's looking at the car. She stands with her ankles crossed like a messed-up ballerina and her arms around her skinny chest like she's a twist the wind could just pick up. There's something about her—

how she's absent and focused at the same time? I don't know. I envy her. She doesn't seem fake.

"So could you fix *anything* on a car?" one of the twins asks—well, even if they're not twins, I can't tell which is which.

"Well, almost anything on a car *can* be fixed. But some things are so expensive that it'd cost more to have them fixed than to buy another car."

"But, like, if we tried to fix stuff on this car and we messed it up, could *you* fix it?" She looks anxious.

"How about this: I can fix *almost* anything. But I promise that if you do something to this car that I can't fix, it's still fine."

"Yeah?"

"Yep. This car is just for showing you guys stuff, so it's no big deal. It's a, what do you call it, learning tool."

They all seem to relax a bit after that. It's fun to show them stuff about cars—things that've become such second nature to me by now that I don't even remember when I first learned them. All week at work, while I was doing repairs and maintenance, I imagined how I could best translate that stuff to explain it to the kids. What would be useful for them to learn. What they would think was cool or interesting.

While we're working I forget about everything except their questions and trying to keep up with their jokes, which all seem to start out being about the car and end up being about sex. And something about how they're trying to come up with a better nickname for me but none of the characters the actor they have in mind for me has played have interesting names, only Jack and James.

All the while, I keep reaching for tools and trying to do things with my right hand, forgetting that it's messed up. I definitely need to change the bandage when I get home because now it's filthy. In fact, by the time 1:00 p.m. rolls around, all our hands are grubby from the insides of the Beretta and a few of the kids have endearingly comical smudges of grease on their faces.

Rafe assures the kids I'll be back next week when they seem reluctant to leave.

I try to catch Ricky's eye to say good-bye, but she doesn't even say good-bye to her friends, just drifts away, kicking at the pavement with her heavy black boots.

"Any interest in going for a run?" Rafe asks.

"Yeah, sure. But I don't have any stuff with me. I drove the Beretta here so I was just going to grab the train home."

"I have gear in my car. We can run near your place and you can get changed, okay?"

We walk the few blocks to his car in silence. Rafe seems distracted by something, and now that I'm not, I can feel how much my hand hurts and I become aware of the dull throb in my head.

I like the way Rafe drives. He's so tall that even with his seat all the way back, his head still nearly touches the ceiling. He keeps his hand on his knee, holding the steering wheel loosely in a few fingers, maneuvering through cross-town traffic smoothly.

I change quickly at my house, eager to run away yesterday and last night. I'm practically vibrating with the need to move.

"You don't have to hold back today," Rafe says. "I know you were taking it easy last time." I nod. "If you pull ahead, just circle back for me."

Right from the start, I'm pushing hard. Each pump of my arm sets my hand throbbing, but within minutes it's coalesced into a constant ache I push to the edges of my attention, alongside the throb in my head and the lingering roiling in my stomach. All I care about is that as I move, my breathing thing disappears and I feel like I can outrun my own body, slough it off like a rusty coat of paint. Rafe's keeping up with me, his long stride helping him, but I can tell he's not going to be able to maintain this pace for more than another mile or two.

After a while, I loop us around Wilson Park, the faded grass mostly worn to dirt from baseball and rain and neglect, and turn us so that Rafe has a straight shot back to my house.

"Go ahead," he says. "I gotta slow down a little."

"Just go that way and I'll meet you back at my place. I'm gonna loop around." The desire to just reach out and throw myself on Rafe wells up suddenly, so big it's almost irresistible. To fight, to fuck—I don't know, but I know I need to run, run away from it.

Rafe nods and I leave him behind in minutes. He's a good runner. But no one can touch me when I feel like this. When I need to get away.

About a mile from home, I can tell I've pushed too hard. My stomach is in my throat and there's a metallic taste in my mouth. My ears ache and my thighs and calves are burning so much I don't even notice my hand anymore.

Rafe's been sitting on the porch long enough to catch his breath when I stagger to a stop in front of my house. I have just enough time to catch the edge of a smile when he sees me before I bend over and retch onto the ground. There isn't much to come up—just a little coffee and the remnants of the peanut butter sandwich I ate last night—but it burns through me and feels like my whole stomach is coming out my throat.

Rafe's hand on my back is cool against my flushed skin. He's holding me up by my shoulders, steering me toward the porch.

"Jesus Christ," he says. "What the hell, Colin?"

"I'm fine," I insist, pushing his hand away from my face. "Just happens sometimes if I go really hard."

Rafe's messing with my bandage, which I forgot to change before we left. It's pretty gross: all dirty and, now, sweaty. He pulls me to my feet by my biceps. It takes him no effort at all, even though I'm practically dead weight.

Inside, I find myself at the kitchen table, a little spaced out, water next to me and my hand on the table. Rafe unwraps the bandage and jerks his eyes up to my face.

"You are an absolute fucking mess, do you know that?" he says, and he sounds pissed.

"Thought you liked lost causes?" I say, but it comes out with none of the levity I intended.

Rafe opens his mouth and closes it again. "I have a proposal," he finally says, voice very calm.

"Is it indecent?"

Not even a smile.

"I propose that you take a shower while I go out and get some food. I think your hand needs stitches—no, hold on," he says when I start to argue. "If you don't want to go to the hospital"—I shake my head definitively—"I can do them. If you're comfortable with that."

Now it's my turn to gape. Um. *Who* the fuck would be comfortable with a random stranger sticking a needle into their flesh?

"Uh, are you… a paramedic or something?"

He shakes his head.

"But you know how to do stitches."

He nods. Well, shit, I guess it can't really be worse than it is now….

I shrug my assent and Rafe nods. I stand to go to the shower and immediately start to sway. Rafe catches me with one hand on my back and the other around my shoulder. My head is swimming, and I want to just collapse. And somehow, I know Rafe would catch me. I've never felt like that about anyone. I mean, maybe Pop when I was a really little kid… but, no, he would've just told me to shake it off….

I shiver at how close Rafe is, and he gives me a little squeeze. I press my forehead against his shoulder before I'm even aware I've done it and pull away as soon as I notice. But when Rafe runs a hand up my back I have a much worse problem.

I try and shift my hips away from Rafe so he won't feel it, but he pulls me back toward him and tips my face up. His eyes are burning. For a second, it's like everything is suspended—Rafe's arms around me, his warmth, his smell, that damned hair I keep wanting to touch. I feel like he could do anything to me. I want him to. Want to just float away from myself and let him do what he wants—no responsibility, no repercussions, no blame.

Then he leans back and the moment is over. He shakes his head, like I've done something confusing, and takes a deep breath.

"Okay," Rafe says. "I'll be back in fifteen."

I nod and close the door without meeting his eyes. When the hot water hits my cut hand, it feels like razor blades. After soaping up, I slap my stupid dick, trying to get my hard-on to go away. No dice. I can't get the feeling out of my head—Rafe surrounding me. The warmth of his chest, his heavy arms around me.

"Fuck," I groan, getting more turned on just thinking about it.

I grab my dick and stroke hard, my hand slick with soap. I picture Rafe pushing me up against the wall, eyes blazing, hair wild. He'd give me no choice, just hold me there, pinned like a butterfly—no. I shake that image off, replacing it with Rafe biting my neck, hands all over me. I stroke faster, so hard it's almost painful, and that turns me on more. After only a few more strokes, I come, a pathetic, gasping orgasm that leaves me light-headed. The moment it's over, hot shame rushes through me and I squeeze my eyes shut to try and disappear.

I can't believe I just jerked off in the shower thinking about a guy I'm going to see in five minutes. But, more, I can't believe I feel the same way I always do after some stranger sucks me off: so fucking ashamed I want to die.

I blast cold water for a minute and drag myself out of the shower. I hardly ever look in the mirror if I can help it, but catching a glimpse of myself as I brush my teeth confirms that I look as bad as I feel. Jesus,

I look tired. The kind of tired that a good night's sleep won't ease. The shadows under my eyes are matched by the ones under my cheekbones, sharp and dangerous looking.

My mother's eyes look back at me, but where hers were a soft blue, mine just look empty. I have her light brown hair, too, but it's usually buzzed so short you can barely tell what color it is. Rafe is right, though. I haven't had it this long in years—maybe an inch long—and it's lighter even than I remember. My brothers all have Pop's dark hair and pale skin. Daniel has green eyes, though, where Brian and Sam have brown, like Pop. I'm not sure how Daniel ended up with them. It's like genetics conspired to mark him as different.

By the time I throw on some sweats, Rafe is back. I don't know how I'm going to look him in the face after what I just did, so I linger in the bedroom, zipping my sweatshirt up to my neck and running a cautious finger over Shelby's sleeping back.

I drink some water while Rafe showers. My hand hangs at my side, a giant, throbbing heartbeat of pain, and my legs feel weak and shaky. I sip the water slowly, and my stomach is so empty that I can feel the path the water takes as it trickles down my throat and into my intestines. I feel... miserable.

Dangerously miserable.

I haven't felt quite this bad in a while, and last time—

"Okay." Rafe's out of the shower, his hair braided back. I've never seen him wear a braid like that before. He sits down next to me and settles a hand gently on my wrist, turning my hand to examine the cut.

"It's swollen, so this is going to hurt. Are you sure you don't want me to take you to the hospital?"

"Naw, man, just do it."

The sting of the alcohol takes my breath away and makes my stomach clench.

"What'd you do?" Rafe asks, probably trying to distract me.

"Oh, I leaned onto a saw blade that was next to a truck I was working on." *Yeah. Because I was thinking about you and your comment the other night. Stupid.*

He threads a curved needle with ease.

"They have this glue now," Rafe explains, "where you can stick the edges of the skin together, but I don't have any. These are the dissolving kind, though, so they'll just melt after a week or two."

"Seriously, how do you know how to do this? Do they just sell this stuff at the drugstore?"

"Nah. I learned at a workshop on radical nursing."

"Uh, what?"

"Radical nursing. It was about basic home care, like sutures, remedies for the flu, how to pack wounds, bind sprains, treat infections, that kind of thing."

"Sorry, radical as in, like, hey, man, far out, or...."

"Radical as in invested in a break from traditional hierarchies of knowledge and embracing modes of transmitting knowledge other than the official, sanctioned ones."

"Whoa."

"Okay?"

I blow out a breath. "Okay."

Rafe puts on gloves and rests my hand on a paper towel on his knee. "Let me know if it's too much." His concentration is intense.

I look away when the needle pierces my skin with a punching sound that makes my stomach heave, and try to distract myself by naming every sound I can hear. The hum of the refrigerator. The buzz of the overhead light. Neighborhood kids playing. A car driving past that has an exhaust problem. The sound of Rafe's deep, calm breaths.

"One more," he says. It's not so much the pain that's getting to me; I just feel queasy.

"All done." He strips off the gloves and peers at me. "Shit, you're green. I should've had you eat first."

I shake my head. "I'm okay." The stitches are in a perfect line, uniform and straight. "Wow. You should be a doctor or something."

He smiles and bandages my hand, then squeezes my shoulder. "All set," he says softly, moving his hand up to my neck. He clears his throat. "I didn't know what you liked so I got cheesesteaks."

"That's fine. Thanks."

Rafe unpacks the food but doesn't say anything. I can't stand the quiet. The wet sounds of chewing and swallowing.

"That kid, Anders. He reminds me of my little brother, kind of," I say into the silence.

"The one you work with at the shop?"

"No, the one who just moved away."

"The professor. How so?" He's turned back to the food, but I can tell he's interested.

"Um, just, like, last week, the way he was really into *Harry Potter*. Daniel was like that—always wanting someone to read to him. My dad always babied him, you know. Treated him like he was delicate or something."

"I think that happens a lot with youngest kids."

"Nah. It's like he didn't expect him to be as tough as the rest of us. Like he knew even before Daniel told him."

"Told him…?"

"That he was gay."

"Wait, Daniel's gay?"

I nod. "After he told Pop, Pop coddled him even more, you know. Like, he was so polite to him. He'd never be that way with me."

"You mean if you were to come out to him?"

"What? No! Just, in general."

"So, your dad was fine with Daniel being gay?" Rafe asks. He sounds confused.

"Well, no. I mean, he thinks it's disgusting—freakish. But once Daniel told him, Pop started treating him all… I dunno. Like a girl or something."

"Like a girl?"

"Just—you know, not wanting to offend him or hurt his feelings or something. Like he was a—"

"What?"

"A sissy. A faggot."

Rafe's eyes flash. "I don't like that word, Colin."

"Sorry, sorry. I just mean, you know, he started treating him like he wasn't a man."

"I see." The silence feels like it lasts hours but is probably only minutes.

"So, um," I say, trying to break the silence. "You said people know about you?"

"That I'm gay? Yeah."

"Like, your family and stuff." He nods. "And they're cool with it?"

"Cool." He laughs a little bitterly. "No, not cool. My sisters are fine with it, though they don't quite believe it because I've never brought a boyfriend home or anything."

"Not even Javier?"

Rafe's face goes instantly blank.

"Javier wasn't my boyfriend," he says. "We were never lovers. Though—" He shakes his head, like he's embarrassed. "My mom has come to accept it, I think. It's gotten easier for her. Especially once she had grandchildren to worry about. I know she wishes I would just settle down and have a family of my own, but...."

He's staring off into the distance, like he wishes for that too.

"Your dad?"

Rafe clucks his tongue. "No. My father would *not* be okay with it, but he hasn't been in the picture for a long time, so."

"What's his deal?"

"He was pretty much gone by the time I was twelve or thirteen. He went back to Zamora—Mexico—with some of his cousins and left my mom with three kids and no money. Not that we were sad to see him go, since when he was around all he did was make us wish he wasn't." He shakes his head in disgust. "So, what did your mom think about Daniel being gay?"

"Nothing. She died when I was twelve."

Instead of the empty "sorry" most people say in response, Rafe just moves closer to me and squeezes my arm.

"What *would* she have thought, do you think?"

What would she have thought? She always wanted me to have a wife. A family. Like Rafe's mom, I guess. Maybe all moms want that. Would she have been disgusted if Daniel told her... that? I don't know. He was her baby and she loved the crap out of him. I know that. Fuck, I don't know.

"I think... she would have loved him," I choke out, and it isn't what I meant to say.

"And your dad. Does he still love Daniel?"

"I don't know."

"But he loves you."

"Yeah."

We eat in silence for a bit, and though I'm clumsily using my left hand to avoid getting food all over the nice, clean bandage Rafe put on, so far I haven't actually slopped food onto myself.

"So, what's the deal with you and your brother?" Rafe says, blatantly changing the subject. "I mean, you seem angry with him. But I would think that if you're both gay, you would've stuck together."

"Hey! I'm not—I never said—I don't—"

Rafe has this glint in his eye, like maybe he's provoking me on purpose. But, as usual, even if he is trying to throw me off balance, there's a core of sincerity. And I don't know how to answer him. Am I angry with Daniel?

"I'm not *mad* at him. I barely even see him," I insist.

"But you think about him all the time. You talk about him a lot."

"Not usually. I don't usually talk about him at all."

"Well, I'm glad you feel like you can talk about him with me." I don't know how Rafe can say this touchy-feely shit and still sound tough. "So? Why are you so upset about him? Don't bother saying you aren't. You get this look on your face whenever you mention him."

"What look?"

"Just a kind of… jealous, pissed-off brother look, I guess."

"I'm not—I just." Jealous? Ugh. I'm too tired to talk about this shit. But Rafe keeps looking at me expectantly, like he's daring me to finish the sentence.

"Daniel didn't care, okay? It was easy for him to risk us all hating him because he was gonna be out of there. He had nothing to lose. I mean, he didn't even want to hang out with us, so no big deal. He didn't want to work at the garage, so who cares if no one wanted him there. He didn't give a shit about Pop, so whatever if he thought he was a freak. Well, that's great for Daniel, but I—"

"You do care."

"Of course I fucking care if my own father thinks I'm disgusting."

"Is that what he thinks? That your brother is disgusting?"

"I don't—look, why are we even talking about this? Are you, like, obsessed with my brother or what? You keep bringing him up."

"No. I'm not obsessed with your brother." He gives me this long, amused look, but I don't know what's so fucking funny.

"Anyway, thanks for the food."

"Come here." He pushes his chair back and stands up.

"Why?"

"Come here, Colin."

So fucking bossy. I glare at him and he comes to me instead. As he gets closer, my stomach flips and my neck feels hot. This close, the air between us is so charged it seems alive.

He takes my hand and my heart starts to pound.

"I know you feel it." Rafe's voice is so soft it's almost a whisper. My gaze jumps to his face and I can't mistake the heat in his eyes.

"Feel what?"

"This." Rafe closes the distance between us, looking at me intently. I look away.

"This," he insists, and before I know what's happening, he backs me up against the wall.

My breath comes in a gasp, but it's not my stupid breathing thing. It's something very different.

Rafe's eyes go sleepy and dangerous, his gaze tracking down my body as he presses up against me. I close my eyes. It's too much. I'm shaking my head and I didn't even realize it.

"This." He runs his palm from my neck to my chest to my stomach, and I'm shivering, so freaked out and so turned on that I don't know what to do. I close my eyes and tip my head back against the wall.

"Tell me what you want," he says in my ear.

I'm shaking my head again, but lifting my chin, trying to get him to just kiss me. To get us out of this awkward damned position.

"Do you want this?" He squeezes my hips, pulling me into him, and I gasp as I feel the evidence that he wants me. I shake my head over and over, because I'll be damned if I'm having this conversation right now, and each time I do, he pulls away and I chase his heat, angling my face toward him and then away.

I'm nothing but points of electricity threatening to fly apart. Rafe groans and leans his hands on the wall on either side of my head, his breath hot on my neck, his erection pressing into my stomach.

"I need you to make a decision, Colin. I need to know you want this. I won't do it any other way."

I pull him closer to me but then drop my arms. I'm so turned on I can barely breathe. Every inch of us is pressed together, from chests to feet, and I feel like if he doesn't kiss me, I'll stop breathing completely. He'd crush me against the wall and kiss me so hard it'd bruise. Pull me against him in a whirlwind of sensation that would go to my head like whiskey on an empty stomach, lighting me up and slowing me down and warming me through and through.

Instead, he's talking again.

"Colin," he says, his lips soft in front of my ear, "tell me."

I want to hit him. Yell at him. He knows what I want—I can tell he does. The sound that comes out of my mouth is more groan than yell. Rafe pulls back, one hand on my shoulder, the other on my neck. His voice is almost mournful.

"Call me when you're ready to tell me what I need to hear," he says, his eyes on fire and his hands hot on my skin. And goddamn him, he kisses me gently on the cheek and brushes the spot with his thumb. Then, with a tight jaw, he turns his back and leaves.

Chapter 5

THE SECOND I step in the door, the kids are on me, Rafe trailing defeatedly behind them.

I texted Rafe last night to make sure we were still on for the workshop even though I hadn't told him anything about… what he needed to hear. Though there was no way I was touching that one, I'd been picturing Ricky, black-tipped fingers tapping her skinny hips in anticipation of what she'd learn; Anders, maybe, like me, wanting the distraction that working on the car would provide. I'd wanted to see if DeShawn would be wearing all white again, and if Mikal's brightly colored outfits always matched his lip gloss.

He wrote back almost immediately: *Definitely. Looking forward to it, Colin. Just a warning, though—the kids have decided on your nickname & I don't think you're going to like it.*

What is it?

I won't steal their thunder. But there was dissent in the ranks.

Mysterious, I wrote back, and I found myself grinning.

"Twilight!" Carlos exclaims, like he's trying it out. Immediately, the rest of the kids start talking at once, but I can't make any of it out.

"Uh. What?" I look to Rafe for clarification, but he's got his forehead in his hand, massaging his temples.

"Twilight," Carlos says again, as if this means something.

"Your new nickname," Rafe says through a tight smile. "Welcome."

"Well, we couldn't call you James," Sammi or Tynesha says. I think it's Sammi; she's taller. "It's a stupid nickname, 'cause, like, it's an actual name."

"Uh, who is James? What are we talking about?"

Mikal comes forward and takes my arm; I resist the urge to jerk out of his grasp, but he must feel me tense because he takes a step back. His T-shirt is purple with black splotches on it and it has a row of gold spikes on each shoulder. Tight jeans bag a little around his skinny thighs and threaten to fall off his hips. He hitches them up, then puts that hand on one hip and looks up at me.

"James is a character from *Twilight*. It's a movie about—"

"It's a *book*, Mikal," Dorothy calls from across the room. "A stupid book," she adds.

"Fine, dear," Mikal says, rolling his eyes. "It's a *book* about this vampire who falls in love with a human girl, and…." He shivers, hugging himself. "And they're, like, made for each other because he can't hear her thoughts."

"Oh wait, is this that movie where the vampire dude sparkles?" The preview for it came on once a few years ago while we were all watching TV at Pop's, and Sam admitted that Liza really liked it.

Rafe's eyes meet mine over the kids' heads and he smiles. It's a strange, private smile, and it does something to my stomach.

"Omigod, you *know* it?! That's totally a sign, you guys!" Mikal is practically swooning with excitement.

"So, wait, you think I look like that sparkly dude?"

"No, no." Sammi—I'm pretty sure it's Sammi—wrinkles her nose. "Not Edward; James. You look *just* like him." She points to me. "Especially when you squint your eyes like that." She looks to the group for confirmation and Mikal and Tynesha nod emphatically, staring at me. I try to stop doing whatever I'm doing with my face.

"Y'all're nuts," a voice says from the back. It's one of the kids who came for the first time last week. I think her name is Mischa. She stands out in this group because she looks like she should be playing soccer in an orange juice commercial or something. She doesn't dress interestingly like Mikal or DeShawn; she doesn't have dyed hair or piercings or tattoos, like Ricky and Dorothy. Hell, even Gap Model looks… um, gay. At least, he does now that I know he is.

Mischa has straight honey-blonde hair pulled back in a smooth ponytail, a slight tan, and light blue eyes. She isn't pretty, exactly, just really healthy looking. She's wearing a green tank top and jeans and looks completely, blandly normal.

She moves closer, assessing me.

"He's not James; he's totally Dean."

"Dude, you just want it to be true because Castiel has your name," says Gap Model—Edward, I correct myself.

"Dude," Mischa shoots back, "you just want him to be Twilight because Edward has *your* name."

I look to Rafe again and his shoulders are slumped a little, like we've gone to a place he would've liked to avoid.

"Wait," I say, "James Dean? I can live with that."

A few of them smile, but the rest look at me blankly.

"James Dean," I repeat. "James Dean?" I look to Rafe who shakes his head, amused.

"You guys have to know James Dean. He was a total badass. But mostly because he had a totally epic car story. He bought this Porsche 550 Spyder: a really cool little car that looks kinda like a bullet. James Dean loved cars; he did some racing too. Anyway, the story is that he showed the car to Alec Guinness—" I look around at them and don't see recognition on any face except Rafe's. At least he looks interested.

"Alec Guinness." Nothing. "You guys. Alec Guinness? Obi-Wan Kenobi?" Some of them nod. "Anyway, apparently he showed Alec Guinness the car and Guinness took one look at it and said he thought the car was evil and if James Dean drove it he'd be dead in a week. And he was. Exactly one week later, he crashed the Spyder into another car, out in California, and the car just *crumpled*." Rafe has perked up and he's giving me a warning look. Uh, yeah, I guess describing gruesome car accidents to kids isn't totally on point.

"Um, anyway, people think the car is haunted because after he died, anyone who came in contact with it got in a car crash or had some tragedy."

"Shut. Up." It's Mischa again, but she doesn't sound upset; she sounds disbelieving. "Oh my god, y'all, it's perfect!" She's looking at the group. "I am so right I can't even *stand* myself right now!"

"Oh shit," says Dorothy. "I get it. It's that one episode."

"Uh, *yeah!*"

"Which episode?" Carlos asks.

"Dean and Dean!" Mischa says. "Ohmychrist, I didn't know it was about a real person, though. Okay, so, it's the one where Sam and Dean are tracking this, like, cursed car that kills everyone who owns it and Dean's all excited because of James Dean—that makes so much more sense now—and they have to look at the engine to see if it's the real car, and then later they're at the wax museum—omigod, *so* good because—"

"The one with Paris Hilton in the wax museum!" Mikal chimes in.

"*Yes*, where it's so funny because in real life Sam was in that *House of Wax* movie with Paris Hilton, *right*?"

"Oh shit, I didn't even think of that," Mikal says, grabbing Mischa's hands and almost jumping up and down with her. "And Dean and James Dean and cars and—" He looks at me and back to Mischa. "And he is all about cars and he knew about James Dean and the haunted car!"

I have absolutely no idea what's going on.

The rest of the kids have been following this exchange like a tennis volley, heads snapping back and forth between Mikal and Mischa.

Finally, Dorothy nods. "Damn, Mischa's right."

And it's like her word is law because everything stops. Mikal pulls out an iPhone crusted with glitter and those plastic gemstone things.

"Final ruling," he says, and after flipping around on the phone for a few seconds, he holds the screen up to the group. They all look at the screen, then at me, even Rafe.

"Damn," says Carlos. "You *are* right." He shakes his head at Mischa. "Look at what he's wearing right now."

I look down at my jeans, black T-shirt, and black work boots.

"Winchester," Carlos drawls, in the same voice he used to greet me with "Twilight" a few minutes before. "Yeah, that's got a ring to it."

"Uh, like the rifle?" I say.

"*Supernatural*," DeShawn says when no one else answers me, too caught up in talking about... whatever the hell they're talking about.

"Huh?"

"It's a TV show about two brothers, Sam and Dean Winchester, who drive all around the country fighting supernatural forces."

"Oh. Well, one of my brothers is named Sam," I offer.

Mikal and Mischa look like they might die of excitement.

"Oh. My. God," Mischa whispers. "This is the best thing."

"Hey," says Carlos, nudging Mischa. "Tell him the car."

"It's a 1967 Chevy Impala."

"You know cars?" I ask Mischa. She rolls her eyes.

"No, duh. On the show."

"The car Sam and Dean drive is a Chevy Impala," DeShawn explains, bless him.

"Oh yeah. Cool car," I say, picturing it. "Triple tail lights. Sixty-seven, you said? Nice. The X-frame gets replaced by a full perimeter frame, angled windshield, full-coil suspension, Coke-bottle styling...."

Ricky, who hasn't said anything during this conversation about *Twilight* and whatever the hell show they're talking about, perks up when I start describing the '67 Impala, but everyone else looks dazed and I trail off.

"So, um, you think I look like this dude who drives an Impala and fights supernatural forces? That's pretty cool, I guess. Way better than some sparkly vampire."

Mikal fits himself to my side and holds up his phone for me to see. On the cracked screen is the guy they've been looking at. He's wearing jeans, black work boots, and a black T-shirt, and is standing in front of a sweet four-door hardtop Impala. He has my coloring, though his hair's darker than mine. And I guess I can see the resemblance. Honestly, though, this guy is way better-looking than me. I give the phone back to Mikal. They're all looking at me expectantly, except Ricky, who's staring off into space.

"Uh, okay?" I say. Mischa grins and Mikal winks at me. Even Dorothy's smile looks satisfied, and Carlos is nodding like order has been restored.

"Okay," he says. "Twilight's out and Winchester's in."

Rafe mumbles something I can't make out.

"What's that, Conan?" Carlos says.

"I said his nickname's better than mine." Rafe looks like one of the kids, slouching with his hands in his pockets.

"Aw, Conan, don't pout," Carlos teases, and Rafe straightens up, back in control.

"So," I say, "we gonna actually look at the car or just talk about them?"

Ricky starts walking toward the car before I'm even done with the question, and we follow her.

We're talking through how to do an oil change when Rafe puts a hand on my upper arm, causing me to break out in goose bumps despite the warm weather.

"Hey, I need to go deal with something," he says, low, nodding to the doorway where someone is looking toward us expectantly. "Will you be okay by yourself for a bit?"

"Yeah, course." I try to focus on the car instead of the line of Rafe's back as he walks away, but before I can get back to what I was saying, the kids clump in around me. At first I think it's to see better, but only Ricky is still focused on what's going on under the hood.

"Okay, Winchester," Carlos says. "Spill."

"Huh?" I look down to the oil pan to see if I spilled, but I haven't started to drain it yet.

"Are you dating Rafe or what?"

"What?" I say, my heart starting to pound and a coil of sick fear unfurling in my gut. "No!" DeShawn is shaking his head at the group, but the rest of them are still waiting like I haven't said anything. I start to cross my arms and catch myself just before I get oil from my hands all over myself. "Why do you think that? Why do you even think I'm...? I mean, I thought you had plenty of straight volunteers."

"We have a few," Mikal says, looking confused as to why I'd bring this up.

"So, why do you think, like... um."

"Why do we think you're gay?" Carlos chimes in.

The word hits like a fist.

"Not cool, man," DeShawn says softly, shaking his head again.

"What—I'm just asking," Carlos says. "Winchester ain't gotta answer if he doesn't want. Right, Winchester?"

I don't know what to say. The kids are looking at me and now it's like what they need from me has nothing to do with cars and everything to do with me. With something that I don't know how to give them. Anders, who hasn't said anything all day, is looking at me expectantly. Dorothy, arms crossed over her chest, has her eyes narrowed at me like I'm disappointing her. Like I'm pathetic and a liar. And I guess she's right. These kids are all here to be honest about who they are. And they're *kids*. I'm a grown man and I can't even say it out loud to a bunch of teenagers. Pathetic.

"Hey, man," Carlos says, and his voice is gentle, like he's sensed that he upset me. "It's cool. You don't have to talk about it either way." Nice kid, giving me an out. "It's not like I'd think you were gay if I saw you walking down the street or anything,"

"Definitely not," Dorothy scoffs after looking me up and down, somehow managing to make it sound like a bad thing.

"Yeah, but, I mean, you wouldn't think that about Rafe either, right?" adds Mikal.

He's certainly right about that.

"So, then, why...?" I start again, but stop, unsure if I want to know the answer.

"It's how Rafe looks at you," Carlos says, sounding serious now. "How, like, in tune you guys are." The rest of the kids all nod, even DeShawn, who stops himself the moment he notices he's doing it.

I can feel my chest heat up and hope that it doesn't show above my collar. I want to know how exactly Rafe looks at me, but I can't ask.

"Totally," says Mischa. "It's like he's completely focused on you. Protective."

"Possessive," says Mikal, and he mock swoons against Mischa's shoulder.

"And Rafe would *never* go for a straight guy," Carlos says.

"How do you know?" I could kick myself the second the words are out of my mouth. I can't believe I'm pumping a bunch of kids for information about Rafe's love life. Ugh. My stomach tightens at just the thought of Rafe loving someone else. Like Javier—perfect, revered Javier: the ghost I could never hope to compete with. I shake my head in disgust.

"Because he's not self-loathing," Dorothy mutters, and DeShawn elbows her.

"He just wouldn't," says Carlos, like it's obvious. "Besides, DeShawn's uncle is, like, the hottest guy you've *ever* seen, and Rafe doesn't look at him the way he looks at you." DeShawn looks embarrassed but everyone else nods their assent.

"Wow, *seriously*," says Mikal, staring off into the distance dreamily. He shakes his head.

"Well, he never really dates anyone," Carlos starts to say, but Mischa cuts him off.

"Okay," she says, "but how do you know he just wasn't attracted to DeShawn's uncle? That doesn't mean he'd never go for a straight guy."

"Um, no offense," says Mikal, "but you've never seen DeShawn's uncle so you don't know what you're talking about."

Mischa looks confused.

"He's fine," Dorothy says. "Like, for real, undeniably."

"I still don't get how—"

"Rafael touches us if we touch him first," Ricky says, her voice flat, her gaze distant, and I know she means the other kids, since she doesn't touch anyone. "Only for two seconds. Then he stops. He shakes hands with grown-ups but never touches them even if they touch him first. You have never touched Rafael. But Rafael touches you at least five times every workshop. And you're a grown-up."

Everyone stares at her in silence, including me.

"What did I miss?" Rafe's voice cuts through the crowd as he walks back over to us and puts a hand on my shoulder.

"The viscosity of oil changes based on temperature so you have to use a multigrade oil to account for heat fluctuation." Ricky doesn't miss a beat, and her eyes stay glued to the engine block the entire time. There's general throat-clearing and knuckle-cracking and then Mikal starts to laugh.

"What?" says Rafe, and everyone just shakes their heads.

"SEE YA next week, Winchester," Carlos calls as the group fractures and everyone goes their separate ways. Okay, I guess Winchester is kind of a badass nickname.

The kids all basically told me that they know I'm—that Rafe and I—whatever—and nothing happened.

Nothing happened at all.

"So, um," I say to Rafe once everyone's gone. "Do you want to run?" I brought my running clothes in case he did, so we wouldn't have to go back to my neighborhood. It seems only fair.

Rafe looks conflicted.

"I can't today," he says.

I didn't realize how much I was counting on him saying yes. The idea that now we're going to go our separate ways makes me feel twitchy and wrong. But why would he want to hang out with me? I didn't call him and tell him what he needed to hear. I came and did the workshop and never mentioned it. Even fourteen-year-olds have more balls than me. And Rafe deserves that. Um, not a fourteen-year-old, I mean. Someone who isn't a coward and a fucking phony.

"No problem," I say. "I get it. Um, see you next week?"

Something flashes in Rafe's eyes. Gone is the even-tempered guy who was here during the workshop and in his place is the intense one that the kids were talking about. Rafe steps up to me and slides one hand around the back of my neck, shaking me lightly.

"This has nothing to do with that," he says.

I just shrug.

"I'm serious, Colin. I meant what I said. You let me know when you're ready. Everything's fine."

Hunh. That's not actually what he said.

"Why don't you come with me?"

"What? Oh, nah." Jesus, the last thing I want is to tag along because Rafe feels sorry for me. Of course he has shit to do and real friends.

"Look," Rafe says, putting a little bit more pressure on my neck. "I'd like to spend time with you, but there's somewhere I need to be. If you come with me, I get the best of both worlds. What do you say?"

It must be nice to have somewhere you need to be. Besides work, I mean. And I don't really want to go sit at home the rest of the day, so I find myself nodding.

"Okay."

He smiles and leans a little closer and says, "You don't even know what you just signed on for," his tone managing to make his words seem filthy.

Jesus. Rafe glances down at the front of my jeans and his smile turns predatory.

"Careful, Colin." His hold on me turns to a caress, fingers stroking the nape of my neck. His eyes may be teasing, but the heat there is real. What would he do if I leaned up and kissed him? If I wrapped my arms around him? God, have I ever hugged a man before? When Mom died, Pop hugged me, I think. Luther did at the funeral, too. But not since then. A few girls have hugged me at bars. Flirtatious pressings together that I think were mostly about rubbing their tits against my chest. The idea of Rafe hugging me—shit, even the word sounds childish—pressing against me, holding me, our whole bodies in contact—makes my heart beat faster.

"What?" Rafe asks, studying my face. "What were you just thinking about?"

I drop my eyes to the ground. "What? Uh, nothing," I say, and I pull away from him. "So, that Mischa is pretty chatty."

Rafe nods and runs a hand through his hair, releasing the scent of something spicy.

"She just moved here from Georgia. She knew Mikal from some Facebook thing."

"Does she play soccer?"

"I don't know," Rafe says, cocking his head. "Why?"

I shake my head. "No, I just—doesn't she look like she should play soccer?"

Rafe smiles. "I guess I can see it."

"Anyway."

"Did you drive or train?"

"Drove."

"You want to follow me or leave your car?"

"I'll follow you. Where are we going?"

"West Philly. Books Through Bars packing session."

"Uh. What?"

"You'll see."

Rafe winds through Saturday traffic: up past the art museum and over the river, then through University City into a neighborhood I haven't been in. We park in a lot between a community garden with a huge mural on the wall, a bar with outdoor seating strung with lanterns, and a Vietnamese restaurant with its windows open wide enough for the smells to make my stomach growl.

"You need a snack?" Rafe teases. "There's usually bagels and stuff inside."

I shake my head. It's only a working theory, but my stupid breathing thing seems to be better when I'm hungry.

"There's only an hour and a half or so left," Rafe's saying. I nod, still not sure where we're going. Outside the entrance, card tables are filled with haphazardly stacked books, with signs that say *Free* and *Help yourself.*

The second the door clangs shut behind us, several voices call out, "Rafe!"

He picks his way between long tables crowded with chairs on either side, at which people are busily writing, stacking books, and wrapping them in brown paper. Almost everyone seems to know him, half of them shaking his hand, hugging him, or patting him on the back. At least three seem to have urgent things to talk to him about, but the scratch of packing tape being torn and the ripping of paper grocery bags makes it hard to hear the conversations.

"Hey, bud," says a man in shredded jeans, a worn T-shirt, and purple hiking boots. He claps a hand on Rafe's shoulder. "Haven't seen you for a few weeks. How've you been doing?" The guy says this like there's a special meaning to it, and I feel my neck muscles tense up.

Rafe glances at me sheepishly but just says, "Not bad. Stuff at the YA's been a little crazy lately." The guy's expression turns even more sympathetic and he pats Rafe on the arm. He's probably in his midforties, but his expression is as sincere as a little kid's.

"Colin, this is Tony," Rafe says, cutting the guy off before he can say anything. I stick out my hand automatically, tensing since the cut is still a bit sore, but Tony's handshake is gentle, if overlong. "It's Colin's first time," Rafe says, "so I thought I'd just get him situated and take him through a few packages. Then I'll make those calls."

"Great, great. Good to see you. We're being a bit careful with tape today because of those packages that got sent back. Well, and because we're running out, like always." Rafe smiles and nods. "Okay. Glad you're here, Colin," Tony says, and then he's called away by a skinny girl in jeans and about three layers of flannel even though I'm starting to sweat because the small room is so crowded.

"So," Rafe says, walking over to a corrugated plastic mail bin full of letters. "People who are incarcerated across Pennsylvania write to us and request books." He rips open the letter. "They say what kinds of books they're interested in—sometimes a specific book, sometimes a genre or a subject. Like, here." He hands me the letter. "This man wants a dictionary and books on World War II."

The handwriting in the letter is the neatest I've ever seen. It looks like an old-fashioned love letter or something, every loop perfectly formed. I guess you have a lot of time to practice penmanship in prison.

Thank you for the books you sent on dogs, the letter says. *I have read them three times so far. I enjoy the pictures too so if there are histories of this war with pictures then great!* The paper is thinner than the lined paper I used in high school.

"Once we know what he wants," Rafe continues, "we go look up which prison he's in and see if there are any restrictions on what we can send." He follows a line on the sign taped to the wall with his finger. "Okay, no hardcovers." He grabs a paperback dictionary from a stack of fifty or so against the far wall and then gestures for me to follow him down a steep staircase. "Dictionaries are a really popular request so we get them wholesale. The rest of the books are donated." He hits a button and the basement illuminates in a crackle of dusty, mismatched bulbs. It's a lot cooler down here, and it smells like mold.

"All the shelves are labeled by topic. Fiction's upstairs and nonfiction's down here." He points to the right. "World War II" is written in faded blue bubble letters on a sign laminated with tape.

"Rafe, what is this? Why are these people sending books to people in prison?" I'm overwhelmed by strangeness. Like I've gone to sleep and woken up somewhere I shouldn't be.

"Well, people in prison want to read too, Colin."

"Aren't there libraries?" I know I've seen that in movies.

"There are. But they're extremely underfunded and very small. And copies of popular books—dictionaries, popular fiction, anything with sex or violence in it—have a way of disappearing. Besides, a lot of incarcerated folks have read everything in their prison's library, so this gives them a chance to request things they couldn't get otherwise."

Rafe's voice is animated, passionate.

"I get that," I say. "But, I mean, aren't they supposed to be being punished?"

Rafe pulls himself up straight and it's only then that I realize how often he leans in toward me. He seems more remote, and when he speaks, he sounds impatient.

"People make mistakes, Colin. That doesn't mean they deserve to suffer forever. Besides, self-education will be an advantage to them when they're released."

I nod, feeling like I've waded into waters that are deeper than I suspected.

"I didn't mean to piss you off," I say. "I just didn't know this was, like, a thing."

Rafe touches my shoulder lightly, turning me toward the books.

"Don't worry about it," he says. "Do you want to pick a book for him? A softcover."

I don't really get what we're doing here, but I flip through a few books on World War II, looking for one that doesn't seem too dry. Finally, I find a good one and hold it out to Rafe.

"He said he wanted pictures," I say, and Rafe smiles.

Upstairs, Rafe grabs us the corner of a table and shows me how to respond to the letter and package the books for mailing. The other people at the table all seem to know each other, and Rafe introduces me.

"So," a girl with artfully styled hair says, "do you live in the neighborhood?" She's just trying to be polite, I know, and make conversation, but though the people don't all look the same, they all look different than me and I'm hyperaware that I don't know what I'm doing.

"No, I live in South Philly," I say. Then, because these are Rafe's friends—or acquaintances, at least—I add, "You?"

"Yeah, I live at 48th and Kingsessing." She points south. "So, like, what's your story? I haven't seen you here before."

I fucking hate that question. *What's your story*, like the person expects you to entertain them or something. I think of all the conversations I could start, the topics I could bring up, and the jokes I could make to get in with them and find that none of them really seem suited to this crowd. In fact, I have no idea how to make them like me.

"Um, no story, man. I'm an auto mechanic."

"Oh. Cool. I've always wanted to do a skillshare about how to fix cars. Neat." But she keeps looking at me like she's waiting for me to explain myself and my presence here and I don't know what she expects. And what the hell is a skillshare?

"So...." She tries again. "Have you been involved in prison justice and decarceration before, or...?"

"Uh... what's decarceration?"

She seems puzzled and looks around at the others. "Oh well, it's trying to get the state not to funnel any more money into building prisons and to eventually release incarcerated folks from prison, you know?"

Everyone else at the table nods as they pack their books.

"Um, is that... I mean... you don't really want to release people from prison, though, right? Like, what about murderers and rapists?"

Every head at the table snaps up to look at me. A few start to say something but then look at Rafe and look at each other, puzzled.

"How's it going, Colin," Tony says, coming to lean over me on the table.

"Um, fine." I lean away from him.

"Cool, cool." He hesitates. "Okay, well, just let me know if you get stuck."

"Am I doing something wrong?" I ask Rafe quietly.

He shakes his head. I meant with the people at our table, but Rafe says, "He's just making sure, since it's your first time."

"Dude, stop saying that. You make me sound like a virgin."

I'm joking, but Rafe's expression changes quickly and he swallows hard. Which, of course, makes my stupid dick sit up and take notice again. Rafe clears his throat.

"I'm gonna get another." I gesture to the letter bin. This letter is from a woman. It's dumb, I guess, but I never thought about the fact that there are women are in prison too. Her name's Jane and she wants romance novels set in Scotland. I wander into the room with the fiction, where it quickly becomes clear not only that a *lot* of the romances are set in Scotland but also that you can tell just by the covers, all of which feature plaid, bare-chested men in kilts, or both.

I grab a few of the least tattered ones, but instead of going back to my table I veer right and go in the basement, hoping to delay the moment when I have to make small talk with the other volunteers. Okay, they seem friendly, and obviously they're doing a nice thing, but... I don't know, there's something about them that I'm clearly missing. Like, they all seem to agree with each other without saying anything, but I'm not sure what they agree about. And Rafe clearly agrees with... whatever they're doing, and I don't like not getting something about him.

I lean against a shelf marked "Prison Abolition" and look at the books I grabbed. The first one is called *Kiss of the Highlander*, and the cover shows the bottom half of a man's face and his bare shoulders draped in plaid. I can't tear my eyes away from the cover because the mouth looks kind of like Rafe's mouth. I've never read a romance novel, never even seen one except when people are reading them on the train. Curious, I flip it open to read just the beginning.

I startle at a hand on my shoulder and practically decapitate myself jerking around to look up at Rafe.

"Jesus," he says. "I thought you left."

"Sorry," I say, pushing myself up and holding the books behind my back. "Just, um, getting some books."

"What'd you get?"

"Oh, just, you know."

"Nope, I don't." He looks quizzical.

"Um." I hold out the books.

Rafe laughs. "Very steamy, Colin. So." He leans in close. "Do highlanders do it for you?"

"Well, I saw the movie. Queen. Best soundtrack ever."

"Mmhmm. Well, it's about time to go, if you want to come finish up this last package."

Thank god. "Sure."

Back at our table, a skinny guy wearing a bike helmet is talking loudly about how everyone should come to a film screening later that night. Everyone nods like they already know about it, but he never says what the movie is. I keep my head down and write back to Jane.

Hi Jane, I write. *I have to admit I've never read a romance novel so I hope these are the kind of thing you were thinking of. I read the very beginning of the time travel one just now and it seems pretty cool and mysterious. Then the other one says on the back that it's supposed to be funny so I hope it is. Nothing worse than when someone says something's funny but it's not. Have a good one. Colin.*

I nudge Rafe. "I don't know what to say. Is this okay, or…?"

Rafe reads it over my shoulder and he bites his lip.

"I can—"

Rafe bumps my shoulder. "It's perfect."

I WAKE up on Sunday in a shitty mood. I don't realize how shitty until I go to make coffee and Shelby darts in front of me and I have to basically throw myself against the wall to avoid stepping on her.

"Fuck!" I punch the wall in a flash of hot anger, which, it turns out, just hurts a lot. It's not a good start to the day, and every little thing irritates me more than the last. I have a voice mail message from Sam from last night, asking where I am and accusing me of "never being around anymore." Yeah, like he's ever around since he married Liza. We used to hang out all the time, but once they moved in together, he always wanted us to come to their house. And it wasn't the same. I'm out of fucking milk, so I shove handfuls of cereal into my mouth from the box while slumped on the couch.

I have nothing to do today but stare at the wall. I bet Rafe has things to do. Letters to write to prisoners and kids to inspire and fundraisers to plan, or whatever they were going to do when they left to get dinner together last night. Rafe invited me but I didn't relish the idea of humiliating myself further by having approximately zero to contribute to their conversation about systemic racism and cultural biases and all the other stuff they were discussing in the parking lot before I left. Rafe had started to explain, but I waved him off.

I scrub my hands over my face and consider just going back to bed and sleeping until work tomorrow morning, but I'm all fidgety and I know I won't be able to sleep.

I hate Sundays. It's not just that I have nothing to do. It's that it doesn't matter what I do. If I watch a game on TV or go running or do laundry or clean the house for the third time this week, it just doesn't fucking matter. I've decided on cleaning the house again when my phone rings.

"Hi, Colin." Even through the phone, the way he says my name does something to me.

"Hey."

"I'm sorry we didn't get to go running yesterday. If you're free today, we could go."

Part of me doesn't want to give him the satisfaction of knowing that I'm basically free all the time.

"Um, yeah, I could do that."

"Great. I'm already in the car, so why don't I come to you?"

"Okay."

I try to shake off my crappy mood before Rafe arrives, though thirty-six years of history should have told me that was impossible.

Rafe shows up cheery and energized, and I try to say as little as possible so I don't ruin it. I'm in no mood to push myself today. I feel sluggish even though I got enough sleep, so Rafe and I are well-matched for pace. Def Leppard pumps me up for a little while, but the second we're back at my house, I'm pissy again. I let Rafe shower first. My own shower reminds me of the other day when I jerked off thinking about him, and I'm swallowed up by a dark, tarry cloud.

What the fuck am I doing with him? What does this mean? And what happens next? Rafe's made it clear that he expects something from me, and I... don't like it.

I rub the towel over my damp hair. I still haven't shaved it.

Rafe's in the living room playing with Shelby. "So, what's up with you?"

"What? Nothing. Why?" Mistake. Never ask why. Just deny.

"You've just seemed pretty quiet. And you look sad."

"I'm not allowed to be quiet sometimes?"

Rafe raises his hands in the universally irritating I-am-blameless gesture. "Okay, Colin. Okay."

Yeah. Damn *right* it's okay for me to have nothing to say.

I walk into the kitchen and start making a peanut butter sandwich to have something to do with my hands. I hold the jar up to Rafe in question when he follows me.

"Sure."

"I don't have any jam."

"Got any honey?"

"Dude, gross."

"No, it's good," he insists.

I shake my head but gesture toward the cabinet.

When he takes a bite, honey oozes out of the side of the sandwich. "Want to try?"

I shake my head. Then I get curious and pull his plate toward me. I take a bite and the mark my teeth leave in the soft bread overlaps with Rafe's. I chew suspiciously. It's disgusting.

"Ugh, too sweet."

Rafe chuckles and reclaims his plate. "I like sweet." He winks at me and I feel my chest flushing for no reason.

"My brother used to eat peanut butter and cheese sandwiches," I say.

"Which brother?"

"Sam."

"That's the oldest."

I nod.

"That doesn't sound good. What about Brian?"

"Peanut butter and grape jelly."

"Grape jelly. That's pretty bad too." I nod. "And Daniel?"

"When he was younger, he liked this marshmallow fluff that one of the guys who worked with my dad used to bring over. Now, I think he likes peanut butter and cinnamon." Well, I don't have any idea about now, I guess. I haven't shared any meal but Thanksgiving with Daniel in years.

"And you like just plain peanut butter, huh?"

"Dude, it's not dream analysis or anything. I just like it."

Rafe smiles; then his expression turns serious.

"Listen," he says. "I'm really glad you came with me yesterday, but I hope I didn't put you in an uncomfortable position."

He touches my arm and I'm reminded of what Ricky said. I count, but even after five seconds he doesn't take his hand away.

"Um. Well, no, but I just didn't fit in. Obviously." I snort, remembering the way everyone stared at me.

Rafe nods. "I know it probably seems that way. Really, though, the people there are pretty diverse. They've just been working toward the same goals for a long time. Sometimes...." He runs his hand through his hair. "Sometimes I think we forget that we had to learn about all these issues too. You know? It's easy to talk to people who are already coming from the same place, politically. But the true test is whether we can effectively communicate those ideas to people who aren't familiar with the issues."

Rafe gets this intent look when he's talking about this crap.

"They're really good people, though. And Tony told me at dinner that he was glad I'd brought you."

I laugh but it doesn't sound right. "Yeah, dinner. I can picture that conversation. 'Hey, Rafe, I'm glad you brought the stupid car guy who didn't know what he was doing.'"

"Hey." Rafe's expression is serious. "Don't do that."

"What?"

"Don't turn something I said into a weapon you use against yourself."

My ears heat. I grab a beer from the refrigerator and hold one out to Rafe before I remember he doesn't drink, and he shakes his head tightly.

"Seriously, Colin. They're not like that."

"Yeah," I say, leaning against the fridge and looking down at the floor I scrubbed the other day. The new bleach-to-water ratio I used definitely helped with the yellowing. "Yeah, I'm sure they're perfect and you all volunteer at soup kitchens together and shit." My voice is a snarl and I sound childish even to myself. I don't know why I do this.

"Actually," Rafe says, leaning forward in his chair, shoulders tight. "I do sometimes. What are you trying to say?"

"Whatever," I mutter, wishing I could take it back. Why the hell does it piss me off so much that he volunteers at a soup kitchen?

"No. You think I haven't seen this before, Colin? Someone trying to make me feel as if the work I do is suspect. Make it seem like my commitment to my politics is about feeling superior?"

And that's what it is. Like every good thing he does just underlines how I'm no good to anyone.

"You *do* feel superior, though. Don't you? To me, anyway. I can see what you think. I'm a selfish little bitch who doesn't do anything for anyone but himself. Hell, who couldn't even—"

"Stop it right there," Rafe says sharply, out of his chair in an instant. "Don't tell me what I think. Don't put words in my mouth."

I put more beer in my mouth instead, tossing the empty can and using the time when my back is to Rafe to get myself under control.

For a while we just stand there. Finally, he says, "You know, you volunteer too. At the YA."

Yeah, I want to say. *At the YA where the kids think I'm fucking gay because of the way you look at me.* Except he's not looking at me that way now. Now he just looks… disappointed. And fuck me, my stupid breathing thing is back.

I crack open another beer and slump against the counter, trying to get a deep breath. I have no idea what to say, and Rafe's obviously not going to help me out this time.

"I'm going to leave," Rafe says finally, as I finish the beer.

Ugh, I'm furious with him but I want him to stay. I'm a total monster right now, but I want, somehow, for him to choose to spend time with me anyway.

"Yeah? Got to go find someone to hang out with who's a saint like Javier, huh?" Shit. I did *not* mean to say that. I can't meet Rafe's eyes. He stands slowly, like he's making an effort to stay calm.

"No. But I can't be around you when you're intoxicated."

"Pssh, I am not intoxicated."

"It's not negotiable," he says with this superior tone that makes me feel like a worm.

"Jesus Christ, man, can you take it down a notch? It's just a few beers. It's not like I'm a fucking junkie or something."

Rafe straightens to his full height and looks me right in the eye.

"Yeah," he says. "Well. I am."

Chapter 6

"UH," I say, anger swallowed up by surprise. "What?"

Rafe sighs and runs both hands through his hair, making it fall around his face in messy waves. "Shit. This isn't the way I wanted to tell you."

He starts looking around the kitchen like a door might magically open in the wall. Finally, he sighs again and stands up straight, as if he's forcing himself to be still.

"Look, okay. I had a drug problem." Rafe's voice is quiet. A little shaky. "I was… into some bad shit and I…. It's still a struggle for me sometimes, and one thing that helps me keep it under control is not being around people who are intoxicated."

I have no idea what to say to that. It's not hard to picture Rafe being into some bad shit. I've noticed the way people look at him, like he's a threat. When he walks at night, he's told me, women will cross the street so they don't pass him, and I know it bothers him even though he understands it. No, it's the idea of Rafe being helpless, out of control, that doesn't fit with the way I think of him.

He glances at me uncertainly, and I'm suddenly aware that I haven't said anything.

"Um. Okay." I want to be reassuring, but I'm pretty sure I just sound confused. I try again. "But you stopped?"

Rafe winces, his expression half resignation and half shame. "I kicked it in prison." He says it quickly, like he can throw the words away.

Wait, what? This is like some really bad after-school special where the totally normal soccer coach confesses that he used to be a drug addict and was in a cult and had accidentally killed a whole village with a bomb or something.

"Uh…."

When Rafe walks over to me, he looks incredibly tired all of a sudden. "Look, I'm sure you have questions, but I can't talk to you about this right now. Honestly, I didn't want to get into it yet at all. It's not something I'm proud of, and I'd like to know someone better before I talk about it. But it came up and I...." He shakes his head. "Anyway, I need to take off."

He hesitates for second with his hand raised like he might touch me—shake my hand or clasp my shoulder—but it never lands. He just turns away and walks into the living room. I'm pretty sure there's something I should be doing. Some protocol I should be following for how to be a good friend when someone confesses something to you, but I have no idea what it might be. The beer sits heavy in my stomach, the taste like metal in my mouth.

All of a sudden the sending books to prisoners thing makes a whole lot more sense. And I stood there and told him that people in prison were supposed to be being punished. Jesus, I'm an asshole.

And not just for that. But because, honestly, it makes me feel a little bit better to know that Rafe's fucked things up in his life too.

"So WHAT'S up Pat's ass these days?" Xavier asks after we order breakfast.

"Eh, he's pissed because I've been taking Saturdays off."

"Jeez, it's about time, man. The benefit of working in the family business is supposed to be that you don't *have* to bust your ass working six days a week—or seven, when you take those extra jobs Pat doesn't know you do."

"Yeah, I guess." X doesn't like Pop. Even as a teenager, he didn't warm to Pop's back-slapping, jokey brand of charm. Most likely because Pop often called him Jamal. Jamal was our quarterback, and the only thing he had in common with X looks-wise was that he was also black.

"So, why are you? It's great and all, but very un-Colin of you."

"Un-Colin?"

"Well, face it, man, you're an unrepentant workaholic. I can't even imagine what could tempt you away from working Sat—wait, is it—did you meet someone?"

Xavier sounds so hopeful that for a second I allow myself to imagine what it'd be like to tell him.

"What? No, man, no. I just wanted a little more free time. You know how it is."

X narrows his eyes. "You hate free time."

I roll my eyes. He knows me pretty well.

"I've been, um, volunteering. At this youth center. I've been teaching the kids about cars, basic repairs, that kind of thing."

"That's great, man," X says, looking genuinely pleased. "But I don't get it. Why would Pat have a problem with that? It's not like there aren't enough hands around the place on Saturdays, right?"

"Oh, well, I didn't tell him about that. It shouldn't matter why I want the time, right? I mean, I'm a fucking adult; he doesn't need to know where I am twenty-four-seven."

X nods, but his eyes narrow again like he doesn't quite believe me.

"So, how's Angela?" I ask before he can say anything else.

He leans back in his chair, his expression so familiar that I'm flooded with warmth for him. It's the same combination of affection, frustration, and puzzlement that he used to get about girls when we were sixteen.

"She's all right." He clears his throat. "She, ah, she wants us to have a baby."

"Oh shit. Are you into it?"

X smiles a little and cracks his knuckles. "Maybe? I dunno, man. Kids are great; it's just…." Kids *love* Xavier. He always picks them up and flips them upside-down and stuff, and they scream with laughter. I can definitely see him as a father. "I don't know what my problem is. Every time she brings it up, I panic. Not that I don't want to go for it. More, like, I just can't picture what shit would be like with a kid, you know?"

I nod. Yeah, I definitely know. But, then, if you'd asked me if I could picture myself volunteering at a queer youth center, I probably would've punched you. And picturing myself spending time with someone like Rafe? No way.

"Anyway, she's pissed because she says I'm desperately clinging to my youth as it recedes and that it's time to get my head out of my ass." It's clear from the way X says this that he's quoting Angela. She has a particular way of speaking. She never stumbles in her speech or has to pause to search for her words. Everything's delivered like a line from a play.

X changes the subject, telling me about some of the guys we used to play football with who he's been in touch with on Facebook. The diner is filling up, and my mind doesn't stay on Kyle Healey and Jackson White and whatever the hell they're doing now.

"All right, Colin, get to the point, would you?"

"What?"

"Come on, man, you're taking time off from the shop and being all secretive about it, and you call me up, ask me to meet you for breakfast—which you never do—and now you're zoning out. You got something to get off your chest, just say it, 'cause your... whatever is making me nervous."

He gestures to the table in front of me where I've forced everything—sugar packets, condiments, jelly pods, napkins, crumbs, and cutlery—into a tight grid pattern. I clear my throat and try to force myself to mess it up, but X waves me off.

"You okay, bro?"

I nod, but now that we're here, I don't even know exactly what I want to ask him.

"Um. You don't—do you know anyone who's been in prison?"

"You in trouble, C?" Xavier's immediately on guard, leaning in to me, his expression fierce. I relax a little. This is the guy who's known me since we were freshmen in high school, the guy who's always had my back.

"Nah," I say. "Just, like, do you think... do you think someone who's been in jail is... super fucked up?"

X looks confused. "Well, yeah, in some ways, because prison is terrible. But I don't think only fucked-up people end up in prison if that's what you mean." He sounds like he's measuring his words carefully.

"Fuck, I don't know what I mean. I just, um—" I can't tell Rafe's personal business, even if it is to Xavier.

"Does this have something to do with these kids you're teaching about cars?"

"Kind of."

"Ah, look, C. It's cool if you don't want to tell me what's going on. But, can I just—" He leans in, sounding almost apologetic. "Look, man, you're... white."

I laugh. "You only noticing that now?"

"Just, you know, you hear prison and maybe you think, yeah, the person did something wrong. But folks go to jail every day for the shit that white guys get away with. Like, remember, that cop caught you and Brian smoking weed in the park and let you off with a warning? My ass would've been in deep shit. For real. So, do I think people who've spent time inside are necessarily criminals? No way.

"Angela's stepbrother served six years in Georgia for hot-wiring a car and driving it around the block. Only, right before he got it back, he got stopped because one of the taillights was out. He freaked and the cops thought he seemed suspicious so they pulled him out of the car and searched it. There was an unlicensed gun in the glove compartment and he had an ounce of weed on him. He was charged with grand theft auto, possession of an unlicensed firearm—even though it wasn't his—and possession with the intent to distribute. It was total bull. Dude should've gotten a misdemeanor for joyriding and they never should've searched shit."

"Jesus."

"Yeah. Angela was so pissed because he didn't call her for advice and got some shitty public defender instead. She said if she'd gotten him a real lawyer, they could've gotten that time way down. Anyway. I mean, as for what can happen to people in prison… yeah, I think it's pretty fucking grim, man."

"Yeah."

"So, if one of these kids is in trouble or something… I don't know, maybe Angela could help? At least help hook them up with a criminal lawyer." I always forget what kind of lawyer Angela is. Something with building permits, maybe?

"Nah, it's not like that, but thanks, man. Yeah, I've just been thinking about it, I guess."

"Yeah, okay, C." X looks suspicious, but thankfully, he doesn't push.

"Hey," I say. "Thanks, man. Thanks for meeting me."

"I'm glad you called, bro. You should come to the house sometime. Come for dinner or to hang out. Watch a game?"

"Aw, man. I just—Angela hates me. You don't have to pretend she doesn't. It's awkward, you know?"

X sighs and rubs his temples. "She doesn't hate you. But… you're never serious in front of her. You don't act like you do with me. You act like you do at the bar. So, she thinks you're a player and she doesn't like when I go out with you because she… you know."

I snort. "Seriously? That's what she thinks? That we're, like, picking up women?"

X chuckles. "I know. I tried to tell her you're not into it, but, hell."

My breath catches. "What do you mean, not into it?"

X freezes and tries to cover it up by rubbing his nose. "Oh. Well, you know, just like, that you aren't like that." He laughs but it sounds forced.

AT THE YA, in the dimly lit basement, I help Rafe set up tables and a platform and move large speakers onto the risers in the front of the room.

I called him after work to make sure he knew we were still… friends or whatever, and to see if he wanted to run, so when he said he had to set up for some event they're having here tonight, I said I'd come help and then hung up before he could tell me not to. He's avoided looking at me since I got here, though, lifting and dragging like a machine. And every time he gets near me, it kindles a flame in my stomach, making me want to reach for him, feel his warmth, smell him.

"So," I say as we're setting up the last chairs in rows. "The kids say you never date anyone."

This is the tidbit that's stuck in my mind. Carlos said it almost as a throwaway comment, but I've been thinking about it ever since. For all that Rafe obviously has a lot of people in his life who need something from him, it seems like maybe he doesn't need anyone.

Rafe stops, a chair in each hand. "And you trust teenagers to have the scoop on my intimate personal life?"

"Well, do they?"

Rafe sighs, puts the chairs in place, and sinks down on the platform we set up. "Well, I'm busy and people have a lot going on," he says vaguely.

"So, they're right. You don't… date or whatever?"

"Yeah, it's been a while," he says slowly, leaning back on his palms.

"You were in love with Javier, huh?"

He sits up quickly.

"What? Why would you think that?" He's studying me intently.

"Um. Just your face when you talk about him." I used to watch Pop's face when my mom would get home from the grocery store or from work. The way his eyes followed her every movement, keeping track of even the smallest gesture like it was important. The way he smiled with his whole face and his shoulders relaxed when she was near him.

"No. Well, yeah, at first. But then…. He was the best friend I'd ever had. The only person besides my mom who looked at me and thought I could be someone. Even my mom…. After—" He looks sideways at me. "After I went to prison, she never looked at me the same. But Javi….

Maybe I was just desperate for someone not to think I was a scumbag junkie criminal, but, man, I would've done anything for him."

I sit next to him, our knees almost touching. It's a strange kind of closeness, like we're kids sitting on a curb or something, swapping secrets in between games.

"I was a kid when we met. Twenty-four. But I already felt like my life was over." His voice is strained. "Felt like, who was gonna hire me after they saw that checked box on the job application. It'd just go right into the trash. And—" He leans forward, knees on his elbows, staring blankly. "—who was ever gonna want to be with me? Make a life with an ex-con." He spits the word out, shaking his head.

It's the other phrase that gets me, though. *Make a life.* It's the first indication I've gotten of what Rafe wants. What he hopes for. How he thinks things work—like a life is something you can create rather than something that's dumped on you.

"I didn't want people to be scared of me," he continues. "But they were. Anyway. Javi… got me. Man, without him I would've been just like all the shitheads I'd been hanging around with when I got sent up.

"He was my sponsor at NA. The relationship between a sponsor and a sponsee is intense. Intimate. You lay all your shit down for that person. You have to. And he didn't judge me. He didn't treat me like a kid. He gave me his shit in return. It was the first time I'd talked honestly with another man about being gay."

He looks at me and his expression is open. This is the most I've heard him say at once.

"Um, you said 'at first'—you were in love with him at first?"

Rafe looks down, embarrassed, but then he laughs. "Yeah. It was so embarrassing." He shakes his head. "One night after a meeting, he asked me to help him take some boxes from his car up to his apartment. When we were done, he got me some water or something, and when he turned to give it to me—" He grimaces. "—I kissed him. I don't know what I was thinking. That he'd used the boxes as a ploy to get me into bed or something. Hell, I don't know. He dropped the water, the glass smashed, and he pushed me away. I was fucking mortified. I worshipped him. Thought he had it all together. I wanted to *be* him. But right then, fuck, I had never felt so stupid."

"What did he do?" The notion of Rafe wanting someone that badly makes me tense, like I'm running out of time for something.

"Oh, he was really kind about it, of course. He's the kindest person I've ever met. He didn't mean to make me feel bad, but he said it wasn't right. He was my sponsor, and I hadn't been clean that long. Besides, he said he saw me as a little brother."

"Wait, he was old?" I've been picturing some really hot variation on Rafe, I realize.

"Not old, but older than me. I was twenty-four; he was about forty." Rafe's smile is fond. "This big old leather daddy."

"What the hell is a leather daddy?"

He glances sideways at me, looking a little embarrassed. "He was a big, beefy guy with a beard and slicked-back hair who always wore jeans and biker boots and a leather vest. Ate burritos or hamburgers for every meal."

"So, um, is that, like, your type?"

Rafe snorts. He looks right at me and takes my hands in his. Ugh, I think mine are all sweaty.

"No," he says. When he lets go of my hands, the disappointment hits hard. Suddenly touching him seems crucial. "Anyway, I got over it. Javi was great. He acted exactly the same around me after that, so I didn't feel so awkward. Never stopped hugging me or hanging out with me. Eventually, I forgot it ever happened, really. He was… my mentor, my sponsor. My best friend."

Rafe looks down at his hands.

"And now he's just… gone. And I don't know what to do with that."

He doesn't try to play it off or cover it up or act like he's okay when he isn't. He… feels it. And I wish so fucking bad I could be like that. My heart feels like it's beating out of my chest and I'm sweating, but I can't help myself. I need to touch him, breathe him in, absorb some of the sadness that feels so familiar.

I push up onto my knees and gently touch my lips to his. He startles at first, like he didn't think that's what I was going to do, but then he relaxes and lets me kiss him.

I can't believe I'm kissing a man.

I can't believe I'm kissing Rafe.

And shit, I must be doing a terrible job, because Rafe's sitting stock-still. After a few seconds, though, one hand slides up my back and the other cups my cheek. And he starts really kissing me. I mean, holy hell is he kissing me.

I've kissed women before and it was fine. Nice, sometimes. But it didn't turn me on like this. Each time Rafe's mouth moves over mine, bolts of sensation shoot straight to my groin. I'm hard in seconds—embarrassingly hard—high school hard—and my whole body is buzzing with energy. Then something inside me lets go, and it feels like I'm drunk. Everything's melted into a soup of darkness and fog and I'm suspended there, where the only thing I'm supposed to do is to kiss Rafe. Nothing could have prepared me for this: feeling like I'm in the right place, with the right person. Like a weight I didn't even realize had always been pressing down on my chest has suddenly vaporized, leaving me ungrounded but free.

Rafe makes a sound in the back of his throat and I realize I have my arms wrapped so tightly around his neck that I'm probably choking him.

"Sorry," I mutter. He doesn't let me pull away, though, and just shakes his head. We're both staring at each other, breathing heavily. Rafe's eyelids are heavy, his lips slightly parted. He pulls me closer, pulls me down so I'm basically straddling him.

"Oh fuck," I mutter as he settles me on his lap. I'm aware of my body in a way I only ever am when I'm running. Connected. I could come with just a touch, which makes me start to panic. I feel helpless like this. Ashamed and nervous and so fucking turned on that I can't pull away.

Rafe runs his hands down my arms, his touch electric. I can smell the warm spice of his hair, and I lean closer, chasing the scent. My nose is next to his neck and I breathe him in. Fuck. Rafe smells like a warm, velvet darkness that I want to dive in to and never come out of.

He leans back slowly, pulling me down on top of him. He spreads his legs and cradles me with his hips as my legs slide between his.

I make a humiliating broken sound, and Rafe kisses me until I'm light-headed and out of control. He pulls my groin tight against his muscled stomach and I know I'm gonna lose it. It's like I'm coming out of my skin. Every nerve ending is electrified, all the pleasure routed to my dick.

I try to push myself away from him, terrified that I'll come all over myself.

"You are so fucking hot like this." Rafe's words send a wave of equal parts shame and joy through me. I gasp and squeeze my eyes shut. "Keep your eyes on me." He angles his hips up, intensifying the pressure between us.

"Don't—" I beg. "I can't—I have to—I'm gonna—"

Rafe catches my scrabbling hands and winds them around his neck, kissing me silent. I shiver when his hands run up my back.

"Look at me." His voice is thick and terrifying, and my body responds to it. Rafe's eyes are almost black in the dim light. Too intense. I concentrate on the light sprinkle of freckles across his nose instead.

His hand moves to my lower back, right above my ass, and I tense, eyes flying to his. He pushes down slowly and grinds our hips together. The pressure is incredible, his arm like a vise. I can feel it begin, little uncontrollable trembles of pleasure skittering from my balls and my spine and my stomach and my thighs like the electric arms of those plasma balls at the museum where I went to on a class trip before Mom died. I put my hand to the glass and the tentacles of electricity jumped to my fingers like magic.

Rafe presses me down harder and harder, his strength inexorable and his eyes ravenous. He runs his other hand up my side under my shirt, the light touch to my ribs a shocking whisper compared to the engulfing pleasure between my legs. Then he cants his hips up and pushes me down as if he could press us into one body.

One second I'm staring at Rafe, his mouth set in concentration, his eyes heated, and the next, my whole body tenses, seized with pleasure. Rafe's hand is immovable, holding me to him even as every muscle clenches. He's looking at me as I come, and his face is pure satisfaction. His eyelids go heavy, and he bites his lower lip between sharp, crooked teeth and shudders against me.

Then he pulses his hips up once, tightening his stomach muscles until his neck cords, and comes, his head thumping back against the platform, his mouth open, breath caught. He looks so vulnerable suddenly. Like I could do anything to him.

My thighs tense over and over and my stomach flutters, seeking the last shadows of shivery pleasure.

I want to kiss Rafe's throat. My mouth is right there and I can smell him, warm and earthy. But then he moans softly, and his hand slides from my lower back down to my ass. He barely touches me, but I tense up automatically, bad memories tumbling it all down, the delicate, dreamlike fog turning tarry and black.

Rafe freezes and inches his hand up to rest on my back once more.

And I hate it. I hate that he made me feel so good and then I probably made him feel like shit. I hate that I just had the best fucking orgasm of my life and then I ruined it. I hate that I wanted to kiss Rafe's neck and instead I'm freaking out. I hate it. I hate myself for fucking it all up. I hate myself for being such a mess that I can't even get off without wanting to punch myself in the face.

Rafe slides his hand up my back soothingly. It's not sex anymore. He's rubbing my back like Mom used to do when I couldn't sleep. I take a deep breath and force myself to relax. His hand moves up to my head, stroking the short strands of my hair. I let out the breath I've caught and lie back on him, trying to recapture the feeling of relaxation from a minute before.

But I'm also sticky, and with each passing second, it's all I can think about, and the more I think about it, the twitchier I get. I need to get washed up, like, now.

"Where's the bathroom?" I croak into Rafe's neck.

"You all right?"

"Yeah, I just… um… sticky."

Rafe chuckles and my face burns. I feel gross. Sticky and dirty and a little shaky. I clamber off of him, probably squishing something vital in the process. Before I can get away, though, he grabs my shoulders.

"Colin?" He sounds almost shy. I look at him, but I'm jonesing to get into the bathroom. He leans in so slowly that I have every opportunity to pull away. But I don't. I let him kiss me softly on the mouth. "I'll go with you," he says, gesturing to the door.

I don't want him to. I need a little distance, some space to think, but I nod.

Under the fluorescent lights, I look like crap. My face is flushed and my eyes are too bright. I want to put the door of a stall between us, but I force myself to stay at the sink and clean up. Every time I glance into the mirror, Rafe is hovering behind me, a slight frown on his lips. I don't know why. It's not like this is new to *him*.

I get myself cleaned up enough that my skin isn't crawling, but I have no idea where to go from here. A door slamming outside makes me startle and drop the wad of damp paper towels. I swipe at them but miss, leaning on my knees and trying to get a deep breath. Fuck. Every good feeling rushes out of me. The weight on my chest is back and it doesn't leave room for anything so warm or delicate as the things Rafe makes me feel.

"I didn't say that about Javi to make you feel sorry for me," Rafe says. He's regarding me uncertainly in the mirror when I stand up.

"I don't feel sorry for you, man. I mean, of course I'm sorry you lost your friend. But you've got a job you love, lots of friends, shit to care about, your family. Those kids worship you." I shake my head. "From where I'm standing, you've got everything."

He drops his hands from my shoulders and looks at the tile floor.

"Yeah. Yeah, you're right. I'm lucky. Luckier than I have any right to be."

Chapter 7

SINCE MONDAY, Rafe and I have talked a lot, and it's been easy. He doesn't pretend that he's into the same things as me. He doesn't like horror movies, doesn't know anything about cars, and doesn't follow sports except for the World Cup and the occasional hockey game. He did give me shit when he found out I played football in high school, though. Said he was surprised I turned into a runner because didn't most football players try their damnedest not to run more than a few yards at a time. So I guess he does have a sense of humor.

Well. Not really. And he doesn't want me to entertain him the way I would with someone in a bar. In fact, when I try to joke around to fill the silence or make light of something, he doesn't seem amused. He's not rude or anything. He just takes things seriously, I guess.

It's a strange feeling. I've spent so many years shooting the shit that I kind of forgot that I had things to say.

I've been remembering it lately, though. Remembering people I used to talk to. There was this kid I knew in seventh and eighth grade. Charlie Lancaster. He was kind of strange, always talking about morbid stuff like death and skeletons and plagues. But I liked listening to him. I liked how he didn't care that people thought he was weird. And after Mom died, all the things he was talking about kind of made sense to me.

His parents had been killed in a car crash when he was ten, and he managed to sit with me and talk and not spout a bunch of shit about how sorry he was for me. Useless comments that made me want to scream and punch people right in their weepy, sympathetic mouths. But Charlie and I talked about what it meant for someone to suddenly cease to exist. About the space someone can leave behind. About where you go after you die—we never agreed on that one: he thought you just disappeared as if you'd never existed, lingering only in the memories of the ones who knew you; I thought there had to be… something. Now, though, I think Charlie might've been right.

But the thing I haven't thought about since freshman year, when I joined football and started hanging out with Xavier and the other guys on the team instead of Charlie, is how I felt when I was near him. How we'd sit, side by side, against the half wall separating the school from the service entrance off the street when it was warm, or against the lockers in the southeast corner of the third floor in winter, talking. How sometimes our shoulders would press together and neither of us would move away. How I was aware that Charlie always smelled like clean laundry, mint, and sweat. How I'd look forward to lunch because it meant seeing Charlie and hearing about whatever he'd been thinking about lately.

And how, sometimes, on really bad days after Mom died, I'd feel a strange compulsion to let my head drop down on Charlie's shoulder, like maybe touching him could leach off some of the poison I felt snaking through my veins.

After Rafe and I, um… well, after Monday, I expected to feel some kind of seismic shift. But it didn't happen. If anything, it's more as if a mess that seemed really jumbled has shaken out into a pattern I can recognize.

"Hey," I say to Rafe, ignoring the terrible movie we've been not really watching. "Did you—when did you realize you were…?"

"Gay? When I was ten or eleven, there was this group of guys in my neighborhood. They were—" He shakes his head. "—trouble. But there was something about them that appealed to me. The way they carried themselves. Their style. They looked tough. Like they could look out for themselves. They were probably only fourteen or fifteen, but I thought of them as being grown. I wanted to be like them. Look like them, dress like them, have a group of people to watch my back like them.

"My dad was a mean fucker. I think, partly, I had this idea that if I had friends like that, they could teach me how to be someone he wouldn't mess with so much. So, I watched them. For years. And I really believed that's what it was—that I wanted to be *like* them. It wasn't until I was thirteen, maybe fourteen, that I realized I just wanted them. By that time, I did have people to watch my back. But it wasn't anything like I imagined. And, well, you know how that turned out."

I nod. The guys who pulled Rafe into their group were affiliated with a gang in his neighborhood. He told me about it haltingly on the phone last night. How he didn't realize what their friendship meant until it was too late. Until he was so deep into taking and selling drugs with them that there was no way he could step away from it without a hell of a lot of fallout.

"They all talked a lot of shit about how many girls they'd been with, even at thirteen or fourteen. Some of it was true. I don't know how much. But I went along with it. Until high school, when it was really clear who was… you know, screwing, because it'd happen at parties, in the backseats of cars, or in bathrooms." He winces. "I kind of… had to."

"With girls."

He nods. "It was a shitty thing to do. Anyway, it's not like it was terrible or anything. It just felt wrong. And then, when I first slept with a boy. Fuck. I knew for sure then. I mean, we were sixteen, so it was clumsy and fumbling, but, damn. It was like all the things I'd been feeling and questioning about myself finally made sense."

"Who was he?"

"Mm, Benny. Benito. He went to a different school, but his cousin went to school with us, so he was always around. He had this really light coloring—almost blond, with grayish-bluish eyes—and everyone joked that he was secretly white. He was… sweet. Which didn't really go over well in my neighborhood. But somehow, people left him alone. Like they could tell he was good." He shakes his head. "I don't know. I don't even know what ever happened to him. But one night at some party, I was standing in a corner, watching everything. I was blitzed. Benny came over to me. He took my hand and led me to this tiny bedroom that had probably been a pantry originally.

"He was smaller than me, but he pushed me up against the door and looked right at me. Didn't say anything. Finally, he leaned up really slow and kissed me. It was like he'd read my mind. I was so shocked that I pushed him away at first. But he kept standing there, looking at me. He knew. He was totally sure of me. And I was so relieved because he proved something to me that I probably would've sat with for a long time, never knowing."

Rafe's smiling. And I'm fucking jealous. Not of this kid Benny, but that Rafe got his questions answered at sixteen, by someone sweet. Rafe likes sweet.

"Do you remember the first time you were attracted to a guy?" Rafe asks.

"I wasn't—I didn't realize that's what it was until just now, I think. This guy Charlie. I dunno what happened to him either. When we went to high school, I kind of lost track of him."

No. That's not true. More like I started ignoring him and didn't step in when I saw people messing with him

A familiar sinking feeling begins, like I'm slipping beneath the surface of something unfathomable, every moment I sit here pressing me farther into a blackness that I want to pull around myself and wrap up in until I can't see or hear anything.

I bite my lip. I can't let myself go to the place where I hate myself. I never know how to come back.

Then Rafe pulls me close and starts rubbing my scalp, kind of the way he pets Shelby. My skin prickles and my breath comes short. I squeeze my eyes shut so tight the room feels like it's spinning.

"God, what are you *doing*?" I groan.

Rafe's hand stills on my hair. "I'm sorry. I was just—"

"No! I mean, what the fuck are you doing here? What are you doing with me? Why do you even give a shit? Fuck!"

I curl in on myself, trying to contain the churning hurricane of fury, shame, and fear in my stomach, but I can't. Liquor will melt me further into it, a razor snap me out of it—for a few minutes, anyway.

Rafe makes a choked sound and turns, going up on his knees and dragging me tight against him.

"You don't feel this?" He presses his palm to my spine, my chest to his. The hurricane in my stomach settles a little as my heartbeat slows down to match the steady, calming thump of Rafe's.

"I feel—I don't know...."

"We... respond to each other, Colin. There's a connection." He presses his face into my neck and I shudder, my body wanting to move closer even as my itchy mind shies away. He breathes me in and his exhalation is warm on my neck.

I feel it. I do. But I don't know what it means. I shake my head.

"I'm fucked up," I mutter, turning away from him. "You'll see."

He chokes out a laugh. "I knew you were fucked up the moment I saw you."

"Shit," I mutter, sliding my arm over Rafe's side and pressing closer to him. "What the hell are we doing?" My voice shakes and he squeezes me tight.

I want to go for the whiskey in the kitchen. Instead, I kiss the corner of Rafe's mouth even though I don't deserve it. Even though all I ever do is hurt people. He snakes his arm around my back and turns his head to chase my mouth. Kissing him feels as warm and intoxicating as the whiskey would.

"Come here, doll," he says breathlessly, shifting me so I'm straddling his lap.

I choke. "God, don't call me that." That's... what the fuck is that? Then I shiver. Rafe's eyes are intense, but soft just for me.

"I can feel how much you like it," he murmurs, pulling me closer. I shake my head. It's... filthy. Embarrassing. "No?"

One palm skates up my spine under my shirt and I shudder hard. I shake my head again, but Rafe's smile is knowing.

"Mmhmm," he says, like he knows better. Which is irritating as hell, but also kind of hot. Damn it. I stop thinking about it when he presses his mouth to mine.

We kiss so slow it's like melting together. My face and neck are hot, and my whole body is buzzing. Rafe strokes up and down my back, and I slide a hand down the back of his shirt, his skin warm under my fingers and slightly rough. He tips my head back and kisses my throat, and I press my hips into him.

"Fuck, Colin, I'm so hot for you, you don't even know."

I choke trying to get a breath in. I don't know what kind of pheromones are coming off Rafe right now, but he's got me tied up in knots with one sentence.

He lays kisses along my throat and sucks at my neck. I shiver every time he touches the place where my neck meets my shoulder.

"You like it here?" Rafe licks the spot he kissed and scrapes his teeth across my skin. My hips jerk forward and I nod frantically, grabbing at him.

"Where else?" he asks, tightening his hand on my throat. "What else do you like?"

All the breath leaves me, and I look away from him. I don't want to stop to think about it because if I do, I'll have to think about how I have no fucking clue what I like, really. Only what I don't. And then I'll have to think about how wrong everything went the last time I messed around with anyone like this. And I really, really don't want to think about that.

"Tell me," he says, voice intense. "I want to make you feel good."

I shake my head, trying to banish the thoughts, and Rafe's hand softens slightly in my hair. I kiss him again, but I can't get back that mindless intoxication from a few minutes before. The one I could lose myself in.

"I want you to tell me what you like and what you don't, okay?" Rafe's expression is serious and I feel ridiculous. I shake my head and kiss him again in an attempt to shut him up.

"So you like kissing. Noted," he says.

"Asshole." I roll my eyes, but he just looks amused.

"Okay, so it's hard for you to tell me what you like in bed."

God, I just want him to stop fucking talking about it and *do* something. I can feel my face heat.

"All right," he says. "I have some ideas. I just need to make sure that I'm not misinterpreting."

"Misinterpreting what?"

Rafe looks almost uncertain for a moment.

"Come here," he says, his voice low and commanding. "Put your hands on my shoulders and kiss me."

I do, and I squeeze his shoulders, loving the strength of his muscles, the solidity of his frame.

"Closer," Rafe says, and I press my chest to his, getting as close as I can while still kissing him. "Put your arms around my neck," he murmurs against my lips, and I do, running my fingers through the hair at his nape. Rafe leaves one hand on my neck when he leans back against the couch, and when he looks at me this time, he's nothing but confidence and certainty.

"I just had to make sure," he murmurs. He looks me up and down. "Damn, that's beautiful."

"Uh, what?" I'm lost. And turned on. Why'd he stop?

"You like it when I tell you what to do."

My head snaps up. "What?" I sure as hell do not like anyone telling me what to do.

"Not ordinarily. I mean in bed." His hand is soothing on my back.

"Uh...."

He leans in and kisses me deep. I melt against him, winding my arms back around his neck.

"Which is incredibly hot," he says against my lips, "since I like telling you what to do in bed."

"I—but—um."

"Lie back," Rafe says, easing me off his lap and onto my back on the couch. He looks almost amused as he leans down to me. "What do you want me to do, Colin? I'll do anything you want. Anything." He kisses me, then pulls away. "Well?"

"Um... I... I don't know."

He leans back down so our hips are pressed together and murmurs in my ear, "Colin, I'm going to slide my hand down your pants and jerk you off until you scream my name."

"Oh fuck!" My hips jerk up, desire sharp in the pit of my stomach. Rafe half smiles at me. "See?"

"God damn it." Why does that turn me on so much? Great, one more way I'm totally fucked up.

"Come on, doll," he says, kissing the corner of my mouth and sliding a hand down to my hip. "You're so hot for this." He grinds our hips together and a sweet pulse of pleasure spreads through me. I thrust my hips up again, chasing the sensation.

"Rafe, fucking come on," I moan. I'm trembling, like my skin can hardly contain my reaction to him.

He slides a hand around to my ass and I jerk into the couch cushions, startled.

"What is it?" he asks.

I shake my head, trying to focus on Rafe rather than on shit from the past. "Nothing. Feels good."

Rafe sighs. "Colin." He's searching my face. "I need you to be honest with yourself. It's really important to me, okay? I can't—*can't* do something you're not okay with. Please don't put me in that position." His touch on my stomach is soothing. "We have plenty of time. Okay?"

I nod. "I swear, I'm fine." Lie. Total lie. But I don't know what else to do. I want this. "I just don't really know what the fuck I'm doing, okay?" Hopefully that will be enough of the truth to satisfy Rafe.

"Okay." His voice is calm. "Can you tell me what you want right now?" He runs a hand over my hair.

I squeeze my eyes shut so I can pretend he's not looking at me. I want to stop thinking about it. I want to stop talking about it. I just want to be caught up in it. "I... I want you to do... whatever."

That didn't really come out how I wanted, but Rafe shudders like it totally does it for him and lets out a breath, running fingers over my lips.

"You tell me if you want me to stop, okay?"

I nod and grip his shoulders as he slides a hand inside my pants. He palms my erection, and I cry out and grab for him.

"One thing," he says, pulling back, and I groan. "You want me to be in control of this, you have to do something for me." He looks serious as he takes my hand. "Words are hard for you. So, if there's ever anything I'm doing that you don't like and you want me to stop, and you can't tell me, then you tap me three times. Like this. And I'll stop."

I nod and clear my throat, but my voice sounds all messed up. "Okay."

"I'll stop. Whatever I'm doing, I'll stop. It doesn't matter if it's a kiss or a touch or I'm five seconds from coming. I will always stop. Tell me you understand."

"I understand," I choke out.

"And if you just need me to slow down so we can talk about it?"

"Rafe, please. Come on." I'm burning up, straining beneath him to get some contact. Every word he says is turning me on more and more.

"What do you do if you need to slow down and talk about whatever is happening?" Rafe asks again. His voice is calm, but he slides his hand under my back and pulls me to him, grinding us together fiercely. I groan.

"Tell me, Colin. Tell me."

"I—ungh!" His mouth is on my neck and I can hardly think. "I tap three times. Rafe, please. Please! Oh god!"

"You're so fucking hot like this. Struggling underneath me. Desperate to come but waiting until I let you." We kiss until our mouths are bruised. Rafe strokes a thumb along my neck, which leaves me shivering against him.

Shit, shit, shit. I don't understand what's happening to me. I feel like I'm coming apart. And I shouldn't like losing control like this. It's dangerous. Too close to having it taken away. And when that happens—

"Oh god!"

Rafe's hand on me is hot and slick with my own arousal and he's moving so slowly. He runs his other hand up the inside of my thigh and squeezes my balls. I arch off the couch and start babbling. "Oh fuck, fuck. What are you—fuck!"

Rafe groans and squeezes my hipbones, holding me still. I make an effort to relax when I realize I'm gripping his shoulders hard enough to bruise.

"Rafe, Rafe, that's—I—"

"Good?" he drawls. "Or not good."

"Good. Yes. Fuck. Please."

He sinks his teeth into the sensitive spot where my neck meets my shoulder and a jolt of pure lust rocks me.

"Rafe." I sink my hand into his hair and strain up into his body. "I'm gonna…."

He strokes me fast and brutal, and I almost choke as I come all over his hand and my stomach and chest. Rafe ends up half on top of me, face pressed to my neck.

I start to untangle my fingers from Rafe's hair and catch my breath. I want to say thank you, but I know it would sound stupid.

He kisses the corner of my mouth, and then he cups my jaw and kisses me for real. I can feel his erection against my hip, and become aware that he's still fully clothed while my clothes are in total disarray and he's made me come harder than I've ever come in my life.

"You're—do you—what about you?" I finally choke out around Rafe's demanding mouth.

"I'm… okay," he says, easing off the kiss a little. He traces my lips with his fingers, then pulls off me and sits up.

"Come back here." When he doesn't move, I sit up, groaning after being mashed into the couch. "You're so fucking stubborn." Rafe just watches me through half-lowered eyelids.

I frown and tug gently at his shirt. He lets go of me and puts his arms up, allowing me to strip it off him. He's fucking beautiful. The thought falls into my head, though I don't think I've ever had it about another person. He's broader than me: his frame is large and his muscles are rounded. One of my hands comes up and strokes his arm before I'm aware I've moved. Rafe sits, gamely letting me touch him.

"Will you?" I gesture to his jeans, and he immediately slides them down his long legs. His thighs and calves are defined and my eyes keep darting down to the bulge in his white briefs.

"Tell me exactly what you want to happen right now. Not what you think should happen. Not what you think I want. Don't think about it. Just tell me."

I blink stupidly at him, and he leans in and kisses me. I bring his hair forward so it envelops my face, and twine my fingers through it.

"Mmmm," he hums. "Tell me."

I shake my head, not sure what the hell to say, and lean closer to kiss his collarbone.

"Tell me," he murmurs again. "Please."

His *please* sends shivers down my spine.

"I want to watch you jerk off." Oh god, did I just say that?

Rafe groans. "Fuck. Whatever you want." He pushes his briefs down his thighs but doesn't bother taking them all the way off. "Won't take much." He shakes his head and presses his thumb to my mouth, distracting me from staring at his dick, which is thick and uncut, straining against his muscled stomach. "Practically came just watching you." His words are matter-of-fact but his voice is raw, and it fucking gets to me.

He palms his erection and looks at me through lowered lashes. I nod, my mouth dry. Rafe starts to move, slowly at first, like he's trying to make it last, but he's looking at me like he's barely paying attention to what he's doing. His mouth falls open and he catches his full bottom lip between sharp teeth. His eyes keep darting down to my hand so I reach out to him.

I'm expecting him to pull my hand down between his legs, but he just holds it while he strokes himself with the other, squeezing my hand as he arches into his own. It's... shit, it's so hot. Like I'm jerking him off by extension. But then it's not enough and I lean against his shoulder and reach down, tentatively resting my hand on his erection. Rafe startles.

"Hey, you don't have to."

I roll my eyes and shake my head. He releases himself. I move my hand on him and I guess it's not so mysterious, since I do it to myself, but the feel of him, hot and hard and straining, makes my heart pound and sends a jolt of electricity through me. Rafe squeezes my hand and gulps.

"That feels amazing," he says, bringing our hands to his mouth and kissing my knuckles. I squeeze him tighter and stroke him hard, twisting my hand a little over his foreskin. He shudders and groans and his head tips back. I press closer to him so I can feel the tremors running through him.

As I move my hand faster, Rafe lets out a string of curses and clamps his free hand down over mine. He strokes both of our hands up and down twice, and then he's coming with a growl, his muscles rigid, our hands twisted up together.

He hisses as he strokes himself gently a few more times. I turn my head and press a kiss to his shoulder, and he leans into me.

"Thank you," he murmurs. And it doesn't really sound stupid at all.

Chapter 8

OVER THE next weeks, every few evenings after work, Rafe'll come over, we'll go running, eat dinner, and talk through movies I don't care about. Rafe thinks about movies analytically, and he connects everything to politics and social justice. He's explained a lot about the political organizing he's involved with, but to be honest, I don't get half of what he says. Fundraising and campaigns and direct actions and… well, really, a lot of it sounds like a shit-ton of meetings, and I'm not totally clear on what the end goals are. I try to listen but I kinda space out.

One night I guess I failed to hide my spacing out when Rafe was saying something about zoning exemptions, race, and charter schools, and he gave up and asked me to teach him the trick with the coin and the glass I showed the kids one Saturday.

I showed him over and over—coin in the center of the palm, tap the glass, slide the coin down, hit with the glass to pop the coin up and in— but he was hilariously hopeless, fumbling the coin and almost dropping the glass every time. He got frustrated at himself, and I teased him about taking everything so seriously. His very serious protests that he doesn't take everything seriously cracked me up, and I finally got him to laugh too. Rafe doesn't laugh much. Almost never. So when he does, it's a total win. I celebrated by climbing on top of him and kissing him silly, narrowly avoiding shattering the glass.

He's also told me a lot about his family. His two younger sisters are both crazy about him. Gabriela has two kids and is a nurse at Temple Hospital, and her husband, Alejandro, is some big-time contractor. She's always inviting Rafe over for dinner so she can lecture him about settling down.

Luz calls Rafe to ask for advice about men, about problems with her apartment, and to talk about Camille, her fifteen-year-old daughter. Luz had Camille when she was sixteen and Rafe feels guilty about it because he thinks if he'd been home instead of in prison, she never would've gotten pregnant and dropped out of high school. Rafe has a major soft spot for Luz and Camille, though, so I doubt he'd actually want to change anything. Whenever Luz calls asking about a leaky faucet or a stuck window, Rafe goes over and fixes it for her right away, even though her landlord lives down the street.

Saturday workshops have been going well. It's clearer and clearer that the kids are up for learning anything if they like the person who's teaching it to them, but what they really want is a chance to hang out with each other in a place where they feel comfortable. Sometimes Rafe and I end up just standing around while they gossip or talk about movies and music and TV.

Watching them has made me think more about Daniel in the last few weeks than I ever have before. About what it might've been like if he'd had something like YA to go to. He was small for his age in high school—skinny and clumsy. His hair was always a mess and he had this expression when he was pissed off, which was most of the time, that I'm sure he thought was intimidating but really just looked like he was in pain. It was a beacon to anyone who picked on the kids who showed weakness. He was always coming home with black eyes and bruises and split lips. When Brian was still in school with him, we'd sometimes ask who he fought with so Brian could take care of it, but Daniel would never say.

"What're you thinking about so hard?" Rafe asks, startling me. He strokes a hand up my neck and into my hair.

"Um, about Daniel, I guess."

"You always think about him after we're at YA."

"Yeah, maybe. I watch them and the way they are with each other. I don't think Daniel had… friends. Anyone to talk about stuff with."

"None?"

"Well, he never brought friends home." Of course, that could've been because he was embarrassed of us. "And Brian was in school with him when he was a senior and Daniel was a freshman, and he said he never saw Daniel talking to anyone. He got picked on a lot. He was scrawny." I snort. "And mouthy."

"Imagine that," Rafe says and raises an eyebrow at me, which is as close as Rafe gets to teasing.

But he settles onto the couch with me, and it feels right having him here, even if I'm still not clear on exactly what's going on between us.

Earlier in the week, while I was doing the dishes, Rafe's sister Gabriela called. I was half listening to Rafe's side of the conversation,

amused at how often Gabriela cut him off to lecture him about something.
It sounded like it might be about some family dinner. After a few minutes
of being interrupted, Rafe came up behind me and dropped his forehead
down on my shoulder, sighing in irritation. He's too tall for it to have
been comfortable for more than a minute, though, so he wrapped an arm
around my waist and pressed against my back.

"Gabri, no— No, thank you. I appreciate it but— Well, he
sounds— No— *Sí*, but— I'm sure he is— I don't even know what that
means, Gabri— Yes, I'm sure doctors do make a lot of— I don't— *Por
el amor de dios*, sis, stop!— *Porque!*— Fine, because I'm already seeing
someone, okay?"

Rafe glanced at me, but I was careful to give the dishes my full
attention.

I don't know why it freaked me out that Rafe would say that. I
mean, I'm not an idiot. I know that's what's going on. I just don't know
what it means. About me. About the future. Anything.

Rafe was looking at me intently.

"*Hermana*, I have to go—no, I'm hanging up. I'll talk to you later.
Te amo. Okay. Colin?"

"Hm?"

"I think it's clean." He took the dish I'd washed three times out
of my hand and dried it. He tipped my chin up so I meet his gaze. "I
probably should have confirmed that with you before I said anything."

"What? No. I mean, no worries. I know that—that we're... you
know. Sure."

"Well, you're nervous rambling and you can't even say the word
'dating,' so I think maybe it's not fine."

I shook my head and changed the subject, but things were awkward
for the rest of the night and he hasn't brought it up since. Of course,
neither have I.

"YOU WANNA watch the game with us?" Brian asks as work is
winding down.

I search my memory, trying to remember if Rafe is going to come
over tonight. Maybe we'll go running....

"Dude, what is your *deal* lately? You never want to hang out anymore.
You don't come in on Saturdays, and you never stick around after work."

Brian's looking at his feet and twisting his shoulders nervously like he did when he was a little kid. "You too cool for me now, bro?" He says it like a joke and slugs me on the shoulder, but he looks hurt.

And he's right. Usually, I'd hang out here with Brian and Pop after work on Saturdays and a few nights a week. We'd get pizza, have some beers, and watch whatever games were on, arguing about players and stats, adding our bottle caps or beer tops to the jars where Brian and I have measured our rival victories for years, until Pop fell asleep in the permanently reclined recliner. But the last month I've barely seen them outside of work and I hardly even noticed.

"Well, I'm definitely too cool for you," I say, throwing an arm around Brian's shoulders. Brian gives a weak smile but shrugs me off. "Sorry, man. It's not like that. Um, yeah, let's watch the game. Pizza sounds good."

"Yeah, well, we get it from a new place now," Brian says, not quite ready to forgive.

"Okay, whatever you want."

And Brian, incapable of holding a grudge for more than five seconds, grins and starts bouncing up and down on his toes, drumming on my shoulders.

"Sweet!" And he darts away.

It's always been me, Pop, Brian, and Sam. Since Mom died, anyway. Hanging out with them always felt normal, easy. Now, though, the last repair done and the tools put away, following Brian into the living room feels strange. The house seems darker or something. And the smell of beer that starts in the kitchen and gets stronger in the living room seems sharper.

Pop comes in from his room looking like he just woke up, which is strange because I saw him in the shop an hour or two ago. Jesus, for the first time, when I look at Pop, I see an old man. He grunts when he sees me and settles heavily into his chair.

"Son," he says, and he nods approvingly. Warmth washes through me. He immediately turns his attention to Brian.

"You order yet?"

"I'm about to."

"Just not that crap place from the other day. Where'd you find that place, anyway? Pizza tasted like fuckin' cardboard."

Brian looks embarrassed. Guess they don't have a new favorite after all.

As Brian and I walk to the corner to get the pizza and more beer, I ask, "So, what was that other pizza place you tried and how'd you live through Pop's fury?"

Brian blushes. The only time I've ever seen Brian blush is when—

"Hey, did you go to a new place because one of the servers is in love with you?" That's what Brian always says about any girl he thinks is cute: "she's totally in love with me." He's a hundred percent cocky and only about 20 percent accurate when it comes to recognizing when someone's actually flirting with him. But right now he's practically tripping over his own feet to avoid looking up. I catch his shoulder.

"Dude. What's up?"

Brian sighs like he's been desperate for someone to ask. "Aw, man," he says, shaking his head. "There's this girl… I think…. Dude, I think she's my soul mate."

"Okay," I say. Soul mate is a new one. "Who is she?"

"Callie," he moans, like this is the end of the world. "I accidentally barfed on her cat and she was so cool about it, man."

"You what?"

"I was drunk, right, and I kinda wandered into an alley, only it was more like a space between two houses, and there was this nice step and I sat down but then I didn't feel well and I barfed. But I didn't see that there was this cat on the porch—"

"You wandered into someone's *backyard* and sat on their porch?"

"Well. Yeah. But I didn't know that at the time."

I shake my head.

"Anyway, the cat just *sat* there, man. It, like, *let* me barf on it. And then it started to try and lick it up. And this girl came out and saw me and I was like, 'Dude, is this your cat, 'cause he's messed up,' and she was so nice and asked if I needed help, and she's so pretty, bro, like, seriously, the prettiest girl you've ever seen."

I have no words. "Um, and she works at this pizza place?"

"What? No. She's a hairstylist."

"So…?"

"Oh, she recommended it to me. I gave her my phone number and we've been talking."

"That's great, Bri. I kind of can't believe that some girl whose cat you puked on wanted anything to do with you. But that's great."

"Yeah, I haven't seen her again, but we've talked, like, every night for the last three weeks. And when I said Pop and I got pizza a lot, she was like, 'Do you ever go to Blackbird?' It's her favorite. So I got it for me and Pop the other day. And, um, yeah, it did taste like cardboard. She's one of those whattaya call 'ems that doesn't eat anything that comes from animals? So it was that kind of pizza."

"Vegan?"

"Yeah, that's it."

"Oh my god, you fed Pop vegan pizza? That's hilarious, bro. Did he know what it was?"

"Nah. He liked the fake sausage part. But, uh, I thought it kinda tasted like feet." A look of panic crosses his face. "Don't tell Callie, though! If you meet her, I mean. I, uh, I sorta told her that I liked it."

I laugh. "I won't tell her," I reassure him. "But you should probably be honest with her, or you'll end up eating vegan pizza for the rest of your life."

I'm joking, but Brian looks horrified.

"Oh shit, that's no good. Thanks, bro."

THE PHONE ringing jolts me out of a dead sleep, and I almost break Rafe's nose with my head as I jerk upright.

"Fuck, sorry!"

"Hello?" Rafe says, instantly alert. I look over at the clock. It's two thirty in the morning.

"Uncle Rafe?" says the tinny voice on the other end of the call. "Can you come get me?"

"Calm down, Cam. Tell me what's going on."

Her explanation is garbled, but I hear something about a party and her mom being mad and something about a boy that makes Rafe's whole body go rigid.

"Where are you, sweetheart? … Can you ask someone? … Okay, listen. It's going to take me a little while to get there because I'm not at home. I want you to go back inside, okay? Then use the GPS on your phone and text me exactly where you are." Rafe's voice seems to relax Camille the same way it relaxes me.

"Stand by the front door so you can see out the window when I get there. Don't take anything from anyone. Not even water. Not gum. Not a damn ChapStick, Camille, do you understand me? I'll call you when I'm a minute away and then you come outside. Not before that. If someone tries to get you to move away from the front door, you tell them your uncle is coming and you're scared of making him mad, okay?" Rafe is already up and searching around for his clothes in the dark as he hangs up the phone.

"Is she okay?"

"She's stupid and dead, that's what she is," Rafe growls. "Sorry to wake you. I'll call you tomorrow." He leans in to kiss me briefly.

"Wait," I say, climbing out of bed and pulling some jeans on. "I'll drive. That way you can call Cam when we're close and you can just jump out of the car."

"I—okay. Thanks, Colin."

I smile even though I know he can't see in the dark. It feels good to be able to do something for Rafe for a change.

He gives me directions from his phone between muttering about how much trouble Camille's going to be in. "She went to some damn rave with a bunch of college kids. Little idiots with credit cards, I swear. And then went back to a house party with them. I know she took fucking E at that damn rave. And now some boy—"

He breaks off, furious, shaking his head at the idea.

"Has this happened before?"

He nods. "She only calls me when she and Luz have been fighting. Luz isn't off work yet." Luz bartends at some club in her neighborhood.

After a few minutes of silence, he reaches over and runs a hand down my arm. "Hey, how was hanging out with your dad and Brian?"

"It was… okay, I guess. But, I don't know, I didn't feel totally comfortable there… which is strange, because I always used to."

"Did you?"

"What? Yeah. Why?"

"Well, I just mean, are you sure you used to feel comfortable as opposed to just being used to feeling uncomfortable?"

"What the hell does that mean?"

"It means, maybe spending more time not lying about who you are has made you aware of the ways you had gotten used to lying about it." Rafe says this gently, hand on my arm, but it still packs a punch I can't process right now. He squeezes my forearm and lets go, fumbling with his phone.

"Okay, Cam, come outside." He points to a three-story brick house on the corner. At least the neighborhood doesn't look as bad as Rafe seemed worried it would be when he told Camille to stay inside.

The door opens and a pretty girl comes out, walking unsteadily, clutching her phone. As Rafe opens his door and gets out, a guy runs out after Cam.

"Come on, Karen," he calls, laughing, clearly wasted. "We were having fun, right?"

She whirls around to face him and screams, "It's *Cam*, not *Karen*, you *asshole!*"

Rafe catches her upper arms and moves her behind him, nudging her toward the car.

"You." Rafe stabs a finger at the guy, and I can tell the moment that he notices how huge Rafe is through the haze of intoxication. Rafe stalks up to him, radiating murderous fury.

"That girl is fifteen years old, you piece of shit," he snarls. "You fucking touch her, that's statutory rape. You know what they do to rapists in prison, you little prep school fuck?"

The guy is curled up in a ball in the face of Rafe's fury. It looks like Rafe's about to beat the crap out of him. Totally deserved, too. But he smiles instead and it's chilling.

"The next time you see a pretty girl, I want you to remember me. Remember this moment and think about what happens when you mess with shit you shouldn't." He gets right in the guy's face. "Got it?"

The guy nods convulsively, his hands up in a pathetic don't-hit-me pose, desperate to get away from Rafe. Rafe spits at his feet and then comes back to the car, shaking his hands like he can dispel his anger that way instead of through a punch.

"These entitled white boys see you as a hot Mexican girl they can take something from," he says to Cam. His voice is fierce. Poisonous. "Okay? You can't trust them. I'm sorry." She nods and buries her face in his chest. He puts her in the backseat and gets in with her. "This is my friend Colin."

"Hi," says Camille miserably. "I'm sorry, Uncle Rafe! I just didn't know—"

He shushes her and pulls her against him as he gives me directions. The roads deteriorate as we get closer to Cam and Luz's, the space between streetlights measured in blocks rather than feet.

In the rearview mirror, Rafe looks intensely relieved, his hand running absently through Cam's long curls. I pull up where he tells me. It's not a street I'd ever stop on in the middle of the night if I could help it, and I make a mental note to lock the car doors behind them.

"Come inside for a minute, okay?" Rafe says. "I don't want you sitting out here by yourself."

Yeah, that's not humiliating in front of his niece or anything.

"Uh, I'll be fine, man."

Camille says something in Spanish under her breath, and Rafe gives her a warning look.

"Please," he says, and he gives me that look. I roll my eyes because it's a combination that basically makes me incapable of not doing whatever he says.

The building is run-down and smells like mold as we trek up the stairs to Cam and Luz's third-floor apartment. Cam stops at the door, turning a pleading look on Rafe. She bats her eyelashes.

"Thank you *so* much, Uncle Rafe. You're a lifesaver. Maybe I should just go in by myself, though. Mom'll be tired when she gets home from work and she probably won't want a lot of people around, you know?"

She smiles a brilliant smile. It's a valiant effort and I can tell Rafe's the tiniest bit amused by her antics. Before he has a chance to say anything, though, the door bursts open.

"Camille!" the woman who must be Luz yells, then claps a hand over her mouth, like she's just now realizing how late it is. She looks terrified as she grabs Cam and hugs her roughly. Over Cam's shoulder, she looks up at Rafe worshipfully.

She lets go of her daughter and hugs Rafe.

"Thank you," she says over and over, wiping tears on Rafe's shirt.

When she pulls back, she notices me for the first time.

"Hi," she says, giving me a wobbly smile. Her voice is friendly, though, and she shakes my hand. "I'm Luz."

She's just gotten off work, she's clearly been worried about her daughter, and it's nearly four in the morning, but Luz is beautiful. She looks a lot like Rafe. She's tall and has the same strong, clean cheekbones and chin, and the same charmingly crowded teeth.

"Colin," I say, feeling awkward as hell.

Her expression changes and she looks at me more carefully. "Well, aren't you handsome," she says, and I'd think she was flirting with me if she didn't turn to Rafe and wink at him. Rafe snorts and I feel my face heat up.

Rafe's expression turns immediately serious, and he focuses back on Cam, who is currently trying to tiptoe through the open apartment door while the adults are all distracted with each other. She freezes when she feels Rafe's eyes on her and tries a smile.

"We're going to talk later, Camille," Rafe says. "After you've told your mother what happened." Cam opens her mouth, but Rafe glares at her and she snaps it shut. "You and I are going to have a conversation about drugs." He steps so close to her that she has to tilt her head way back to see him. "In case you've forgotten," Rafe says, his voice gentler now, almost vulnerable, "I ended up in prison because of them."

Camille looks ashamed, but before she can say anything, Rafe leans down and kisses her on the cheek.

"Always call me," he tells her fiercely and kisses the top of her head before he pushes her inside.

He lets out a sigh and turns to Luz.

"Rafe, I—"

Rafe holds up a hand to stop her. He leans down and kisses her on the cheek too. "I can't right now, sis. I love you."

And he takes my hand and leads me away.

As we're driving back to my place, Rafe leans his head back against the seat and closes his eyes.

"Thanks," he breathes. When he turns to look at me, his eyes are warm.

"Man. I thought you were going to beat the crap out of that guy. He was so fucking scared of you he was practically shitting himself."

"Yeah, well." After a few minutes of silence, Rafe says, "I can't get in fights. It's, um, it's what I went to prison for."

"Wait. I thought you went to prison for drugs." I realize, though, that Rafe's never told me the story of what happened exactly.

"Yeah, well, I got in a fight because I was high." He sounds so tired. "Bar fight. Idiotic. I was there with guys from the neighborhood. We were drunk, messing around like idiots. I was high so I thought we were hilarious."

Every time Rafe talks about drugs, it's like he's forcing himself to say that he used them. I wonder if that's an NA thing.

"There was a guy there. He was hitting on some girl who wasn't interested and he was being a total jackass about it. Showing off for his friends. Embarrassing her." He shakes his head. "Anyway, I threw the first punch. I don't remember that much of the actual fight. But I... man, I hurt him really bad."

Rafe runs both hands through his tangled hair. "He—I broke a bunch of ribs and one of them collapsed his lung. He had to get his spleen removed. Knocked out a few teeth. Broke his nose." He's reciting it like some horrible grocery list, his voice flat and choked, like he's forcing the words out through sand. "Cracked his skull. Fuck." His fists are clenched against his chest.

I pull up outside my house and turn off the car, turning to look at Rafe. He's holding himself carefully, like he doesn't trust himself not to bolt.

"Well, look," I try, "he was acting the fool, got in a bar fight. You do that, you deserve what you get, right?"

When Rafe turns to me, he looks miserable. He shakes his head. "No. He didn't deserve that. I was out of my mind, Colin. I was a fucking monster."

I can tell he truly believes that. He's pushed himself against the door, as far away from me as he can get. Clearly, he doesn't want to be let off the hook.

"You served your time," I say. "You quit using."

For me, there's nothing else to say. Rafe is the best man I've ever met, and finding out that he's made mistakes… well, it doesn't change that.

He pulls himself together and nods, but he doesn't touch me as we walk inside.

"What was it like?" I ask, not sure he'll answer. He hasn't told me much about his time in prison. I know he doesn't like to think about it.

He sighs, toes his shoes off, and sits down on the bed. "It was boring. And terrifying. Almost always one or the other. Boredom—having nothing to enjoy, feeling like there's nothing to look forward to—it's dangerous. Makes people do… things they wouldn't, otherwise. Half the violence was just boredom, just blowing off steam."

He's looking at the floor as he talks and he trails off for a minute, watching as I get undressed.

"I was a kid," he says. "Twenty-one. When the sentence got handed down and it actually sunk in that I was going to prison…." He shakes his head, eyes distant. "You have no idea how fucking terrified I was. I wanted to cry and hide at my mother's apartment. I'm not kidding. I wasn't rational. All I could think was that I had to run away somehow."

It's so unlike the Rafe I know that I can only imagine how scared he'd have had to be to consider leaving his family.

"And, of course, the idea that I might not be able to use whenever I wanted… that was almost as scary." He sits on the side of the bed and wiggles his fingers at Shelby, who bats at them halfheartedly until Rafe picks her up and cuddles her. Then she takes a swipe at his hand and jumps off the bed. Rafe sucks on the scratches she raised.

"The first night I was there—shit, the first *week*—I didn't sleep. I was so damn scared, Colin. Honestly, I only got clean because I was too scared to try and score in prison. You could do it, but I just wanted to keep my head down. Didn't want to owe anyone any favors, step on anyone's toes. Shit, I barely even talked to anyone. Anyway, it was…. You know, you just… you can get used to almost anything, if you have to."

He sits up straighter and holds out a hand to me, pulling me so I'm standing between his knees. I put my hands on his shoulders.

"Listen," he says, leaning his cheek into my arm and looking up at me, "I'll tell you anything you want to know. But can we be done for now?"

"Yeah, course."

He stands and strips for bed.

"But if you swore off fighting, then why did you help me that night? The night we met. I—I mean, I was out of it, but I saw you. You took those guys apart."

Rafe steps close to me and leans in until his mouth is close to mine. "I couldn't help myself," he murmurs. "I saw you sitting at the bar earlier." He kisses my throat and I lean into him. "You looked so nervous. Miserable. And—fuck, I don't know what it was." He kisses my shoulder. "But I've never wanted anything so much in my life." My heart starts to hammer, and I wrap my arms around his waist. "When I saw you were in trouble, I just—" He pulls me hard against his chest and holds me. "I just ran after you. Didn't even think about it until it was all over."

He runs his hands through my hair, then pushes me down onto the bed and crawls on top of me.

"I just knew I had to get to you."

WHEN I get to the YA parking lot, no one's there. I find everyone in the basement. Rafe catches my eye immediately and he gives me an apologetic look. When I get closer, I can see he looks tired. Stressed. Mikal, Carlos, Mischa, and DeShawn are in a tight huddle, and everyone is talking at once. And what they're huddled around is Anders. And he's shaking.

Ricky's standing off to the side, rocking back and forth as Dorothy tries to calm her down and keep an eye on Anders at the same time.

"I hate your dad!" Mikal yells, clenching his glitter-polished fingers into a fist and snarling. The others echo his sentiment, but Anders just keeps looking at the ground like he doesn't know what to do with his friends' anger. And when he does look up, it's Rafe he looks to. Rafe, who's standing still, whose shoulders are set tight, and who's holding his hands behind his back like a bouncer.

Carlos is the first of the kids to see me. His "Hey, Winchester" is subdued. I've never seen him look so serious.

I'm not sure what's going on, but I can tell Anders isn't going to talk with everyone staring at him. "Hey, guys," I say to the kids. "Let's go outside and I'll let you, um… hit our car with a tire iron?"

Rafe's head jerks up and I shrug at him. Anders' lip starts to tremble a little more, and I gesture the kids toward me. They're reluctant, but I herd them out with promises that vehicular violence will help them get their aggression out. I know I guessed right when, at the door, I turn back and see Anders slowly dissolve into tears, shaking in Rafe's arms the second his friends aren't there to see.

RAFE'S SWING of the tire iron is so powerful that he almost busts through the top of the trunk.

"Holy shit," I mutter.

Mikal, Carlos, and Dorothy went to town with the tire iron before they dispersed, everyone agreeing they weren't in the mood for a workshop, but they were timid and didn't do much real damage. Mischa left right away. DeShawn just stood, bulging muscles tensed beneath his spotless white button-down, and watched the action, arms crossed like he was holding himself in check. Ricky watched out of the corner of her eye, but didn't participate either.

Rafe thought I was kidding when I handed him the tire iron, but since he said he didn't want to go to his boxing gym, I figured it'd help him get some aggression out. He seems almost surprised at his own power and looks at me nervously.

"Go for it," I say. Not like we need to open the trunk for anything.

He looks around to check that no one's going to see, then proceeds to beat in the trunk of the car until it's totally concave. He's breathing heavily, but he doesn't look quite as tense as he did. He clears his throat and hands me back the tire iron, staring at the damage he just inflicted.

"Hey, now it's an El Camino," I tell him, tossing the tire iron in the backseat since I definitely can't get it back in the trunk.

"You want to run?" Rafe asks, drifting close to me but not touching.

"Yeah. By my house?"

Rafe nods. I keep offering, but Rafe never wants to run by his apartment and never wants to hang out there. I get the feeling he doesn't spend much time there, period. He's started leaving running clothes at my house.

He walks to my car with me and sinks into the passenger seat, keeping his eyes closed as I drive.

"Is he okay?" I ask. "What's up?"

Rafe sighs deeply. "No. Not really." He rubs his eyes. "His dad found out he's been coming to YA and he's furious. The kids need parental permission since they're minors and Anders didn't have it, so he can't be here. He started coming with Mikal, and it was right after Javi died. With everything that was going on, I… I must've forgotten to check. Fuck, I can't believe I was so stupid."

"So, what, you just kick him out?"

Rafe glares. "I don't have a choice!"

"But would his dad even have to know?"

"That's not how it works, Colin. YA serves a lot of other youth. We can't risk it."

"But what if—"

"Look." His voice is tight with anger. He's definitely done with this conversation. "It sucks. I know it does. But that's just how it is."

"I guess it's just one more year," I offer.

"What?"

"One more year. Until Anders can move out and then his dad won't have control over him anymore."

Rafe looks at me sharply. "Fathers can have control over you at any age, don't you think?"

RAFE RUNS until he nearly exhausts himself, keeping up with me for the first five miles and then only dropping back a few blocks. Even though it's a chilly day, we're both soaked with sweat by the time we collapse on my porch.

"Goddamn, you're fast," Rafe mutters, like he always does. He turns to me and his gaze is intense, his cheeks flushed. "Take a shower with me?" he asks, running a hand through my sweaty hair. We've never done that.

I nod and Rafe pulls me up, our legs shaky.

Rafe's presence makes my small bathroom feel even smaller as we peel off our sweaty clothes. Rafe steps under the hot water and reaches for me, finally relaxing a little when he pulls me against him. I don't know if I'll ever get used to this—the feel of him against me, around me. It's overwhelming and I shut my eyes against the overstimulation and concentrate on the water.

Rafe's hands are gentle, but I can practically *feel* the energy vibrating off him, and when I look up at him, he's looking right at me. I smile, self-conscious, but Rafe uses his thumb like an eraser to scrub the smile away and kisses me as the water pounds down around us. After a minute, though, he just holds me to him, arms tight around me, clearly still upset.

Rafe sighs and washes his hair with the bar of soap. I really should get some shampoo for him.

He strokes a soapy hand up and down my spine, but his hand lingers on my lower back and I tense automatically, realizing that he's probably seeing my tattoo in the light for the first time. Not an accident on my part.

"Can I look?"

He says it like it's nothing, but I'm so immediately furious it makes my head spin.

Rafe kneels down behind me. He holds my hip and traces a finger over the tattoo, and I struggle to hold still.

"Have to say, you don't really seem the butterfly type," he says.

I spin away, my temples pulsing. I hate the fucking thing. I've hated it for years. I was drunk when I had it done—hell, they should never have let me get tattooed, but it was a piece of shit hole in the wall and they didn't give a crap that I'd stumbled in off the street reeking of liquor and clearly angry and upset.

"Fuck off," I say.

"Hey." Rafe's tone is sharp. "What's the problem?"

Shit. It's not even him I'm pissed at. It's Daniel, who called the other day and made it clear he knew about the tattoo. It's Ginger, Daniel's big-mouthed friend. I went to her to try and have it covered up and she clearly told him all about it. Shouldn't there be some kind of client confidentiality or something? I only went to her because she was the only female tattoo artist I knew of and I sure as hell wasn't going to show some dude that I had a butterfly tattoo. Fuck her. And I'd gone because I didn't really want Rafe to see it. It had never come up before.

I'd been under a car at work the other day when I heard Sam get on the phone and say, "Daniel?" He chatted for a minute about Liza and I tuned him out. Daniel only ever called the shop if he was about to break some news, like that he was leaving. Maybe he was calling to say his fancy job didn't work out and he's moving back. Or maybe he wanted to borrow money from Pop. Pop got on the phone and, after a few minutes asked Daniel what he needed, then passed the phone to me.

I raised my eyebrows at Pop, but he shrugged and tossed me the cordless, an old, paint-spattered plastic thing that was heavy enough to do damage if I didn't catch it.

"Brian?" Daniel asked, and I was immediately irritated. Clearly he wanted to ask Brian something and Pop handed the phone to me instead. I spun around to ask Pop, but he'd gone inside.

"No, it's me. What's going on?"

"Hey, Colin," he said, sounding anxious. "How's it going?"

I hated that. Daniel always sounded nervous around me, and I didn't do anything. It was like he was holding his breath, just waiting for me to fuck up. Prick.

"Uh, fine," I'd said, hoping he'd cut to the chase, but he cleared his throat. "What did you need?" I'd asked, eye on the clock. It was after five and I wanted to get out of there in the next hour.

"Damn, Colin, I don't need anything. I just wanted to say hey. Christ."

What the fuck did that mean? Daniel never called me to say hello. "Well," I said, hesitantly, "hey, then." I paused but he didn't say anything. "I'm gonna get back to work," I said, my mind already back on the cars.

"Oh, yeah," Daniel said, his voice gone poisonous. I'd never heard him sound like that before. "Got to go get some hearts and flowers tattooed to match your manly butterfly?"

My heart had felt like it was being squeezed in my chest. What the fuck? How in the hell had he…? I realized Ginger must have told him.

There was nothing to say. I was right back there. That night years ago. So drunk I didn't even remember leaving the party. Barely remembered staggering into the tattoo parlor, consumed by thoughts of what things might be like if my mom were still alive and some vague notion that the pain of the needle of was, at least, a pain I could choose.

My heart was beating fast—too fast—and my mouth was dry, but I had to silence Daniel's smug superiority.

"Fuck you, you little bitch," I spat out, and I smashed the phone into the wall.

Rafe reaches out to me, but I pull away from him and get out of the shower, wrapping a towel around my waist.

"Nothing. I just don't like it," I say.

"Okay," Rafe says, clearly not buying it. "Did you like it when you got it?"

"I don't remember, man. I was wasted." Rafe's frown deepens and I sigh. "It was for my mom, kind of. It was after high school and I was just having a bad time and—" I shake my head, not wanting to talk about that. "Honestly, I don't remember asking for the butterfly. I must have, but…." I shrug.

The next morning when I saw it in the mirror, bleary and hungover, I was so confused by what I saw that it took a moment for the lines to coalesce into something recognizable. A fucking butterfly. Something delicate and vulnerable and… gay. It was like I'd been branded with an emblem of everything I wanted to hide. And now Daniel knows about it.

Rafe starts to say something but stops himself at whatever he sees in my face and nods, going back to toweling his hair dry. I'm just relieved he's not going to push it. I go into the bedroom, throw on sweatpants, and fiddle with the window, trying to get some air.

"Colin." I startle at Rafe's voice and turn around. He slides his hands underneath my sweatpants and over my ass. He squeezes and I shudder against him. "Mmm. Have I told you what a gorgeous ass you have?"

My face heats up in an instant. Every time Rafe talks to me like this, it turns me on faster than anything. And I'm happy to be distracted.

Rafe pulls me toward him and scoots back on the bed to make room for me between his legs. His mouth is hot and I can't get enough of the way he tastes. When his arms come around me, I let myself relax on top of him, just wanting more contact. Rafe runs a hand down my back as we kiss, but he doesn't stop; he trails his fingers down to the top of my ass and into the crease there. I startle.

"Is this okay?" Rafe asks, looking at me seriously. He stops moving until I nod. I'm not sure if it's okay. Rafe just looks at me. I start to kiss his neck because it's awkward.

"Wait a second, okay?" he says.

Slow as honey, Rafe pulls my cheeks apart, squeezing in a way that makes my breath come short. Rafe's eyes go hot and his eyelids lower to half-mast.

"Good?"

I nod, but my breathing starts to come too fast and I feel too hot. Things I don't want to think about crowd the edges of my thoughts, and I shake my head to banish them.

He slides a finger down and runs it lightly over my hole, and I jerk against him. At first, I can't tell if I'm turned on or freaked out. Both. Definitely both. Rafe doesn't move, just looks at me steadily.

"Bad?" Rafe asks, his voice neutral.

I shake my head, confused. "No, I—" I duck my head to his shoulder, but after a minute, he lifts my chin to look at him again.

"Tell me."

"I don't—uh—I don't have much basis for comparison," I mutter.

"Okay." Rafe kisses me and his voice is soft. "You don't have much. But you do have some?"

And there it is. What I've been avoiding thinking about. Almost like talk of my damn tattoo conjured it.

Rafe's expression is neutral but I can tell he's paying close attention. I look out the window.

"Only once. And it... wasn't a good thing." That's a fucking understatement. Rafe's hands on me tighten, and he bites his lip, like he's waiting for me to go on. "I don't want to talk about it." He narrows his eyes like he's going to push it, and I prime myself to get up and leave if he does.

But then he just pulls me closer and hugs me. After a minute or so, I relax against him.

"Is that what you want?" I ask. My face is near his ear so I only have to breathe the words. "To... to fuck me?" The words feel odd in my mouth.

"Mmm. Well." His voice is a rumble. "I would love to fuck you. But there are lots of other things we can do if you don't want that. I want it to be good for you."

I nod.

"Or you could fuck me," he says. "If you want."

And damn, the idea of being inside Rafe wakes my dick right up. But I don't really want that. Not now. Don't want the responsibility. The idea that I could hurt him is too awful.

"No. Uh, I mean, no thanks."

Rafe smiles. "You want to go watch a movie or something?"

I shake my head and kiss his neck, feeling his pulse speed up beneath my lips. I kiss his ear and down his jaw to his mouth. We kiss slowly at first, but then I bite at Rafe's lip and we start really going at it, feeding on each other's mouths and grinding together.

I need this. Need to feel in control of it. And Rafe's good at that. I take his hand and he curls his fingers around mine as if we were walking down the waterfront hand in hand. I move his hand to my ass and slide down so our hips are aligned. Then I grind hard into him and he grabs my ass just like I knew he would.

"Want to try?" he asks, and I nod. Rafe runs both hands over my ass as we kiss. He strokes fingertips over my hole and the skin around it and I shiver as nerve endings wake up. It's turning me on in the strangest way. A way that has nothing to do with my dick and more to do with the heat that's started buzzing inside me. After a minute, I'm shaking in Rafe's arms and my dick is rock hard. Rafe groans and kisses me desperately. Then he rolls me off him and turns to his side to face me, his erection heavy between us. He runs a hand down my neck.

"I want you," he says. "I want to be inside you. I'll make it good for you, I promise." He sounds so serious. "But we won't do anything you don't want."

Can I do this? I'm not sure. I shake my head.

"Okay," Rafe says. "Then we won't."

"No, I—I was just thinking."

I'm starting to tense up the longer I have nothing to say. I'm just scared, I guess, though I hate to admit it. Scared I'll panic, thinking about before. Scared I won't like it.

"When I touch you here—" Rafe runs his fingers over my hole again and I shiver hard. "Fuck. The way you respond... I think you'll love the way it feels to be filled." He presses against my hole for a second, keeping the pressure light. "The way it feels to be open to me, trusting that I'll make you feel good." He squeezes my ass hard and runs his fingers down behind my balls, pressing in. I jerk against him.

"Mmm," he hums, rolling us so I'm back on top of him. "Hear something you like?"

I can't think of a thing to say to that. He lifts my face away a few inches, looking at me. I don't know how he can keep eye contact the way he does without feeling awkward. I close my eyes and kiss him, hoping he'll just keep doing what he's doing.

"Okay," he says, as if he's answering a question I didn't ask. "Let's go with that. I say or do something you like, you kiss me. Is that easier?" I wrap my arms around his shoulders and kiss him, relieved. He squeezes me back. "Okay."

"Um, am I crushing you?" I ask.

"No." He takes a tube from his pocket. "Spread your legs for me." And, oh god, that should not turn me on like it does.

When he touches me again, his fingers are slick against my skin. I stare at the tube of lube sitting on the comforter next to Rafe's hip, and it's like I've fallen into someone else's life. When the tip of his finger slides inside me, I gasp and my whole body clenches around it. Rafe bites his lip.

"You okay?" I nod. He must be getting seriously sick of asking me that. "Try and relax if you can." He pushes deeper inside me, and I can feel it with each beat of my heart. He strokes up and down my back with his other hand, and I squeeze my eyes closed. But that's no good because it lets me imagine it isn't Rafe touching me and then my mind starts to spiral to places I don't want it to go, so I open them.

Every time he slides in and out of me, I feel these jolts of sensation inside. It doesn't feel anything like the last time. It's pleasure, yeah, but it also kind of feels like....

Heat flushes my cheeks and I pull away.

"What's wrong?" Rafe asks immediately.

"It's—I—is it—"

"What is it?"

I shake my head. "I—it—I don't—it feels like I'm gonna...." Oh god, this is so embarrassing. I cringe away from Rafe's gaze, but he just nods.

"It feels like you have to go to the bathroom?"

I nod, wincing.

"Yeah. You won't, though, don't worry. It's just the sensation of having something inside you. You'll get used to it and it won't feel like that anymore. The more you can relax, the less it'll feel that way, too. Do you want me to stop?"

I take a deep breath and shake my head. I want this over with.

"Try to push my finger out," he says softly, still stroking my back. It's like this isn't embarrassing him at all. He kisses me lightly on the mouth. When I do it, he slides back inside me, deeper this time, and the feeling fades a little.

"Good. You're doing great."

I huff out a laugh. Yeah, right.

He slides in and out of me slowly and reaches between us. He strokes my erection lightly while his finger is inside me and it feels amazing. Like everything is amplified. I kiss him and feel him smile a little into the kiss.

He slides out, and this time when he slides back in, it's more. My breathing is shallow but suddenly I'm so turned on I can hardly think. I kiss Rafe with everything I have.

"Mmm. Good?" he asks. I kiss him again. "How about now?" Rafe shifts his fingers inside me and I nearly scream.

"Oh Christ," Rafe groans.

"Fuck, fuck, fuck, what the fuck did you do?"

Rafe looks amused and turned on at the same time. "That's your prostate," he says against my lips. He's using that voice that I love, the one that sounds intimate and filthy, like a promise. "Can you imagine how that will feel when I'm inside you? When it's my cock touching you here"—he crooks his fingers again and bolts of electricity shoot through me—"instead of my fingers?"

"Oh god."

He's rubbing that spot inside me and I'm writhing on top of him, not sure if I want to get away or feel more.

"I—fuck, I can't—fuck!"

Rafe kisses me deeply, sliding in and out of me slowly, then he slides a third finger in. It hurts for a moment, but my body adjusts quickly. I'm so lost in sensation that I hardly notice when Rafe stops kissing me. His cheeks are flushed and his lips swollen.

"How're you doing?" he asks, running his free hand over my hair. I nod and kiss him.

"I want—I think—can we try?"

Rafe's expression is serious and his hand on my cheek is gentle. "Yeah," he says, voice rough. He kisses me as he eases his fingers out. He eases me down onto the bed like I weigh nothing and takes a condom out of his pocket.

"You, uh, you always carry lube and condoms in your pocket?"

"I put them in the bag with my running stuff. Just in case." He pulls his underwear off and he's hard and leaking. He rubs more lube inside me.

"Oh god, Rafe."

"Roll over on your hands and knees, okay?" He taps my hip. I do what he says automatically, but the second he grabs on to my hips from behind, my stomach starts to lurch. I try to ignore it as he kisses down my spine and puts on the condom. I try to ignore it as he slicks himself up. But then I feel him coming toward me and I can't.

I twist away on the bed, needing to see his face.

"Not like that, okay?" I say, shaking my head, my breaths coming too shallowly.

Rafe's cupping my face, talking to me softly, but I don't hear anything he's saying over the rushing in my ears.

"Come here," I hear finally. Rafe wraps his arms around me and pulls me to his chest. When I let him move me closer, I can feel the steady thump of his heart beneath his ribs, and I try to match my breathing to his. He runs his hand over my hair and strokes my back and I start to feel really pathetic. Then mad as hell at myself for *failing* to have sex.

"Fuck, I'm sorry," I say. "I'm okay." Lie.

"I don't think so." He leans back and pulls me close to his side, stroking from my head to the base of my spine. After a few minutes, I'm breathing okay and the shaking has stopped and I just feel foolish.

"I know you don't want to talk about it, but—"

"I want to try again," I say. I kiss his neck, his jaw, loving the feeling of stubble against my lips as I move toward his mouth.

He shakes his head, but I can feel how turned on he is.

"I don't think it's a good idea," he says. But his eyes are burning into mine and I'm pretty sure I can convince him.

"No, come on. I just—I think I just need to see you. Can we... you *can* do it that way, right?"

"Oh yeah," he says heatedly.

"Just checking," I mutter.

Rafe moves on top of me, kneeling between my legs.

"We're going to go slow," he says, kissing me, "and you stop me at any time. It was good that you stopped me."

I close my eyes, humiliated, but Rafe just kisses me again and I force myself not to think about anything but the feeling of his mouth on mine, the smell of his hair as it spills down around my face.

"Sorry," he mutters, pulling a rubber band off his wrist and moving to tie his hair back. I grab his wrist before he can.

"No, don't. I… I like your hair."

Rafe's smile is sweet and delighted. Is it possible I've never given him a compliment before? I pull his face down and kiss him again to try and say sorry, twining my fingers in his hair. I love the way it feels, thick and soft. It's a little tangled, though, and when I tug gently, I end up pulling his hair.

"Shit, sorry," I say just as Rafe groans. He kisses me hard and slides a hand under my thigh, lifting my leg up around his hip.

He breaks the kiss to study my face as he moves his hand between my legs. He touches me so gently, his fingers sliding in the lube that's still there, and his mouth opens on a breath.

"Okay?"

I nod and he slides two fingers back inside me. My eyes close and my head tips back and Rafe leans in, kissing my throat, then my mouth, fingers playing inside me, finding that spot that felt so good before.

"Ungh!"

He rubs over it, and I dig my fingers into his back, pleasure spreading through me.

"Good?"

"Yeah."

Rafe rolls my hips up, and I start shaking against him, needing something I can't put words to. Rafe kisses me deeply, moaning into my mouth as he moves his hand between us. He puts on a new condom and slicks himself up again. I feel shaky and overstimulated and my dick is leaking down onto my stomach. Rafe stills, just looking at me.

"You are so fucking gorgeous like this," he murmurs, running a hand down my torso, rubbing at the drops of precome that have fallen onto my stomach, and then lightly stroking me until I'm gasping.

"Okay, okay, okay," I say, tangling my fingers in his hair and pulling him down into a kiss.

"Okay," he says, smiling. "You stop me if—"

"God damn it, I know!"

Rafe smiles. He reaches down and guides his dick to my opening, just resting there for a minute.

"Push out," he whispers against my lips.

When I do, he presses just the head inside me. I gasp and nod at him. He kisses me lightly and slides deeper.

"Breathe, breathe," he says. "Fuck." Rafe's voice is breathy, his jaw tight. He pushes in so slowly that I can feel myself opening up to him.

"Oh god," I say. I feel caught between something unbearably good and something terrifying. I squeeze my eyes shut, and Rafe rubs circles on my stomach. His hand is shaking.

"Okay?"

I don't know if I'm okay. I don't know if I'll ever be okay again. Because the feeling of him inside, filling me up, connected with me… it makes me feel like a different person. I squeeze my eyes shut, too overwhelmed to keep looking at him.

"Colin, are you okay? Please, I need you to tell me." His thumb brushes at my closed eyelids and I feel moisture there. I blink it away, nod, then spread my legs farther for him and pull at his back.

"'M'okay. Just, c'mere."

He nods. Then he slides the rest of the way inside me. He groans desperately, but doesn't move once he's inside. I try to keep breathing, but I feel too full.

I scrabble at Rafe's shoulders, starting to panic again.

"Okay, try to relax for me. I know, babe, I know." He kisses me, and as distractions go, it's a good one. His mouth on mine is hungry, possessive, but his hands are soft, rubbing my stomach, stroking up and down my arms. When he reaches between us and strokes my dick, I clench up and we both cry out.

"Oh," I gasp as the feeling of uncomfortable fullness transforms into something so much better. Something deep and powerful. Rafe is frozen above me, an intense look on his face. He's biting his lip and gazing down at me. "I—oh Jesus, Rafe." Because I can feel him throbbing deep inside me. And this feels nothing like the painful, hurried mess of before.

Rafe takes my mouth in a bruising kiss and starts moving. As I relax my muscles, I start feeling these little tingles ripple through my ass, like electricity. Rafe leans back and rolls my hips up, then pushes back inside me, and I cry out as he comes in contact with that spot inside me. He does it over and over and I'm lost in the sensations. My whole body is hot and tense and liquid at the same time.

"Fuck, you feel amazing," Rafe says, thrusting inside me and freezing there, his muscles tight. "How're you doing?"

I'm falling to fucking pieces. I can't even speak. When I open my mouth, all that comes out is a garbled moan that sounds embarrassingly desperate. I just reach a shaky hand into his hair and kiss him with everything I've got. That seems to do the trick. He speeds up, and the smooth slide sends sparks all down my spine. I dig my fingers into his back, needing more.

"Harder?" he asks, and I kiss him again. He groans, then starts thrusting harder, muscles tight with control. I start moaning, these choked sounds that would humiliate me if I could pay attention to anything except the feeling of Rafe inside me. Then he reaches between us and grabs my dick and I cry out.

He's muttering my name and things I can't make out and I don't care because he's stroking my erection in time with his thrusts and heat is curling in my lower belly. The trembling starts in my thighs and then Rafe hits that spot again and I'm coming—an orgasm that starts somewhere deep inside and radiates through my ass and lower back and balls and, fuck, shoots out my dick in thick pulses of pleasure I can't control. Rafe's groaning and muttering sweet filth about my ass and my dick and how hot I am, but I can barely hear him.

"God, babe, you're gonna make me come," he chokes out, then he freezes inside me, moaning brokenly, pulsing his hips over and over, each movement stirring a shiver of pleasure deep inside me.

Rafe moans one last time and buries his face in my neck, kissing me worshipfully. I rub my fingers through his hair. He softens inside me and I squirm.

"Hold on." He drags his lips over my throat. When he pulls out, the soreness hits. I feel tender and a little swollen, but I don't care.

Rafe runs a finger around my hole. "You okay?" he asks. "I didn't hurt you, did I?"

I shake my head, reaching blindly for him so he'll lie down again and stop talking. He gets the message and lies next to me, kissing me softly and running his hand over every part of me he can reach.

"I'll be right back."

I must doze off for a minute because I startle awake to a warm washcloth cleaning come off my stomach.

"Sorry," Rafe says softly, hand on my hip. He drops the cloth on the floor, but I let it go, for once too warm and relaxed to get up and put it in the hamper.

Rafe slides down next to me and gathers me to him. "That was…. Mmm, damn," he moans. And I know I should say something. Tell him he made me feel amazing. That I loved it. But I can't. I'm afraid if I say any of it out loud, think about it for too long, the shame will hit. I just hum against Rafe's shoulder and squeeze my eyes shut, sliding a hand into his hair and absently untangling it until I fall asleep.

Chapter 9

WHEN THE doorbell rings, I'm just getting out of the shower and I almost break my neck getting tangled up in my sweats as I drag them over still-wet skin.

Relief floods me when I see that it's Rafe. I haven't heard from him since he left my house Sunday morning. I even texted him a few times, but he didn't respond, which isn't like him.

I find myself smiling automatically, and Shelby practically climbs the leg of his jeans. Rafe gently detaches her from his leg, but sets her down on the floor without playing with her. Also not like him.

"Hey," I say.

"I need to talk to you." He sounds like he's trying really hard to keep his temper.

"Okay." I back away from the door.

"I'm going to ask you a question and I need you to be honest with me."

I nod. He's still standing just inside the door.

"Do you wanna sit down?"

But he shakes his head. He looks like a different person than the Rafe I woke up to on Sunday morning. The one with the warm, sleepy kisses. The one who told me I was beautiful—even if that did make me blush and smack him. The one who said he liked being at my house because his apartment felt lonely since Javier died. The one who cooked me breakfast and hugged me tight before he had to leave.

"Were you alone with Anders here on Monday night?" he asks, voice tight.

My heart starts to pound. "Uh... no? Not here. But yeah, he came to the shop. Wanted to talk."

Rafe puts his head in his hand and groans, like Anders wanting to talk to me is some kind of horrible nightmare.

"I mean, I'm sure he'd have rather talked with you, but he didn't know where you are when you're not at YA and he knew where I worked, so...."

"I'm not—Jesus, Colin, I'm not *jealous*. I just can't believe you would do something so monumentally stupid! Fuck!" Rafe drops down onto the back of the couch. "What were you thinking? Were you alone with him? Who else was there? Did people see him?"

"Hold the hell on. What are you implying? I didn't... I didn't *do* anything to him!"

"Yeah, unfortunately, that's not the point. That's why there are protocols for working with youth. You have to be absolutely beyond fucking reproach at all times or you leave yourself open to every accusation under the sun. And I'm the one who brought you on as a volunteer, so if it looks like you're being inappropriate with the kids, then it's on me!"

"Well, how do I know this shit? I was trying to help." Okay, my first response had been irritation that Anders had come to the shop, but I got over it.

"You *don't* know so there are times you *can't* help," Rafe says, like I'm an idiot. I hate it when he does this. Acts like there is this whole set of rules that I'll never understand. Not that he's wrong. It'd just be nice not to be reminded that I fuck up everything I touch.

"Look, he wanted to talk to me because I'm not... you know, because people don't know about him. Being gay. Queer. Whatever. Like, he wanted to know should he tell his parents and shit. And I think he just wanted to know how it was for me."

Rafe takes a deep breath like it's all he can do to control his temper. "So, what did you tell him?" he asks slowly.

I'd been finishing up a repair when Anders slunk in. All I saw of him at first were his skinny legs encased in their usual black denim and ending in too-heavy black boots that scuffed the grimy concrete. Pop had left and I had pretty much scared off Brian and Sam by bringing up the idea of proposing more custom repairs to Pop. They'd both done the we-don't-want-to-make-waves shuffle and I'd been pissed at them the rest of the day for being such cowards. So, chances were no one would see Anders, but I'd led him into the office anyway, not wanting to take any chances that we might be overheard.

He apologized about a hundred times for bothering me before I finally got the story out of him. He'd begun coming to YA with Mikal after they connected on social media, and his family had no clue he was queer—his word. He said he hadn't really even talked about it much with any friends. Seemed like he'd been a bit of a loner before he met the other YA kids. He spent a lot of time practicing violin—I guess he played in pretty major competitions. Recitals. Whatever you call them. His dad was some kind of banker and his mother did something with trading stocks. They were Swedish and still spent a lot of time going back and forth to Stockholm so they weren't around a lot. But when they were, they seemed to hold Anders and his brother and sister to pretty exacting standards. Sure, Anders' father's expectations ran more to perfect grades and ten-year plans, but I was familiar with the sentiment.

When his father had found out that he'd been going to YA instead of spending time after school practicing, he'd flipped out. Anders had told him he was just going there to support a friend. That it didn't mean anything. He looked ashamed when he told me that, as if he owed them the truth as some kind of familial tithe. But he knew his parents wouldn't like it. His father especially would be disappointed. Something about business and being the oldest son, Anders said, but clearly beneath it was just the same kind of old-fashioned disgust that Pop had displayed since I was a kid.

And that was the heart of why Anders had come to me, I think. He'd been looking for someone who had the same issue as him. It wasn't very flattering, being sought out because you have the same shit going on that a teenager does when you're supposed to be an adult. It was the adult part Anders was clearly after, though. He knew Rafe better, sure, but Rafe was a damn shining beacon of integrity, whereas I… well, I may have had a similar problem, but I had no solutions. Not even for myself. I wished I could tell him a brave story like Rafe's—always having been honest about who he was and damn the consequences. Hell, I wished I could tell him a story like Daniel's, even. Where he hadn't chosen the moment to tell people he was gay, but when it had happened, he'd taken control over it.

I even started to tell him those stories. As if we were in some soppy movie and my words would inspire him and change everything. But in real life we were just in a messy office at the back of a damn auto shop, and the only perspective I could bring myself to give him was my own. And maybe it had helped, knowing someone else was going through something similar.

I have no clue if Rafe will think I said the right thing, though.

"I told him that his personal shit wasn't anyone's business, not even his parents'. That he'd be out of the house in one more year, and if telling them he was queer meant that he'd have to put up with a bunch of awful shit for a whole year, then it wasn't worth it. He has a lot of time later on to figure everything out. He doesn't have to decide anything right away."

Rafe runs a hand through his hair like he's at the end of his patience, but at least he isn't looking at me like I'm a child molester anymore. He just sighs and doesn't say anything.

"He's pretty pissed, though, man. That he can't come to YA anymore." And hurt. That was clear beneath everything Anders said. He'd finally found someplace where he could feel comfortable, and now he'd been rejected from there, too.

"Yeah, all the kids are pissed. I'm pissed. Of *course* I wish Anders could still come. I wish we didn't need permission from a guardian—it cuts so many youth off from service, or forces them to weigh their desire for an inclusive space against the potential cost of coming out to their family. I wish I could do more for all of them in a thousand ways."

"Then couldn't you just make an exception? He could just tell his dad he was somewhere else?"

"You don't understand how serious this is. It's all so fucking precarious. The slightest whiff of something suspicious, something not aboveboard, and YA could get shut down in an instant. One of the kids says something at school about how we're letting someone hang around adults unsupervised and a teacher overhears? Disaster. I heard fucking *Mikal* telling Dorothy that Anders was hanging out at your *house*, Colin! Who knows who else he might've said it in front of? It doesn't matter if it's not true, it just matters what people will believe. You *cannot* be alone with a minor. End of story. It's for the volunteers' sake too. You just… you can't leave yourself open to any accusations. Not any more than YA can. And it can't be Anders' responsibility, okay? He's a kid, he's hurt, he's confused, and looking for comfort. I know it feels like the worst fucking thing in the world, but you have to be the one who draws the line."

He's ranting at this point, and I never know what to do when he gets this way—furious about a system that he thinks is unjust but unwilling to sacrifice what good is in place to break out of it. I'm not sure if he's angrier at himself for following the rules or the rules themselves.

"YA is *everything* to me, Colin. Javi built it from nothing. And those kids… they're—they've been what I wake up for in the mornings. For years. Helping with them—giving them something I didn't ever have—it's—Colin, it's the only decent thing I've ever done. I can't fucking lose that."

Rafe looks wrecked and it's my fault. It doesn't matter what my intentions were. I fucked up. Most of all, I hate that Rafe is disappointed in me. So I just stand like an idiot in the middle of my living room.

Rafe walks over to me and puts his hands on my shoulders. With his expression tense, the fine lines around his eyes are more visible and the crease between his brows is deep. His lower lip is rough, like he's been biting at it.

"You can't do that again. Okay? You can't be alone with any of the kids outside of the workshops. No matter how much you want to help. I… believe me, I get it. But it's too easy for everything to go wrong. Please." He looks so tired. "Please, babe."

"Okay, I'm sorry," I say. "I thought… I thought I was helping. I wanted—I just hated seeing him so upset." And, yeah, there was the fact that he came to me. That, despite having made a mess of this stuff in my own life, he actually thought maybe I'd have some answers. It felt so good to have someone see me that way. And it's quite a contrast to how Rafe's looking at me now. With fondness, maybe, but mostly like I'm a liability. A fuckup. Like he gave me something precious and I smashed it.

Like I can't be trusted with anything real.

After sitting in strained silence for an hour, watching a movie about some dude in a small town who turns out to be part of the mafia or something, I'm ready to scream. It would've been easier if Rafe had just left, but apparently he didn't get the memo that it's awkward to hang out after fighting with someone.

And then, yeah, my stupid breathing thing starts. I'm just about to get up and go into the kitchen to quietly freak out when I notice that Rafe's watching me. It feels like I'm cheating because I know he can't just sit there and not try and help me. My fucked-up-ness is his damned kryptonite.

He lets out a big sigh and then his hand is on the back of my neck and I close my eyes and try to concentrate on his touch.

"We're okay," he says, but it sounds like he's trying to convince himself.

"Yeah? Well, it feels like shit."

Rafe sighs. "Yeah. Look, I can't condone what you did—it's too dangerous. But I like why you did it. I like that you were trying to help. You're fucking fierce. I like that."

"Thought you liked sweet," I mutter.

"Mmm. Oh, Colin. You're sweet as hell."

"Yeah right."

"Kiss me," he says softly, a peace offering.

I huff and grudgingly peck him on the lips. He snorts and pulls me closer, kissing me deeper.

"There, see?" he murmurs. "Sweet."

I push off his chest and roll my eyes at him.

Rafe's expression turns serious and he moves in and kisses me again. He kisses me like he really does think I'm sweet. As if he has nothing else to do but kiss me.

"I missed you this week," he says, kissing my neck.

"Oh, now you want to be sweet too, huh?"

He puts on a who-me? expression. "I missed being here with you." He kisses my shoulder. "I missed eating dinner with you and falling asleep with you." He kisses my chin. "I like it here."

"So you're just using me for my house."

Rafe nods. "Yeah, and your cat."

"Damn cat," I mutter, looking over at her, and one of Shelby's little ears perks up like she knows we're talking about her.

In bed, we kiss until we're both desperate and pulling at each other's clothes, as if we can ease the tension with our bodies. Rafe strips his underwear off and we both grab for our dicks at the same time. We kiss hard and deep, and it pushes my head into the pillow so there's only softness beneath me and Rafe's hardness on top of me.

I press my hips up into his, wanting somehow to be on top of him and underneath him, inside him and around him all at the same time. Rafe groans, sliding his other hand under my thigh to grab my ass, and squeezes, holding us tightly together. He pushes my hand off of us and I call him bossy and he grins, slowing his strokes and kissing me silent, our bodies rocking together as his hand controls our pleasure.

I tug on his hair and he moans into my mouth and strokes us harder. When my balls start to tighten, I squirm beneath him, trying to get just a little more pressure, a little more contact. I gasp into his mouth and he smiles and slows down his strokes again, bringing me away from the edge.

"Damn it!"

Rafe's eyes are heavy-lidded with lust and nothing I do makes him move any faster than he wants to. He kisses my neck, then bites where it meets my shoulder, which always makes me tighten up, my stomach and my ass clenching.

"Rafe, come on." I pull at him, but he kisses me before I can say anything else. Then he rolls us so I'm on top of him and sucks on his fingers, getting them slick. I start breathing heavy, and Rafe smiles that wicked half smile and raises an eyebrow. I nod and he slides his fingers inside me. My whole body clenches up on top of him, and his dick jerks against mine in his hand.

He groans and starts moving his fingers slowly inside me. I lean down, begging him with my kiss not to stop. He lets go of our erections for a moment to cup my cheek.

"So sweet," he says against my lips, and I can smell us on his hand.

"Oh god, shut up," I gasp, and I thrust against him. Then, "C'mon."

"Mmm."

Rafe fists us again, stroking in time with the movement of his fingers inside me. He starts to thrust his hips into mine, his breath coming short. He rubs that place inside me that makes my whole body spark and I cry out, clutching at his shoulders.

"You going to come for me, Colin?" Rafe's voice is rough with arousal.

"Fuck," I gasp.

"You're so gorgeous when you come," he says in my ear.

"Ungh."

He tightens his hand on our dicks and spreads his fingers inside me, a fingertip still pressing on that spot. Pleasure races up my spine and my orgasm starts deep inside and explodes through me, every stroke of Rafe's hand on us dragging out the pleasure. I shoot between us and he kisses me, catching my cries with his mouth. He keeps stroking even after I'm a shuddering mess, little aftershocks sparking from my balls to the tip of my dick, and I reach between us and grab his erection and then he's coming too, groaning into my neck as his heat hits my stomach and his hips slam up into mine.

"Mmm." Rafe kisses me softly, gently moving his fingers inside me, making me shudder against him. He kisses my cheeks, and I bury my face in his hair, going limp against him. Our come is smeared between us, but I relax into him and he wraps me in his arms.

Finally, I start to feel slimy, so I get a warm washcloth and clean us up. Rafe slides under the covers, but stays sitting up.

"Can I stay?" he asks a little tentatively, the ghost of the earlier tension rearing its head.

"Yeah, course," I say, getting into bed. Then I add, "You can always stay," and Rafe gives me a sleepy smile, confidence back in place. He pulls me to him and the feeling of all that skin against mine is intoxicating. I touch him the way he sometimes touches me, pretty sure he's okay with it. I rub up and down his spine, and he hums contentedly, then rolls onto his back so I'm lying with my cheek against his shoulder, his arm around me. I slide my hand into his hair and absently untangle it as my mind wanders.

"Colin?" Rafe says softly.

"Hmm."

"My sister invited you to Thanksgiving at her house."

He rubs circles on my back before I notice I've tensed up.

"Oh, um, well, that's nice of her. I always go to Pop's, though. He'd be pissed if I didn't show."

"Yeah, I told her you probably had plans with your family. But I wanted to pass along the invitation." Rafe kisses the top of my head, but then he shifts so he can look at me. "I'd really like it if you'd come to dinner with my family."

His voice is soft and even, but I can hear how serious he is.

"Yeah, sorry, but Pop—"

"I know. I don't mean on Thursday. Look, I know you're not ready to tell your family. I get that you're not comfortable going out with me in public. But my family already knows about us. You met Luz. I just…. It doesn't have to happen right now. But I need to know that we exist outside these walls."

"Rafe, I…." But I have absolutely nothing to say to that.

"Just think about it. Okay?" He kisses me and settles me back against him. He falls asleep in a few minutes, but I lie awake for a long time, my fingers in Rafe's hair, wishing real-life shit was as easy to untangle as the knots there.

I LIKE the city on holidays even though I don't care about Thanksgiving. Fewer people around and everyone's less rude, like they remember we're all someone's family. A few older ladies at the bus stop actually nod to me when I walk by on my way to Pop's.

The Eagles are playing this afternoon, but I'm going over in time for the early game, which is Detroit and Chicago. I grab more beer on my way, but when I get to Pop's, it's clear I didn't need to bother. The whole refrigerator is a tetris of cases, cans, and bottles.

After he invited me for dinner, Rafe explained that his family doesn't really celebrate Thanksgiving. For them, it's just mandatory family time, and they cook a huge traditional Mexican meal at Gabriela's, since her place is the biggest. When I told him it sounded nice, he said I could still come.

But we both knew I wouldn't.

After sitting on Pop's couch for a few hours drinking beer, I'm starting to have second thoughts. I'm starving and there's no food. The Bears are playing like shit. And Brian keeps throwing drained beer cans at the TV in anger, so the entire living room reeks.

When I crack open my fifth beer, I realize I'm pretty drunk. My decreased tolerance is a reminder that I haven't been drinking much lately because I've been spending so much time with Rafe.

It's like sliding into a warm and comfortable hole, though. My arms and legs feel heavy, like doing anything but sitting on this couch would be impossible, and my head's fuzzy.

And apparently my fuzzy head only wants to think about Rafe. Like, why, exactly, did I come here, to this sad place, when I could be with Rafe, eating delicious food and seeing him interact with his family? But then Brian grins at me and holds out a couple stale crackers he found in the kitchen, and I know I have to be here.

Halfway through the Eagles game, Daniel calls. While Sam chats with him, I find myself wondering where he is for Thanksgiving. Maybe I do wish I were with Rafe instead of being here, but at least I have somewhere to be. I don't like to think of Daniel alone in Whereverthefuck, Michigan. Sam holds the phone out to me, but I shake my head.

I drunk text Rafe, *I wish I were with u.*

He texts back almost immediately: *You can still come if you want. Lots of food.*

My stomach growls. *U wdnt like me now*, I write. Rafe's made it really clear he doesn't want to be around me when I drink.

I always like you, Rafe texts, and I can't help but smile. Then a minute later, he writes, *Be safe. I can drive you home, if you need.*

I walked, I send. Then, *Thanks.*

Liza shows up an hour later with half a turkey—really, you never know with Liza; she said she had it because of something to do with work, but she's a florist, so I have no idea. I barely taste it, though. I keep looking around at all of them—Pop, Brian, Sam, Liza—and asking myself what the worst-case scenario is. Like, what exactly might I lose that's worth not being able to make Rafe happy by agreeing to go to dinner with his family. Or take him out to dinner. Fuck, the guy was practically begging me to go on a date with him and I said no. I'm the worst... whatever on the planet.

Brian and Pop are drunk too; Sam and Liza are tipsy. When I'm coming out of the bathroom, Pop and I nearly collide in the kitchen. He pats me on the back, practically knocking himself off balance in the process.

"You're a good kid, Colin," he says. "Good son. I'm goin'ta bed." He squeezes my arm as he shambles past me.

"Yeah, me too," I say.

I play the moment over and over as I stagger home, and all I can think as I fall into bed alone is *that's* why. That's why I can't be with Rafe outside these walls. And even if I did, there's no guarantee that things would work out. Knowing me, shit probably *won't* work out. So, what if I gambled it all on Rafe—my family, my job—and then I fucked it up like usual. Maybe Pop's an asshole sometimes, but he raised me, Daniel, Brian, and Sam after Mom died, kept food on the table, gave us jobs. I know he loves me. I think he does, anyway. But if he found out... he'd never say anything like that to me again. He'd never look at me like that, with warmth, appreciation. Love me? I don't know. But respect me? Be proud of me? No.

And, god help me, I don't think I can live with that.

THE NEXT week, everything seems off. Work is normal, I guess, but nothing feels satisfying the way it used to. Every time I hear Pop or Sam tell someone we don't do specialty repairs, every time I'm stuck changing a flat tire or explaining to some know-it-all who looked up engine trouble on the Internet what's actually wrong with his car, I'm wishing for... more.

That's what I want, lately. Just more. I want work to be more interesting, more of a challenge. I want to be able to do more for the kids at YA, give them more of what Daniel never had. I've thought about Anders a lot too. Wondered what he decided to do about telling his parents—if he's decided yet at all.

And fuck me, I want more of Rafe. More of everything to do with Rafe. When I'm with him, things feel… good.

But I don't think Rafe feels the same way. When he got to my place earlier, I asked him if everything was okay and he said it was, but it seems like there's something he's not telling me.

Ever since he asked me to come to dinner with his family, things have been strained. I think he's getting frustrated with me. Impatient. He wants something that I'm not giving to him.

We're on the couch and I'm leaning into him, enjoying his smell and the feeling of his arms around me. I'm making stupid comments about the movie—some eighties action thing—and he doesn't respond but he keeps touching me. Small touches like you might reach a hand out to your bedside table to check that something you put down is still there.

Then he lets out a sigh and my stomach goes hollow and tight. It feels like he's trying to work up to saying something, and that is never good.

"Rafe," I say when I can't take it anymore, "just tell me whatever the hell is wrong. You're freaking me out."

He looks a little sheepish. "Have you given any thought to what I said?"

"What you said when?"

"About having dinner with my family?"

"Oh." I knew it.

"Look, it was great seeing everyone at Gabri's last week. They're crazy and intense and they drive me nuts sometimes, but it's home. Something was missing for me, though, because you weren't there. My mom would describe some cat video her coworker showed her and I'd want to tell you that it reminded me of Shelby. Or Camille would use text speak and I'd want to laugh at you because you never know what the kids are talking about at YA when they use it. I just… wanted you there."

On the surface it sounds perfect: exchanging knowing glances over the dinner table or laughing gently at private jokes. That's what you're supposed to do, right? But it leaves out the part where I'm cringing just thinking about being introduced to Rafe's family. About what it would mean. About us. About me.

He stops me from saying anything with a thumb to my mouth. "I know you couldn't—that you already had plans. Family obligations. I respect that. And it's not the point. It's that I don't know if you'll ever be there. I don't know if I'll ever get to go out to dinner with you or… go on vacation with you or…."

He's obviously sincere, but it's kind of hard not to bristle at what's basically a list of all the ways that I'm failing to live up to Rafe's standards.

"I didn't expect to feel this way," he says, his voice more vulnerable than I've heard it. "I didn't know that I wanted those things. Or, I didn't think about it. Didn't let myself think about them because I didn't think—anyway. I know it hasn't been that long. I'm not saying I need those things right now. But I want them. In the future. And"—his voice gets softer—"and you don't think much about the future."

"I—" I'm caught between relief that Rafe isn't ending things and the sudden choking anxiety that his words bring. I guess it's true that I don't think about the future much. I've never had anything to look forward to, so there didn't seem much point. Lately, though….

"I… um. We can go to dinner at your family's. I—that sounds good, okay?" That's what he wants, right? And it wouldn't be in public where anyone could see. I can give him that if it means things will stop being so awkward.

He nods, but he doesn't look happy. "Okay. I'd like that."

He's clearly waiting for something more, but I don't know how to make promises about the future. Not when, for the first time, the present finally feels almost… okay.

"I don't—I don't know what you want me to say," I mumble.

Rafe shakes his head. "I don't know either."

"I… I don't want to tell them," I choke out. Because that's what he really means, isn't it? Even if he says it's not the point. I think about what I told Anders when he came to the shop. About how his personal shit is no one's business and how it's not worth making your life miserable just to tell people about it.

"I'm not asking you to do that," Rafe says sternly. "I've never asked for that. It's your family and your decision."

"Okay, so then…."

"All I mean is, there's a huge part of you that's a secret to all the people you care about. And that means you can't think about what the future will be like. You're suspended in the present. Getting through each day without anyone finding out about you. Running hard enough that you feel okay. Drinking enough that you forget about the world long enough to fall asleep and wake up to a new day. Only it's the same thing then, too."

My life in his words makes me want to puke. Because he's right: that's how I feel most of the time. But… not when I'm with him.

"And I understand that. Truly." He brushes his thumb over my lips. "It's how I got clean. You need to focus only on the present moment so you *can* get through it. But… that's not where I am anymore. I've already gotten through enough days. It's all I did for so long. And now… I try to work *toward* things instead. Build things. With social justice work, with YA. It's what I need to do. And it's… it's what I want for us."

I pull away from him as anger shoots through me. *Now* he tells me these things? I feel like I just spent months building an entire car out of scraps and Rafe is now telling me that he wants me to build a truck instead.

It's taken me a long fucking time to admit to myself that I want him. That I want him in my life, in my house, in my bed. And he's saying, what? That those things don't matter because I haven't thought about going on vacation with him? What the fuck? I want to hit him.

"So, what? What do you want me to do? What do you want me to be working toward?"

"I don't know, babe," he says, his voice infuriatingly calm. "Only you can answer that."

"What the hell, Rafe! Are you a fortune cookie or something? I—you—we—what the fuck do you want from me?" I'm yelling and he's still, watching me impassively. "I've already—fuck!—I've already let you do everything to me. What else can I do?"

He's up like a shot, fury I've never seen blazing in his expression. "Stop right there. I haven't done anything that you didn't want. I would *never*!" He looks offended. Outraged. Like he cares more about seeming beyond reproach than about what I'm actually saying.

It's like the anxiety and anger and uncertainty that have been hanging over us boil over, and I'm utterly furious with him. The kind of furious that usually ends with me punching the shit out of someone.

"Oh yeah, I know," I spit out. "Saint Rafe would never do anything wrong. You just want to make the world a better place."

Rafe's expression is ice, his fists clenched.

"I have done things wrong. Things I can't ever take back. Things I wake up with every day and go to sleep with every night. Don't you dare judge me for what I do to try and live with them."

"And you feel so fucking guilty that you'd do anything to atone for it," I snarl at him. "All your projects and your soup kitchens! You work so hard to make the world a better place for everyone else but you don't even care about living in it. And now you're too scared to ever break the rules, even when it would help Anders."

Fuck, where did that come from? Rafe's mouth falls open and still I don't stop. I'm all twisted up inside and I just want to hurt him.

"You don't think you deserve to just be happy and you want me to—I don't know—be your next cause. Well, I'm not one of your fucking projects, okay? So, don't treat this"—I gesture between us—"whatever it is—like we're going to have committee meetings or whatever the hell you guys spend your time doing."

I'm shaky with the same poison I felt every time I hurt Daniel. I'd try to hold back the tide, but then I'd see a glimmer of something vulnerable—hope or faith that this time I'd do the right thing. And in that instant of knowing for a fact how truly misplaced that hope was, how it made me responsible for him when I didn't want to be, I'd strike the killing blow and the poison would flow through me. I'd hate myself for hurting him, but more, I'd hate him for letting me do it. For making me into a monster who hurts everyone I come in contact with.

I want Rafe to take a swing at me so I'll stop. Or so I can hit him back. But he just stands there glowering and vibrating with a punch he doesn't throw.

I can't stop. I never can.

"But, hell, maybe that's why you're here in the first place, huh? Right? You took one look at me and thought, 'Hey, there's my cause of the month. I guess I should hook up with him and fuck him happy!'"

Rafe's face is completely shut down but his eyes burn with something I hardly recognize and I'm careening right toward it.

"Is that it, Rafe? You want to fix me? You always said you wanted to be like Javier. Is that what you're doing? You want to be my sponsor? Turn me into someone you can point at and say, 'I did that'?"

Rafe hisses and I know I'm so far over the line I can't even see it. I catch a glimpse of my reflection in the window. I'm spitting mad but my face is white.

Rafe steps right up to me and he's shaking, his quiet words cutting deeper than any yell.

"Don't talk about him," he says, and for the first time, I can see the man he might have been. Dangerous, menacing, cold. I can see him choose to control himself, but it's clear he could've gone the other way.

I wish he would. I wish he would hit me, shove me, do anything to me. Anything would be better than this distance, this cold. He's looking at me like we don't even know each other.

"You," he says, "are lying to yourself if you think you're living in the world. You're barely making it through. You know what you want but you're too scared to go after it. You think being gay is what makes you weak?" He shakes his head, and there's pity in his face. "Living a lie when you don't have to. Acting like you're the only one affected by your decisions. Those are the things that make you weak. It's just fear."

Something shifts in Rafe's face. He lets go of something, or... or maybe he just doesn't care anymore.

"You know what you're really scared of, though? You're afraid of what will happen once you don't have a secret to hide behind anymore. Once you're just you. Strip away your fear and what's left? I don't think you even know."

My heart is beating so hard that I feel like I'm going to pass out. I know now that I've been waiting for this moment since I realized how much I wanted him. The moment when he figured out what a waste of time it is for him to be with me because I'm fucking nothing.

"Fuck you," I bite out, the response automatic.

Rafe nods once, like he wasn't expecting anything more, and it hits me like a sonic boom. His total dismissal. But when he walks out— when he leaves me standing in the middle of my immaculate living room feeling like the fucking walls are coming down and the blackness beyond them is swallowing me whole—the sound of the door shutting behind him is almost silent.

Chapter 10

WORK IS just like it was yesterday. And the day before. And the day before that. And I don't care anymore. I try to lose myself in the vehicles. Distract myself by picturing their beautiful circulatory systems. The way each piece has a job to do. How every system is necessary to keep things running smoothly. But I'm just going through the motions. Waiting for something that might snap me out of this fog. Everything Brian, Sam, and Pop say pisses me off, and I've been walking around with my fists clenched in a constant state of readiness to fight during the two weeks since Rafe walked out my door. I feel like I'm sixteen again.

This morning I woke from smothering dreams, still half drunk, the sheets twisted and sticking to me with sweat, and I dragged myself up to run. The sidewalks were cracked, the remains of the snowfall a few days ago hiding dangerous uneven patches that can turn an ankle. I felt heavy, my legs useless like in dreams where I'm being chased—as if the pavement is quicksand, sucking my feet down no matter how hard I try to propel myself forward. I cut over to the track behind my old high school, shut down three years ago in budget cuts. The track's just dirt now, really, but I didn't trust myself to pay attention running around the neighborhood.

I zoned out as I ran, but the second I stopped, everything slammed back into me like the nasty return of punching bag when your head's turned. My legs were shaky and weak, my stomach roiling, and my ears numb with cold.

All of that was nothing compared to the fishhook of pain lodged somewhere between my chest and my stomach, throbbing with each beat of my stupid, pathetic heart.

As I come through the door of the garage with a second cup of coffee—an attempt to wake up after almost melting a mess of wiring with the soldering iron—Sam nearly slams into me and the mug falls, shattering on the cement, splatters of coffee mixing with oil, paint, and grease.

"What the hell," I mutter.

"Pop!" Sam yells, his voice panicked like I've never heard it. "Call 911. Call 911 now!"

I bolt toward the office as Luther grabs the phone. On the floor of the office strewn with paperwork lies Pop, one hand clutching at his chest, the other clawing at Sam's arm. He's covered in sweat. His face is gray and terrified.

The only time I've seen him look so lost is after Mom died. When he wandered through the house like a child, picking things up and putting them down as if, maybe, she wasn't gone, but simply misplaced.

"They're on their way," Luther calls.

My heart races like I'm still running. "Pop?" I croak out, and I sink down next to him. He mouths my name but no sound comes out.

Before I can figure out what we should do next, paramedics are pushing us out of the way. Pop loses consciousness before they get him out of the office.

"What—what—Colin, what happened? Pop?" Brian runs up to the shop as the paramedics are putting Pop in the ambulance, late as usual. "What's wrong with him?"

I remember that edge of panic to Brian's voice. I remember it from when Mom died and Brian came home from school to find Pop crying in the kitchen.

But I can't talk to Brian. It's taking every bit of energy to drag air into my lungs. Luther pushes Sam into the ambulance with Pop, but they can't take us all.

"I'll drive you." Luther grabs Brian's arm with one hand and mine with the other and puts us in his truck. This too is familiar. Luther was there, especially those last few weeks when Pop was with Mom in the hospital most days.

The ride to the hospital is a blur of Brian crying and Luther talking and traffic lights changing and horns honking, and then we're in the waiting area. Brian's chewing on his lip, his knee bouncing and his head swiveling every time someone walks by. Sam is slumped in his chair, eyes straight ahead, cradling his cell phone. Luther is half watching us and half watching the nurses' station. It's too bright and too quiet and too loud to feel anything.

We're probably getting motor oil and grease on the waiting room. Mom never let Pop sit on the couch without changing his clothes and taking a shower. She insisted that oil still managed to get on things even when he did. The price of loving a mechanic, she always said, smiling.

I close my eyes, trying to picture her. Trying to remember how she smelled. I know her perfume was some kind of rose—her favorite flower—but I can't conjure it. There's only sweat and oil and stale recycled air.

TEN MINUTES later it's over.

Pop's dead.

A heart attack, the doctor says.

I DON'T remember getting back to Pop's. Luther must've driven us, but I don't know how long ago. Sam is a robot as he makes arrangements with Vic, a guy from the neighborhood we've known forever whose cousin runs a funeral parlor. Luther makes a bunch of other calls. I don't know.

"We have to call Dan," Sam says tiredly.

"I gotta go home. Gotta feed the cat," I mumble, stumbling to my feet. I hold up my cell phone to say they can call me if they need me.

"You have a cat?" Sam's saying as the door closes.

WHEN I get home, I try to call Shelby over, wanting to drop my face into her fur and hug her to me like a stuffed animal. She lets Rafe cuddle her like that sometimes. She comes close, but when I try and grab her, she swipes at me, claws raising red lines on my hand. It doesn't hurt enough, so I try again. She thinks we're playing and rolls over onto her back. I rub her belly. She always likes it for five seconds before she attacks. She claws lines of heat down my forearm with her back feet and latches on to my wrist with her teeth. When I try and lift my hand away, she comes off the floor with it, wrapped around my arm. When she gets tired of playing, my forearm is crisscrossed with scratch marks oozing blood, but I don't feel any better.

I pull myself up, looking at my stinging arm. Picture Pop's arm as he clutched at his failing heart, lying on the floor of the business he built, staring up at me like I could help him. I can't even help myself.

My interactions with Pop in the last month? I didn't say one word more than absolutely necessary. Didn't stick around one second longer than I had to. Didn't pay attention to anything but my own work. I can barely swallow around the guilt clogging my throat.

The first gulp of bourbon trails fire behind my breastbone, the second warms my stomach, and the third goes down like water. So does the rest of the glass.

I'm exhausted but I can't be still or I start to focus on my breathing, on how my stomach is a whirlpool.

Shelby's scratches weren't enough to ease the pressure. In the bathroom, careful not to look in the mirror, as always, I turn on the shower so the bathroom fills with steam.

The razor blade parts my skin easily, blood welling, then dripping down my chest. Every cut sends a rush of heat through me, relaxing my stomach a bit, making my breaths come easier, as if I can draw in oxygen through them like gills. It's been a while.

Under the hot water, my head starts to swim. I hardly notice what's happening until I'm gasping for air on the floor of the shower, sobs turning me inside out.

Any recognizable feeling is so far out of reach that it may as well be a distant star I'm clawing at as I spiral through the vastness of space.

I wander from room to room, picking things up and putting them down again because there's nothing that can help. Finally, I crawl into bed with the bourbon and put up the hood on my sweatshirt. The heat's up high but I can't stop shaking.

The bourbon hits me all at once and the room is spinning. Distantly, I register that Shelby has jumped onto the bed and curled up on Rafe's pillow. On the pillow Rafe always uses, I mean. It doesn't smell like him anymore. I checked.

But Shelby's sense of smell is stronger than mine. Maybe she can still find a trace of him in the fabric.

I WAKE up to my phone ringing in the other room. I have no idea how long I've been out. Everything is dark, but it's because my hood's over my face, which is damp with tears or spit or the condensation of breathing into the fabric. I know if I try to get up to get my phone I'll puke, so I pull the covers tight around me and slip away again.

THE NEXT time I wake up, it's to Brian shaking me. My head feels like it's splitting apart, and my stomach gives a warning heave when Brian jostles my shoulder. I groan and bat his hand away.

"You okay?" Brian asks, his voice rough. I try and pull the covers back over my head, but he doesn't let me.

"Come on," he says and holds out a hand. He looks wrecked. "You'll feel better if you puke."

I groan at the word, but I know he's right. I'm sweating bullets and my mouth is so dry I can barely swallow, but I stick my finger down my throat and vomit what feels like acid until there's nothing left in my stomach. I move to brush my teeth, but when I catch sight of the bloody razor sitting on the sink next to the soap, my stomach heaves again. I must've been really out of it to leave it there.

When I stagger out of the bathroom, Brian passes me a beer and I sip it until my stomach settles.

"I was calling you all day yesterday and you didn't answer."

He kneels and holds out a hand to Shelby, who comes and sniffs him delicately. Then she rubs her head against his fist and sits to let him pet her, rubbing her face against his knee.

"God damn it, Shelby," I say under my breath.

"What?" Brian asks, looking up at me as he scratches Shelby between her shoulder blades, making her purr and lean into him. I actually start to fucking tear up because the damn cat likes everyone better than me. Then she makes a sound that I haven't heard before, like she's whining.

"Nothing, man," I say. "Gimme a sec."

I change out of my sweats, shocked to see it's ten in the morning. Oh fuck. Brian said he called me all day yesterday. That means I passed out hard. Lost a whole day. Missed both of Shelby's feedings.

"Shit." I hurry into the kitchen and tip food into Shelby's bowl. At the sound, she comes galloping into the kitchen and shoves her face in the bowl.

"I'm sorry, Shelby," I whisper. "Fuck, I'm so sorry."

I reach out a shaky hand to pet her, but she twists away.

"Sorry," I murmur again and tip a little bit of extra food into her dish.

"Um, did you call Dan?" I ask.

Brian looks sheepish. "I forgot. Sam called him yesterday. He's driving. Should be here tonight. So, um, do you want to come back to the house? I just thought, you know, we could hang together or whatever."

No. I absolutely don't want to go to Pop's house when Pop's not there anymore. But I'm afraid of what I might do if I stay here alone, so I grab my coat and my keys and follow Brian to his car. I look at my phone to see ten missed calls from Brian, but what I'm really looking for is the call from Rafe that isn't there.

The desire that hits me is a physical ache so strong I wrap my arms around myself to try and contain it. I want to see Rafe. I want to see Rafe more than I want anything at this moment.

SAM, BRIAN, and I slump in the living room in the same configuration as always, the television droning in the background a prop so we don't have to talk. After a couple of beers, I feel better. After a couple more, I feel worse. Liza brings some food over, but everything tastes like sand.

Another beer and I actually close my eyes and make a wish as I snap the pop tab off my beer. I wish that Rafe would, somehow, walk through the door. I want the weight of his hands on my shoulders, the pressure of his arms around me, the smell of his hair as it falls around my face.

But when someone does walk through the door, it's the last person I want to see.

Daniel. And he has someone with him.

The second Daniel says "Hey" and his eyes land on me, I'm slammed by a combination of fury and jealousy so potent it takes my breath away.

"Um, this is Rex," Daniel says tentatively. The guy with him is handsome in a rugged kind of way, and is sticking close enough to Daniel that he could reach out and touch him at any moment. Daniel leans against the wall and looks at us, as if he doesn't even want to get close enough to sit on the furniture.

"Um, so what the fuck happened?" he asks. "Was Dad sick?"

I think back on all the times that Pop disappeared for hours during the middle of the day. The way he went to bed really early on Thanksgiving. I thought he was just drunk, but maybe… was he dying this whole time and I didn't even notice?

"If he was, he didn't say so," Sam says.

"I don't think he went to a doctor or anything," Brian adds, looking at me for confirmation.

"So, he just dropped dead all of a sudden?" Daniel snaps, like he's talking about a stranger. "Can you please tell me what happened?" He directs this to Sam, like Brian and I know nothing. My heart rate is kicking up and my skin is buzzing. As usual, Daniel sets me on edge with barely a word. He cares more about hearing the story than he even does that Pop's dead.

I can hear the tears in Sam's voice as he explains.

"Shit," Daniel breathes. "So, the doctors said it was a heart attack? What else did they say?"

What does he want from us? Pop's dead. We'll never see him again and Daniel wants to show up and play I'm-smarter-than-you, as usual.

"Are you a fucking medical doctor now, too?" I say.

"No." Daniel's voice is shaking like it always does when he's upset. "I just want to know what happened."

"We're having the funeral tomorrow," Liza interrupts before I can tell Daniel to go fuck himself.

"Jesus, that's fast," Daniel says, frowning.

Sam explains that Vic got us an in at his cousin's funeral parlor. He always was the most patient with Daniel's need to know every fucking detail about every fucking thing.

"Seriously, Sam?" Daniel says scornfully. "Vic's a fucking slimeball." He always used to say Vic was so stupid he couldn't believe he hadn't died in traffic yet. Never mind that Vic's cousin was the one who buried Mom, letting Pop pay him in trade because he couldn't afford anything else.

"Just because you don't like him…," Brian chimes in.

"Dude, he's a criminal. Come on," Daniel scoffs, like we're all idiots.

I think of Rafe telling me how scared he was when he got out of prison that no one would ever want him. That no one would give him a chance because of their stereotypes and fears about people who'd been in prison.

"Well, you weren't here to make other arrangements," I tell Daniel. "So we took care of it. If you're too good to go to the funeral because you don't approve of Vic, then that's your fucking business." The words come out like knives.

"Of course I'm going to the funeral. What can I do to help?"

"Nothing," Sam says. "It's taken care of. It'll be a graveside service. Luther called people for us, but some of Pop's friends can't make it, so we decided we'd have a party at the shop the next day. You know, a wake or whatever."

"Okay," Daniel says. "Well, I'm sorry I wasn't here, but I'll see you tomorrow."

And now he's just going to walk out the door. With the way Rex is looking at him, Daniel is probably in for a peaceful night of sweet cuddling or passionate sex—whichever he wants. Because Daniel always gets what he wants. It's always been that way. He was the baby. Mom doted on him. Pop protected him like he never did me. And Daniel never gave a crap. He did whatever he wanted and damn the consequences.

"Not like you ever gave a shit about him anyway," I mutter.

"You know that's not fucking true, Colin," he says, his voice shaky. "I just didn't have that much in common with him."

At the first sign that Daniel's upset, Rex steps closer to him and puts his hand at the small of Daniel's back. Daniel leans into him for support, and my stomach clenches with that poisonous mix of fury and envy.

"I'm sorry," Brian says to Rex, clearly way behind in the conversation, "but who the fuck are you?"

I stand up to face Daniel. He's the same height as me but he's built much slimmer. Daniel has that look on his face that I know so well. That vulnerable look that says, *This is how you hurt me. Go ahead, it's easy.* And I want to punish him for being so weak. So easy to hurt. For being such easy prey that he turns me into a predator by default.

"Well, yeah," I say. "What would Pop have in common with a stuck-up little faggot? He looked out for you and you didn't even care enough to stick around."

Sam says my name in warning, but I know he won't step in. He never does. Never wants to get his hands dirty.

I'm like a heat-seeking missile trained on the tremble in Daniel's lip that means he's about to cry and the way he lowers his dark lashes over green eyes filled with hurt. I may be drunk but I could take Daniel drunk and one-handed. He's a good fighter. Hell, he should be. I taught him. But his face is so easy to read that I can always tell when he's going to strike. He'd probably do fine if he were fighting someone who didn't know him, but he has no chance against me.

"What the *fuck*, Colin!" he yells. It's the same thing he used to say when he was a teenager. He doesn't even hit me. He shoves me, which he knows is a surefire way to get his ass kicked. He probably doesn't want to actually fight, just look tough in front of Rex. Though I don't know why he's bothering since Rex looks like he wants to wrap Daniel up in cotton and put him in a box like a Christmas ornament so nothing bad can touch him.

I grab Daniel by the shirt and shove him into the far wall, figuring on a hit from Rex. But, though Rex is there in a heartbeat, he just pulls me off.

"Don't. Fucking. Touch him." Rex's voice sends shivers through me. For a moment we lock eyes and his expression changes. Softens. Like he's looked inside me, seen me for the monster I am, and instead of scorn, feels only pity.

"Um," Brian interjects, "so, *who* are you?"

"Rex."

"He's my boyfriend," Daniel says, and the word burrows into my chest, feeding on the ache there. I can't take it. I can't watch them together for one second longer.

"Well, I guess it's obvious who the girl is, Danielle," I say, and I don't know why exactly I'm so set on provoking him.

Sam and I saw some stupid movie when we were kids where all the boys get turned into girls when a magic spell goes awry and, for a few months, thought it was hysterical to call each other girl versions of our names. Sam was Samantha, I was Colleen, Brian was Brianna, and Daniel was Danielle.

Pop did not think it was funny. And later, after Daniel told us he was gay, Brian started calling him Danielle again. Not even really to be mean. More… immature. But when Pop heard him do it, he was furious. He slapped Brian in the face and told him never to call Daniel that again.

Sure enough, Daniel lunges at me. I don't even try and fight him, just let his punches connect. Goddamn Rex pulls Daniel off me before he can do any real damage, though.

"Fuck!" Daniel yells, and I want to say the same thing. Because when Daniel slams out the door like the sulky little bitch he is, he takes my distraction with him.

Rex lingers for a moment after Daniel leaves. When I look up, his eyes are fixed on me.

"He's your fucking brother," Rex says.

And he follows Daniel out the door. Two more people who can't wait to get away from me.

I KNOW what I have to do. There's only one thing that will make me feel better that isn't bourbon or the blade.

The phone rings four, five, six times, and I'm sure he's not going to pick up. Why would he after what I said to him?

But then he's there, and I almost can't believe it. I was so sure he wouldn't answer that I didn't even consider what I would say if he did.

"Rafe?" I say. I sound bad. Shaky.

"Colin," he says, and hearing it makes my throat so tight I can barely talk.

"Rafe, I… can you come over?" I manage, cringing at the words.

"Are you in trouble?"

There's tension in his voice and I can imagine what he's thinking. That I'm bad news. That all he ever does is help me.

He sighs. "Have you been drinking?"

"I—"

"Tell me the truth, please."

"Yeah," I whisper.

"Are you sure it's me you need?"

I almost laugh, because though he sounds like he thinks he's laying down some truth, it's pathetic how much I need him.

"Please, Rafe. Could you…?" I look at the clock. It's before nine. Not too late. "Do you think you could come over? I won't drink anymore, I swear."

I don't know what I'm going to do if he says no. My stomach and chest are so tight that I don't even notice I'm crouching on the floor, hunched around the phone, until he answers. The pause is interminable.

"Okay."

It's not enthusiastic, but it's there.

"Thank you," I say. "Thank you. I'm sorr—"

"I'll be there in thirty minutes. We'll talk then."

I take a shower and brush my teeth until my gums bleed, then put on clean sweats and drink some water, trying to sober up before he arrives.

He knocks on the door exactly thirty minutes after we got off the phone.

I feel a momentary surge of hope just looking at him, but it's immediately extinguished by the memory of the last time we were here and the things we said.

The second Rafe shuts the door, Shelby comes galloping over and climbs him like a tree, licking his cheek and butting her little head against his neck. He's caught off guard and laughs for a moment. She's so glad to see him it makes me sick. I haven't done right by either of them.

"Rafe, I—"

Rafe closes the distance between us in two steps.

"What happened?" he demands. The second he touches me, my throat gets thick. He takes me by the elbow and leads me to the couch, sitting next to me. He puts Shelby in my lap, but she jumps off immediately.

"She hates me," I say.

Rafe runs a hand through his hair and sighs. "She doesn't hate you."

"Pop died." Rafe freezes. "And Daniel's here."

"What happened?" Rafe takes my hand between his, and it's like a dam breaks with his touch. I'm not even really drunk anymore, just exhausted. Tired of hurting and tired of being afraid. Tired of trying to be without Rafe and tired of not being what he needs. Just so fucking tired. My eyes blur with tears, and I squeeze his hand so hard it's probably painful.

"I'm sorry," I mutter. "Please don't hate me. Please."

His arms come around me hesitantly, and he strokes lightly up and down my spine. I don't even have the energy to be embarrassed that I'm crying. I just want to feel something other than the choking fear of this creeping darkness.

Rafe sighs. "I don't hate you," he says softly. "I was upset before. Angry, yeah. But I never hated you." He brushes his fingertips over my lips and up into my hair. "What happened with your dad?"

"He had a heart attack in the shop. Day before yesterday. He died in the hospital. I… I'm all…. I don't know…." I shake my head. I've wanted to talk to Rafe every day for two weeks, but now that he's here, I barely have the energy to speak. I just want to be near him. "Can you forgive me? I said fucking awful things. I didn't even mean them."

His expression is serious but he doesn't seem angry. "Are you sure you didn't mean them?"

I cast my mind back, desperately trying to remember everything I said. It's hard after I spent two weeks shying away from every thought of them.

"What I said about Javier. I'm sorry for that. The rest... I guess I... I guess I probably did mean it, but I didn't mean to say it so awful."

Rafe nods and squeezes my shoulder. "Me too. I meant what I said, but I said it all wrong. I'm sorry for that. Let's not worry about it right now. We'll talk about it later. Okay?"

I nod, intensely relieved that there will *be* a later. Rafe leans in slowly, stroking my lips with his thumb. I kiss his thumb and his mouth goes all soft. He moves his thumb to brush my cheek and kisses me softly.

"Will you stay? Please. The funeral's tomorrow morning. I just—" Fuck, I just really don't want to be alone.

Rafe stands up, pulling me with him like I weigh nothing, and touches under my eyes. "Looks like you could use some sleep."

He's stripped down to his underwear before I realize I'm just standing by the bedroom door, staring at him. He's like a luxury car: everything's perfectly balanced, his lines are beautiful, powerful. He's... he's fucking beautiful.

"You coming in here?" he asks, lifting the covers.

I nod. "Lemme just brush my teeth." I don't want even the slightest taste of beer to linger if Rafe's going to kiss me again.

In the bathroom, I risk a glance in the mirror. Dark circles are under my eyes, which look almost violet from the redness of crying, like an old bruise. There's an actual bruise on my cheek from where Daniel hit me earlier. My hair is the longest it's been since high school and it's a mess. I've only seen myself with a buzz cut for so long. I look like a different person with it longer. Softer, maybe.

When I slide under the covers with Rafe, he plucks at my hood. "You're sweating."

I kick off my sweatpants and pull my sweatshirt over my head, feeling better when the cold air from the open window hits me. My landlord sets the heat way too high.

"You not been eating?" Rafe traces my collarbone with his finger. "I dunno."

His gaze immediately goes to the cuts on my chest and he runs a finger over them, jaw tight.

"It's been bad," he says, and I nod, closing my eyes. He leans over me and presses a kiss to the cuts on my chest. "Okay."

He pushes the blanket all the way off so he can look at me. He runs a finger over the scratches Shelby left on my arm, and I throw my other arm over my eyes. There are warm kisses on my stomach and my hipbones. Hair brushing my thighs.

Looking down my body in the light from the window, I can see that he's right. I have lost weight. My stomach muscles are almost cartoonishly defined and my hipbones jut unhealthily beneath them. The muscles of my thighs are tight, but my knees look knobby and too big. I've never liked the way I look, but at least I've always felt strong, ever since the summer before high school, when I started lifting weights. Now, though—god, I look a mess. I move to pull the covers up so Rafe doesn't have to look at me.

He lets me pull them up, but he keeps a hand on my stomach, stroking gently. He kisses my cheek, then rolls onto his back next to me, relaxing into the mattress.

"Who hit you?"

"What? Oh. Daniel." Rafe tenses. "I deserved it."

He shakes his head but I guess he's not going to fight me on that right now. I turn over and rest my cheek against his shoulder, wanting to absorb as much of his presence as I can before the inevitable moment when he leaves.

"I was terrible to him. I just—I don't know why he makes me so mad. Even when he doesn't do anything. He—I look at him and I...." I shake my head. "And he brought this guy. His boyfriend. They were standing there, in Pop's living room. Like it was nothing. Like, now that he's gone, Daniel can—fuck, I don't know, man."

Rafe runs his hand along my ribs. When he speaks his voice is gentle. "Maybe you get so mad at Daniel because he gets to have something you don't."

"I mean, his boyfriend's handsome and all, in a lumberjack-y way, but you're way hotter."

I can feel Rafe's smile. "I mean that Daniel gets to be honest about who he is and who he cares about to his brothers. He accepted the consequences of the truth and he told it anyway." The words cut, but Rafe wraps his arm around me, pressing me against him, and kisses my temple. "I think sometimes the people we get angriest with are the ones who have the things we want the most."

"So, then, who do you get angriest with?"

He rubs my back, shifting me closer against him. "My sister," he says finally.

"Gabriela?"

He shakes his head. "Luz."

"But I thought you guys got along really well?"

"We do. But when she calls me to fix something for her or she wants me to give her advice…. It's not that I mind fixing things for her. I don't. And I like that she wants my advice."

"So… what, then?"

"I guess I'm jealous that she has me to go to," Rafe says slowly, like he's still thinking it through.

"You mean you're jealous because you want… yourself?"

"No. Well, yes. I'm jealous that she has me to call because I know that I'll always be there for her, and I…. That's what I want. Someone I know will always be there for me."

His voice sounds smaller than I've ever heard it, and it puts a lump in my throat.

"My sisters are there for me. I know that. But they have their own lives. They have kids. They're not…." He shakes his head again, dismissing the subject. "So, the funeral's tomorrow?"

"Yeah."

"Do you want me to come?"

My heart starts to race. I don't want to fight again, but I… I just can't deal with worrying about Brian and Sam asking questions about who Rafe is, and I—

"Hey," Rafe says, "calm down. I'm not trying to fight. I'll be there if you want me there. If you don't, I won't. It's as simple as that."

I nod. "I want you there," I say. "But I can't…."

"Okay," he says. "It's okay."

All I can do is nod. I throw an arm over his chest, hoping we can stop talking. Rafe rubs my back, and I twine strands of his hair around my fingers. It's the kind of wavy it gets when he braids it wet from the shower.

After a while, I kiss his neck and slide my hand down his chest to his stomach. I feel his intake of breath, and his hand tightens on my back. With a hand on his cheek, I turn him to me so I can reach his mouth. The kiss feels so right—familiar and warm—and I deepen it.

Rafe turns on his side so we're facing each other and kisses me, softly at first, then more urgently. This. This is what I need. I need to forget everything except the feeling of Rafe against me, his mouth on mine, his hair between my fingers, his hands on my skin.

"Rafe," I murmur into the kiss. "Please. I need...."

"What?" He strokes my cheek. "Anything."

"You—I... I need you."

I try to pull him on top of me, needing to feel that he's really here. "Yeah?"

I nod. He's studying my face, and I try with every last bit of energy I have to show him how much I want him. How much I need this.

"Okay," he breathes, and relief rushes through me.

"You're so handsome," he says, kissing my neck. I snort, and he covers my mouth with his fingers and goes on. "I didn't think about it until the kids started talking about it, but I can see what they mean." He runs a finger down my cheek, over my chin, down the bridge of my nose, and over my eyebrows. "I watched the show. *Supernatural*. Last week." He looks a little embarrassed at this confession. "I was missing you and... anyway, I see the resemblance."

He kisses me before I can argue with him, sliding a hand under my neck to control the kiss. It's hot and hard and I pull him down on top of me. My exhaustion evaporates, replaced by need. Our hands are everywhere as we kiss. Rafe is like a tornado and I meet it with everything I have, until we're straining together, sweaty and shaking. Until I'm obliterated. Gone.

SOMEHOW LAST night with Rafe, I forgot everything. I forgot that Pop is dead. I forgot that, in the last few months of his life, I didn't even notice anything was wrong because I barely saw him. I forgot that he died terrified and alone in a room of doctors. I forgot that I'll never see him again, that I'll never have the chance to earn his respect or... or.... But now it all comes rushing back.

Brian is a mess when I pick him up. He's in Pop's bed, eyes red and clothes stinking of beer. We meet Liza and Sam at the cemetery, and after a few minutes, Daniel walks over slowly, Rex at his side. They both look put together and pressed. Daniel doesn't even look sad. His green eyes are clear, and though he's a little pale, he mostly looks impatient, as if this is all just an inconvenience to him.

And with him is Ginger, his best friend. The two of them put their heads together, and when Ginger says something, Daniel looks over at me with a half smile on his face. As if it's not bad enough that Ginger told Daniel about my tattoo, it looks like they're laughing about it. I'm still furious with myself for going to her to ask about getting it covered up in the first place. She was the only female tattoo artist I could think of, and it seemed less embarrassing than having another man see the butterfly. My stomach clenches.

During the funeral, I can't look away from the coffin. Pop's coffin. The words being said about Pop don't matter. This guy didn't know him.

Hell, I'm not sure that I knew him. I wrack my brain, trying to think of things I know about him.

I could read his mood, sure, since it was necessary to surviving in his house. Tell when he was pissed off and I should leave him alone. When he was in a good mood and I could approach. When he wanted to teach me something and when he wanted me to figure it out for myself. I know what beer he liked, and what rum. I know which teams he rooted for and which radio stations he listened to. I know his socket wrench of choice and which brand of oil he'd recommend to a customer.

Yet I can't think of a single other thing about him.

And he didn't really know me either, did he?

I'm shaking with cold and nausea as they turn the crank that lowers Pop into the ground. I wrap my arms around my stomach, trying to keep from puking. Trying to pretend that they're Rafe's arms around me, like they were when I woke up this morning. Even though I'm the one who told him not to come, everything in me cries out for him.

As the coffin sinks deeper and deeper into the earth, something dark inside me follows it down. I can't stop the tears from coming no matter how hard I try to squeeze my eyes shut against them.

Rex is holding Daniel tight against his side, and an uncontrollable fury rips through me at the sight. I think about what Rafe said, that my anger is really desire for what he has. And I nearly double over with pain when I realize he's right.

Because I haven't just lost Pop. I've lost the chance to ever know for sure. To know if Pop would still love me if he knew the truth about me.

I did everything he ever wanted. I worked with him on the cars he loved. I advertised the shop and put together our website. I made sure Brian kept on the straight and narrow at work and didn't let Sam turn into a corporate douchebag. I lived nearby and drank with him, watched sports with him, went to baseball games with him even though I hate baseball. I did everything he wanted, lived the life he wanted for me, and I still don't know. I don't know if one simple confession—a confession Daniel made at sixteen—would have changed everything.

And now I'll never have the chance to find out.

Daniel's leaning into Rex and staring off into space the way he does when he's pretending to be somewhere else. It's an expression he's worn since he was about thirteen years old. When he decided he didn't care about us anymore. When he decided we were too stupid, too low-class, too crude to want anything to do with us.

After, Luther hugs me and I practically throw up. I don't want anyone to touch me. I don't want to talk to anyone. I just need to get out of here. I need something that isn't dark and foul and miserable. I stumble away from my brothers, from the pile of dirt covering Pop. I don't know where I'm going, just that I need to get out of sight so I can lose it. I fumble with my phone, but my hands are shaking too hard and I drop it on the wet ground.

"Fuck!"

I pick it up, but before I can dial it, I hear my name and look up, confused, to see Rafe coming toward me.

"Hey," I croak, and he catches me before I stumble.

"Oh, babe," he murmurs and wraps me in his arms. He guides me into some kind of storage shed, leans against the wall, and pulls me to him.

"It's okay." He's talking low, saying soothing stuff I'm not listening to because all I can do is clutch at his shirt and try not to shake apart.

"Tighter," I say, and he squeezes me so tight it's almost painful. But I start to calm down a bit. Stop shaking so much. Breathe. "Rafe, I don't even know if he would—if he'd known that I'm—that I—that we—I just—I don't even know if he would—fuck!"

"Colin," Rafe says softly, and I look up at him. "I'm sorry. I'm so sorry."

I nod. There's nothing else to say. And there's nothing I can do. I missed my chance. I just have to try and live with that.

Rafe is warm and solid, and I can almost pretend we're back in my bed, waking up slowly as Shelby pads over our legs.

Suddenly, Rafe freezes, and I turn around to see what startled him, blinking away tears in the dim light.

When I see Daniel, every muscle in my body tenses. Rafe's hand is still on my shoulder, but I am a tiny, cringing thing alone in the universe.

"Holy fucking…," Daniel mutters, staring between Rafe and me. I can see the exact moment he realizes what's going on. He drops into a crouch, like the force of his surprise drives him downward, elbows on his knees, looking up at me in shock.

I see my hand reach out toward Daniel as if it's not even attached to me. My whole arm is shaking, and Daniel looks like he's about to crumble.

"Look, Dan," I say as he stands back up. My voice doesn't even sound like my own, and before I can get any words out, he launches himself at me.

"You fucking *liar*," he screams, grabbing my coat and pulling me closer to him.

For the briefest second, his anger doesn't register and I think he's going to hug me. Even when he starts hitting me, I can't quite make sense of it. Because it's not just anger. It's something that seems like… grief. But Daniel doesn't care about me. I can't believe he even cares enough to hit me. Sure, he gets angry and wants to fight when I start shit with him. But I didn't even do anything.

I only realize Daniel's crying when I hit the dirt and he lands on top of me, his tears dropping onto my face as he punches me. He's practically screaming. I shake off my surprise enough get in a few hits, but he is powered by some kind of unholy rage. For the first time, I see that all those feelings that make him so easy to read, when pushed further, have power.

He slams my shoulders to the ground and chokes me with his forearm. I jab him in the kidney, the mouth, the stomach. And then we're just wrestling. I'm trying to get Daniel off me without hurting him too bad, but he's trying to do real damage. His fist slams into my mouth just before he's pulled off me, still screaming that I'm a liar.

It's Rex dragging Daniel backward, holding him tight as Daniel shakes with anger.

I pull myself up and blood splatters the dirt floor when I spit. I concentrate on it so I don't have to look at Daniel's face. At my little brother's face so contorted with grief that I know I've made a huge miscalculation in thinking he didn't care.

"I—I—please, Danny," I say. I haven't called him that since he was a kid. Since I was the one he'd come to in the middle of the night when nightmares about Mom's death woke him. Since we'd sing along to the radio together and I'd walk him to school. Since he used to look up at me with something like admiration, the only person to ever look at me like that.

"Don't fucking call me that, you fucking *liar*," Daniel yells, his voice just a scratch, and the only thing that keeps him from launching himself at me again is Rex holding him back.

"But," I try, "can I—"

"How *could* you?" Daniel croaks out. Tears are running down his cheeks and his eyelashes are spiky with moisture, just like they were when he was that little boy. He's looking at me like he used to when I stomped on his sandcastles at the beach. Anger, shock, betrayal.

I'm underwater again. I can't breathe, and this time, I don't want to. Then his face changes to the expression I'm more familiar with. Scorn. He just shakes his head at me like I'm nothing. Like I've failed to live up to his standards so completely that he can't even think what to do with me.

He turns to leave and a new panic grips me.

"Dan," I choke out. "Don't tell Brian and Sam. Please. Please," I whisper. Tears are running down my face, and I can't even lift my hand to wipe them away. For a second when he turns around, something nasty flickers in Daniel's eyes, and I feel a flash of relief. Relief that Daniel's as petty as I thought. Relief that if he hurts me, then it means, for once, maybe I'm not the worst one.

Relief that the choice is being taken out of my hands.

But then he takes a deep breath and his shoulders droop, the victim once again. He nods once and closes his eyes like maybe he can forget I ever existed. Rex follows him out, as close on his heels as a shadow.

"Oh god," I choke. I stumble to the doorway of the shed and gag, throwing up the toast Rafe made for me this morning. Then I'm just dry heaving and gagging.

The world has narrowed to a single drop of blood that fell on the dirt from my nose as I puked. It's an ocean, trying to swallow me up. And I want to let it.

"I wish I was dead," I whisper, too soft for anyone to hear, and Rafe's hands on me falter.

Chapter 11

THE GRAY of the ocean is one shade darker than the sky. The waves roll in, crash, and pull back in an endless rhythm. It's like as long as the outside is moving, then things inside me can stay still. The sound of the ocean is so constant that everything we say sounds softer here, makes me feel tipsy or sun-drunk.

We're in Ocean City, on the Maryland coast. I hardly remember getting here. After the funeral, Rafe packed a bag for me, grabbed Shelby's litter box, and put us in the car. Then he just drove and I slept.

The house was Javier's and he left it to Rafe when he died. It's right on the beach, up on stilts so that you take stairs up from the entrance to the first floor high off the ground. A kitchen and breakfast room open onto a large deck that looks out over the ocean. Upstairs is a master bedroom that also looks out on the ocean and a small front bedroom with windows out onto the tourist town of Ocean City: donut shops, fried fish and chicken restaurants, tiki bars, and bowling alleys that are all deserted in the winter.

On every side table are arrangements of shells that seem too perfect to have come from the beach outside, smooth stones that sparkle with mica, and coasters printed with starfish and sand dollars. In the bathrooms are dishes of small blue and green and pink soaps in the shapes of shells that have never been used and towels with beach umbrellas embroidered at the hems. Paintings of palm trees and herons in seashell-crusted frames are scattered around the walls of the breakfast room. The trivets look like they've had shells pressed into them to leave imprints, and there are vases in the corners filled with tall, stalky grasses.

The bedspread in the master bedroom is striped in shades of blue like the ocean and the sheets are the color of the sand on the beach outside. Last night as I fell asleep, I imagined that I was lying on the beach and the blanket was the ocean slowly covering me, pulling me into its dark.

Rafe ordered pizza, and though I can taste it, I can't remember eating it. He's talking about Javier, and I don't know if I asked him a question or not. Then I realize he's talking so I don't have to. To distract me.

He tells me how Javier bought this place with his partner before the area was developed. When the beach was empty. How he'd tease Clive for the way he decorated: like the beach took a shit in the house. How Javier brought Rafe out here and it was the most peaceful place he'd ever been.

How the ocean makes him feel small. "You look out over the ocean and you know that the water you're seeing, no matter how far out you look, is only the very edge. It's like space or something. Scary big. It's kind of strange to know you're only experiencing the very outside of something. All those kids in the summer, wave-jumping, swimming, surfing in the sun. They're just playing on the very edge of this giant monster. But I like it. The sense that there's something bigger than me that connects me to someone far away, on the other side, looking out over the water thousands of miles from here, from a totally different place, living a completely different life."

It's how I think about cars sometimes. That I have a hand in something that someone is going to drive far away, into another life.

Rafe's arms slide around my waist from behind and he rests his chin on my shoulder, squeezing me. For a moment, I think the rushing in my ears is a sign I'm feeling woozy, but it's just the waves outside, ever-present, even with Rafe's breath in my ear.

"How are you doing?" Rafe asks softly, and the sympathy in his voice is almost painful.

I shrug and his arms tighten around me, holding me up when I sag back into him.

"COLIN! COLIN! God damn it!"

I'm wrenched around and yanked against Rafe's chest. He's squeezing my wrists hard enough to bruise but I don't even feel it.

"What the fuck are you doing?" Rafe shakes me, looking down into my face fiercely.

"I—I'm—nothing."

The lightening sky is white and the ocean is gray, the world like a black-and-white picture.

Rafe shakes his head, teeth gritted and jaw clenched. He drops his forehead down on my shoulder, shaking.

"Come in. It's freezing out here."

The sand coats my wet feet as we walk out of the ocean and up the beach onto the deck. I'm shaking with cold, my feet and legs numb. Rafe tries to brush the wet sand off of them but only succeeds in getting it all over his hands.

Finally, he just pulls me inside and upstairs, stripping off my underwear and T-shirt and shoving me into the shower. He takes off his coat and the flannel pants and T-shirt he was sleeping in, and steps under the water with me. If I close my eyes, I can almost pretend that the too-hot water pouring down on me is the too-cold water I was wading into. Rafe's arms are wrapped around me and he's murmuring something in my ear, but I can't hear it because the shower is even louder than the ocean.

He dries me off like I'm a kid or a stray dog and wraps me in the bedclothes. The ceiling is that weird stucco that looks like someone bounced a ball into it while it was wet, leaving little smacks of texture. We lie there in silence for I don't know how long.

When Rafe finally speaks, his voice is tight, weary.

"You could've died," he says to the ceiling.

I shake my head, the sound of my hair scratching the pillow almost deafening.

"Oh, you don't think so?" Rafe goes up on one elbow and turns to look at me. "You walked into the ocean in December in your fucking underwear, Colin!"

He smacks the bed with his palm and slumps back onto the bed, hands fisted over his eyes.

"Is that what you want?" he asks softly.

"Hm?"

"To kill yourself. Is that where we are? Because that's something I need to know."

I laugh nervously.

In the month after Maya and her father came to Pop's house and they all agreed we'd get married because of the baby, I tried to kill myself twice. Kind of. Is there a word for just not trying very hard to avoid ceasing to exist? It was more like that. The life I could imagine for myself, Maya, and a kid, was just a yawning blackness, so I may as well have wandered into another kind of blackness. An easier one. One without responsibilities and expectations that filled me with hopeless panic. There were the nights I walked alone in places I knew I shouldn't, or went to parties and drank so much I blacked out, or shoved down my throat or up my nose whatever pill, paper, or powder was passed to me.

Then there were the other times.

There was the time I walked along the train tracks after football practice, still shaky from running sprints, and stood with my back to an oncoming train, the shudder of the rails growing stronger and stronger through the soles of my sneakers, the whistle finally startling me off the track almost against my will, where I stumbled down the rocky slope and retched.

There was the time I looped Brian's ratty Eagles scarf over the bar in my closet and tied it around my neck. When Pop asked how the bar broke, I told him I was trying to do chin-ups, and he smacked me for thinking it would hold my weight.

WHEN I wake up, it's dark. I find Rafe in the kitchen staring out the glass door at the beach, a bowl of cooked spaghetti next to an unopened jar of sauce on the counter.

"Pop used to always make spaghetti when we were kids," I say as I pour the cold sauce on the noodles.

Rafe fills his own bowl and sits on the stool next to mine, but he doesn't touch the food. "The night we met," he says. "That wasn't the first time I saw you at The Cellar."

I eat without tasting the food.

"People talked about you, you know."

"What?"

"The pretty guy who wanted to get the shit beaten out of him. They said they thought you got off on it. Like a fantasy of getting jumped or something."

I shake my head. Everything feels fuzzy and confused, and that damn ocean sound, like the rushing in my ears, makes everything feel unreal.

"Yeah, I didn't think it was a fantasy." He looks down at his hands, twisted together in his lap. "You looked so damned miserable. And now that I know you...." He leans toward me so I have to look at him. His brow is furrowed and his eyes are sympathetic. "I don't expect you to be okay. But I need to know where you are. I can't worry every time I close my eyes or leave to get food that I'm going to come back and find you dead. So if that's where you are, I can handle it, but I need to know it."

"I wasn't—I didn't mean…. I don't know what happened. This morning. I didn't—I just remember you being there, but I don't know…."

"Okay." After a long silence, he says, "Is there anything I can do to help?"

Which is ridiculous, because all he's done since we met is help me. Here we are in this beach house, far away from the grime of the city, and he's been helping me with everything. I gesture around us helplessly, trying to convey this, but Rafe catches my hand and holds it between his.

"You make it better," I murmur, but I don't meet his eyes. If I knew what would help—if I *ever* knew what would really help—I'd do it.

"Maybe you need a distraction." He runs a hand up my neck and squeezes. "Just something to focus on." His thumb brushes my mouth.

It would sound like a cheesy pickup line if Rafe weren't looking at me like he'd turn himself inside out to make me feel better.

"Okay," I say against his thumb.

"Leave that," he says as I start to put my bowl in the sink.

Rafe runs a bath, tipping something into it that looks like the rock salt we use on the sidewalk outside the shop when it's icy. He helps me ease into the steaming water. It's warm and relaxing, but I feel silly with him just sitting on the closed toilet seat, watching me. He's probably afraid I'll try and drown myself in the bathtub or something if he leaves. I reach out a hand trying to indicate that he should get in, but it's not really big enough.

He sits on the floor next to the tub, pulls off his sweater, and dips a hand into the bathwater, then trails his fingers up my arm. The only light comes from the lamp in the bedroom.

"Close your eyes. Just relax."

I'm worried he's going to leave, but he keeps his hand on my shoulder, and every time the water starts to cool a little, he lets some out and adds hot. I must doze off for a minute because when I wake up to the sound of the ocean and the sensation of water it takes Rafe's hand sliding gently under my neck to figure out where I am.

"Ready to get out, or you want to stay a little longer?"

I shrug.

"Stay right there for a few minutes."

I hear him moving around in the bedroom and then he's back, holding a large towel open and helping me out of the tub. As Rafe helps me to the bed, my movements are so sluggish it feels like I'm still in the water.

Rafe kisses me slow and liquid, his hand on my hip. If he wants to distract me with sex, I'm happy to go with it, but when I try and pull him down on top of me to deepen the kiss, he eases back, just kissing me like we have all the time in the world.

I'm not even turned on, really. Just warm and relaxed, like after I've run until I can't run anymore. Rafe lies down next to me, and I turn on my side to face him. His hair is a mess—tangled from the wind outside probably—and I work the knots out as he kisses me, leaving it soft around his face. It sticks in stubble I haven't shaved since before the funeral.

Rafe's jeans and T-shirt are rough against my water-softened skin, and I tug at them. He pulls his shirt off slowly, the lamplight behind him turning his torso into a sculpture. He comes back down to me naked and kisses me deeply.

"I love how you taste," he says against my mouth.

"I probably taste like spaghetti sauce."

He presses my shoulders back down to the mattress, and something warm and dark unspools in my gut. As long as Rafe's in charge, I can't fuck up.

"Just let me touch you," he says. "I want to." I nod. He kisses my ear, my neck, the hollow of my throat.

Then he has my hips tilted up and my thighs spread while I'm still lost in the feel of his tongue tracing my jaw.

He slides fingers down the crease of my ass and around my hole, watching me, then sliding inside. Every touch of his fingers inside me makes me crave more. When he leans in and kisses my open mouth, he looks mesmerized.

"You love this," he says. "Me inside you. Filling you. Opening you up."

I can't speak for the sudden wave of lust that washes over me when he talks like that. Says out loud the things that I could never express. Would never say. And I don't have to say anything because he just keeps kissing my mouth and my neck, his fingers trailing fire inside me.

Then he pulls away and my eyes fly open. "No!" I say, trying to grab his wrist.

"I'm just getting lube," he says, but I shake my head and pull him back. He fucks me with his fingers, and every few thrusts he curls them and pleasure slams through me. "God, you're so beautiful like this. The way your body just lets me in. Fuck," he groans, dropping his head onto my chest, stilling for a moment while he takes a deep breath.

He kisses down my stomach and scrapes his teeth over my hipbone, and I curl into the sharpness of his mouth.

Rafe buries his face in my crotch, breathing me in, kissing and sucking at the crease where my thigh meets my groin and the base of my dick. Everything feels like it's happening in slow motion. Like every minute his mouth is on me unfolds to hours and all I can do is lie here, caught perfectly between his hot mouth and his fingers inside me.

It should be impossible to be this relaxed and this turned on at the same time, but I keep spacing out even though I'm aware of the physical sensations.

One night, weeks ago now, Rafe and I woke in the middle of the night and brought each other off in the dark, both half-asleep, our legs entwined and his hair in my face. I feel almost like that now. Dreamy and liquid. This time, though, Rafe's focus is intense and everything about him is urging me to be open to him. To let him do as he pleases. It's a heady feeling and one that still makes me cringe if I think about it.

I let out a shaky sigh, and Rafe groans into the crease of my thigh. "I love this," he murmurs.

"Don't stop," I choke out. "Please." Rafe licks up my dick, swirling his tongue around the head. His hair tickles my stomach, and his mouth is a tease of heat I try to chase, pressing my hips up, desperate for more contact, craning my neck to watch my erection slide between Rafe's lips. He looks at me, hair falling around his face, dark eyes soft, and it goes right to my gut.

Then he starts to move more quickly, and I drop back onto the bed, unable to focus on anything but his hot mouth and his fingers inside me and the bloom of pleasure that opens me up and breaks me apart. Little spasms start deep inside, where Rafe's fingers stroke into me. Bolts of sensation zing from my balls to my dick. Then it's huge, my entire body clenching. My mouth is locked open as the heat of orgasm washes through my groin, my belly, my thighs. Shudders of pleasure tear through me, and my ass contracts around Rafe's fingers as I spill into his mouth.

Rafe moans, and I feel his muscles tighten as he jerks himself off.

Then his hand is on my cheek, his lips on mine. He whispers something but I don't make sense of it because I'm too blitzed to think.

Everything else has melted away. The only problem in the whole world right now is that I'm cold and I want Rafe wrapped around me.

I try and lift my arm to pull him down, but I can't coordinate the movement. Rafe's thumb brushes the corners of my eyes and I can feel the moisture there.

"What's wrong, sweetheart?"

It feels like I'm held in a cloud, everything soft and fuzzy. But it could evaporate at any moment, leaving me in free fall.

"Cold," I finally get out.

We're lying on top of the covers, but Rafe flips the edge of the blanket from the other side of the bed over us. We lie like that for a minute, Rafe stroking my face. Loneliness shoots through me even though he's right there, and I start to shake. Then I start to cry. Then I'm sobbing and Rafe wraps himself around me, murmuring nonsense.

THE NEXT week passes like a dream. We wander along the beach, nap, and eat. But something's different. I feel calm in a way I never have before. Like the moment I'm in is bearable. I don't know how long it will last, but I'm clinging to it while it does.

This morning when we woke up, Rafe told me my brothers have left me a bunch of voice mail messages. I didn't notice that I hadn't seen my phone in a while, but I guess he's seen the calls come through.

I try to work up the nerve to listen to the messages. I bet Sam's going to rip me a new one for missing Pop's wake. And I can already hear Brian's confused voice, hurt because he doesn't know where I am. There are dozens of missed calls from both Sam and Brian and the messages I expected, Sam sounding increasingly irritated and Brian more and more hurt.

It never occurred to me that Rafe meant Daniel, too.

But after Sam's and Brian's are two messages I didn't expect. From Daniel.

"Hi, Colin," Daniel says as if he were actually talking to me instead of leaving a message. "I'm so angry with you because you cheated me out of a brother. I don't understand why you never told me. I mean, I can think of lots of reasons, but I don't know what yours was. No matter what it was, though, I think it sucks. I think it sucks that you let me think I was alone in this, when I wasn't. I wasn't, was I, Colin?"

Then from last night, "Colin, it's Daniel. Look, I'm mad at you, but I still want to talk to you, okay? I want to know what the fuck's going on with you. Why were you so horrified when you found out I was gay? Because I know you weren't faking that. You wanted to kill Buddy when you found us together. I just want to know why. Please call me back, okay?"

Rafe sinks down next to me. "What's up?"

"I think… I think he really didn't tell them."

"Daniel?"

I nod.

"What did he say?"

"He's mad. He, um, he doesn't get why I was upset he's gay since I—" I shake my head and drop the phone onto the end table. Rafe takes my hand in his and kisses my palm.

"I just…," I start, but I can't pull my thoughts together. I play Daniel's messages over again in my mind. He sounded genuine. Not pissy, just… hurt. "I just don't get why he cares, I guess. He hasn't cared about my opinion since we were kids."

"Are you sure?" Rafe asks in that way where he makes me really, really think about it.

And I just don't know.

Rafe's kiss tastes like cinnamon.

"So, listen," he says, handing me a bowl of cereal. He runs a hand through his hair. "My mom." He looks up sheepishly. "She'll kill me if I don't show up for Christmas."

I must look as confused as I feel because Rafe says, "It's the day after tomorrow."

"Oh. Shit, man, you should've said something."

Rafe sits back down next to me, and Shelby, who has been staring out at the ocean, mesmerized, starts eyeing my cereal from her place on the floor.

"I am saying something," he says, turning me to face him. "I'd rather be with you than watch the monsters tear into their presents and then complain about what they didn't get."

I didn't even think about Christmas. Christmas without Pop... that's... I can't imagine what we'd do. The idea of going back to Philly and sitting in that house with Brian and Sam, watching sports and getting drunk while we... I don't know what we'd do. We never did much for Christmas anyway.

One year, when Daniel was ten or eleven, he asked Pop if we could get a tree and make Christmas cookies. It sounded kind of nice. Not that any of us would've known how to make cookies. But a tree seemed okay. Pop looked so pissed. And guilty. I could tell what he was thinking. That he took care of us—cooked and gave us money for clothes and shit—and Daniel was pointing out this way that he'd failed as a father. I couldn't stand the look on Pop's face, like he was worried he was doing everything wrong, so I just laid into Daniel, telling him only girls baked Christmas cookies and trees were for snotty Rittenhouse shitheads who have nothing better to do than sit around and stare at them.

Daniel's face fell, then his lip started to quiver, then his eyebrows wrinkled, and he walked away before he started to cry. Pop clapped me on the shoulder in thanks and Daniel never mentioned anything about Christmas again.

Rafe's looking at me, concerned.

"You'd be welcome at Gabriela's," he says.

I shake my head. The last thing I want is to meet Rafe's family when I feel like this.

"I just... I know I said I'd meet them, but I'd be lousy company right now," I say.

"I understand. Another time."

"I—do you think...? Never mind."

"What?"

"Could I maybe... stay here? Over Christmas? I just don't think I can handle my brothers right now."

A flicker of fear passes over Rafe's face, and I know he's thinking about the other morning in the ocean. But he takes a deep breath and nods.

"Yeah, you could do that. I don't like to think of you alone on Christmas, though."

I bump his shoulder with mine. "I don't care about Christmas. I'll be fine."

I RUN until my legs shake, then sink down into the cold sand and look out at the water. It smells clean and wet, and the waves drown out my panting breaths. It's like running along the edge of the world. Mostly, it's the sound I like. The way it covers things up. My shitty breathing and my stupid thoughts.

There's this one thought that's rattling around, though. This one thought that the waves can't quite drown out. It was there when I woke up a few days ago. Rafe's arms were around me, his face tucked into the crook of my neck, and I was too comfortable to move. I stared out at the sun rising over the water and it was just… there.

I'm free.

I'd almost fallen back asleep when Rafe shifted in his sleep, pulling me to him like a stuffed animal. He fumbled for my hand and held on and I just smiled. I didn't have to get up and go to work. Didn't have to pretend anything with anyone. Didn't have to worry about how to act because Rafe already liked me, god help him.

I fell back asleep pretty soon after that, but over the next few days, it kept popping up.

Now, without Rafe to pay attention to, it's back. *I'm free.* Pop is dead and I feel shitty about it, but also, for the first time, I think… maybe things could really be different. Maybe there's a chance *I* could be different. Feel different.

Back at the house, I pick up my phone to check the time and see an unplayed voice mail from last night.

"Colin," Daniel says, and he sounds freaked. "I have this memory. At least, I think it is. I'm not totally sure it really happened, but… if it did…. It's—it was a snow day at school and I came home early. You were in bed, drunk, and I remember Dad's pills, for his back. Anyway, I remember a lot of them, Colin, and I just. I wanted to make sure—I wanted to see if…. Look, just don't do anything fucking stupid, all right, you asshole? Because I…. Just, please be okay. Okay?"

My heart races. Pop's pills. Buddy…. I know the day he's talking about, though I'd almost forgotten about it until now.

It was the first time. Well, no. I'm not sure I was really trying that time. Mostly, I just wanted the screaming in my head to go away and the only times it did was when I was blaring music, lifting weights until I couldn't think, or out of my mind wasted. That day, music hadn't helped and I lifted until my arms gave out, but it was all still there. I drank as much of Pop's rum as I thought I could get away with, but that didn't help either. I found his pills in the medicine cabinet. He'd slipped a disc a few months before, but he stopped taking them because he said they made him feel like he was going to piss himself.

I don't know if I meant to or not, but once I'd taken the first handful, I climbed into bed and the bottle was just out of reach. I couldn't make myself move enough to grab it, just fell into a dreamless oblivion where things were okay because there was only blackness. I remember Daniel hovering over me, but that's about all. He just did that sometimes.

"WHAT IF it's an emergency?" Rafe asks. He brought his mother's tamales and stories of her arguing with Luz about letting Cam hang out with boys back with him last night.

We're walking down the beach at sunset—Rafe's idea—and I've just ignored a third call from Daniel. I guess I shouldn't have texted him to tell him I'm alive after all. But he sounded so scared in his message.

"I'm never the one Daniel would call if he had an emergency. Besides, he's in Michigan."

Rafe just raises his eyebrows at me, but he gets distracted by the sunset. He seems to have kind of a thing for them.

After dinner, I get Rafe to watch *Cabin in the Woods* with me. He got it at the video store before he went back to Philly and clearly didn't think he'd have to watch it. He's holding Shelby in front of his face to block the movie and then pretending like he's just playing with her.

"You can turn it off," I tell him finally. "I've seen it. I mean, thanks for getting it for me and everything, but you don't have to watch."

"Shit'll give me nightmares," he mutters, but he doesn't turn it off.

WHEN I get out of the shower the next morning, Rafe's sitting on the side of the bed looking guilty as hell. I freeze.

"What?"

"Um." He cuts his eyes to the bedside table, but the only things that're there are my phone and a half-empty glass of water.

"Dude, you're freaking me out," I tell him. "What's going on?"

"I talked to your brother last night. Daniel."

"What? Why?"

"He called at one in the morning, babe, and I just—I was worried. He obviously really wanted to get in touch with you."

"So?"

Rafe reaches out a hand and pulls me to stand between his knees. "He's in Philly. Staying with his friend Ginger. He says he's in town until the day after tomorrow and he'd really like to see you. Talk."

Rafe strokes up and down my sides, then settles his hands on my hips, looking up at me. "He didn't...."

"What?"

"He didn't know where you live."

"Why would he need to know where I live?" I lean away from Rafe, but he grabs my ass and pulls me toward him, pressing his chin to my chest and looking up at me.

"Rafe," I warn.

He sighs. "I told him he should come to your house tomorrow evening so you two could talk."

"What the hell?" I pull away from him, and this time he lets me. Out the window, the ocean pulls itself against the sand again and again like always.

Then Rafe's arms come around me from behind. He rubs his lips against my hair and it drags through his stubble. I should really cut it.

"What are you thinking?" he asks.

A simple question but it seems impossible to answer—like a row of dominos I'll knock over if I touch one. That I've always thought of Philly as home, but the idea of going back makes my heart race and sweat prickle under my arms. That work is the one thing that's always been a constant in my life, and now it's gone. Or different, anyway. That I don't know how we'll keep the shop going without Pop. Will one of us take over as the boss? Do we just go on with it like nothing's changed? Or could we take the opportunity to make some changes? Jesus, what kind of a son thinks of his father's death as a chance to make business decisions? But it's not about the business. Not really. It's the future.

Brian and Sam were horrified when I brought up the idea of taking on different kinds of clients. But was that them, or was it just because they didn't think Pop would like it? Will they feel different now? I don't know. I don't even know how they are. I hope Brian hasn't been sitting around Pop's house all alone. I guess it's his house now. Shit, is the house paid off? I don't know. Does Brian know? He helped pay the bills, but I don't know if he had anything to do with the mortgage. I should ask Sam. But should I—

Rafe spins me around by my shoulders and cups my face so he can see my eyes.

"Tell me what's going on," he says, tapping my temple.

I open my mouth, not sure what's going to come out. "I don't want to leave."

Rafe nods. "I know. You needed to escape for a while—have space to deal with some things." He runs his thumbs over my eyebrows and cheekbones. "I've liked escaping with you," he says softly. "But it's not real. You know that. The real test is whether this feeling can exist side by side with your life." He rubs my shoulders, his voice serious. "You have to ask yourself what you want your life to look like."

I snort out a laugh because he sounds like some kind of shitty self-actualization guru.

"I don't even know what that means," I say. It comes out mocking and short.

But Rafe seems dead serious.

"It means there's nothing noble about handing the reins of your life over to someone else, Colin," he says. He doesn't raise his voice, but there's an edge to it that he gets when he's trying not to snap at me. "You have a chance now, you know? To do something different if that's what you want. To have a different life."

A nervous laugh escapes even though my lips are pressed tight together, and I shake my head. It's kind of like he read my mind.

"Don't laugh at me," Rafe says, voice intense. "You think it's stupid to reinvent yourself? You know what my life would've looked like if I'd taken the one that people were willing to hand me?"

Now he's worked himself up. He starts pacing, long legs eating up the sand-colored carpet. It's like he's hardly even talking to me anymore. He speaks quickly, the words bitten off and full of anger and loathing I've rarely heard from him.

"I was a fucking convict. A criminal. I would've had a minimum-wage job at some shitty fast-food joint. I would've gotten bored, or thought I could make a little more than minimum wage, so I would've started bartending at some thug bar. Little by little I would've gotten so used to seeing people smashed or high, that my sobriety would've felt like too much work. I'd have gone back to using, and when the money I made at the bar wasn't enough, I'd've fallen back in with the guys I used to run with. Doing favors. Enforcing debts. I would've been right back where I started, only worse, because there wouldn't have been any second chances. If I'd gotten picked up, I would've gone to prison for ten years, or fifteen. When I got out, I'd have been a fucking middle-aged loser. Too old to be useful to the gangs or the bars or any-fucking-one. Too hard to be of any use to my family, even if they *had* wanted anything to do with me. My nieces and nephew would've grown up thinking I was a worthless loser. My sisters wouldn't have even mentioned my name. My mother—"

He shakes his head, takes a deep breath, and sinks down onto the side of the bed, looking out at the ocean.

"But that's not what happened," he says like he's trying to soothe himself with the truth of it. "That's not what happened because I met Javi. Because I woke up that first morning after I got out and I thought, *Hey, idiot: no one is going to give you anything good. If you want it, you're going to have to make it happen.* And yeah, because I was so scared of ending up like my fucking father that I wanted to do anything not to abandon my family and run away to something that felt easier."

He takes a deep breath and looks at me. "That's where you are, babe. It's the morning after you got out. You have some decisions to make. And I know it's hard and it's scary as hell, but… the morning after you get out… well, not deciding to make a decision is the same as making the decision not to change your life. Not to take responsibility for what happens next."

"I wasn't in prison," I mutter, looking away.

The anger is gone from Rafe's voice; now he just sounds sad.

"You were as much in prison as anyone I knew there, Colin. Only you created it for yourself. Your father paced out the cell and your brothers fit the bars and you turned the key in the lock and buried it somewhere only you know. And you stared at Daniel through the bars and cursed him for being able to walk out the door. But he's not the one who did something wrong. All he did was save himself. And you can too. But you have to find that key and unlock the door."

I'm shaking my head compulsively. That's the stupidest thing I've ever heard.

"I made my own choices," I say. "No one forced me to do anything."

"Things could be different now," Rafe says urgently. "Maybe getting shit square with Daniel is the first step. Something *has* to be different when you go back to work with your brothers, or what's to stop everything from being exactly the same?"

I turn and look at him, eyes narrowed.

"And, then, what about us?" he says. He's going too fast. I don't know what we're talking about anymore. "Where do we go from here if everything's exactly the same? If you're still not able to feel like yourself? If we're hiding in your house all the time, not even able to go to a restaurant together? Does that feel good to you?"

"I don't—what are you saying?"

Rafe catches my hands and pulls me down on the bed next to him. He kisses me fiercely on the mouth, pulling me toward him and wrapping me in his arms. He keeps kissing me; then he pulls away and regards me seriously, as if he's made his point.

"I just…. It feels different here or something," I mutter, wishing he'd just kiss me again and stop me from saying stupid shit.

"Yeah, because we're far enough away from real life that it feels like there are no consequences." His hands keep moving on me, rubbing my back, running over my shoulders. "But what if it could feel like this all the time? What if there *were* no consequences to being with me?" He sounds so hopeful. Like that's actually possible. "What if… what if we could just… care about each other all the time and that was okay?"

His expression is still warm, but there's an urgency to what he's saying and his grip has tightened just a little.

"You… you want that," I say, still trying to figure out what exactly we're really discussing. Rafe pulls me closer.

"I already feel that, Colin. I already care about you all the time."

"Why?" I spit out. I didn't mean to say it, but it's what I've wondered every time we were together. How someone as amazing as Rafe could ever want me.

Rafe narrows his eyes, puzzled.

"I don't…." I look out the window, but Rafe guides my gaze back to his with a hand on my cheek. "I don't understand why you care. I… I believe that you do. I feel it, but…." I shake my head, frustrated. "But I don't get how you can. About me. When you're… when you're so much more…. When I…."

I think about Daniel and how I couldn't protect him. About the women I've fucked over because I didn't care. Because I was too scared to admit why I didn't want anything to do with them. About how I abandoned Pop in the last few months. How I can't even take Rafe out to dinner like he wants.

"I'm not a good person," I whisper, closing my eyes.

Rafe pushes me backward and kisses me hard.

"I see you," he says fiercely, cupping my face. "All the shit, that's…. I understand why you needed it, you know?"

I shake my head. I really don't.

Rafe rolls us so we're lying on our sides, facing each other. He throws a leg over my hip, anchoring me to the bed, and rests a hand on the back of my neck.

"In prison, people build themselves up. They construct a… a version of themselves that they think is most likely to get them out of the situation with as little damage as possible. It's not a lie, exactly, but they emphasize some traits, cover some up. They say certain things but keep others private. And it's armor, just like doing push-ups and lifting weights to build up their bodies. And you just… I don't know, if you pay attention, you learn to translate it. You see which parts are armor and which parts are weapons."

He strokes his thumb against my neck. Our faces are so close I can feel his breath warm on my cheek, see the jagged scar that breaks his eyebrow and the frown lines on his forehead.

"Armor," he goes on. "Armor's not dangerous. That's for survival. It's weapons you have to watch out for. And you—" He strokes my lips with his thumb. "It's mostly armor, Colin. And when you're with me, the armor falls away. Who you are without it… it's beautiful."

Chapter 12

DANIEL LOOKS different. He was always kind of skinny, with a pointy chin and prominent wrist bones. But he looks healthier. Like he's filled out, put on a little muscle, maybe. His clothes fit well, and his usually messy hair isn't quite so all over the place, and longer than I've seen it. He's wearing black jeans and a thin red sweater under his leather jacket. With his green eyes, it looks strangely Christmassy.

He gives me a nervous smile and shoves his fists in his pockets, ducking his head a little so his hair falls in his face.

"Hey," he says.

"Hey."

I open the door wider and he shuffles in, the toe of his boot catching on the doorjamb.

"Oof, sorry," he mutters as he knocks into me. He takes a look around and gapes at me. "Um, whoa. Should I take my shoes off?"

"Sure."

"Nice in here. Clean." He yanks off his boots.

"Yeah, well."

"Uh… so… how are you?" he says, shifting from one foot to the other just inside the door. His socks don't match.

"Yeah, okay. You?"

He nods, smiling a little. "I'm good."

We sit at opposite ends of the couch, Daniel scrunched into the corner and leaning against the arm like he wants to get as far away from me as possible. He plays with my couch cushion and looks everywhere but at me, like he's hoping I'll start talking. But he's the one who wanted to come see me, so I'll be damned if I'm going to figure it out.

"So, uh—I… um…," he fumbles. His cheeks start to flush, and he gets that familiar pissy look. For the first time, though, I can see that he's pissed at himself, for not finding the right words. Embarrassed, not scornful. And it makes me think of what Rafe said about armor. How Daniel kind of doesn't have any. He thinks he does—hell, maybe strangers even think he does—but with me, with Brian and Sam, with Pop, he's naked. He's naked and vulnerable and so, so easy to hurt.

And I guess when it came down to hurting Daniel or hurting myself, I hurt Daniel every time.

"Um...," he starts again, looking around wildly like someone might appear to bail him out.

Then, like she read his mind, Shelby comes sauntering into the living room, all mussed from sleep.

"You have a cat? Come here, kitty," he coos. Shelby looks at him and sniffs delicately, then jumps up onto the back of the couch and butts her head against his fingers.

"Aw, you're so cute." He scratches between her ears, and she rubs her face all over him. Then she jumps into his lap and plops down there, letting him pet her.

"Oh, for fuck's sake!" I say.

"What?"

Daniel cups his hand around Shelby—around *my* cat—like he can protect her from me.

"My own cat hates me and loves you. That's perfect."

I push off the couch and go to the kitchen, putting water on to boil and grabbing Rafe's tea from the cabinet out of habit.

Daniel leans in the doorway, arms crossed, frowning.

"Do you want some fucking tea?"

"Okay."

I stare at the kettle as it boils. When I turn back to Daniel, he's got his scared face on again and this time I can't help it.

"Look, I'm not gonna hit you or anything, okay?"

"Uh, I didn't think you were."

"Well, then why are you fucking cringing over there like I'm about to beat the crap out of you?"

"I'm not cringing. I'm leaning. And it's not like you *haven't* beaten the crap out of me before."

"Well. I mean. Okay, but we were kids. We were just messing around."

Daniel narrows his eyes at me. I hand him a cup of tea and sit at the kitchen table. He hesitates, then sits across from me.

"Are you serious right now?" He sounds genuinely puzzled.

"Yeah."

"You're sitting here, drinking tea, and telling me that the times you beat the shit out of me—when I was, like, thirteen and weighed a hundred pounds, and you were nineteen and the size you are now—we were just kids messing around. That's really what you're going with?"

Daniel's eyes are wide and there doesn't seem to be a good answer to that.

"Okay, well what about when you found me and Buddy McKenzie in the alley outside the shop? That wasn't just messing around." He wraps his arms around himself like he's giving himself a hug. At Buddy's name, my ears start to buzz and I go clammy with sweat.

"That's—that wasn't—he—I was… just looking out for you."

"Dude. No way." He's gaping at me, clutching his tea.

"Look, that was a long time ago, so, um…."

Daniel shakes his head like he can't even think of what to say. Then he gets up and starts pacing.

"So, why does your cat hate you?" he finally says as Shelby wanders over to her food dish.

I shrug, and Daniel rolls his eyes and crouches down to pet Shelby.

"I… forgot to feed her one day," I say finally.

Daniel looks up. "Why?"

"I was drunk. It was after Pop died."

He nods, curling Shelby's tail around his hand.

"She already didn't like me very much, though," I admit. "She loves Rafe. And you, apparently."

Daniel's chin jerks up and he comes back to the table. "Rafe. That's the guy at Dad's funeral?"

I nod, but I can already feel my throat tightening and more sweat slicks my spine. I hadn't meant to bring Rafe up at all.

"And he's the one I talked to. On the phone?"

"Oh. Yeah."

"And he's… and you're… together."

I nod and start cleaning up the tea.

"I, um, I didn't know you were such a neat freak," Daniel says. I wheel around and glare at him. He holds his hands up. "Clean, I mean. That you were so clean."

"Look," I say, leaning back against the counter I just cleaned. It's exhausting, tiptoeing around each other like this. "What do you want?

I mean—" I correct myself when Daniel bristles. "—what are we doing here? Because this sucks."

And there it is again: that hurt look. But then he shakes it off and squares his shoulders.

"What do I want. Okay. Well, I want to know why you treated me like shit for my entire life for being gay when you're gay too. That's what I want."

My grip on the counter turns slippery. It feels like it's a thousand degrees in here.

"I didn't—" I start to say, and Daniel's eyebrows shoot up into his hair. We're like dogs with their backs up, circling each other, growling at every word. Daniel sighs and he forces himself to relax.

"Look, let me start again." He eases a small piece of paper out of his pocket and smooths it out on his knee, hiding it under the table and glancing around the kitchen like he's not looking at it. He clears his throat nervously, then tries to sound totally natural.

"So, you're gay right? Or, you know, into dudes? Just to clarify…."

"Are you reading that off a piece of paper?"

"What? Oh, well… um, so, you are, right? Rafe?"

"Yeah, okay, yes, Rafe." I grab the all-purpose cleaner and start wiping off the table. I pick up Daniel's tea and move to wash it.

"I wasn't actually done with that."

I slam it back down on the table in front of him and tea sloshes over the sides. I grit my teeth and wipe it up.

"Dude," Daniel says, shaking his head. He glances down at his knees. "Um, so, how long have you known you were interested in men?"

"Daniel, seriously. Are you reading that off a piece of paper?"

"Uh…." He laughs nervously. Then he starts laughing harder, cracking up at something. He spills the tea and jumps up before it can drip onto his lap. "Shit, sorry."

I shake my head and wipe up the tea. Then I clean the table again. And still, Daniel's laughing at me.

"Fucking what!?" I snap.

He laughs until he wheezes, hands on his thighs, then holds the paper out to me, incoherent with laughter. It's crinkled and a little damp, so the ink has bled in places.

"What is this?"

"I… stayed up all night… making a list…," he blurts out through his laughter, "of questions and… topics of conversation." He snorts. He used to do this as a really little kid: laugh until he started snorting. Not as cute as an adult.

"Uh, why?"

"Ginger said I should write them down so I didn't forget," he says, wiping at his eyes. "Oh god. Sorry. Okay. I'm fine. Shit. You may as well just read it now, I guess." He shakes his head. "Hey, listen, do you have any food? I'm starving."

I gesture toward the fridge where Rafe put some groceries earlier while I was cleaning. "I'm not sure what's in there. Can you cook?"

Daniel starts giggling again. "No, not really. Rex has been trying to teach me, but… I'm kind of hopeless."

I read the paper while Daniel digs through my refrigerator.

1. Double-check he's actually into dudes. And since when? Dated other guys? Women?

2. If so, why so freaked about me? (Self-hatred? Hates me? Closet/ Fear? Dad? Just a homophobic asshole? AOTA?)

3. You made my life miserable. Why always so cruel?

4. We were kind of close once, right? What happened?

I swallow hard at the last two.

"What does 'AOTA' mean?"

"Huh?" Daniel says, pulling something out of the fridge. "Oh. All of the above."

I lean against the counter, and Daniel puts out an apple and some cheese.

"Can I eat this?"

I nod, frowning.

"Um," he says, sounding nervous again, "so… you can just go in order if you want…."

He gets out a plate and a knife and proceeds to cut the apple and the cheese into perfectly uniform slices and pile the slices on the plate, which he offers to me, looking pleased with himself for a second. But I definitely can't eat anything. *Why always so cruel?*

"Soooo?" he says.

"I don't understand," I say, sitting down carefully. I put the paper in the middle of the table and point to number three. "How did I make your life miserable? You didn't want anything to do with me—with any of us.

You were never around. You… were ashamed of us. I don't… I mean, you didn't care…. You thought we were losers and you were so much smarter…."

"That's not true," Daniel says furiously. "*You* guys never wanted me around because you thought I was a pansy—*your* word. All you ever cared about was cars and sports, and the second that I wasn't good at that stuff or didn't want to do it, you totally wrote me off, like if I wasn't just like you, I was fucking worthless!"

"But you *were* good at that stuff. You were good with cars and you were great at track. You just decided you didn't want to do them because they were too… you know, not classy enough for you."

Daniel jerks in his seat, then runs a hand through his hair, messing it up. "I only ran track because I thought Pop might pay attention to me for, like, a second if I did a sport. Not that it worked. He thought track was for sissies. So I quit. I didn't like it, anyway. And I never thought I was smarter than anyone. I just wanted to learn shit and you guys acted like I fucking betrayed you or something."

We sit in silence, Daniel pushing the slices of apple around on the plate, me looking anywhere but him.

"Was it just…?" He looks down at his untouched food. "Was it just because I'm gay that you hated me?"

"We didn't hate you," I scoff.

"I'm talking about you," he says softly. "You… hated me. Hate me? I just—I don't remember exactly when it started, but I… I… we weren't always like that. I—when I was little, you let me hang out sometimes. When you'd be listening to the radio. And I thought, you know, like, you thought I was okay. But then…." He shakes his head. "Then you hated me. So. Was it the gay thing? Or was it just… me?"

"I… I… I…."

Daniel shakes his head and makes a sandwich with apple and cheese. He only takes one bite before he puts the food down again and squirms.

I don't know what to say. The story he's telling… it's like someone summarizing a movie you saw but hitting only the points you barely noticed. Daniel has his arms wrapped around himself again. It reminds me of Ricky and the way she pulls herself tight, shoulder blades spreading like wings.

"Uh, so how long have you and Rafe been together?" he asks finally.

"Since October, I guess. Around then."

"How'd you meet?"

"Oh, well. I've been helping him out at this place he works. For kids. I've been teaching them shit about cars."

"Really? That's cool," Daniel says. "Where at?"

"The Youth Alliance, in Northern Liberties."

"The queer youth program? Seriously?"

"You've heard of it?"

He nods.

I miss the kids. It's been weeks since I've seen them. I wonder how they are. If they think I forgot about them.

"There's a kid there that reminds me of you," I say. Only Anders isn't there anymore. I wonder how things are going for him.

"Oh yeah?"

"Yeah, he just… he's kind of scrawny and he's really into *Harry Potter*. Anyway, it just reminds me of how you were when you were a kid. Always wanting people to read to you and stuff."

"Yeah, and then Brian would rip up my library books."

I swallow hard. I don't remember that.

Daniel shakes his head. "I don't get it, man. So, when I told you I was gay, you punched me in the stomach so hard I puked and told me that I shouldn't ever admit it. But now you volunteer at a queer youth center and you're all fond of these kids and shit?"

My head is spinning. "I didn't tell you not to admit it—I just… I didn't want you to be… gay… because I didn't want anything bad to happen to you."

"Why did you think something bad would happen to me?"

"You were with fucking *Buddy* and he's…. And I—you were so little and I didn't think…. I just wanted to make sure you could take care of yourself."

Daniel's looking at me like I'm speaking another language. He opens his mouth to say something, but I cut him off.

"That's why I taught you to fight in the first place. It's why I tested you sometimes. You know? To make sure that if you needed to, you could protect yourself. That's all."

"I was sixteen. I wasn't a little kid," Daniel says, but he sounds like he's choosing his words carefully.

"You were *little*. And he was—" Fuck! I don't want to talk about this. "Anyway, you just did whatever you wanted and you didn't care how much Pop sacrificed to take care of us."

"Uh. What?"

I don't say anything. I want this to be over. I want to go back to the moment Rafe told me he thought I should talk with Daniel—all warm chest and strong arms—and I want to tell him to shove it.

"Colin, seriously, what the hell? What do you mean, Pop *sacrificed*? What do you think he sacrificed?"

Daniel's biting his lip, and he looks pale against the bright red of his sweater and the near-black of his hair. It's only a little darker than Brian's and Sam's, his skin only a little lighter, but with his green eyes, the contrast is a lot more noticeable.

"He was a fucking fall-down mess after Mom died."

"Yeah, I know," Daniel says.

"You *don't* know. You were a kid. You didn't have a clue."

"I know he drank himself to sleep every night for months. I know the school counselor had to call him because I showed up in the same dirty clothes for weeks and the kids wouldn't sit next to me because they said I stank. I know Sam ordered pizza every day for so long we practically puked at the smell of it. I know Pop cried every time Cindy Lauper's 'Time After Time' came on the radio even though he didn't want anyone to see. And I know after a year or so he got his shit together but he was never the same. What I don't know is what the hell you think I could've done about it."

I had forgotten about that Cindy Lauper song.

"You just—" I shake my head and start cleaning the floor around Shelby's food and water dishes. It gets dirty so quickly. "You didn't have to make his life *harder*! That's what I'm saying. He barely kept it all together and you were right there showing him all the ways he was failing. All the ways he wasn't good enough. And then you tell him you're gay—"

"*I* made *his* life harder?" Daniel stands up, hands on the table. "So you're saying, what, that because he lost his wife, I should have done whatever he wanted for the rest of my life in an attempt to make him feel better? To make him feel like he succeeded at being a parent even without Mom? That is so intensely *fucked*, Colin! And in case you somehow missed it, he *didn't* succeed. He was a *shitty* father! He was cruel and petty and he made me feel like a worthless piece of garbage *all* the time."

"Yeah, right!" I stalk toward Daniel. "He *babied* you so hard. He *never* did that shit with me. If I'd pulled half the shit you did—"

"*Babied* me! What shit did I pull? You're insane! All I did—all I *ever* fucking did—was tiptoe around you all so I could get my homework done and get out of the house without a slap or a punch or having you look at me like I was disgusting."

"You *were* disgusting!" I yell in his face. "Prancing around like you were better than everyone. Like you didn't care about your responsibility to our family. Like all you wanted was to get as far away from us as possible and live your perfect fucking life with your perfect fucking boyfriend and never see us again!"

Daniel blinks quickly, his green eyes huge and his face pale. I can hear every swallow he takes.

"What family?" he says softly. "What family is it that you think I had, *brother*? You and Brian and Sam, Dad, you were a family. You loved him. I know that. And you all had your cars and your sports and your beer. What the fuck did you want from me? I wasn't part of that. Any time I even tried—if I asked how your day was, if I asked how the shop was—you made it clear you didn't want me to be a part of your family. My family died the day Mom died, and you blame me for trying to be honest about who I was? There was *nothing* for me at home, but you think I should've pretended to like it there? Lied about what I wanted? About who I wanted it with? I didn't even care about telling Dad and you guys that I was gay. I only did it because you saw me with Buddy and I knew that if I didn't tell them before you did, then you would present it in the most disgusting way possible."

"No! I would never have told Pop because I knew it would break his fucking heart to have a—"

Daniel takes a step toward me, his arms wrapped around himself.

"To have a what? To have a faggot for a son?" His voice is eerily calm. "Well, I guess you'd know."

Heat rises in my face and my breathing goes bad. I keep trying to swallow the lump in my throat, but it won't go down.

"You can't even say it, can you? You can't even look me in the eyes and say you're gay." He shakes his head. "Jesus Christ, Colin," he says, his mocking voice crawling deep into my gut, "does he have that much power over you?"

I open my mouth, but nothing comes out. This is not how this was supposed to go. This is not how this was supposed to go at all.

"Shit," Daniel says softly. He backs away a step and looks at me. "Shit, he does, doesn't he? And he always did," he goes on, like he's talking to himself. "Jesus, you were talking about yourself, weren't you? That's what *you* did. You played the role of the son you knew he wanted because you thought you could make it okay for him. That you could make him feel like he was an okay parent even without Mom…."

I'm concentrating on my breathing, pretending Rafe is here, his hand on the back of my neck helping me breathe in and out, in and out.

Daniel's muttering to himself and pacing, his mismatched socks crisscrossing my spotless kitchen floor.

"And then when I—fuck, you knew you were gay, didn't you? All that time. And after you saw how Dad reacted to me, there was no way you could…." He's chewing on his lip, looking at me through the hair falling in his face every time he runs a nervous hand through it.

Jesus, that hand through his hair is just like Rafe.

"Are you okay?" Daniel asks. He's standing a step away from me, his hand hovering near me like he's afraid to touch me. My breaths are so short it's making black dots shimmer in the edges of my vision. "Shit, Colin? Do you wanna sit down or something?" I shake my head.

The doorbell rings and a second later I see Rafe's shoes walk into the kitchen. They're the same beat-up Pumas he was wearing when we came back from the beach this morning, so he didn't even go home and change. I joked when he left that we should have some secret signal like they do in the movies in case I wanted him to come interrupt my conversation with Daniel. Only I wasn't actually joking. And like always, I guess he could tell.

"He's—I'm—we were—and—I don't know what's wrong," Daniel says, and he sounds like a little kid again.

Rafe doesn't say anything to Daniel, just steps right in front of me and pulls my arms around his waist, crushing me to him.

"Okay," he says in my ear. "You're okay." He rubs a palm up and down my spine, holding me tight against him with the other hand. I try and time my breathing to the expansion of his rib cage. I breathe in his smell and imagine his hair spreading out around me, veiling us both in our own little world.

Little by little, my breathing normalizes and the black spots recede from my vision. Rafe's hand is cradling the back of my neck and my face is buried in his jacket.

The second I realize I'm okay, though, the mortification hits. Because Daniel just saw me a hundred percent lose it. I squeeze my eyes shut, wishing I could just hide in Rafe forever, then open them and see Daniel's feet, one navy blue sock and one black, hovering a couple feet away.

I pull away from Rafe, my eyes still on the floor, then look up at Daniel quickly, like ripping off a Band-Aid. He has one hand at his mouth, chewing on his thumbnail, and the other wrapped around his stomach. He looks scared, the way he used to.

"Are you okay?" Daniel's voice breaks on every word.

I nod and look down. An awkward silence settles over the kitchen until Rafe clears his throat.

"I don't want to interrupt," he says, "but I brought dinner."

Daniel's looking at Rafe very strangely, head cocked and eyes slightly narrowed.

"I, um." He gestures to the apple and cheese sitting untouched on the kitchen table. The apple has started to go slightly brown and the cheese has gone slimy. It looks disgusting.

"I'll just grab it from the car."

Daniel and I look at each other, and his expression of terror at prolonging this get-together mirrors my feelings so perfectly that I almost laugh.

"I'm not really hungry," I say to the floor.

"Yeah, I'm fine," Daniel says quickly, but then his stomach gives a loud growl. He squeezes his arm around it even tighter and rolls his eyes at himself.

Rafe chuckles and Daniel's head jerks up.

"I'll be right back," he says again, looking between Daniel and me.

Daniel perches tentatively on the edge of the counter. "I didn't know you got panic attacks," he says softly.

"Well, you don't really know anything about me," I snap, but it comes out sounding a hell of a lot milder than I intended.

"Yeah. You're right," Daniel says. "We don't know each other at all, do we? I don't know Brian or Sam either. And I sure as hell didn't know Dad."

"Me either," I say softly.

Daniel snorts. I shake my head and close my eyes again.

"Wait, what do you mean?"

The adrenaline from a few minutes ago has drained away, leaving me exhausted. I can feel a headache coming on.

"Well, he didn't really know me, did he? So I don't know how he would've felt about me if he did."

"He didn't...." Daniel fumbles around for words.

"I don't even know if he would've loved me if he knew who I was, okay!"

Daniel swallows hard. "You mean because you saw how he didn't love me once he knew I was gay."

Shit. "I didn't mean that."

"No, I know." He's fiddling with something in his pocket and rubbing a hand over his chest absently.

After a minute of awkward silence, Rafe comes back in and lays out food from the Greek place I like down the street.

"Oh shit, this is so good," Daniel says with his mouth full. "My—um, Rex, my—um, he loves to cook."

"Your boyfriend?" Rafe asks.

Daniel nods, but he gets this doofy look on his face like he's a thousand miles away, and he rubs his chest again.

"So, Daniel," Rafe begins politely, and I can tell he's about to initiate some kind of getting-to-know-you chatter, but Daniel interrupts him.

"We're—I'm—we're moving in together," he blurts out, looking at me. "Oh, sorry," he says to Rafe, realizing he interrupted. Rafe just smiles at him and shakes his head. "He asked me. At Christmas," Daniel says softly, nervously fiddling with his fork. Then he shakes his head as if he's irritated with himself for saying it.

I don't know what to say. I kind of hated Rex on sight, but, you know, there were extenuating circumstances.

"Congratulations," Rafe says once it's clear I'm not going to respond.

"Thanks," Daniel mutters, clearly embarrassed at the attention even though he's the one who brought it up.

Daniel and I both shove food in our faces for a minute to avoid talking, and Rafe looks between us, saying nothing.

Rafe puts his hand on my thigh under the table and squeezes. Daniel stares into space as he eats, his mind clearly on something else.

"Wait," he says after a while, eyebrows wrinkled in confusion, "I was little and he was… what?"

"What?" I say.

"Buddy McKenzie. You said you were worried something would happen to me because I was little and he… what?"

"What? Nothing. He was an asshole. And way too old for you."

"I thought he was your friend?"

"No." I put my fork down, my appetite gone.

"But… wasn't he?"

"No. Well, once."

"I just don't understand—"

"Look, I thought he was hurting you, okay? What else is there to understand?"

Every muscle in my body is rigid, and I'm vaguely aware of Rafe tensing beside me. He can always tell when something's wrong.

"But, I mean, I was…." Daniel blushes. "You know, I was the one… going down on him, so—"

"Yeah, so I saw," I bite off.

"So… okay, so then, why—"

"How did I know you wanted to do that? That he didn't manipulate you into it!" I put my hand over my mouth as Daniel's eyes narrow.

"I don't…. Wait, did that… happen to you?" Daniel asks. "Oh shit. Did that happen to you with Buddy? Is that why you weren't friends anymore?"

I forgot this about Daniel. The way he takes little pieces of what you say and fills in the blanks to make whole stories. It's why I never used to want to answer him when he'd ask me about my day or try to get me to talk about shit. Because I knew that in his head, he was weaving it all together and getting more out of it than I ever intended to let on.

"You *were* friends," Daniel murmurs. "I remember."

"You were a kid. You don't remember shit."

He shakes his head like I haven't even spoken.

"What the fuck did he do?"

Rafe is motionless beside me.

IT WAS the beginning of senior year. We'd been in football together for years, but we weren't exactly close. There was just something about the way I felt when we were together. Something that was different than my other friends. Different even than Xavier. There was this... energy between us. I didn't know what it was at first.

One afternoon we were drunk at his cousin's house, where Buddy lived in the basement for a reason I never quite understood, and he came into the bathroom while I was taking a piss. I thought he walked in on me by accident, but then he looked down at my dick and grinned at me like he could read my mind.

At first I was just terrified that he knew my secret. That he was going to tell everyone that I sometimes got hard-ons in the locker room. But then he unzipped his jeans and pissed into the toilet with me. I started to say something, but when we were finished, he reached for me. I startled, but he grinned the way he did when we were playing video games or when he made a good block, blue eyes scrunching up, tongue just showing between the gap in his teeth. He put my hand on his dick and we stroked each other off. It felt good, losing it between us, his rough hand on me. But the second it was over, I was so terrified, so ashamed that I practically ran out of the bathroom.

The next time I saw Buddy, we both acted normal, but the second we were alone, he pushed me against the wall and started fumbling with our pants and I got hard in about three seconds.

We never talked about what we did. We never touched anything but each other's dicks. Never kissed or caressed. That would've seemed totally weird. But it was clear that we both wanted it, so.... That whole month, whenever we were alone together, we jerked each other off, fast and hard, and then got drunk like it never happened and watched football or played one of his cousin's video games. He would hang around the shop sometimes, shooting the shit with me and Sam. He was into cars too, so it was no big deal.

After another couple months, it was clear what he wanted. He wanted to fuck me. When I got annoyed at him trying to pull me down onto the bed, he'd just act like it was a joke and we'd finish up like we always had.

One day, though, he lost his temper. He was a smiley guy. Big and blond, and when he smiled he looked like he wouldn't hurt a fly. But when he got pissed, his whole face and neck turned red and his eyes squinted and his mouth turned to a snarl. That day, when I tried to laugh it off, he crowded me against the wall. "You know how easy it'd be for me to tell everyone about this?" he said. I kind of laughed again and rolled my eyes, but his expression chilled me.

"I'm serious," he said. "Let's just help each other out, okay?"

I was shocked at what he was saying, but he was still Buddy. Still my friend, and I didn't think he'd really say anything.

"Come on, man," I said. "What are you talking about?"

"Nothing, bud. I'm just saying there are things that feel a whole hell of a lot better than a hand job, you know?" And he smiled at me like he always did. "Look, just think about it." Then he backed off like he knew he'd gone too far.

A few weeks later, I'd almost forgotten about it. Written it off to being drunk and horny and stupid. He called, asked if I wanted to hang out, and I went.

And it was fine. We drank a few beers, ordered pizza, watched a game. No problem. Same thing the next time. It was all fine.

Then he started bringing it up again. Casually. How good it'd be. How it was no big deal. Just getting off. Just between friends. And how easy it'd be to slip up and tell someone about what we did together.

Finally, one night, he was more explicit than usual and I was tired of going around in circles. So I agreed. Because he was my friend. Because people finding out seemed like the worst thing that could possibly happen. And because maybe Buddy was right and it would be good. Maybe also because I wanted to know for sure. Because sex with Maya had turned into a nightmare, but that was my only experience with it. So yeah. I said okay.

He got that familiar grin on his face. My friend. Happy because I was doing what he wanted. He patted me on the back like I'd made the right decision, and he fumbled our pants down and pushed me down on the bed.

"Cool, man," he said. "This'll be awesome."

But it wasn't awesome. I couldn't relax and it hurt and when I wanted to stop—

"Don't pull that girl shit, man. You agreed. We had a deal."

So. Afterward, we never did it again. I didn't go over to Buddy's house anymore and he didn't call me again.

But then one morning, I came out to the garage, coffee mug in hand, to see Buddy there, talking with Pop. It had been more than four years, but at the sight of his blond hair and rounded shoulders, I felt queasy and light-headed.

He was going to be picking up a few shifts at the garage, Pop said.

"Hey, man," Buddy said to me, clapping me on the back. "Long time no see, huh?"

When Pop walked into his office to do some paperwork, I rounded on Buddy.

"What the fuck are you doing here?"

"Aw, come on, bud, don't be like that," he said. "A job's a job, right? And I need this one."

I shook my head. "You gotta get outta here, man."

His eyes narrowed and his smile disappeared in an instant. "Look, bud, I don't think you're in any position to be telling me what to do," he said, and he nodded at Pop, coming out of his office. "Just a few shifts a week. No harm, no foul, am I right?" And he walked over to Pop to finalize arrangements.

DANIEL LOOKS stricken at what I've told them. Sick. And Rafe is still frozen beside me. He does that sometimes. He told me once that in prison, if you were still while others were moving, you were less likely to get pulled into a fight. It was easier to avoid being seen. To take a time-out until you can decide what to do.

I go into the bathroom and splash some water on my face, trying not to think about how, a month after Buddy beginning his shifts at the shop, I'd found Daniel—younger than I had been when Buddy and I started hooking up—blowing him in the alley.

How Buddy's dirty hand was heavy on Daniel's hair, Daniel's sharp shoulders barely visible behind the bulk of Buddy's thighs. How red Buddy's face was or how Daniel's hands fluttered on his own knees like he wasn't sure he was allowed to touch Buddy with anything but his mouth. The sick fury that had unfurled in my gut, blinding me to everything but one imperative: get Buddy the fuck away from my brother.

I brush my teeth twice and force myself to walk slowly back to the kitchen. Rafe's cleaning up the food and Daniel's sitting on the floor, his back against the refrigerator, clutching Shelby like she's a stuffed animal. She's letting him, but I can tell she's losing patience quickly.

"You're about to get scratched," I tell him.

"Huh?" When he looks up, he's alarmingly pale and his eyes are unfocused. "Ow, shit!"

"Told you."

Shelby runs to Rafe and rubs her face against his shins.

"Look, I'm really tired," I say. "I'm gonna head to bed."

"Colin...." Daniel stands up and comes toward me, but I look over his shoulder. I can't see the hurt in his face, even if it is mostly on my behalf. I can't see the sympathy. The soft, vulnerable look that I know will be there. I can't be mad at him right now. It's just too much.

"Your socks don't match," I say.

"Huh?" Daniel looks down. "Oh. Shit." He looks like he's about to say something, but he changes his mind. "I'll um—I'll get out of your hair," he says finally, walking to the front door. He jams his feet into his boots while standing, nearly losing his balance, and pulls his jacket on. Then he turns to me.

"Um." He runs his hand through his hair, messing it up. "Thanks. Thanks for agreeing to talk with me. I didn't... I... thanks. And thank you for dinner," he says, looking to Rafe. "And for...." He shakes his head. "Anyway. I'll.... Can I maybe call you sometime?"

For a second I think he's talking to Rafe and I bristle at the idea. Then I realize he's looking at me.

"I guess," I say, and he nods, like that's more than he was expecting.

He opens the door and shivers.

"Bye, cat," he says as Shelby sniffs at the fresh air. He blocks her with his foot.

"You all right to get home?" Rafe asks.

"Huh? Oh, yeah, sure," Daniel says, like he's confused as to why Rafe would ask.

IN BED, I try to pull Rafe down on top of me, but he resists, kissing me chastely on the cheek. I roll close to him and try to kiss his mouth, but he just grabs me and holds me to him, tucking my head under his chin. When I change tactics and try to reach down to his underwear, he growls and rolls us, pinning me to the bed.

"Please," he says, holding my shoulders down. "Please don't. Please." He's stroking my hair and my face and my neck, looking down at me.

Screw this. If he doesn't want me, fine. I roll away from him and bury my face in my pillow. I just want to fall asleep and forget this day ever happened. I wish we were back at the beach house. Wish it was the sound of waves I could hear and not the sounds of traffic. Wish tomorrow I could wake up and have breakfast with Rafe, looking out at the gray ocean instead of dragging myself over to Pop's to make sure Brian hasn't gotten scurvy or something from living on only beer and crackers.

"Colin." Rafe's voice is gentle, his lips warm at my ear. He kisses my shoulder and rests a hand on my bare hip.

I huff and roll farther away from him, but when he moves toward me again, pulling me back against him, I press my ass into his crotch and hear his breath catch. The hand on my hip turns to a caress, and I throw my head back. Rafe kisses my neck, his hair tumbling over my face. I roll onto my back and pull him down on top of me.

"Fuck," he mutters, and I can feel his dick stiffen against my hip, so I take advantage of it and kiss him hard, thrusting up against him. Though he tries to pull away at first, he finally sinks down against me, his hands running over my thighs and my ribs as we kiss.

"Are you sure now's a good time to do this?" Rafe asks, his breath labored. "You sure you want this?"

"Look, just because that thing happened with Buddy, like, a hundred years ago, doesn't mean I'm some little girl who got raped or something. Would you just fuck me?"

Rafe freezes.

"It doesn't have anything to do with whether you're male or female," he says, and he sounds pissed. "You think men can't be hurt? Can't be raped?" His voice is shaking. "Do you know how many men I saw get—" He cuts himself off with a shake of his head and pushes off me, dropping onto his back on the bed and putting one arm over his face. "And the fact that you don't see it—that you don't see what he did to you…." He shakes his head. "If you don't feel like it was rape, then… then, I'm glad, I guess, but…. Colin, he *coerced* you. He threatened to tell your father and your brothers that you were gay if you didn't let him have sex with you when you didn't want it. That's… that's—well, whatever you want to call it, it's fucking wrong. And I hate that it happened to you."

I run a tentative finger down his arm. He's vibrating with anger. Coerced. Yeah, that's the word I was trying to find earlier to tell Daniel what I thought might have happened the day I found him and Buddy in the alley. But it wasn't that. Not for him. And I'm glad. Glad the ugliness didn't touch him.

"And I fucking *hate* that you didn't tell me about it before," Rafe says, turning to me, his face fierce and his hand on my hair gentle.

I shake my head, trying to find the words to explain that I wanted things to be different with him. I wanted to start that side of things over, as if shit with Buddy had never happened. That I didn't want to think of what I did with Rafe as even being in the same category as things with Buddy.

But I don't come up with any words at all. I just reach for Rafe, wanting the warmth of his skin, his scent, the weight of him. Wanting to be connected with him. It's not even exactly sex that I need. Just something to let me feel close to him.

"Please," I hear myself say softly. Rafe lowers his mouth to mine and kisses me, sweet and slow. "Please."

"Colin." He moves on top of me, stroking my face and neck.

"Please."

"Are you sure?"

"You think it's fucked up?" I say around a lump in my throat.

He shakes his head. "I think it's fucked up that I want you right now."

"Why?"

"Because I"—his voice drops to a whisper—"I don't want to be like them. The men. The ones who hurt people."

"You're not."

"Sometimes I'm not sure," he says.

"No way."

"Don't you get it?" he says finally. "I want to tear the fucking world apart to find the people who hurt you. I want to pull them apart with my bare hands and watch them whimper while I tell them what they're being punished for." He's squeezing my shoulders too tightly and his eyes are focused inward, like he's not even looking at me.

"'S not the same," I tell him. But he shakes his head.

I reach up and run my fingers through his hair, untangling every snag I encounter, as he calms down. Gradually, my hands find their way from his hair to his neck, then down the corded muscles of his back to rest on his ass, drawing him against me.

We kiss for a while, moving together slowly. When Rafe leans back to pull his shirt off, he's looking at me strangely.

I want him to obliterate the past and blot out the future. I want to be so completely full-up with only Rafe that everything else falls away. I want to become the person I feel like when he's touching me. And I also want to show him that he isn't those men—the ones who hurt people.

"I want—I…. Listen. I trust you," I say. Rafe runs his knuckles down my jaw, eyes half closing. "I want you to touch me however you want." I can see the arousal shoot through Rafe in the tightening of his muscles and it makes my heart beat faster. "I want you to… do whatever you want."

Rafe bites his lip and frowns but the way he's looking at me leaves no question that he wants this. His pupils are huge in the warm brown of his eyes and his forehead is damp. "Yeah?"

I nod. He kisses me, and when I reach a hand up to his nipple, he presses my wrist into the pillow above my head. When I reach my other hand down to where his erection is sticking out of the band of his underwear, he presses that wrist to the bed too.

He pauses just before kissing me, lips an inch from mine. "Is that okay?"

I nod, gasping for breath.

"Mmmm. You *can* trust me." I nod. There's something almost desperate in his voice. "I won't hurt you."

"I know."

He kisses me again and I go wild beneath him, testing the strength of his hands on my wrists.

"Fuck, you look so beautiful like this." He rolls my hips up and my wrists slide from his hand. I whimper at the loss, and he rolls my hips up until they come off the bed.

He licks into my hole like a starving man, and I don't even recognize the sound that comes out of me, part scream and part whimper. A drop of my own precome lands on my chin.

Rafe opens me with his tongue, pressing down even harder on my arms, and groans when my hole relaxes.

"So fucking sweet here," he mutters against my ass, and then both his hands are spreading my cheeks, practically bending me in half, and I can't move, can't do anything except moan as his mouth moves on me.

Rafe grabs one of my hands in each of his and moves them so I'm holding my legs open for him. He sucks on my hole and runs his tongue around it, then licks his way to my balls, taking each one in his mouth. I feel ridiculous. Awkward. Totally at his mercy, my ass and balls and dick exposed for him.

He licks up the length of my erection, swirling his tongue around the tip, where I'm leaking. He sucks me until I'm moaning and trying to thrust deeper into his mouth, but my position won't let me. He pulls off, presses a kiss to the inside of one thigh, a bite to the other, and moves back to my ass, burying his face there and spearing his tongue into me until I'm a quivering mess.

He eases my legs down so my feet are flat on the bed and rolls on the condom. He grabs my wrists again and holds them fast over my head. "Put your legs around me," he says breathlessly.

Rafe sinks into me in one slow, deep thrust and I almost scream. With my legs around him, thighs pressed nearly to my chest, his entire weight is bearing down on me. He's all around me and inside of me, and any way I move, he's there.

He catches my scream in his mouth, kissing me, feeding me the taste of myself on his tongue until I have to wrench my face away to gasp in breath. A bite to my throat. His tongue at my pulse. The scrape of teeth along my jaw. Then we lock eyes and he starts to move. In this position, I'm so tight around him that he feels huge, on the edge of painful, like every time he slides out of me it seems impossible he'll be able to thrust back in. Confused pleasure skitters through my body and lands at the base of my dick, trapped between us. I can feel him in my stomach, my chest, my throat.

I wiggle my hips, desperately trying to get some contact for my erection, and I tighten around Rafe. He roars, slamming into me until we're locked so tightly together that I can't move, can only let out a choked moan. He squeezes my wrists and presses his other palm to my cheek, his eyes burning into me.

"The sounds you make fucking kill me, Colin." His hand ghosts over my face, shakily tracing my lips, by brows, my cheeks. "You—Jesus, you just kill me," he chokes out. Then he kisses me before I can say anything, the sweetness of his mouth a contrast to his powerful thrusts.

"Rafe, I—oh god! Please!" I'm spewing nonsense and my dick is spewing precome as Rafe takes over my body. Everything is his and I force myself to relax beneath him. To make good on my promise. That I trust him. That I want him like this.

My legs are wrapped around him, and he's deep inside my ass, one heavy arm trapping my wrists while the other hand maps my face and throat. His hair is in my face, his mouth owns mine with kiss after kiss, controlling even my breath, and his weight presses me into the bed. We're tangled into a knot so complicated I wouldn't have the first clue how to undo it.

Still, he won't touch my dick. I'm so painfully hard that each beat of my heart throbs in my erection.

"Please, Rafe, please, please," I whine, begging him for just that tiny stroke that I know would bring me over the edge. He shakes his head, buries his face in my neck, and groans. Then kisses his way back to my mouth. As he kisses me, he thrusts deep, and when his balls are snugged up against my skin, he freezes there, pulsing inside me. He licks my mouth like an animal, tasting me while he's inside.

I'm caught there, speared open on him, held down by him, whimpering.

"You're fucking mine. Do you hear me?"

I cry out as I feel his dick swell inside me at his words. I nod frantically, not even sure what I'm agreeing to.

"Your body," he says, rocking against me, his weight pressing him deeper inside me. "Your sweet fucking heart." He rests his palm against my chest and I feel my eyes fill with tears.

His face softens and he starts to let go of my wrists to wipe at my tears. But that's the last thing I want. I want to be tucked safely inside the cage of his body, his flesh and taste and scent and the sound of his voice filling every opening.

"Don't let go!"

He squeezes my wrists. "I won't." He leans down, and when his mouth is almost touching mine, he says, "You like this? Us close like this? Me in charge of your body?"

I nod quickly. That's exactly it. He's in charge of every inch of me like this.

"Because I fucking love it." Then he starts thrusting hard and my eyes roll back in my head.

"Look at me," Rafe says.

I look back at him, and he brings his hand up to my throat.

"I won't hurt you," he says, sounding more sure of himself this time. "Tap my shoulder and I'll stop."

With each thrust, he tightens his hand on my throat a little more. I can still breathe through my nose, but it's hard. Pleasure pulses inside me as he thrusts, and as he presses harder and harder on my throat, my dick starts to throb harder.

Then he takes his hand away, and I gasp in a breath and groan my disappointment. He kisses me passionately.

"Okay?"

I nod, but he looks down at my throat and frowns, then drops a kiss there. This time, he brings his hand up and covers my nose and mouth.

"I don't want to leave a bruise," he mutters, kissing my throat again, and I smile against his palm. Lick it. Then he presses his hand tight and starts to move again. The pleasure boils through my groin and stomach and everything in me strains to take a breath. As I try and fail, a new feeling starts in my dick—a buzzing, tingling pleasure, as if someone's stroking me or licking me with a rough tongue.

Then Rafe moves his hand and I drag in a deep breath, the buzzing receding. I cry out in frustration and Rafe bites his lip.

"So hot—feeling you squirm against me while I'm inside you, fucking you with my cock and my hands and my mouth. I can't wait to feel you come. Can't wait to feel you lose it, squeezing me with that tight little ass as you lose yourself. Fuuuck." He rotates his hips and I clench around him. "Yeah, just like that."

It happens faster this time. He cuts off my air and I sink into it, the buzzing sensation creeping from my balls to my dick. When Rafe hits my prostate, fireworks shoot through me and his hand muffles my groans. Then something shifts inside me. I try to take a breath but can't, and instead of fear, what I feel is elation. Instead of air, all I take in is Rafe. The tingling intensifies and my vision goes a little swimmy and then I'm coming, a huge, wracking orgasm that swallows me up in blackness.

My dick is pulsing with pleasure and my stomach and chest are heaving and my ass is spasming around Rafe's dick. I'm gasping in air and Rafe is moaning into my neck, and then he's coming so hard I can feel it, and he crushes me to him, the sensation of his body all around me a rush all its own.

My heartbeat slams in my temples. My skin feels exquisitely, almost painfully sensitive, and I'm shivering, but I just want to hang on to the feeling of being completely flayed in Rafe's arms for one more minute.

I open my eyes to find him looking at me, holding my face in his hands. I nod and there's relief in his trembling lips when we kiss.

As he pulls out, I groan at how sore I am. Not just my ass and my legs, but my arms and my stomach and even my mouth. I didn't notice any of it when Rafe was holding me, but now I feel... wrung the fuck out. I wince as I straighten out, irritated that something that could feel so amazingly, transcendentally good one minute can leave me feeling like shit the next.

Rafe lies down next to me and reaches out to help me, but I bat his hand away, grumbling.

He looks a little guilty but also a little pleased with himself, so I slug him in the shoulder.

"Ouch," I say, and he lets out a relieved laugh, wrapping his arms around me and sliding a leg between mine.

"That was amazing," Rafe murmurs. He strokes a warm hand up and down my spine. "You okay?"

I nod, shivering just remembering the things he did to me. I stammer, then shake my head, giving up any attempt to explain how he makes me feel.

"What?" he asks softly, stroking my chin so I'll look at him. I just shake my head, and Rafe huffs and pulls me on top of him, nestling his mouth near my ear. "Tell me." He squeezes me tight and I shudder and wince, my legs falling open around his hips. I wrap his hair around my fingers and kiss the warm skin below his ear.

"Tell me, Colin. Just say it, whatever it is. Say it quick."

I squeeze my eyes shut and breathe in the smell of his hair.

"I think... I need you."

"What?" he asks gently, cupping my face and moving me so he can see me.

I bite my lip, and I'm sure my face is bright red because I can feel the heat there.

"I don't know what's fucking wrong with me," I say, trying to explain, "but you do something to me and I...." I shake my head, the words coming out in a muddle.

Rafe's hands are warm on my face, his eyes gentle, but he doesn't bail me out. He just listens.

"Before, I was—before I met you was... terrible. Everything was terrible. I was... terrible. I didn't mean to be. I just... I couldn't—and then I met you and now, I can't—if you weren't—I don't... I—"

I'm shaking and Rafe takes pity on me.

"I need you too, doll," he says, squeezing me tight. "I need you too."

Chapter 13

"WHERE THE fuck have you been?"

Even though there's no one else here, Brian is sitting on the floor in front of the television, where he usually sits when Pop or Sam takes the recliner and I take the couch.

His face is puffy and his eyes are vacant and there are beer cans strewn all over the living room. Even through the mustiness, the yeasty metallic smell tells me the cans have been sitting here awhile.

Though I've always let myself in to Pop's house before or come in through the garage after work, it feels weird to just walk in. Like I'm intruding.

"Had to get out of here for a bit," I say, defensiveness rising immediately, even though the whole reason I came over here was to apologize for disappearing and to make sure he's okay.

I cross my arms and pinch myself to try and set myself back on course.

"So, listen," I say, sinking deep into the busted couch cushions. "Um, we need to figure out what's going on with the shop. Do we want to keep things the same for a bit or start accepting different kinds of business? Do we want to take a little time?"

Brian's not even looking at me.

"Callie didn't call me back," he says softly.

"Huh? Who's Callie?"

"*Callie*. I told you about her!" Brian's voice rises an octave.

"Call—oh, the girl you puked on."

"I didn't puke on her!" Brian whines. Then he mumbles, "It was on her cat. I don't think she likes me anymore." Brian's eyes are unfocused and he sounds like a second grader. A drunk second grader. He reaches out blindly for a beer can and takes a swig. He immediately sputters and gags.

"Not from today?" I say as he wipes his tongue with his sleeve.

"Ugh!" He throws himself down so he's lying on the floor.

I trap my hands beneath my thighs so Brian can't see they're in fists. It took all the energy I had to get over here today so we could figure shit out about the shop. I really don't feel like hearing about Brian's latest random obsession.

"Uh. Right. Anyway, about the shop...."

"Are you still gonna let me work there?"

"What? Of course. What are you talking about?"

"Well, everyone knows I'm not good at it the way you and Pop and Sam are. Hell, even Daniel was better with cars than me."

He's right. He's not great with the complicated fixes and doesn't have the focus the rest of us do, but... I didn't actually think he knew that.

"You all just send me to make coffee and pick up the old ladies anyway. Probably doesn't pay enough to keep the house now that it's only me."

"Bri," I say, "that's—I mean, you're—we...," I start. He snorts. "This is a family business, is what I mean. And you're part of it. Okay, yeah, maybe if you were a stranger, I wouldn't hire you over someone else. But that's not the point. You know the business and you're one of us, so shut up about that shit."

I was shooting for comforting, but the way Brian's looking at me, I think I may have missed the mark.

"What if—what if I didn't want to do it anymore?" Brian says softly. "The shop. What if I want to do something else?" His voice is almost a whisper and he's looking at me like he's afraid of what I might do.

Brian's always done what we told him to, but I always thought it was because he liked it that way. Liked not having to worry about figuring shit out on his own. He's looking at me expectantly, nervously. And I can't help but think of what Daniel said. About how the things I said had an effect on him when I always thought he didn't care.

"That... would be okay."

Brian's eyes go wide and his face relaxes. "Yeah?"

"Well, yeah, man. It's your choice. Do you know what you wanna do instead?"

"I—you're gonna think it's lame," he says. I shrug. "I want to be a bartender." I look at him, unsure what to say. "Well, okay, I thought maybe someday I could have my own bar."

"That's... that'd be cool, man. Really."

"Yeah? Yeah."

"Why didn't you ever say anything before?"

Brian's eyes immediately cut toward the recliner. "Yeah, 'cause Pop *wouldn't* have totally killed me. And he definitely wouldn't have let me keep living here." His face falls and his lip starts to tremble all of a sudden. He looks around, like he's just remembered Pop isn't here anymore.

"Colin," he says, and it comes out as a whisper. "I… I'm a total loser, man. No wonder Callie doesn't want to be with me. I mean, I don't even—I don't even fucking know how to take care of… anything." He gestures around the house. "Pop always…." He shakes his head and he looks so lost.

"Told you what to do," I finish for him. He bites his lip like he thinks I'm about to make fun of him, but nods. "Yeah, I know, man. But, look, maybe… well, maybe Pop wasn't the best at knowing how to take care of everything either."

Brian looks surprised.

"Just, you know. You can do it." Yeah, I'm definitely not very good at these pep talk thingies.

He nods again, but he's already distracted by something else. "Hey!" he says. "Who's the guy?"

"Um. What? Who?"

"The big guy with long hair."

My stomach drops.

"I don't—what?"

Brian rolls his eyes. "The guy who was at your house. I swung by your place yesterday because no one had heard from you—hell, I even called Daniel!—and I saw this guy. I, uh, I remember you got mad the last time I just showed up without calling, though, so I didn't ring the bell."

My heart is hammering in my throat, and I feel like I'm going to puke. I keep opening my mouth to try and say something, but nothing is coming out.

Brian saw Rafe. In my house.

My breathing stutters and my mouth goes dry.

What's confusing, though, is that I feel something treacherous and unfamiliar trying to claw its way out. And I have to get the fuck out of here, because what's trying to get out is the goddamn truth.

I try to stand up casually. "Gotta take off," I say, already halfway to the door. "I'll talk to you later." And I rush out before he can say anything.

I drive home on autopilot and get in the shower. My hands are shaking and I can't figure out where that impulse came from. Tell Brian about Rafe? That's crazy.

Isn't it?

By the time the water goes cold, I still have no clue what's going on with me. I'm shaky and fidgety and every time I start to calm down, I get really aware of my breathing and then I start sweating and my stomach hurts. I want to call Rafe, but he's at work and I don't want him to think I can't even get through a day without him.

Finally, after clicking over to his number for the third time, I throw my phone onto the couch and grab the whiskey from the cabinet. I just need something—anything—to make this feeling stop. After two drinks, I feel a little calmer. After four, I start to panic because I know Rafe hates when I drink. So I try and tell myself that it's no problem: I just won't see him tonight and he'll never know I've been drinking. But then the idea of not being able to see him makes me feel panicky and fucked up. And *that* requires another drink.

Finally, I can't stand it anymore and I call Rafe.

"Hey," he says when he picks up. "I'm actually on my way to your house—that okay?"

"Yeah" is all I get out before he says, "See you in a few," and hangs up.

"Shit, shit," I mutter. I wash my face and brush my teeth three times to try and get rid of the whiskey on my breath, but I can't make myself call and tell him he shouldn't come, even though I know he won't like it. I need to see him.

I fucking need him.

Oh god.

"HEY," RAFE sighs when I open the door. He looks tired but happy to see me. I still can't get over the way he's actually *happy* to see me.

"What's wrong?" he says, immediately wary as he looks at me closer. "Did something happen?"

He reaches a hand out to me and I stumble as I go to him.

"Sorry," I say. "Sorry, sorry, but Brian saw you, and he asked who you are and I don't—something's wrong with me because I wanted—just, I don't know—and I had to get out of there, and—"

"And get drunk," Rafe says, holding me at arm's length.

I squeeze my eyes shut. A child's logic that if I can't see him, then I can't be seen. He sighs loudly and lets go of me, going to sit on the couch.

"I'm sorry," I say, sitting on the other side of the couch. "I know you're mad. But I didn't mean to. I just... I was freaking out, and I couldn't—look, don't be mad, okay?"

He shakes his head tiredly.

"No, I know you are," I try. "I mean, you seem mad. And I'm really sorry. But—"

"It's not about you, Colin."

"Yeah, I know, it's about drinking. You don't like it. I know. I'm sorry. I'm really sorry, but—"

Rafe shakes his head again, not looking at me, and bites off a bitter laugh.

"No, I mean, it's not actually always about you, Colin!"

"I—what?"

"Do you know why I was on my way here when you called?"

Oh. Shit. I didn't even ask. I shake my head and he grabs my wrists, looking right at me with such intensity that I want to look away.

"You said you needed me. You said you *needed* me, Colin." Heat rises in my face at how desperate I was with his arms around me and his breath on my neck. "And what did I say to you?"

I search my memory, but all I come up with is how safe he made me feel. Well, and how hard he made me come.

Rafe winces. "I said that I need you too." He pushes me away and starts pacing the living room. His hands are on his hips, and I notice for the first time that his hair is coming out of its braid, like maybe he'd forgotten it was tied back and run his hands through it anyway.

"I—did something happen?" I ask.

"Do you know what that means to me?" he asks.

Shame washes over me when I remember the conversation we had before Pop's funeral. Rafe said he was jealous of his sisters because they have him to go to. Because they know that he'll always be there for them. Because that's what he wants: someone who he knows will always be there for him. Fuck.

"I needed you tonight," he says softly, and the hurt and disappointment in his voice make my stomach curdle.

"Tell me what happened." I reach for him but he shrugs away from me.

"I don't want to talk to you when you're wasted," he says.

"I'm not. I swear. Not anymore. I can listen, I promise."

He narrows his eyes. "You don't understand." His hands are fists at his sides and his teeth are clenched. "When I'm around it… any of it…. I still want to use, okay?" He sounds disgusted with himself. "It's always there, at the edges of my mind. As an option. As a thing I'm *not* choosing. It's never just… gone. Even after all these goddamned years, I still remember what it felt like." His voice goes dreamy. "What it feels like to get away. To escape. To breathe because it's not all my responsibility. To make a move without thinking through every possible consequence. To take something because I want it. To shrug and have every fucking thing fall away."

He shakes his head and shrugs for real, like he hopes it'll have the same effect. When he meets my gaze, he looks ashamed.

"I'm sorry," I whisper. "I'm so sorry. You can count on me. You can."

It sounds hollow even to me, and Rafe's face makes my heart sink because I can see how much he wants it to be true and how much he doesn't believe me.

"I'm not sure I can do this." Rafe's voice is the shocked whisper of someone confessing a secret he has only just now realized.

My heart starts to pound so hard it makes me light-headed.

Rafe puts his hand over his mouth.

"Oh god," he murmurs. He sinks down to the floor, looking up at me, his hand still over his mouth. "Oh god, I'm not sure I can do this."

"Rafe, no," I say, kneeling in front of him.

He's trembling, his eyes wide.

"Rafe?" I put a hand on his shoulder. His eyes have gone distant, like he doesn't even see me.

"I want you all the time," he says. "I would do anything for you. But—" He bites his lip and shakes his head. "—but if I have to worry that every time something is hard, you'll…. And if I don't even have…. Oh god. Colin…."

Rafe's eyes are wild. Desperate. I've never seen him like this before, and a kind of panic I've never felt before rises in me. It's huge. And instead of feeling like darkness, like sticky tar, it's just need—need that I can't let go. While I'm used to the darkness, I don't know what to do about needing someone. About a yearning for something beyond myself so strong that it wants to push out through my skin. He's there on the floor and everything in me is sparking toward him, like a live wire, desperate for a ground.

"*Rafe.*" I hardly recognize my voice. His eyes snap to mine. "Please. Please, just tell me what happened." I have this idea that if only I can get him talking, then this won't be happening. If I can figure out what the problem is, then I can solve it. Like a leaky valve or a cruddy engine. He won't leave me. He won't give up on us.

"It's all over," he whispers. "I just didn't expect it all at once."

"Tell me!"

"I failed all of them. And Javi. He trusted me, but everyone else…. They think I'm trash. Just a fucking criminal. I should've known. I can't… I can't believe I thought they actually had faith in me."

"Who? What happened? Please."

When he doesn't answer me, I straddle him and put my hands on his shoulders, forcing him to look at me. He looks surprised to find me so close.

I lean in and kiss him, just a soft touch of our lips, and his eyes flutter closed. I kiss his cheeks and his chin.

"What happened?"

He squeezes his eyes shut, his hands settling on my hips automatically. I'm dead fucking sober now.

"Youth Alliance has a board of directors. They don't really do much day to day, but they're in charge of grant writing and the budget for programming and salaries, and writing press releases or providing info to other groups who do similar work. And they're in charge of keeping records for all of the kids and the staff and volunteers at YA."

"Okay," I say, not understanding the problem. Rafe's shoulders slump.

"Javi hired the original people who worked there. The board came later, once YA grew. After it became a 501(c)(3). A nonprofit," he explains at my blank look. "Javi hired me long before there was a board or any official process for hiring. I started out volunteering, then just kind of segued into working there part-time. They needed all the help they could get. The board knows me, of course, but I've never been involved with them. When Javi died and I started, you know, doing more, we didn't really talk about it. Things were crazy and I was the one who knew the kids, knew how everything worked because I'd always been with Javi. Nothing was official. We were just trying to… keep it all together.

"But today," he says, "Carly, the board representative, called me and asked if I'd have a meeting with them. They found out that I'm a… that I have a record."

"They didn't know?"

"Javi didn't put it in my file. They do background checks on everyone now, but since I'd already been there…. In my file Javi'd written that he knew me from church." Rafe snorts. "And they all trusted Javi, so no one questioned it, I guess. After he died, they were just glad someone knew what needed to be done."

"So, why did they check up on you now?"

"Anders' father told them." The muscle in Rafe's jaw tightens. "After he found out Anders had been coming to YA, he looked into me. It's public record." He shakes his head. "He was angry. Looking for something to discredit YA. Make us look bad. And there I was. A fucking ex-con and an addict working with youth, and the board didn't even know. Honestly, I'm lucky they didn't call the cops on me."

"Oh no."

"I…." His voice trembles. "I just don't know what I'll do without them, and—"

When I pull him against me, he's shaking.

"And not having you either—I—" He closes his eyes.

"Don't say that. Please don't say that. I'm sorry, Rafe. I'm so sorry. I'm—fuck, I'm sorry about all of it. But you can't—I mean, I—we—it's—just, please, don't."

Rafe leans back so he can see me. He strokes my cheek, my eyebrow, my lips. I can't read his expression at all.

"I… need some time to think," he says softly, pressing his thumb to my lips.

"Rafe, no," I say, but his thumb makes the words sound garbled.

He stands, pulling me to my feet.

"Please," I try again, "what do you mean you don't have me? You—" But he cuts me off.

"Colin. I need to make sure I'm doing the right thing. The right thing for *me*. Because I can't go much deeper before—" He rakes his hair back, then looks at me seriously. "I thought maybe talking with Daniel might help you see how much you have to gain by being honest."

"I—what?"

"I just need you to know," he says slowly. "That it's a lot. For me. The secrecy. If this is how it's always going to be—a secret, a lie. It's a lot, Colin. It's a lot if I don't have any hope that things might be different someday. Maybe…. It may be too much. Too much to live with and not… I just have to think. Okay?"

My head is spinning and my stomach's churning, but he kisses my forehead before I can say anything, and walks out the door.

The words echo after he's gone, though. *Secret. Lie. Too much.*

They echo for a long, long time.

Chapter 14

WHEN I was sixteen and broke my arm, the doctor at the hospital asked me to rate the pain on a scale of zero to ten, with zero being no pain and ten being the worst pain I could imagine. I wanted to look tough, sure. But also I could imagine oceans of pain so vast and incalculable they tipped this to practically nothing. So I told him it was a four. He smirked at me and gave me a pain pill anyway. What was worse than the pain, though, was the fear. When I first crashed Pop's car, all I felt was pain, and I didn't know what it meant. Was I going to look down and see that my arm had been torn off? Once I knew it was just broken, even though it hurt the same, it didn't feel as bad. Broken bones heal. I knew that.

Every second since Rafe walked out my door has been a pain so different it's shocking it can even be called the same thing. And rather than reacting like I usually do—wanting to disappear, wanting to obliterate myself—cut and punch and run and puke until there's nothing left—now I feel like I need to *do* something. I'm vibrating with restless energy. I'm waiting for something and I don't know when it will come. I'm teetering at the edge of a cliff, and a breeze from one direction or the other could end or save me.

In an attempt to fall in the right direction for once, I went back to work right after New Year's, desperate to get out of the house, only to find that no one had been coming in since Pop died. I don't know what Sam's been up to because he hasn't called me back about the shop. Luther took the week off to go to some aunt's house or something. Brian's been out, mostly. He says he's following up on bartending gigs, but he has the manic look he only gets when he's scheming about a girl, so I assume it has something to do with Callie and her puke-cat.

Alone in the shop, I've worked twelve-hour days and still wanted to do more. After I finished the repairs that had languished with Pop's death, I cleaned up the whole shop, putting in order things that've been a mess for years. I've thrown away busted tools and organized good ones, shredded dozens of boxes of useless papers in Pop's office and redone his filing system (less of a system and more of a stack, really), scrubbed every corner of the garage until the floor was clean enough to eat off of, and repainted the walls a blue-gray color that reminded me so much of the ocean outside Rafe's beach house when I went to the paint store that I couldn't help but buy it.

I've oiled every hinge and plastered every crack. I've cleaned the ductwork and installed a new phone with an intercom system from the office to the shop floor. I've sifted through every piece of hardware and organized it all. Ball bearings separated by size; hinges, gears, cotter pins, and springs categorized by type; wire neatly bundled. Every screw, rivet, nut, washer, O-ring, and shim has a home.

The messages start coming while I'm painting.

I'd given Anders my phone number back when he came to the shop needing to talk. I figured in case shit went seriously wrong at home, at least he could call. He'd never used it until now, though. *I'm so sorry about your dad* is all he writes. Rafe must've told the kids.

Before I can even write back to say thanks, another message comes through. *Death effing sucks. Sorry Winchester ;) oh this is Carlos.* Anders clearly gave him my number, too.

Then: *So sorry sweetie. Let me know if U need cheering up!!! xoxoxo Mikal.*

And: *Condolences Colin. You don't seem like a flower guy so I didn't send any but I'm sorry for your loss.* That one is unsigned but clearly from Mischa, echoing her parents' country club style.

Then, from Mikal again: *DeShawn says it's totes innappropes to text U w/o permish. Sorry bb!!! We just <3 U! xoxoxoxoxo*

The idea that I may not see them again—that without Rafe working at YA, I have no reason to be there—settles in my stomach like cement. It quickly becomes clear that Anders, DeShawn, Mikal, Carlos, and Mischa are all together because they begin to text me in a flurry of tangled responses I can't keep up with.

Finally, they get irritated and call me instead.

"Dude. Dude. Yo, Winchester! Take the phone away from your ear, man, it's Facetime."

I pull the phone away and see them huddled together on a perfectly made bed. The green-and-white checked blanket and bright white walls dotted with framed pictures hung on green ribbons mark it as Mischa's room, I'm pretty sure. Carlos waves at me and grins. Mikal claps excitedly. Anders and DeShawn are still and serious, leaning against the wall. Mischa walks in the door holding a bag of apples and a box of crackers and nods at me like I'm in the room.

Then they dive in with no preamble or pleasantries, all talking at once, and I can't help but smile at the familiarity of them interrupting each other, elbowing each other, and nodding in approval.

The long and the short of it is that they're devastated Rafe got fired, have a lot of questions about his past, which I evade, and are furious with the board. Not only because of Rafe but because, they assure me, all of the board members are lame to hang around with. Then they start giving me messages to give to Rafe, and my stomach clenches when I have to tell them that I'm not sure when I'll be able to pass them on.

"Did you guys break up?" Mischa asks.

God damn it. Trust teenagers to cut right to the gossip. I just shake my head, trying to come up with something.

"Oh no!" Anders cries, sounding like he's in pain. DeShawn turns to him immediately. "You can't break up. You guys are, like, my OTP. If you can't make it, there's no hope for me!"

He sounds genuinely upset. What the hell is an OTP?

"Look," I say, "the point is that I'm sure Rafe would want to hear from you, but there are, uh, protocols and things, so you'll just have to wait and see."

"That's shit, Colin," Mikal says in a bitter voice, rolling his eyes. It might be the first time he's called me by my name instead of "sweetie" or "boo." It doesn't bode well. "Let me guess. You broke up because you're still in the closet and Rafe finally lost patience, right? Well, fucking man up and get the job done."

"That's *super* sexist," Mischa says.

"It's *bullshit*," Mikal insists. "You guys are, like, like, *perfect* together. You're all—" He gestures wildly. "—and he's all—" More gestures. "—and I can't *believe* you!"

Then they're all talking at once and there's no way I'm wading into it. I should be pissed that I just got called out by a teenager, but I already feel so shitty and mixed-up about things with Rafe that I can't even muster any indignation.

As they move from the shambles of my romantic life to ranting about how they'll force the board to hire Rafe back, it's Anders I can't stop looking at. His hands are clenched in his lap, his skin and hair almost ghoulishly pale against his black clothes. He's leaning into DeShawn's shoulder just a little, and DeShawn keeps glancing down at him.

Watching them, I'm reminded of something Anders said when he came to the shop to see me. He talked mostly about not wanting his parents to be disappointed in him, but just before he left, he said that it helped to know maybe someone could still like you even if you couldn't quite be totally open yet. I'd been embarrassed at the idea he was talking about me and Rafe. But now I wonder if he was thinking about DeShawn. If Anders was relieved to think that maybe they could have a chance to be something even if he didn't out himself.

I'm still thinking about Anders days later. I know Rafe probably wouldn't approve, but I texted Anders the night I talked with the kids and asked him how things were with his family.

He responded within seconds. *I don't think I can tell them. I don't know what my dad will do.*

I was furious for him and nervous for him and I told him that was fine. That if he didn't feel like it was okay, then it was better to protect himself. That the most important thing was making sure he was safe. He texted back a *Thanx* and a smiley face, and I sat on my bed and stared at my phone for hours.

Because I already was safe. I could protect myself. Rather, there was no one in my life I needed to protect myself from. Not really. Not anymore.

XAVIER OPENS the door and immediately pulls me into a hug.

"I'm so sorry about Pat, bro. So sorry." He squeezes me, then thumps me on the back.

"Thanks," I mumble into his shoulder.

"Why didn't you tell me about the funeral, man? I would've been there."

"I—well, I mean, you guys didn't exactly get along, so I didn't figure you'd care that much."

"I would've wanted to be there for *you*, you fucking idiot," he tells me, shaking his head and gesturing me into the kitchen.

"Oh. Sorry. Thanks. I guess I didn't really think about it like that."

X rolls his eyes and sits me down on one of the stools at the bar that separates his kitchen counter from his living room.

He grabs a beer out of the fridge and slides it in front of me.

"Oh, um—thanks, man… but I'm not, uh—I'm taking a break for a bit." I push the beer away with one finger even as I can taste its icy bite in the back of my throat.

"Yeah?" X immediately takes it away from me and puts it back in the fridge. "That's… shit, that's good, man. Really good." He sets a lemonade in front of me instead and takes one for himself. "It's this lemonade from Lancaster that Angela's obsessed with. Pretty good, actually."

"She here?"

"Nah, she's out with some of her girlfriends. Oh, hey, you know who I could swear I saw the other day? Daniel."

"Um, yeah, he was in town. We… uh, we hung out, actually."

"You don't hang out with people." X snorts. "And you definitely don't hang out with Daniel. What's the deal?"

"Well, I just… he wanted to talk about some stuff, so…."

"I always liked Daniel."

I roll my eyes like I always do when he's said this over the years. But then I stop and remind myself that I don't have to feel that way about Daniel anymore.

"Hey, Colin," X says, which is weird because he almost never uses my full name. "I'm real sorry about Pat, but… you look good, bro. I mean, you look—don't take this the wrong way, but you look better."

Xavier's looking at me totally sincerely. My oldest friend. And all of a sudden, nothing makes sense. It makes no sense that I've lied to him all these years. That I've shied away from ever talking about anything real with him, since he's obviously seen a lot of it anyway.

"Colin! Dude, are you listening?"

"I'm gay," I blurt, my voice echoing wildly in Xavier's spotless tiled kitchen.

I take a huge sip of too-sweet lemonade and choke on it. When I can get a breath, I say, "I get if you don't want to be my friend anymore—" but X punches me in the shoulder before I can finish my sentence. "Ow, shit!"

X stands up and starts pacing in front of me. "That what you fucking think of me, you asshole? That I'm a damn bigot who'd throw away twenty years of friendship?"

I shake my head, looking up at him.

"God damn it, Colin!" he yells. "I can't *believe* you!" He shakes his head. "This is—this isn't a new thing, is it?"

He's got his hands on his hips, staring down at me, and I stand up so I don't feel quite so small.

"I—um, well, yeah, but I—"

"I could *kill* Pat!" Xavier roars.

"What?"

"See, I knew it."

"Huh?"

X throws himself down on the stool next to me, looking thoughtful. "I always knew it was something. I even wondered if it was that you were gay, but then you always had such a problem with Daniel...." He shakes his head. "Fucking family, man. I get it. A lot of my family, they don't... get me anymore. They think since I married Angela and started my job... like, that I'm not real anymore. You know? They think I'm putting on airs or something. It's... you know, it's bullshit—ignorant bullshit, but it still hurts that they think that. They think Angela's a gold digger or something. Like, that she wants us to be all rich and living in the suburbs or some shit. But they don't even know her. They don't want to get to know her."

The relief—no, the gratitude—that X is just talking like usual is so sharp that my throat gets thick and tears prick my eyes.

"And sorry to speak ill of the dead," he's saying, "but I didn't just hate your dad because he was a racist dick. I hated him for this, too. The way you were always scared of disappointing him. How nothing you did was ever good enough. Man. I *hated* him for that." X's voice is fierce and I'm reminded of all the times he had my back.

"Thanks," I say. "For not hating me."

X glares at me. "I'm gonna try really hard to remember that you're freaked and not take it super fucking personally that you thought I might care." He shakes his head at me like I'm the biggest idiot to walk the earth. "So, who's the guy?"

"What? What guy? Why d'you think there's a guy?"

"You're not the confessional type, C. Not a big sharer, ya know. So I figure there's a reason for you to tell me after all these years." He winks at me. "Unless of course it's because you finally want to confess your love for me."

I smack X, spilling lemonade on the counter in the process, and he cackles.

"Nah, it's cool, bro. I'll keep it on the DL with you." This time when I move to push him off his stool, he wards me off, suddenly serious. "For real, if I mess up this kitchen, Angela will have my ass."

We both crack up at the same moment, and when we've finally calmed down, X toasts me with his lemonade, walks into the living room, and flips on the TV, settling back against the couch like things are exactly as they've always been.

X KNOWS. The kids at YA know. Daniel knows. And no one cares. That's what I've been saying over and over to myself for the last few days. No one cares and I feel… better. Not just because people know I'm gay. (I can't get used to that phrase no matter how many times I think it.) But because I'm *doing* something. I'm not just sitting around waiting for things to happen the way I always have.

The next thing that has to happen? I have to tell Brian and Sam. Not because of some bullshit like they deserve to know. But because I'm so fucking tired of how much energy it takes to keep it a secret. I was thinking of Anders and all the work he has to do. He had to tell his parents that he was just going to YA with Mikal in support. Had to sneak around to meet up with his friends. Keep his phone turned off and in his pocket whenever he was at home in case a text came that would give everything away. And all of it just to feel safe in his own house.

In one of the texts Anders sent me a few days ago, he said he wanted to start practicing a new violin piece for a recital that's coming up but because of all the lies and the fear and the way he's constantly on guard, he just didn't have the energy.

That hit me hard. Made me wonder how many things I might have done if I hadn't spent so much energy hiding.

Now I feel like I'm going to puke with nerves and I can't stop jiggling my knees and cracking my knuckles as I wait for Sam to show up. He thinks we're meeting to talk about the shop, and when he walks through the door, I actually think I might pass out.

"Hey," he says. "Been a while."

He looks tired, or maybe just still sad about Pop.

We go into the kitchen to make coffee and the smell of it nearly turns my stomach. My knees are like jelly.

I can hear Brian in the shower, but the idea of standing there with Sam until he gets out is unbearable. I pound on the bathroom door. "Brian, can you get out here for a minute?"

"Dude, what the hell?" Sam asks, pouring coffee into the lumpy green mug he always uses.

I shake my head and pour my own coffee.

"What? What's wrong? What's up?" Brian says, crashing out of the bathroom with a towel wrapped around his hips and a spot of lather in his wet hair. He blinks confusedly at Sam and me drinking coffee in the kitchen. "You okay?" he asks.

"Don't look at me," Sam says, nodding at me.

"Yeah. Yeah, fine, I just wanted…."

"Okay, business stuff—it's cool," Brian offers, and I jump on it.

"Right, so. Are you guys cool with expanding or whatever to take on vehicles Pop never liked working on?"

"You're the one who's good at those repairs, bro," Sam says. "It's fine by me, but it'd mostly be on you."

"Yeah, fine by me," Brian echoes. "I'm not really involved anymore, anyway."

"Okay," I say, staring at the floor.

"Um," Brian says, "that it? 'Cause…." He gestures to his wet hair.

My throat feels tight and my mouth is clamped shut. I squeeze my eyes shut and picture the icy calm of the winter ocean at Rafe's beach house—the way the waves broke on the shore and were pulled back together every time.

"I… I… I'mdatingaman," I spit out, my heart pounding with relief as the words linger in the air.

"Um, what?" Brian says. "Sorry, didn't catch that."

I turn to Sam, whose eyes are narrowed in confusion. He shakes his head too.

"I… um, I've been… um… I'm dating a guy."

Brian lets out a nervous laugh and looks between Sam and me, his face panicked.

I realize I've been holding my breath and I make an effort to let it out and breathe in again. Think of Rafe, think of Xavier, think of the waves. In and out, in and out.

"I don't—I don't get it," Brian says finally.

"It's not a joke," Sam says. His voice is poisonous.

"I—Sam—" I start.

"No, I get it," Sam says. Standing here, in this kitchen, he looks so much like Pop. He and Brian both have Pop's dark hair and eyes. And the expression on Sam's face—a kind of irritated contempt—looks so much like Pop's that for a moment it's like having him back. "Pop's dead so now you can finally spread your goddamned wings and soar like a butterfly, right?" My heart lurches into my throat. "You'll just change the shop to the way you've always wanted it to be. Prance off to the Pride parade like nothing ever happened. Great. Just fucking great. Lucky you. It's like he never existed at all."

"I don't—what?" I say.

"Jesus, man, you think I didn't know you liked dick?" He lets out a disgusted, vicious little laugh. "Come on, Colin. You've never had a girlfriend." He's counting things off on his fingers. "You never talk to women. Even in high school, you never went out on dates, just hung out with your football friends. All you ever wanted was Pop's approval and to hang out with all his friends. Then Daniel came out and it was like you hated him. You made it your mission to shit on everything that made him happy. Anytime *anything* about him being gay came up, you stomped on it in a total panic. And Jesus save him if he said anything about it in front of Pop. It's like you thought you needed to protect Pop from it all, like *he* was the kid and Daniel was the one doing something nasty."

"I—but... I...."

"Fucking pathetic, man. It was goddamned depressing to watch you. I was so relieved when you finally moved out. Thought maybe you'd grow a pair and stop squirming under Pop's thumb."

"Me!" I yell, the anger finally breaking through the shock and shame. "What about you? You were always too fucking scared of Pop to say one word against him!"

"No, brother," he spits out. "That's where you're wrong, as fucking usual. I wasn't scared to speak against him. I just. Didn't. Care." He bites off each word like he's going to spit it at me. "Because this business is just a job to me. A job I like, but a job." He snorts. "Shit, Pop was miserable after Mom died. He was gonna be miserable no matter what. So I didn't get my damn feelings hurt when Pop shot down an idea, because I didn't fucking care. I've got my own life and my own shit to take care of, so

Pop could run this place however he wanted. But you…. Oh, man, you practically dug your own grave every time he shot you down. Pop and I got along fine because he knew to keep his nose out of my business. But, Jesus, Colin, you two were wrapped up tighter than a square knot."

"I… so… but—" I stammer.

"I don't give a shit who you sleep with, man. I really don't. You never cared about anyone but yourself anyway, so I don't know why I'd think that'll change now. Never cared what anyone but Pop thought, anyway."

"Sam, I…."

"You what, man? You don't care, so why don't you just admit it?" Sam bites his lip. "How many times has Liza invited you over for dinner but you never come. You never ask about anything outside of the shop. Ever."

Sam's face is angry but his eyes are hurt. He looks really, really tired.

"Are you—did something… happen?" I ask, a shot in the dark.

"Yeah," he says, biting his lip. "Yeah, something fucking *did* happen, actually. Liza was pregnant and she lost the baby last week." Sam's lip is trembling and he looks down at the floor.

"Fuck, Sam. Shit, I'm so sorry."

He pours his coffee down the drain and sighs. "Thanks."

"No, seriously. I'm sorry. About… Liza and the baby *and* about being so… whatever. It's been… made really clear to me lately that I'm not good at seeing what the hell's going on, so…."

"B-b-but…." I hear from behind me. I'd almost forgotten Brian was here. "I don't—I don't understand." His voice is small, like when he was a kid. Like when Pop died. "I don't…. If you're… if you… but then why were you so mean to Dan? Why did you…?"

Brian's shaking. His wet hair is dripping onto his bare shoulders and he's covered in goose bumps. He's hugging himself against the chill, his eyes darting from me to Sam and back again.

"I, um, I apologized to him," I say lamely.

Brian's eyes are wide.

"But… but I was *horrible* to him. I was fucking horrible to him because I thought that's what *you* wanted! You were always so miserable and it was, like, the only thing I could do that seemed to make you feel better was tease him. And so I-I-I did. And now… you—and…. *Fuck!*"

Brian grabs at his wet hair. He looks like he's going to be sick.

"I'm sorry," I whisper. "I'm so goddamned sorry."

"Can you go?" Brian says. "Just…." He shakes his head and walks into his bedroom, the spot of lather still in his hair, leaving Sam and me standing in the filthy kitchen.

"I DID it. I told Brian and Sam. I fucking did it!"

Shelby cocks her head to one side and then rolls onto her side on the floor to clean her own ass.

"Yeah, that's about right," I mutter and flop onto the couch.

I can't stay sitting down, though. I'm jittery with excitement and fidgety with nerves. In one way, it's as if everything was leading up to this—to me telling Brian and Sam. In another, though, the person who had the real power to break me when I told him is the one person I can never tell. In any case, it feels totally anticlimactic because I still don't have Rafe. I'm not sure what I expected. That he'd snap back to me like a rubber band the second I told them? I pace around the living room, trying to figure out what to do. After an infuriating few hours of pacing, cleaning, sit-ups, showering, more pacing, and more cleaning, I call Daniel.

"Dude," he answers the phone. "Congratulations."

"Huh?"

"You did it! You came out to Brian and Sam, right? I'm proud of you."

Daniel's voice is light, but his words settle comfortingly in my empty stomach.

"Wait, how did you know?"

"Oh, um, well, I got a very distraught message from Brian basically apologizing for treating me like shit all these years, and blaming you for it. No, I didn't mean—I'm kidding."

But I know he's not kidding. Neither was Brian. He didn't mean it like that, but he's right. I never gave it a moment of thought. But Brian would never have treated Daniel that way if what he said wasn't true. If he hadn't been trying to somehow do something for me. Brian can be an idiot, but he's not mean.

"I'm sorry, man," I say. It hangs in the air.

"No, I—that's not what I—I wasn't trying to—"

"No, I know. I get it. But still."

"That's why you called, right? Because you did it?"

"Yeah. I—well, not exactly. Rafe's upset with me. Thinks he can't trust me to… well, partly to be honest about… you know, our relationship, but also, like, to be there for him. He said he needed time to think. And I don't know how to… like, show him that he can. Trust me, I mean."

There's a pause before Daniel says, "*Can* he?"

"What? Yes!"

"Are you sure?"

"What? Fuck you, man! What, because you're—"

"Would you put a lid on it, Colin? I'm trying to help you. Explain it to me. Tell me why Rafe can trust you."

"Damn, man, why d'you have to be such a dick about everything?"

"Why do *you* have to get so defensive about everything?"

"I don't—" I take a deep breath. "Fine."

There's murmuring on the other end of the phone.

"Rex says don't be a dick to me or he'll have to defend my honor," Daniel says.

"Psh, yeah, I'd like to see him try," I say, instantly pissed again.

"Dude. I was kidding. A joke. Just calm the fuck down. Did you ever think that maybe *you're* the one freaking Rafe out enough that he thinks he can't trust you. If every time *he* asks you a question, you fly off the handle, then maybe—"

"Yeah, yeah, yeah, I get it. Jesus. Fine."

"So, explain it to me."

"I can't."

"Why."

"Because. It's—you're—I—we. It's private."

Daniel chuckles. "Fine, don't tell me. But if I were you, I'd tell Rafe. Not just *that* he can trust you, but *why*."

Daniel rambles on for a while about him and Rex and it all gets a little bit therapy for my taste, but then he says something that strikes a chord.

"If Rafe's what you want, then you have to fight for him the way you'd fight someone who was trying to take something away from you. You know how to fight. You've just got to figure out what are the right moves to win this one."

Chapter 15

SO THAT'S what I've spent the last two weeks doing. Fighting. But not for me this time. For Rafe.

I called the board of directors and talked to the chair, Carly, who seemed friendly enough at first. Once she realized who I was, she began by thanking me for working with the kids and even snuck in a fairly subtle suggestion that the shop might want to donate money for programming in the future. But when I turned the conversation to Rafe, she was cold. Not unsympathetic—hell, she'd known him for years—but absolutely decided. I tried everything I could think of to get her to give him another chance. I even sent her testimonials I had the kids make, but she was immovable. Under no circumstances could they have someone with a record working with youth. She was, she told me, frankly horrified that Javier had hired him in the first place, and they were now undertaking a thorough review of everyone he'd vetted.

I went back to Books Through Bars, where I'd been with Rafe, and talked to people there about what his options might be for working with queer youth. They were full of righteous indignation about him getting fired, which was at least satisfying, but they explained in no uncertain terms the realities of how having a record made you nearly unemployable in any job involving youth. Of course it was delivered alongside impassioned monologues about racial disparity in incarceration, the school-to-prison pipeline, and an ex-inmate shadow economy that rivals that of undocumented workers—not to mention several articles that someone e-mailed me from their phone. Still, the takeaway was clear. There wasn't much I could do.

Now I'm here. At Rafe's apartment, where I've never been invited. To tell him that I fought.

And that I lost.

The pounding of my heart in my ears is louder than my knock, and it speeds up as the door squeaks open and Rafe fills the doorway. He looks awful. His hair is dirty and coming out of its hair tie, and there are dark circles under his eyes. Worse, he looks defeated. Every muscle is slouched inward like they're curling around him, a last-ditch protection against the world. In his threadbare gray sweats, he looks like he's back in prison.

Worst: he does *not* look pleased to see me.

"I told you I needed time."

"I know," I say. He's blocking the door. "You look like shit."

He narrows his eyes at me but backs up just enough to let me in, like he doesn't even have the energy to tell me to fuck off.

His apartment is an efficiency, with a kitchenette that connects to the living room-slash-bedroom, and a bathroom off to the other side. It's dark and musty and everything is brown and a yellowish color that was probably once white.

He has a couch backed against the kitchenette, with a card table in front of it and a small TV on an upended wooden crate. On the card table are his phone and a beat-up old laptop. Taking up most of the rest of the space are a mattress and box spring pushed against the far wall and a small dresser next to them, stuffed to capacity. There's no closet, so a few dress shirts and a suit are hung from a hook next to the window and his shoes are lined up along the wall. A shelf between the kitchenette and the living room holds a few stacks of books, some DVDs, and random odds and ends piled among framed photographs of what must be his family.

Several posters for political rallies and groups hang in the living room, among them one for Books Through Bars. Other than the posters, the only decorations look suspiciously like craft projects. Maybe things his nieces and nephew made him? But no, looking closer at the amount of glitter and the preponderance of rainbows, they have to be from the kids at YA.

Rafe drops down on the couch and I sit next to him, sinking deeper into the worn couch than I expect to.

"Are you... okay?" I ask like an idiot. He's clearly not.

"Nope," he says flatly, staring straight ahead. "I'm exactly what I never wanted to be. An unemployed ex-con addict who sits around his apartment all day wishing he could get high and forget everything." His voice is so blankly hopeless that he doesn't even sound like the same person.

"No," I start to say, but he turns to me and grips my forearms.

"*Yes*," he snarls. "Those are true things. You can't hide them by keeping me a secret from everyone. I'm a fucking loser. So why are you here? I didn't call you." He drops my arms and turns away.

Rafe is pushing hard. I've done it so many times but never quite seen what it looks like from the other side: forcing someone to see you the way you see yourself. Forcing them to press their face right up to the ugliness inside and then make the decision about whether they want to go or stay from there. Most people go. But Rafe saw me at my ugliest and he didn't go. He asked for time and I gave it to him, but now I'm done. Done messing around. Done sneaking around. Done making excuses for either of us.

"Okay, yeah. You are unemployed. You went to prison so you are an ex-convict. You had a problem with drugs. And maybe you have been sitting around thinking about getting high. God knows you smell like you haven't left your apartment in weeks. So sure, those things are true."

His shoulders soften a little bit.

"Listen," I tell him, deciding to jump right in to what I came here to say. I'm not much for comfort at the best of times. "About YA. I'm so fucking sorry, man. I really tried to get them to give you your job back. The kids did too. Jesus, the shit they said. But…." I shake my head.

He turns to face me. "What?"

I tell him about talking to Carly and how I asked the kids to write testimonials about how important Rafe had been to them. When I tell him that instead of writing them, they recorded videos on their phones, he almost smiles, and mutters, "Of course they did."

"I can't believe you did that for me," he says finally, and shame settles in my gut at how clearly Rafe expected absolutely nothing of me.

"Sorry it didn't do any good."

"It did," he says softly. "Thank you."

"I get it more now. How freaked you were about the thing with Anders. How scared you were to break any rules. I—" I roll my eyes at myself. "—read some articles about all that stuff. How difficult it is to get hired when you have a record and how hard people come down on anything you do that's not perfect." I trail off, not really knowing how to talk about this stuff. "It's so damn unfair."

"Fuck, Colin," he says, and he takes my hands. "I don't know what I'm going to do without them. I just… I haven't felt this… untethered since…." He shakes his head and slumps back into the couch.

"Look, everything sucks right now, but you'll figure it out. You will," I insist as he starts to turn away. "When I met you, my life was utter garbage. No, it was. You changed everything for me, man. If you can do that for me, you can do it for yourself. Hell, maybe you'll start your own version of YA. Or whatever. I don't know. But you've got all this experience and you know tons of people who'd want to help. Maybe you can't do the same job. But that doesn't mean your life is over."

Rafe bites his lip and doesn't say anything, and I go up on my knees on his stupidly uncomfortable couch and put my hands on his shoulders. "I know my timing's shit," I say, forcing him to look at me, "but I want to be with you. For real. I want to... go to dinner at your mom's or whatever the hell."

"You do?" Rafe says suspiciously.

"Well, okay, no, I don't actually *want* to go to dinner at your mom's, but I will. If you want. And yes, I want to be with you. I just... I need you to tell me shit that you want. Like going to dinner. And I'll try. I know I haven't been very good at that, but I'm going to do better.

"And, like, we might each need different things, but that's normal, and if we can tell each other what those things are, then we can try and... you know... give them to each other, and...."

I trail off, embarrassed. Rafe's looking at me with narrowed eyes and a slightly open mouth like he has no idea what to say to me, which is fair, given that I totally garbled that.

"Uh. Fine. Daniel told me a bunch of that stuff, but it's true, right?"

Rafe almost smiles, then lets out a long sigh and scrunches up his eyes. "You're not really letting me wallow in my misery here, babe."

I grin. "Yeah, I guess I'm not as good at that as you are with me. Besides, you've been wallowing for weeks, looks like. So go on, then. Tell me what you need." I cringe at sounding like a self-help book.

He runs a tentative finger up my arm, and I brace myself to listen to what Rafe's conditions are. "I need you not to be drinking, mostly. A beer every now and then, sure. A glass of wine with dinner once in a while, okay. But I... I can't see you drunk. I just can't. And I can't know that it's your coping mechanism. I can't be honest with you if I know that I might potentially be the cause of you going off and getting wasted to cope with what I've said, even if you do it where I can't see. I can't know that's what I might trigger. It's not something I can live with. And I need to be able to be honest with you, so...."

"I get it," I say. "I—it's just something I've always done. I—Pop was always a drinker, and my brothers, and so...."

"I know a lot of people who could help you with it. There are meetings. A lot of support."

I shake my head. "Nah. I mean, no offense to the twelve steps or whatever. I know it helped you a lot. But I don't want to talk to people about that shit. I haven't had anything to drink since that night. The night you left. I can do it. I promise."

Rafe traces my mouth with his finger, but he doesn't look as hopeful as I'd like.

"That's good. That's really good. But... you can't promise something like that, okay? I mean, promise that you'll try, but it's a big deal. A process, not a onetime decision. And it's exactly because you've always done it that it's going to be hard. Because it's not only about stopping. It's about finding other ways to cope with stressors and problems when they arise. Do you see?"

I want to fight him with everything I have. Want to assure him that I *can* promise this, since it's the thing he says he needs. But I know he's right.

"But if I can't promise, then... are you saying you don't want to...?" I gesture between us, and Rafe catches my hand and kisses it.

"No, I'm not saying I don't want this. I'm saying that's one thing I need, and if you can promise me that you're going to work on it, then thank you."

I nod. I can do that. I can fight for that. "Okay, so what else?"

Rafe slumps back into the couch like he didn't expect me to agree or something.

"I missed you," he mutters. "I hated not being with you."

"Yeah. I—look, I know I fucked up. I'm going to prove to you that you can trust me. That I can be your, um, your you." He looks confused. "You know. Like when you said you were jealous of Luz because she had you." Rafe's expression softens and leans a little closer. "I know I've been a mess since you met me, okay? I do know that. But you can talk to me about the shitty stuff too. You don't have to wait until it gets this bad."

"I tried," he says.

"Yeah, maybe. And I probably fucked it up. But there have been other times. When you've been upset about things or feeling shitty about stuff and you didn't tell me. Like you thought I couldn't handle it. But I can."

"Yeah?"

I nod once. I think it's even the truth.

"Er, and I have to tell you something. You might be mad." Rafe tenses immediately but schools his expression. "I, um, I gave Anders my phone number that day that he came into the shop, and he gave it to the other kids and we've been texting. Especially me and Anders. Not in a creepy way, I don't mean. Just, I've been thinking a lot about all the shit he's going through. All of them are going through, really, and then we were texting, and anyway, I know it isn't protocol or whatever. But there are records or something, I'm sure, so it's not like anyone can accuse me of being inappropriate."

I've said all this in basically one long sentence so Rafe can't say anything, and now he groans and collapses onto me.

"Jesus Christ, Colin, I thought you were going to say... I don't know. Don't fucking scare me like that."

His body against mine for the first time in so long feels exactly right. I breathe him in and he smells—well, he smells bad, honestly, but underneath the not-showered, hiding-in-my-apartment mustiness, he smells like Rafe. I put my fingers in his dirty hair.

"I told Brian and Sam that I'm gay," I tell him quietly.

It feels like I'm peeling off my cards one by one and throwing them down on the table for Rafe. It's shock and awe and I'll be damned if I'm leaving here without getting Rafe on board. Something about seeing him this low, this down about everything, makes me finally feel like I have something to offer him.

"You *what*?"

He jerks away from me, and I start laughing at the look of total shock on his face. It may be slightly on the hysterical side because once I start, I can't stop. He's staring at me like I'm nuts, mouth hanging open ridiculously, which makes me laugh harder. He sputters.

"But... you... but, why?"

"Because of Anders' stupid dad," I get out through my laughter, "and because of Daniel, and because—because I fucking love you," I cackle. "I think. Maybe. Probably."

"What!"

He sounds so exasperated and looks so affronted that I laugh until I have to sit up so I don't choke. "Well, I don't know! I've never... *you* know." I gesture between us.

"Oh my god," he mutters, shaking his head, and starts laughing. Then he lunges at me and kisses me until I'm gasping for breath. He kisses my neck, and his hair falls in my face.

"You're filthy," I say. He makes a noise in the back of his throat. "No, I mean, when's the last time you took a damn shower, seriously?" I feel so light, so buoyant in the moment that I can't put any heat behind it. And honestly, I don't care.

"Mean," he murmurs and pulls me off the couch and onto the mattress two steps away.

"Ow! God damn it!" I roll to the side to escape the stabbing spring that Rafe just threw me onto.

"Sorry," he says, but he goes right back to attacking my neck.

"Jeez, no wonder you want to stay at my house all the time. All your shit is uncomfortable as hell."

"Mmhmm." He nods into my throat.

We kiss hotly, grinding together, and I roll us until I'm on top of him. I slide our pants down but that's all I can do before we're pressed together again, drinking the breath from each other's mouths and losing where one of us ends and the other begins, all playfulness dissolved in desperation.

We both fumble between our bodies, working our erections. Bolts of pleasure rocket through me and I grab at Rafe's arms as he drives our hips together. I've missed this so much. Forgetting myself in his body, his smell. Rafe's usual finesse is nowhere to be found, and it's as if a wall has dropped between us. He's wild, overwhelming, his weight pressing into me, his ragged breaths in counterrhythm with the groaning of his horrible mattress as we hump against each other. After only a few minutes I lose it, shuddering hard against him, shooting onto his stomach, crying out into his mouth, and pulling his hair harder than I mean to. He moans and comes with a few more strokes, heat blooming between us, and collapses next to me, sweaty and flushed.

When his breathing evens out, he pushes up on one elbow and kisses me sweetly—barely a kiss at all. More an innocent press of lips. A teenager-on-tiptoes impulse. We lie on our backs, our faces turned close together. I look at the freckles scattered across his nose and cheeks, and his eyes linger on my mouth. Rafe twines our fingers together and squeezes my hand, eyes fluttering shut.

Despite the saggy mattress and the stickiness coating my belly and thighs, I'm almost asleep with my face in Rafe's dirty hair when he cups my cheek.

"I love you too," he says. And I don't have to see his face to know he's smiling.

Epilogue

"THANKS FOR coming with me," I tell Rafe as we walk to the restaurant where we're meeting Daniel and Rex for dinner. They're moving here next month so Daniel can take a job teaching at Temple, and they're in Philly to find an apartment.

"Well, it's the least I could do since you're coming to Gabriela's birthday dinner with me this weekend," he says, smiling.

"Uh, I am?"

Rafe spins me around the corner and presses me against the wall in an alley between a parking garage and a 7-Eleven.

"Please?" he says, leaning in to kiss me softly.

"Hmm," I murmur against his mouth.

He runs a hand down my neck and presses a thumb against my lips. "I can make it worth your while," he whispers, and he slides a muscular thigh between mine, making my breath catch.

"Hmm?"

"Oh yeah. Never doubt it." Then he kisses me until I'm clutching at the back of his shirt and pressing against him and we're both breathing heavily.

"We'd better go to that restaurant right this second or else I'm taking you home," he says heatedly. "Besides, it's filthy in here."

I look around. It's definitely… an alley. "Hey, you dragged me in here. Besides," I say, bumping his shoulder, "don't knock it. We met in an alley just like this."

"Yeah, and if I remember correctly, I wanted to take you home that night too." He kisses me again, then pulls me against him so he can look into my eyes, his expression suddenly kind of… sappy. "I knew you were something special that night, Colin. Even though you didn't."

"Aw, man." I can feel myself blushing. "Well, I thought you were basically a dick." Way to ruin a moment. Rafe laughs and grabs my hand, pulling me toward the restaurant.

There should be a word for living a life so different from anything you ever thought was possible that you don't even recognize yourself in it.

The last few months have been hard. Rafe didn't adjust well to not being able to see the kids, and in an attempt to fill the space they'd left behind, he threw himself into political organizing projects so aggressively that I wouldn't see him for weeks at a time. Which made me think he didn't want to be around me. Which made me act like an asshole and insult his work when I did see him. Which made him *actually* not want to be around me.

Things were awkward for me at the shop. I'd told Luther and the other guys about being gay since it seemed ridiculous to keep it a secret when Sam knew. Though Luther didn't care much, the others' reactions varied and some of them ended up quitting.

Finally, though, after some epic fights and a particularly dark moment of Rafe's when the only thing that made any difference was forcing him to watch the video testimonials that the kids had recorded for the YA board, things have turned a corner. Rafe has had a bunch of meetings with people who are interested in helping him start a support group for queer youth and young adults who are currently incarcerated in Pennsylvania. They're only in the planning phase, but some of the calm satisfaction that he got from working with the kids at YA is already back.

And I've been trying to integrate our relationship more into my life outside my house. That's Rafe's term for it, anyway. Which basically just means keeping the promise I made about being willing to go out to dinner or the movies, and to meet his family.

They clearly weren't sold on me the first time we met. Except for Luz, who I think would like anyone Rafe liked, the consensus seemed to be that I was a boring white dude who didn't want kids and therefore brought very little to the table. His mother warmed to me a bit when she found out my parents were both dead, as if it was her responsibility to step up and force-feed me. Which, honestly, was irritating as shit, but I just smiled and let her do it, a decision that earned me epic sexual favors from Rafe. So I guess that was okay.

We also went to Xavier and Angela's for dinner. It was intensely awkward for the first half hour or so, with Xavier trying to play host and Angela asking all kinds of intrusive questions that made me want to punch her. Rafe was on his best behavior but was clearly uncomfortable because he'd given me permission to tell X he'd been in prison. Finally, Angela broke the tension by telling me she'd never liked me but now she felt like she was meeting me for the first time, and I told her I'd never liked her and actually nothing had really changed about that, and everyone laughed and she wasn't even mad about it. Which kind of made me like her a little bit.

Daniel and I have texted and talked on the phone some, and I saw him when he came to Philly to interview for the Temple job. He was a mess—nervous he wouldn't get the job, possibly more nervous that he would because he was convinced that Rex didn't really want to leave Michigan and move with him if he got it. It took Ginger to calm him down finally, practically shaking him and then snatching his phone and calling Rex to extract assurances that, yes, he really would move to Philly if Daniel got the job, and no, he wouldn't resent Daniel forever for making him leave his cabin in Michigan.

Daniel may be cool with me now, but despite working together to calm him down that night, I'm pretty sure Ginger still hates me on his behalf. And after years of hearing stories where I was the boogieman, I guess I can't blame her. Of *course* Daniel insisted she and the guy she's dating come to dinner with us too.

I shake Daniel's hand awkwardly when we get to the restaurant. I can never tell if that's what I'm supposed to do or if I'm supposed to hug him. Ginger snorts with amusement and I ignore her and let Daniel make the introductions.

Christopher's handshake is as warm and genuine as his expression. He's got bright red hair, freckles, and a boyish smile. Everything about him seems friendly and nonthreatening, and I find myself wondering if Ginger eats him alive.

I expected the restaurant Daniel chose to be kind of snobby, but Little Nonna's is a small Italian bistro with brick walls, mismatched table settings, and a view to the kitchen. The waiter leads us down a twisting hallway and out onto a back patio where there are larger tables. There are barrels of wine stacked at one side and what look like vintage aprons tacked on the wall amid strings of twinkly lights.

"This is nice," Rafe says, looking around.

"Christopher knows one of the chefs," Ginger says as she and Christopher slide into the table across from each other. I'm trying to figure out what configuration will be the least awkward. Daniel's looking around at the table, seemingly as baffled as I am. Rex finally takes the chair next to Ginger, but instead of sliding onto the bench across from him, Daniel sits down next to him. I must wait too long because Rafe just slides in next to Christopher and gives me a weird look.

We all sit in awkward silence as the waiter comes up and pours our water. Then Ginger shrugs and says, "So, Colin's gay now, we all have boyfriends, and Colin and Daniel are friends. Who'da thought?"

My face turns hot at once, and I want to kick her under the table, but Daniel just laughs and goes, "Right?" like he was thinking the same thing.

"Hey, did you ever invite Sam?" Daniel asks me.

"Yeah, I asked him at work." I hesitate and Daniel rolls his eyes.

"Dude, it's not like it could be worse than what I've heard from you guys my whole life." Rex puts his hand on the back of Daniel's neck. "I just—uh, sorry—just... what'd he say?"

"He said, 'I'll just let you two hang out since you have so much in common now.'"

"Has he been... shitty to you?" Daniel asks.

"Nah, he's been fine at work. Normal. But every time... like, when I said you were moving back, he was just kind of whatever about it."

Daniel sniffs. I used to think that sniff was him being prissy, but I've realized it's one more of the things he does when he's trying not to show he's hurt.

"Yeah," he says, "well, he didn't care before; why would he now?"

"I think maybe he's just being grouchy 'cause he's got his own shit going on at home," I say. I'm not sure if Sam would want me to tell Daniel this, but Sam's not here, so.... "He and Liza were trying to have a baby and she had a miscarriage."

"Oh shit," Daniel says. "That's awful."

We make polite small talk about Daniel's job and about the shop, though I stop myself from going into detail when Daniel's eyes start to take on the faraway look they always got when Pop or me, Brian, and Sam would talk about sports and cars. Instead, I tell them about Ricky, who's started working with me.

"She's awesome. She's this kid from YA—uh, the Youth Alliance—and she's a genius with cars. She asked me some question about a carburetor once, for a science project or something, so I brought her to the shop to show her. She's just…. She loves it, man. She's so into it, so I asked her if she wanted a job and she jumped on it. She's… not autistic…." I look at Rafe for the right description.

"She was born addicted to meth, and some symptoms that are on the autism spectrum go with that."

"She's just kind of vacant with people, but she's amazing. Dude," I say to Daniel, "remember when Pop would open the hood and have us see if we could guess what was wrong?" Daniel nods, a slightly pained expression on his face. "Well, asking Ricky's like running a human diagnostic. She inputs all the stuff that's wrong and she remembers every detail about the make and model's system and she, like, spits out the most likely scenario. She can't really talk to customers, but who cares."

Rex looks at me consideringly. "It's great that you gave her a chance even though she isn't… great with people," he says, his voice low. I remember Daniel telling me he used to be really shy. I didn't notice it at first since he throws up such a protective vibe, but I can definitely see that shyness tonight.

Ginger's telling a story about a client who came to her shop today when there's an obscenely loud sound of something vibrating against wood. Daniel jumps, jerking out of his chair, and fishes a battered flip phone out of his pocket.

"Jesus Christ, sorry, guys. I thought it was on silent." He shakes his head, looking awkward as he sits down. Then he flips open the phone and gets a kind of puppy-dog look on his face. "Aw, poor Leo—sorry, Ginge."

"Ooh, what's the latest in the tale of our young bizarro Daniel?" she asks. "Daniel made friends with this kid in Michigan who's basically exactly like he was as a teenager," she says to me with a wink, as if she assumes I know what she's talking about.

"Poor Leo," Daniel says, shaking his head in amusement. "He's, like… how would you explain it?" he asks Rex. Rex thinks about it for a minute before saying anything, like he and Daniel are alone.

"He's exactly who he seems to be," Rex says finally. Daniel nods, like this is exactly right, but I have no idea what that means.

"Yeah, there's no mask or anything. He's guileless," Daniel says, seemingly satisfied with that description.

Rex shakes his head.

"Oh," Daniel says, "yeah, he's totally genuine—like you said. So he's just really easy to hurt, I guess. Vulnerable. You know?"

"That is just like you, then," I say.

Daniel looks surprised. "What? No! What?" He looks between me and Rex. Rex gives him this barely there smile, but the way he's looking at Daniel... it's like there's a whole history behind it. Daniel blushes and looks down, mumbling something I can't make out.

"Um, anyway, he's only eighteen—no, nineteen now, I guess—and he's got this huge crush on Rex's friend... ex-boyfriend, really," he says, his nose wrinkling in distaste.

I shoot Rafe a look to say *Why the hell do we care about this shit?* but he gives me that stern eyebrow raise that means "You're being a dick," so I just shut up and listen.

"Will. And Will's—how old's Will, twenty-six?" Rex nods. "They met in Michigan when Will was visiting his sister, but Will lives in New York. Anyway, Leo was devastated when he left and I guess they kissed.... Leo's very secretive about what actually happened." Daniel trails off like he's trying to put a bunch of pieces together and has distracted himself by doing it. "I don't know," Daniel muses finally, "maybe when Leo goes to school in New York...."

"I don't think so, baby," Rex says softly. Daniel shrugs and leans into him.

When the waiter comes to take our order, Daniel and Rex are whispering, pointing to things on the menu like they're planning a covert military action or something, and then Daniel orders for both of them.

Once the food comes, things are a little less awkward. Daniel starts leaning over Rex to answer Ginger's questions about when he starts teaching at Temple and something about Christopher's cousin, so Daniel and Rex switch seats.

"Daniel was telling me that you built the cabin you guys live in," Rafe says to Rex, who's paying a lot of attention to finishing Daniel's plate of spaghetti and meatballs.

"Yeah," he says. "Well, not from scratch. It was... it was going to be torn down, so I started working on it. I saved what I could, but it was kind of a mess."

"Do you know where you want to live in Philly?"

"Um, well, I'm not real familiar with things here," Rex says, "but—"

"That's bullshit," Daniel interrupts, tuning back in to the conversation. "Rex took one look at the map and knew the city in, like, ten minutes."

"Well," Rex says, shaking his head, but he's smiling a little, so maybe it's true. "We were talking about… is it called Fishtown?" he asks Daniel, who nods.

"Yeah, there are all these converted industrial spaces—like, living space over what used to be an ironworks or a welding place. So Rex could turn that space into his workshop. We're looking at some more places tomorrow."

Rex nods and then starts eating again, clearly uncomfortable being the center of attention.

"You know," Christopher says, "I have some friends who are opening a bar near my shop and they're looking to do custom built-ins. A bar, some shelves, a few booths. I wonder if you could talk to them about putting in a bid for the work?"

Rex's head snaps up and he nods immediately. "Yeah. Yes. That'd be great. I could do that. Do you… they'd want a… formal bid, I suppose?" His eyes dart to Daniel, who just smiles.

"I think you could probably talk with them first, then write down whatever you agreed on later," Daniel says.

Rex lets out a breath and nods. "Thanks, Christopher. That'd be great. Really great."

"Rex," Rafe says, "I know you'll have your hands full, with your work and moving and a new city and everything, but if you ever have some free time, maybe you'd want to run a workshop at YA? I know the kids would love to learn some carpentry and woodworking. It would need to be stuff that isn't too dangerous, but if they got permission slips…."

I squeeze Rafe's knee. It's not surprising to me at all that he'd be thinking of ways to help the kids even though he can't work at YA anymore.

Rex looks a little anxious, but he smiles. "Yeah, I—I think I could probably do that." He turns to Daniel. "It'll give me something to do while you're hanging out at Ginger's shop."

"Yeah, seriously, babycakes," Ginger says, "I've missed out on, like, a whole year of you, so you'd better be ready to hang hard."

Christopher says, "Yeah, I don't know what *I'll* do when these two kick me out. Maybe I can come hang out at YA too?"

"Maybe," Rafe says. "What do you have to offer?"

"Um. I make sandwiches." It's clear Christopher's joking, but in the pause that follows, I can almost hear Rafe scouring every last corner of his mind to think of how he can translate that into anything but a workshop that would imply he thought the kids were going to work at McDonald's someday.

"Well," he finally says, "you could just volunteer to supervise programs they've already got running."

"I can supervise with the best of them," Christopher says, smiling. Ginger snorts.

"What? I can!"

"Yeah, sure, babe. That wasn't you the other day totally letting your cousin walk all over you. And you definitely don't let your employees get away with showing up late and taking extra time off."

"Okay, okay," he says, "so I'm a lenient boss."

"It's no way to run a business," Ginger says, her eyes narrowed intensely, like probably this isn't the first time they've had this conversation.

"I think I'm doing fine," Christopher says, his tone lazy. He leans back, looks her up and down, and winks at her. "Yup, I'm doing just fine."

I swear, if there wasn't a table between them, they'd be making out right now.

"Um," I say, desperate to change the subject, "did you see Brian since you've been back?" Brian's guilt over the way he—we—treated Daniel growing up was out of control for a while. He kept calling Daniel to apologize. So often that I think eventually Daniel just told him he forgave him to stop the incessant phone calls. After which, Brian showed up at my door one evening and was so relieved that he didn't even notice Rafe, just said, "Dude, it's okay now!" and plopped his ass down on the sofa with the remote while Rafe and I eyed each other over his head.

"Yeah, I went by there last night." When Daniel heard that Brian was looking to bartend, he put him in touch with his old boss. "Dude, he's wrecked!"

"Huh?"

"That girl? Callie?"

"Oh yeah."

"So, Brian fell for this girl he met, like, once," Daniel tells Ginger and Christopher. "And he blurted out that he loved her over the phone, so obviously she freaked."

"Obviously," Ginger agrees.

"But now they're dating and he's all… mushy."

"Mushy?" I ask. I haven't seen Brian at work much since he's not in the shop anymore. He's still living in the house, though. The mortgage was paid off and Pop's insurance money was enough to get Brian through a few months of expenses before his job turned full-time.

"Yeah, he's all… squishy about it. He was talking about buying her… something, and I don't know. He's kind of an incoherent storyteller; have you noticed?" Daniel asks me.

"Um. Not really. Well, when he said the thing about puking on her cat, I was a little thrown, but—"

"He puked on her *cat*?" Ginger says so loudly that everyone turns to look at our table. She just gives them a grin and ignores it.

"He… yeah."

"And cat is a euphemism for…?" Ginger asks me.

"No, he vomited on her pet cat," Daniel explains. "I know, I know, it's better the other way." Ginger pouts and nods. "Anyway, he was basically raving. I think he might do something insane like propose in a hot air balloon or… with skywriting or whatever. He's out of his mind."

"So, what are you going to do?" Rafe asks us.

"Uh, about what?" I say.

"Brian." Rafe looks at Daniel this time, but Daniel just raises his eyebrows and looks from side to side, like a kid who got called on in class but doesn't know the answer.

"Um…."

Daniel and I look at each other for clarification, but we both shake our heads.

It's like a scene in a movie where everyone has a gun pointed at someone else: we're all silently looking around, all sure we've misunderstood. Finally, Rex and Rafe lock eyes and both start to laugh. It's Rafe's real, genuine laugh, not his polite, on-my-best-behavior laugh, and Rex has this low, warm chuckle. Rafe kind of gestures between me and Daniel and they nod. Daniel and I look at each other blankly and they laugh even harder.

THE KIDS are jammed together in the gazebo that they've decorated with streamers and glittery feather boas for Mikal's birthday. Dorothy sees us first and waves. She jabs Mischa, who jabs Carlos, who spins around and yells, "Conan! Winchester!" as the others scramble toward us.

"Ow!" Mischa says as someone elbows her to get to us.

Rafe is grinning hugely as they all jump on us and start talking at once. When Mikal texted me to invite us to the party, Rafe was clearly thrilled but he talked all this shit about it not being appropriate for us to go, clearly wanting me to talk him into it. When I told him he was being an idiot and of course we should go, he looked relieved and agreed in about five seconds. What I didn't tell him was that they were having the party in a park at the Wissahickon even though it was still kind of chilly outside precisely so he *could* come, because when Mikal had asked for permission to have the party at the YA, it was made clear to him that Rafe was not, under any circumstances, allowed on the premises.

"Happy birthday," Rafe finally says to Mikal, who's decked out in an entirely glittered outfit—sparkly leggings and a T-shirt with a print that looks like an Easter card of a pastel kitten that's covered in rhinestones. His eye makeup is glittery. He even has glittery shoelaces in his purple Keds.

"Yaaaay!" Mikal says, bouncing on his toes. "You're here! We're just waiting for—"

Mikal breaks off as a guy I've never seen before walks up, hands in his pockets, looking around suspiciously. He looks older than the other kids and he's limping a little.

"—Philip, yay!" Mikal calls out, bouncing over to the new guy and drawing him into the circle. "Philip, this is Rafe and Colin."

We shake his hand, but he doesn't quite make eye contact.

"Philip's my new friend from school. You should totally start coming to YA," he says to Philip. The guy doesn't say anything, but he keeps his eyes on Mikal.

"Okay," Mischa says, clapping her hands together like a camp counselor. "The stations are: sponge-painting T-shirts at this table and nail polish at that table. And snacks and drinks are right here. Go for it!" Then she pushes a button and disturbingly upbeat music pours out of speakers plugged into her phone.

"Omigod, Colin, can I *please* paint your nails. I see you in purple—maybe a purple ombré?" Mikal's looking up at me, his eyes bright.

"I—um, well… I—" I look to Rafe, who seems totally relaxed and amused by this turn of events.

"It's his birthday" is all Rafe says, smiling at me warmly.

"What's wrong with you?" Dorothy says to Mikal. "He doesn't want that." I take a deep breath and turn to Dorothy in relief, ready to give her whatever she wants for getting me out of it. "Look at what he's wearing! It's gotta be gray. Ooh, maybe use the crackle topcoat," she says, nudging Mikal with her shoulder. Then she looks up at me and winks, nodding. I shoot her a look and she just laughs and goes to the sponge-painting station.

"Well, who's gonna do Rafe's, then?" I say, and the smile on his face becomes slightly forced.

"Me!" Mischa yells. "Please, me," she says to Rafe. He nods at her and sinks down on the bench next to me.

Of course, within five seconds all the kids are gathered around us, not doing anything but eating snacks while they watch me and Rafe get our nails painted.

"Colin, your hands are *so* messed," says Mikal.

"What?" I say, mildly offended. My hands are spotless. "Dude, have you seen most mechanics' hands? Mine are the cleanest you'll ever find."

"Oh, um, right. No, sorry, Colin. They're nice," Mikal says, patting the back of my hand and shooting a look over my head. "There you are!"

DeShawn walks over and nods at everyone, setting his white backpack down carefully in the corner of the gazebo. Anders creeps along at his side, his all-black outfit an almost comical inversion of DeShawn's.

"Happy birthday, Mikal," DeShawn says, kissing him chastely on the cheek, and Anders follows suit.

"DeShawn, I got white especially for you," says Tynesha from the other side of the nail polish table.

Once they have DeShawn and Anders settled at the table, Carlos says, "Hey, maybe Anders should get white and DeShawn should get black. Or you could mix them." He winks at them both lewdly. DeShawn braces himself on the table and pushes himself off the bench slightly, leaning into Carlos' space. I've never seen him the slightest bit aggressive before and everyone freezes. He keeps eye contact with Carlos, his expression never even changing. After about thirty seconds that feels like an eternity, he sits back down and picks up the white nail polish.

"Sorry, bro," Carlos mutters and DeShawn nods peacefully, placing the black nail polish in front of Anders.

"Aaaanywaaay," Mischa says. "So, I'm thinking of doing galaxies on Rafe. It's awesome 'cause his hands are so big that I'll be able to get really good detail. What do you think?"

The table agrees, but I stopped listening the second she mentioned Rafe's big hands because all I can think of is waking up to them all over me. Recently, he likes nothing better than to wake me up by slowly stroking me to an aching hardness and then going down on me the second I'm conscious enough to nod okay. It's basically the hottest thing ever and suddenly I'm feeling extremely self-conscious to be sitting at a table full of teenagers. I shake my head to clear it and avoid eye contact with Rafe.

When I tune back in, Rafe's fully engaged in a conversation with Mischa about the intricacies of a galaxy manicure and DeShawn is weighing in about the relative scale of the cosmos. Mikal is pushing on the skin around my nails with something that looks terrifyingly like an instrument of dental torture, and has apparently selected a gray nail polish for me.

"Dude," I say, "you're gonna paint my nails the color of a dirty floor?"

"It's avant-garde!" Mikal insists.

"Whatever. The gray trend is saturated and over," Mischa says.

"No way!" Mikal insists, clutching the bottle to his chest.

"Um, never mind," I say. "It's cool. It's... uh... oh, it's like um, rims—tire rims. It's cool."

"Dirty rims," Carlos mutters under his breath, but when I shoot him a look, he raises his hands in peace. "What should I do, Mikal?"

Mikal looks Carlos over. "Um, neon green?"

Carlos grins.

"Hi."

I look to my right and Ricky's standing a few feet away.

"Hey, Ricky. How are you?"

She looks at the floor and cocks her head.

"I'll be right back," I tell Mikal.

I'm very careful not to bring up anything personal when Ricky's working at the shop. Rafe was the one who first mentioned it, and it quickly became clear that he was right. That Ricky just wants to work on the cars when she's at the shop. That she can only focus on that one task and that if I try to ask her about other things, she gets flustered and upset. As a result, though, this is the first time I've seen her outside of the shop since she started working there. I crouch down so Ricky's taller than me.

"Hey," I say. "You're doing great at the shop. Really great. You liking it there okay?"

She nods, but she unwraps her arms slightly, bouncing gently on her toes.

"I'm gonna get ginger ale," she says and walks over to the snack table, but I think I see the ghost of a smile.

The kids paint nails peacefully for a while, trading friendly barbs and compliments like always as their music pumps in the background.

"Holy…," Rafe mutters, and his eyes are on his nails. Mischa has actually made them look like pictures I've seen of outer space. Black with swirls and clouds of white, stars that blaze yellow and blue, and smatterings of dusty particles. "That's amazing," he says to Mischa.

"Dude," Mikal says, "there are, like, a thousand tutorials on YouTube. Get a meme."

I smile at Rafe. I should've known that it wouldn't matter if it was actual astronomy or nail polish technique. Rafe is captivated by anything that takes skill. I'm so distracted by how handsome he looks that I don't notice my own nails until Mikal says, "All done!"

He's changed the color somehow. My fingernails look like broken glass, with white shattered over the gray.

"What the…?"

"You like?" Mikal asks.

"Dude, that's… kind of awesome. Looks like a broken windshield."

"Good call on the crackle topcoat!" Mikal calls to Dorothy.

She salutes him, then says, "An announcement, then cake."

"Ooh, there's cake?" Mikal asks, and she just shoots him an offended look that says *You would dare to doubt me?*

Dorothy nods to DeShawn and everyone falls into a circle, their attention on him.

"I wanted you all to be the first to know," DeShawn says, but his gaze is split between Rafe and Anders. "I got into MIT. I just found out."

Rafe lets out a whoop and is across the gazebo in an instant. He grabs DeShawn and squeezes him in a hug so tight DeShawn's feet come off the floor.

"Dude, dude, you're gonna get your galaxies all over his shirt!" Carlos yells.

Rafe unhands DeShawn, but he's grinning wide.

"I'm so proud of you," he says to DeShawn. "So damn proud."

DeShawn is nodding and looking at the ground, seemingly overcome. Anders is standing against the wall. He doesn't look surprised, but he's watching DeShawn intently and he has his arms wrapped around himself.

All the kids are whooping and patting DeShawn on the back, carefully keeping their freshly painted nails away from his white clothing, and Rafe looks like he's close to tears. His eyes are wide and unfocused, and his hands are shaking at his sides, galaxies vibrating.

Finally, in all the jumping and yelling, Rafe's eyes find mine and everything in him pulls at me.

I don't care that we're in public, don't care we're in front of twenty teenagers and that god knows what bubble-gummy dance music is blaring in the background. Rafe needs me, so I take a step toward him and keep my eyes on his.

"Colin," he says, his voice shaky. I nod at him and he grabs my shoulder. DeShawn had a lot of trouble over the last few months. A bunch of family issues arose, and his uncle was concerned about his mental health and turned to Rafe for some support. Since DeShawn is eighteen, Rafe felt okay being involved, and they'd ended up talking a lot about DeShawn's future, and what he hoped for if he got into MIT. Rafe's pride in DeShawn is radiating from him. He's practically glowing.

He pulls me to him and buries his face in my neck. My arms come around him automatically and I hold him tight. Then he tilts my chin up gently and kisses me. Just a light brush of our lips, but his thumb strokes my cheekbone and he's looking into my eyes like he doesn't see anything else at all.

And suddenly it goes dead quiet except for the pulsing backbeat from the stereo.

"Um...."

"Uh...."

"So...."

The kids who already knew about Rafe and me are grinning. The others are staring at us and looking around at each other.

"Oh. My. God. I *totally* called it!"

"Dude, me too—I knew it!"

"Um, yeah, we all *knew* it."

"But—"

"And—"

Then it's just more clapping and squealing and the kids are bouncing around us. Someone has thrown their arms around us in an excited hug. Someone has turned the music up and the kids are dancing. Someone has thrown glitter up in the air and it's falling down on us like rain.

Through the backbeat and the nail polish and the goddamned glitter, Rafe puts his hands on my shoulders and my eyes find his. He holds me there, at arm's length, like we're kids at a middle school dance. But his smile is as warm as I've ever seen it. His dark hair falls around his face and his skin glows against the collar of his white T-shirt and he's looking at me like I'm the only thing in the world.

"Hey," I say, "Rafe. Move in with me."

Rafe freezes for a moment, then relaxes. "I basically already live there," he says over the music, his eyes dancing. I roll mine and look at him expectantly. He pulls me into a hug and I press my nose into his neck, breathing him in.

"So? What do you say?"

His laugh is pure joy. "Do we have nail polish remover at home?"

Afterword

DECARCERATION REFERS to the process of ending mass incarceration in the United States, acknowledging the entrenched political, historical, and social systems that produced it, addressing the damage it has done to our communities, and investing resources in alternatives.

If you're interested in learning more about decarceration, prison education and literacy programs, or queer youth programs like those mentioned in *Out of Nowhere*, here are some places to start:

Check out Michelle Alexander's book, *The New Jim Crow: Mass Incarceration in the Age of Colorblindness* (www.goodreads.com/book/show/6792458-the-new-jim-crow).

Decarcerate PA (www.decarceratepa.info) is a grassroots campaign working to end mass incarceration in Pennsylvania.

In the Philadelphia area? Books Through Bars (booksthroughbars. org) distributes free books and educational materials to prisoners. You can volunteer and donate books or money. Not near Philadelphia? Find a similar program near you at Prison Book Program (prisonbookprogram.org).

The Attic Youth Center (www.atticyouthcenter.org) is an independent LGBTQ+ youth center in Philadelphia. Visit their website for more information and to donate, or you can find a community center in your area at www.lgbtcenters.org/Centers/find-a-center.aspx.

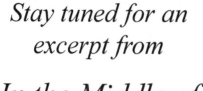

Stay tuned for an excerpt from

In the Middle of Somewhere

Middle of Somewhere:
Book One

By Roan Parrish

Daniel Mulligan is tough, snarky, and tattooed, hiding his self-consciousness behind sarcasm. Daniel has never fit in—not at home in Philadelphia with his auto mechanic father and brothers, and not at school where his Ivy League classmates looked down on him. Now, Daniel's relieved to have a job at a small college in Holiday, Northern Michigan, but he's a city boy through and through, and it's clear that this small town is one more place he won't fit in.

Rex Vale clings to routine to keep loneliness at bay: honing his muscular body, perfecting his recipes, and making custom furniture. Rex has lived in Holiday for years, but his shyness and imposing size have kept him from connecting with people.

When the two men meet, their chemistry is explosive, but Rex fears Daniel will be another in a long line of people to leave him, and Daniel has learned that letting anyone in can be a fatal weakness. Just as they begin to break down the walls keeping them apart, Daniel is called home to Philadelphia, where he discovers a secret that changes the way he understands everything.

www.dreamspinnerpress.com

Chapter 1

I TOSS my bag in the door of my rental car and practically throw myself in after it. Once the door is safely closed, I slump into the seat, close my eyes, and curse the entire state of Michigan. If Michigan didn't exist, then I wouldn't be sitting in a rental car at the edge of Sleeping Bear College's tiny campus, having a premature midlife crisis at thirty.

I just spent the day interviewing for a job at Sleeping Bear, a small liberal arts college I'd never even heard of until six months ago. My interview went well, my teaching demonstration went even better, and I'm pretty sure I never let my cuffs slide up to show my tattoos. I could tell they liked me, and they seemed enthusiastic about hiring someone young to help them build the department. As they talked about independent studies and dual majors, I mentally catalogued all the bear puns I could. Of course, what they'd think if they found out that I associate bears' hairy chests and lumbering gaits with large men drinking beer instead of the college, the nearby dunes, and the animal they are named for, I can't say.

I've been working my ass off to get where I am today, and all I can think is that I'm a fraud. I'm not an English professor. I'm just some queer little punk from Philadelphia who the smart kids slummed it with. Just ask my ex. Just ask my father. Ask my brothers, especially. God, what the hell am I doing here?

Sleeping Bear is the only college where I got an interview and it is in the middle of fucking nowhere—near some place called Traverse City (which is definitely not a city, based on anything I've ever seen). I had to drive for nearly four hours after I flew to Detroit to get here. I could have gotten closer with a connecting flight in a tiny plane, but I'll be damned if the first time I ever flew I was going to crash into one of the Great Lakes. No, overland travel was good enough for me, even if the flight, the rental car, and the suit I bought for the visit put me even deeper in the hole than I was before. At least I saved a hundred bucks getting the red-eye from Detroit to Philly tomorrow night.

I shudder when I think what my credit card bill will look like this month. Good thing I can turn the heat off in my apartment in a few weeks when it gets above forty degrees. Not like there's anyone there except me. My friends from school never want to come to my neighborhood, claiming it's more convenient to go places near campus. Richard, my ex, wouldn't be caught dead in my apartment, which he referred to as "the crack house." Asshole. And I only see my brothers and my dad at their auto shop. Still, I love Philly; I've lived there all my life. Moving—especially to the middle of nowhere—well, even the thought is freaking me out.

Now, all I want is to go back to my shitty little motel room, order a pizza, and fall asleep in front of crappy TV. I sigh and start the rental car I can't afford.

I have to admit, though, the road from the school to my motel is beautiful. All the hotels near campus are cute (read: expensive) bed and breakfast joints, so I booked in at the Motel 6 outside of town. It's down a two-lane road that seems to follow the tree line. To my left are fields and the occasional dirt road turnoff with signs I can't read in the near-dark. God, I'm starving. I haven't eaten since an ill-advised Dunkin' Donuts egg sandwich at the airport.

It's really cold so far north, but I crack the window to breathe the sweet smell of fresh air and trees anyway. It's actually really peaceful out here. Quiet. It isn't something I'm used to—quiet, I mean. Library-quiet and middle-of-the-night quiet, sure. But in the city there's always noise. This is a quiet that feels like water and trees and, well, nature, I guess, like the time my parents took us to the Jersey Shore when we were kids and I hid under the boardwalk away from the crowds, listening to the overwhelming sound of the ocean and the creak of docks.

And peace? Well, never peace. If it wasn't one of my asshole brothers starting shit with me, it was my dad flipping his lid over me being gay. Of course, later my lack of peace came in the form of Richard, my ex, who, while we were together, was apparently sleeping with every gay man at the University of Pennsylvania.

My hands tighten on the wheel as I picture Richard, his handsome face set in an expression of haughty condescension as he leveled me with one nauseating smile. "Come on, Dan," he said, like we had discussed this before, "who believes in monogamy anymore? Don't be so bourgeois."

And, "It's not like we're exclusive." That, after we'd been together for two years—or so I'd thought—and I'd taken him to my brother Sam's wedding.

Anyway, I hate being called Dan.

I grit my teeth and force myself to take a deep breath. No more thinking about Richard. I promised myself.

I glance down at the scrap of paper where I scrawled the directions to my motel. I can almost taste the buttery cheese and crispy pizza crust and my stomach growls. When I look back up a second later, something darts into the road in front of me. I swerve hard to the right, but I hear a sickening whine the second before the car veers into a tree.

ALL I can see is blackness, until I realize I scrunched my eyes shut before I hit the tree. I open them slowly, expecting to look down and see that my legs are gone or something, like in one of those war movies my brother is always watching, where a bomb goes off and the soldier thinks he's fine, laughing and smiling, until the dust clears and he looks down and has no lower body. Then the pain hits. It's like the cartoon physics of awareness: we can't hurt until we see that we're supposed to.

But my legs are there, as is everything else. I do a quick stretch, but aside from some soreness where the seat belt locked in, I actually feel okay. The car, however, is another story. I can already see that I'm not driving out of here. I jam the door open and slide out, a little unsteady on my feet. And then I hear it. A terrible whining noise.

Fuck, what did I do?

The dark seems to have settled in all of a sudden and it's hard to see the road. I take a few cautious steps toward the noise, and then I see it. A dog. A brown and white dog that doesn't look much older than a puppy, though it's already pretty big. I don't know anything about dogs, have no idea what kind it is. But it's definitely hurt. It looks like maybe I broke its leg when I hit it.

"Fuck, fuck, fuck," I say. The dog is whimpering, its big brown eyes wide with pain. "Fuck, dog, I'm so sorry," I tell it, and reach out a hand to try and soothe it. As I reach for its head, though, it growls and I jerk my hand back.

"I know, dog, I'm sorry. I'm not going to hurt you. Hang on."

I rush back to the car for my phone and try to call information so I can find an emergency vet, but I can't get a signal out here at all. I put the car in neutral and try to rock it away from the tree enough so that I can look under the hood—growing up with a family auto shop means you can't help but know how to fix cars, even if you don't want to go into the family business. But there's no way. The undercarriage must've caught on the tree's roots or something.

I grab my bag and sling it over my shoulder, and go back to where the dog is lying, still whimpering. I can't leave it here. It'll get run over by a car in the dark. Or, worse, it'll just lie here all alone, terrified and in pain. The sound it's making is ripping my fucking heart out. I can't believe I did this. Christ, how did I even get here? I ease to the other side of the dog and gently run my fingertips over the soft fur on its head. It whines, but doesn't growl.

I keep petting it, talking low as I ease my arm underneath.

"Okay, dog, you're okay. Don't worry, I've got you. Everything's going to be fine." I'm saying things I haven't heard since my mother said them when I was little. Words that are meant to comfort but mean nothing.

I roll the dog into my arms and it whimpers and growls as I jostle its hurt leg. I cuddle it close to my chest to keep it immobile and try to stand without falling over and hurting it worse. I'll just walk a little ways. There has to be a gas station, or a house, or something, right? I'll just ask someone to call a vet. Hell, maybe this is what police do in a nothing town like this. Rescue dogs that get stuck in trees, or something? No, wait, that's cats. Cats get stuck in trees. Right?

I walk for what feels like forever. The dog has gone quiet, but I can feel it breathing, so at least I know it isn't dead. What it is, though, is getting heavy. I stop for a second to check if I have phone service for what feels like the millionth time. I haven't come across a single gas station and I'm not sure how much longer I can walk.

"Okay, dog; it's okay," I say again, but my voice is as shaky as my legs, and, really, it isn't the dog I'm talking to anymore. Still no service. Fuck.

Then, off to my right, I see a light. A shaky beam of light that's getting closer. Just as I pull level with the light, a man steps out of the woods. I rear away from the large form, and the dog whimpers softly. The man looks huge and the way he's shining the flashlight is blinding. My heart beats heavily in my throat. This guy could take me apart. Squaring my shoulders and setting my feet so I look as big as possible, I plan how I can set the dog down without hurting it further if I have to fight. Or run.

Then a warm voice breaks the silence that stopped feeling peaceful the second I swerved.

"You okay?"

His voice is deep and a little growly. For half a second, all the puns about bears that I was making earlier dance through my head and I laugh. What comes out sounds more like a hysterical squeak, though.

"Do you mind?" I say, squinting and hoping my voice sounds more threatening than the noise I just made. He lowers the flashlight immediately and walks toward me. I take a half step back automatically. All I can really see in the dark, with the ghost of the flashlight leaving spots in my vision, are massive shoulders clad in plaid.

"Are you okay?" the man asks again, and he puts out a hand as he takes the last few slow steps to my side. I nod quickly. His hand is huge.

"I, um."

He bends down and looks in my face. I don't know what he sees there, but his posture shifts, the bulk of him softening ever so slightly.

"I didn't mean to," I try to explain when it's clear he isn't a threat. "Only, it came out of nowhere and I couldn't—" I break off as he shines the flashlight on the dog. It whines and I gather it closer to me, suddenly unsure. "I tried to find a vet, but I can't get a signal here and my car hit the tree so I couldn't drive and I—"

"You were in an accident? Are you hurt?"

"No—I mean, I'm not. I'm... but my car's fucked. Do you have a phone? Can you call a vet?"

"No vet," he says. "Nothing's open this late." It's maybe 7:00 p.m.

"Please," I say. "I can't let it die. Fuck! What the fuck am I doing here? I can't believe I—" I break off when I can tell my next words won't be anything I want a total stranger to hear.

"Come with me," the man says, and turns and walks back into the woods. What the hell?

"Um," I say. Am I actually supposed to follow a total stranger into the woods? In the dark? In the middle of nowhere? In Michigan? I know stereotypes about cannibals who live in the woods and eat unsuspecting tourists are just that: stereotypes. Maybe I've watched The Hills Have Eyes one too many times, but still. Isn't it, like, a statistical fact that most serial killers come from the Midwest?

While I was distracted by regionally profiling the man, he'd come back out of the woods and is now standing directly in front of me, close enough that I can kind of see his face. He has dark hair and eyes, and a sharp nose. That's all I can see in the dark. But he is definitely much younger than I assumed. His low voice sounded older, but he looks like he's in his midthirties. And up close, he is massive, with hugely broad shoulders, powerful arms, and broad hips—how much of that is flesh and how much is flannel remains to be seen. He's nearly a head taller than me, and I'm not short.

"You need to come with me," he says, and his voice suggests that he's considering the fact that I might be an idiot.

"Er, sure," I say, figuring that if worse comes to worst, at least I can run; I have to be faster than this guy, right? I take an experimental step toward him and, in the way it sometimes happens when you rest after an exertion, nearly fall on my face as my body takes longer to wake up than my brain. The man catches me with one easy hand under my elbow and steadies me. Shit, that was embarrassing.

"Here," he says. "Let me take the dog. You take this." He shrugs something off his shoulder and hands it to me. It takes a few seconds to process the unfamiliar shape in the dark.

"Is that a gun?"

"Yeah," he says.

"Why do you have a gun?" I ask warily. Though, I guess I should be reassured that he's handing it to me and not pointing it at me.

"To hunt with," he says matter-of-factly.

"Right," I say. Hunting. Michigan. Michigan.

He gently sets what I can only assume is a rifle on the ground next to me.

"Let me." He slides his hands under the dog. His hands are huge, covering practically my whole stomach as he worms them under my arms. "I've got him," he says.

"I don't know if it's a boy," I say. "I don't know anything about dogs. I mean, I guess I would've been able to tell by looking, but I didn't think of it. But it's really common, defaulting to male pronouns to refer to things of indeterminate gender." Christ, I'm babbling.

He cocks his head at me and walks away. I pick up the strap of the gun gingerly and take off after him, holding it as far away from the trigger as I can. With the luck I'm having today, I'd trip and end up shooting the man. Or myself. Or, shit, probably the dog.

ROAN PARRISH is currently wandering between Philadelphia and New Orleans, drowning out her cat's complaints at riding in the car by singing along to the radio at ever-increasing volumes. A former academic, she's used to writing things that no one reads. She still loves to geek out about books, movies, TV, and music—now, though, she's excited to be writing the kind of romantic, angsty stories that she loves to escape into.

When not writing, she can usually be found cutting her friends' hair, meandering through whatever city she's in while listening to torch songs and melodic death metal, or cooking overly elaborate meals. One time she may or may not have baked a six-layer chocolate cake and then thrown it out the window in a fit of pique. She loves bonfires, winter beaches, minor chord harmonies, and self-tattooing.

You can find her on her website, on Twitter, on Facebook, occasionally on Pinterest, and on Instagram, where she mostly natters on about food. Have questions/comments/pictures of octopi? Want to recommend a strong cheese or express a strong opinion? Drop her a line on e-mail. She'd love to hear from you.

Sign up for her Newsletter to receive updates about new releases, works-in-progress, and bonus materials like sneak peeks and extra scenes!

Website: www.roanparrish.com
Twitter: @RoanParrish
E-mail: roanparrish@gmail.com
Facebook: www.facebook.com/roanparrish
Pinterest: www.pinterest.com/ARoanParrish
Instagram: www.instagram.com/roanparrish
Newsletter signup: eepurl.com/bmJUbr